Carol Ericson is a bestsel[ling author of] more than forty books. Sh[e] [...] true-crime stories, a love [...] for reality TV, all of which [...] her own tales of murder, mayhem and mystery. To find out more about Carol and her current projects, please visit her website at carolericson.com, 'where romance flirts with danger.'

Karen Whiddon started weaving fanciful tales for her younger brothers at the age of eleven. Amid the gorgeous Catskill Mountains, then the majestic Rocky Mountains, she fuelled her imagination with the natural beauty surrounding her. Karen now lives in north Texas, writes full-time and volunteers for a boxer dog rescue. She shares her life with her hero of a husband and four to five dogs, depending on if she is fostering. You can email Karen at kwhiddon1@aol.com. Fans can also check out her website, karenwhiddon.com

Also by Carol Ericson

Also by Karen Whiddon

Discover more at millsandboon.co.uk

CANYON CRIME SCENE

CAROL ERICSON

THE SPY SWITCH

KAREN WHIDDON

MILLS & BOON

First Published in Great Britain 2022
by Mills & Boon, an imprint of HarperCollins*Publishers* Ltd
1 London Bridge Street, London, SE1 9GF

www.harpercollins.co.uk

HarperCollins*Publishers*
1st Floor, Watermarque Building,
Ringsend Road, Dublin 4, Ireland

Canyon Crime Scene © 2022 Carol Ericson
The Spy Switch © 2021 Karen Whiddon

ISBN: 978-0-263-30348-3

0622

MIX
Paper from
responsible sources
FSC™ C007454

This book is produced from independently certified FSC™ paper to ensure responsible forest management.

For more information visit: www.harpercollins.co.uk/green

Printed and Bound in Spain using 100% Renewable electricity at CPI Black Print, Barcelona

CANYON
CRIME SCENE

CAROL ERICSON

Chapter One

The gates to the California Correctional Institution closed behind her, and Lori stepped on the gas as she smeared a tear across her cheek with the back of her hand. The tears always came later. She never gave in to them while sitting across from Danny.

She hadn't been able to bring her brother any good news this time as he endured his sixth year behind bars for a crime he didn't commit. As if Danny would've killed his girlfriend. He'd loved Elena more than anything in the world.

He'd loved her...passionately. The little voice whispered in her ear, "too passionately?" She brushed away the words along with another tear making its way down her face.

That's what the DA had insisted. Danny had killed Elena in a fit of passion. That's why the DA's office had charged him with manslaughter instead of first-or even second-degree murder. That and Danny's confession.

He'd only pleaded guilty to get the deal. Danny had assured her he hadn't done it and she believed him...because of the fingerprint.

She flexed her hands on the steering wheel, her palms sweaty, as she accelerated onto the freeway that would take her back to LA. The police had found a fingerprint at Elena's murder scene that they couldn't identify. They never did ID it but hadn't tried too hard after Danny confessed to the murder.

And Lori had been looking for the owner of that print ever since. After college, she'd been heading for a career in forensics anyway, but the mystery of that print had led her to fingerprint analysis and a career as a fingerprint tech with the LAPD.

She'd just finished a stint on a serial killer task force where she'd made a couple of big contributions and had gotten on the radar of the new captain at the Northeast Division. She worked hard and loved her job, but her brother's case always loomed in the background. She compared every print she came across in her line of work to the one at Elena's crime scene.

Her former boss, Clive Stewart, had caught on to what she was doing, but then Clive had turned out to be the infamous serial killer The Player and now he was dead, so she didn't have to worry about him. The fact that the LAPD had a serial killer working on its forensics team for over twenty years had been a source of embarrassment for the department and Chief Sterling, and they had cracked down on policy and procedure—but there was always a way around that. She should know. She'd learned it from a master—not that her workarounds were remotely in the same league as Clive's. She'd never liked the guy. She'd grown up around enough shady characters to smell one out across the lab from her.

As she left the snow-capped peaks of the Tehachapi Mountains in her rearview, her phone rang. She glanced at the display before putting her cell on Speaker.

"Hola, Mama."

"Did you see him?"

"Just left."

"How does he look? Is he eating right?"

"He looked fine." Except for the prison tat on his neck that he'd acquired since the last time she'd visited. Did he think that was going to help him land a job when he got out, even if she could prove his innocence?

Her mother released an audible, soggy breath. "Is he still too skinny? Tell me, *mija*."

Lori squeezed her eyes closed for a second, seeing Danny's slim frame and concave chest. "He's the same, Mama."

Her mother paused. "He still says he's innocent?"

"He doesn't have to say that to me." Lori's temples throbbed. "I believe him."

"Okay. It's okay, *mija*. I know you do." Her mother's voice soothed like a pat on the head.

Then she started talking about her other children— the ones that mattered—Lori's older brother, Raymund, who was a police officer in San Antonio, and her older sister, Rita, who lived in the Netherlands with her husband, who worked at the State Department.

They'd all given up on Danny when he'd confessed to Elena's murder, and Mom had moved back to Mexico to take care of Abuela, although the old lady didn't really need the help. Dad would've stood by his son, but he'd died two years before Danny's arrest.

That left Lori to fight for him, although some days, like today, Danny didn't seem to want the help.

Lori let Mom ramble on for several miles. What else did she have to occupy her time? The landscape that rolled past her window presented a stark view. The snow from the mountains that had made it down to this elevation had all melted away with the coming spring, and a brown, drab color scheme painted the rolling hills waiting for the greenery of new growth.

Southern California had suffered a hot, dry summer the year before and several wildfires had blasted the region. Those splashes of green in this area might be a long time coming.

She blinked when she heard her mother say her name. "Lori?"

"I'm sorry—what did you say?"

Mom sighed. "I asked if you were still doing okay after finding out your boss was a killer."

"I told you, Mama. It didn't affect me. I wasn't in any danger from Clive."

Her mother tutted. "You always told me he didn't like you."

"He didn't, but he didn't want to kill me. He saw me as a threat to his job."

"*Dios mio.* To be that close to a killer."

"Definitely a creep." Lori slowed down when she spotted a familiar fast-food sign on the side of the road. "Hey, Mom. I'm going to pull in to get something to drink for the rest of the ride home. I'll call you later, and give my love to Abuelita."

Fifteen minutes later with a drink in her cup holder and the radio blasting '80s music, Lori hopped back on the freeway to LA. She'd planned her visit to Danny at the beginning of family time so she'd make it home before nightfall.

As she cruised on the highway, her phone buzzed and she tapped to answer it.

Her boss's voice boomed through the car. "Hey, Lori. Are you anywhere near the station? Please tell me you're not in Big Bear catching the end of the ski season or camped out poolside in Palm Springs getting a jump start on your tan."

"I wish." She gazed out her windshield at the barren hillsides as she swooped down into the Los Angeles basin. "Why would I be in either of those places?"

"Because two of your coworkers are, and I need someone to process prints at a possible crime scene in Hollywood."

Her heart skipped a beat, just as it always did at the mention of a crime scene. "Possible?"

"A guy came into the Northeast Division yesterday to report his friend missing. The desk sergeant told him to come back when it had been forty-eight hours. The same guy called in today to tell us he'd broken into his friend's house and found a mess and some blood. Now we have a possible crime scene."

Glancing at the clock on the dashboard, she said, "I'm driving back into town, but I'm about forty minutes from the station. I'll drop by and get my kit and head over to the crime scene."

Doug said, "*Possible* crime scene."

"Right." She ended the call and put pressure on the accelerator.

She'd lied to Doug. More than an hour stretched between her and the station, but a girl had to do what a girl had to do to stay on top of her game.

BY THE TIME Lori rolled up to the neat stucco house in Hollywood, her bag of tricks slung over her shoulder, LAPD Detective Jane Falco was in the front yard directing traffic.

As Lori jogged across the street to join the gaggle of

CSIs grouped around Detective Falco awaiting orders, she eyed the detective's pantsuit and sleek ponytail, wishing she'd had time to change out of her jeans and sneakers before arriving. Visiting day at the correctional institution didn't demand professional attire.

She sidled up to the edge of the circle, brushing her bangs from her eyes.

Detective Falco pinned her with a gaze and raised her eyebrows. "Del Valle, fingerprints?"

"Yes, ma'am." Lori's heart didn't pitter-patter too much at the recognition. After all, she'd worked side by side with a serial killer and hadn't noticed a thing—until the end. Maybe the detective knew her name because she'd been clueless, not because she'd finally reported her boss for odd behavior.

Falco nodded. "I was just saying, the missing woman's friend tried to make a report yesterday, after checking area hospitals, but Courtney had just skipped a lunch date and the friend couldn't reach her. Knowing he had to wait another twenty-four hours before he could report her missing, he took matters into his own hands today and broke into her house through a back window. He noticed some disturbance and blood in the bedroom and called us."

Lori asked, "Do we have the friend's prints on file to rule them out?"

"I'm going to leave that to you, Del Valle. Do it at the station. The friend—" Falco checked her notes "—Trey Ferrar, is coming in for a formal interview. You can take his prints there."

Detective Falco gave them a few more instructions before turning toward the house next door to Courtney's to start her canvassing of the neighborhood. The department had just transferred Detective Falco to the Northeast Division and the gossip already had her pegged as a by-the-book stickler. Lori didn't mind as long as the detective stayed out of her business.

Lori hitched the bag onto her shoulder and followed the other CSIs into the house. They already knew Trey had broken in through the back window, so she'd start there and get his prints.

The break-in point turned out to be a window over the sink in the kitchen. Trey had jimmied the sliding glass out of its tracks and lifted it free from the frame. He'd left a shoe print in the sink as he climbed into the house, knocking a glass to the floor on his way. Lori dusted the window frame and the counter and lifted both finger and palm prints, as he probably braced himself before he jumped to the floor.

She didn't bother with the rest of the kitchen, as she had no interest in random visitors to Courtney's house. She had to hit the areas where smears of blood had been found, specifically Courtney's bedroom and the door leading to the garage.

Courtney's car was also missing and who was to say the young woman didn't cut herself and drive to the emergency room? Except her friend hadn't found a record of her at any hospital emergency room in the area, and her car hadn't been located.

Lori crouched down to study the blood smears and sucked in a breath. She called out to anyone within shouting distance. "I found a patent print in the blood on the garage door."

Lori hadn't even heard Detective Falco return to the

house, but she hovered over her shoulder now and said, "Good job, Del Valle."

"Ah, you can call me Lori, and Clive Stewart may have been a serial killer but he taught me well." She twisted around to retrieve a tool from her bag, and her gaze collided with Detective Falco's piercing green eyes.

"That's not funny, Del Valle."

"No, ma'am." Lori returned to her task, rolling her eyes. Falco had better learn to lighten up if she planned to work with Jake McAllister and Billy Crouch, the two hotshot detectives at the Northeast Division who played fast and loose and still managed to solve four copycat killer cases and nail the original, her boss, Clive Stewart.

When she finished taking the prints from the house, with the prerogative to return if she needed more, Lori packed up her tools and drove back to the station. There, she'd take Trey's prints and eliminate his and Courtney's from the one she took at the house. She hoped neither of theirs matched the patent print left in the blood. She didn't even know whose blood that was yet, but she'd bet on it being Courtney's.

When she got back to the station, she noticed Trey Ferrar already sitting at a desk, his head in his hands. Lori hesitated and raised her eyebrows at Detective Falco across the room, who gave her a slight nod.

Lori approached Trey and cleared her throat.

The young man's head jerked up, and he swiped a hand across his eyes.

"Hi, Trey, my name's Lori Del Valle, and I'm going to take your fingerprints just so we can rule them out at Courtney's house. Is that all right?" Not that Trey had a choice, but it sounded nicer to ask.

He gave her a jerky nod and said, "Here?"

"I'll take you to the machine." She waved her hand over her shoulder. "We don't have to roll prints these days. We can do them electronically."

He rose to his feet and followed her to a small room where they handled the prints. While she instructed him where to put his fingers, Lori peppered him with questions. "Why did you suspect something wrong when Courtney didn't show up for lunch?"

"Court's always on time and she never misses a date—not with me, anyway." He flicked a black curl from his eyes.

"Are you two…dating?"

Trey's nostrils flared. "I'm not into girls. Court's my BFF. We're each other's confidantes."

"Has she confided anything to you recently about going away or meeting someone new or being scared?"

"She's been…"

"Are you finished in here?"

Lori glanced up at Falco filling the door, her head cocked to one side. What Courtney had been doing, Lori would never know now.

"Yep, all done." Falco must be great at interrogations. She could make you feel guilty with one look from those cat eyes, but Lori didn't feel an ounce of embarrassment for questioning Trey. Maybe he'd let something slip that he wouldn't tell a detective.

She ushered Trey out of the room and went to the CSI lab. Not all LAPD divisions had their own CSI labs, but the Northeast Division had been remodeled recently and the station had gotten a fancy one. The lab handled work for smaller LAPD divisions, and she could count on a steady stream of techs in and out of the room during the week. Sundays tended to be slower, so she and the team that had worked Courtney's house today had the place to themselves.

Lori processed the prints from the house, labeling both Courtney's and Trey's prints for comparison. Her heart thumped a little faster when she realized the print in the blood didn't match either of theirs. Maybe Courtney's kidnapper had been sloppy.

She put together an impression of the print to email to IAFIS but as this was still a missing person and not a homicide, she didn't expect speedy results. She'd send out the email tomorrow morning.

She waved to the remaining tech in the lab, as she left and walked down the hallway. She passed the conference room that had doubled as the Copycat Player task force room, now back to its sedate oval table and chairs, the electricity gone, ready to host the next meeting of the brass on finance or citizen complaints.

She jogged downstairs to the reception area, a loud, irate, totally male voice disrupting the typical somnolence of a Sunday evening. She hid a smirk as the man looming over the front-desk sergeant pounded his fist on the counter.

His voice rose. "I don't care if it hasn't been forty-eight hours. I know my sister."

Not just the words but the set of the man's broad shoulders and the sweep of his dark blond hair gave Lori pause, and she stumbled to a stop and turned toward the commotion.

Sergeant Cerda glanced at her past the irate citizen and lifted one eyebrow.

The imposing figure turned, and Lori pressed her hand

against her chest as she met the smoldering blue gaze of the man who'd stolen her heart.

She'd repaid him for that theft by deceiving him in the worst possible way.

Chapter Two

His blood pressure spiking, Cade Larson spun around mid-rant when he noticed the desk sergeant making faces at someone behind him. His eyes narrowed as he took in the attractive brunette gawping at him from across the room.

A warm flush crawled up his chest and he unclenched his fists. He probably was making an ass of himself, acting like his entitled father, but Summer was worth it.

When the woman finally picked up her jaw from the floor, she took a tentative step toward him and said, "Cade?"

The heat, which had been subsiding, rushed back, engulfing his face.

Cade swallowed hard as his gaze skimmed over Loretta Del Valle's curvy body, snug in a pair of jeans, her hand held up in a tentative wave as if uncertain if he'd remember her. Some nights he'd found her hard to forget.

He reversed his scowl into the smile that could charm an agreement and a signature from the most skeptical of business associates. "What are you doing at a police station, Lori?"

He clenched his teeth behind the smile. Dumb question. This could have something to do with her brother Danny.

She tucked a strand of chocolate-brown hair behind one ear. "I work here. What's your excuse?"

"Are you a cop?" He snapped his fingers. "No, forensics or something, right?"

Her dark eyes widened for a second before she strode across the floor toward him, her sneakers squeaking on the linoleum. She thrust out her hand. "Good to see you, Cade, and it's fingerprints."

He took her hand, the professional gesture throwing cold water on his daydreams, her warm, soft skin firing them up again. "That's right. Fingerprints."

She practically snatched her hand from his and tucked it behind her back as if afraid he'd take it again. "Now that my presence here at the Northeast Division is explained, it's your turn. I thought you lived in…somewhere else."

Cade's heart stuttered in his chest. She knew he lived in New York? He glanced back at the officer behind the counter, whose eyes were glued to a computer screen, while the tilt of his head indicated he'd heard every word exchanged between him and Lori.

"I, uh…" Cade dipped his head, remembering the way he'd been haranguing the officer when Lori happened by. He scooped in a deep breath. "I came out to LA to see my sister, and now she's missing."

Lori gasped and grabbed his arm, squeezing it. "Summer?"

"Yeah, Summer." Cade had two sisters—one older and one younger—but Lori figured right away that it was his younger sister in trouble and not his perfect older sister, Sarah. He and Lori had bonded in high school over the problems of their siblings, except his family had the money to buy Summer out of trouble and Danny had wound up in prison—not that Summer had ever murdered anyone…not that he knew of, anyway.

"I'm so sorry." She slid a glance at the uniform not even pretending not to listen anymore. "How long has she been missing?"

"Since about seven o'clock last night." He gripped the edge of the counter, his anxiety taking hold of him again. "She was supposed to meet me for dinner in Santa Monica."

"Santa Monica? What are you doing at this station?"

"She lives up this way. My hotel is in Santa Monica, and she wanted to go to a place near the pier—only she never showed up."

Lori gestured toward the officer. "That's why the police can't take a report yet. An adult has to be missing for forty-eight hours unless there are signs of foul play."

Cade smacked his palm against his forehead. Hunching over the counter, he said, "I'm sorry for yelling, Sergeant Cerda. I'm worried about my sister."

"I understand, Mr. Larson. If you still haven't located her in the next twenty-four hours, come back and I'll send you right up to a detective."

"Thanks, Gary." Lori tapped on the counter. "I—I can be here tomorrow when you come back, Cade. Just, you know…"

"That would be great, Lori." He stepped away from the counter, and steered Lori away with a hand on the small of her back. "But what's this tomorrow stuff? Are you free now for a drink or a coffee?"

The hand clutching the strap of her bag tightened, but it didn't sport a wedding ring on her finger. Didn't mean she didn't have a man waiting for her at home. Lucky bastard.

"I'm sorry. That was a dumb idea. Y-you're probably busy." And just like that, Lori Del Valle had managed to turn him into a stuttering high school jock again.

She scooted a little farther from the reception area and lowered her voice. "Actually, I'm not busy. I was just going to head home and eat something. I had to come right into work after visiting Danny today, and I'm starving."

He grinned like an idiot. "Perfect—I mean, not that you had to see Danny behind bars or that you're starving or…"

She cut off his rambling with a hand to his chest. "I know what you mean. Do you have a rental car?"

"How else am I supposed to get around LA? Where's your place?" His face warmed. "So we don't go someplace out of the way."

She withdrew her hand from his shirtfront and stuck it in the pocket of her jacket. "I'm not too far from Santa Monica. I'm currently staying in a house in Venice—on the canals."

He raised his eyebrows. "Nice spot."

"Being a fingerprint tech doesn't pay that well. I'm renting the house from a friend at an extremely reduced rate. She insisted. Gave me some story about not being able to rent it out after what happened there."

"What happened there?"

"A murder." She dug her keys out of her purse and waved them in the air. "Why don't we head back to Santa Monica, park in the structure on Third and find a place to eat around there?"

Cade wanted to ask if her house was safe. He wanted to ask her if she had a boyfriend. He wanted to ask her a million questions, but he didn't want to break this spell right now.

Instead of giving her the third degree, he said, "That sounds good. I'll follow you."

They walked out to the parking lot together, and she jerked her thumb at a black SUV. "This is me. Traffic shouldn't be too bad right now, but in case you lose me I can give you my number."

He pulled his phone from his pocket. "Give me your number now, and I'll call you so I have it."

He tapped in her number, she answered and he hung up. "Got it. See you in a few."

He followed her onto the freeway and kept close on her tail. His familiarity with the city matched hers, as they'd both grown up in LA—she on the east side of LA and he in Malibu. They'd attended the same private high school. Lori had gotten a scholarship but fit in as seamlessly as he did. Without the money and the legacy connections, Lori had used her brains and her warmth to adapt to the rich-kid vibe at Brentwood Prep. Despite Lori's good grades and popularity, his parents didn't approve of their relationship. They thought her brother Danny would have a bad influence on her, never acknowledging that they had a troubled daughter of their own.

Cade's hands involuntarily squeezed the steering wheel of his rental. Why would Summer take off without telling him? She hadn't mentioned a boyfriend, but then he didn't know any of her friends. He didn't even know if she had a job. Dad sent her money like clockwork from Japan, where he and Mom had been the past few years, setting up a new business venture.

Dad had agreed to support her financially as long as she stayed in college, but Summer didn't have to send proof of her enrollment. Dad should've known that without accountability, Summer would do what she wanted. She always had, but Mom and Dad firmly ascribed to the adage of *out of sight, out of mind* and were comfortable with the arrangement.

But he wasn't. He'd decided to take a few weeks away from his business and come out to LA to get Summer back on track. Maybe his sister was running away from him. Maybe Sergeant Cerda was right—adults took off all the time without telling people, and they had the right to do so…especially people like Summer. She most likely didn't have a job, wasn't in school, had disposable income…and liked to party, which was a benign way of saying she was a drug addict.

Cade had been able to stay behind Lori and followed her off the freeway and into one of the parking structures that handled the vehicles for the outdoor Third Street Promenade. The area still drew the crowds, even on a Sunday night, but he had no trouble nabbing a parking spot on the same aisle as Lori.

She waited for him by the stairs of the garage and eyed him up and down as he approached her. "Good, you have a coat. On the way over here, I developed a sudden craving for some fresh seafood. Do you want to catch a bite at the fish market on the pier and eat at the tables outside?"

He'd had something a little more formal in mind, but Lori usually went for adventurous over formal. "Whatever you like. I'm the one who strong-armed you into this date."

She wrinkled her nose. "It's not really a date, just two old friends catching up."

Lori seemed determined to put some space between them, or at least to downplay their previous relationship, and he'd honor that. It meant no reliving those steamy nights in the backseat of his car or in a sleeping bag at the beach when they couldn't keep their hands off each other. His gaze wandered to her backside, cupped in a pair of tight jeans, swaying in rhythmic motion as she preceded him down the stairs. Not even the stench of urine that permeated the stairwell could blot out her sweet smell. She must use the same perfume or lotion she'd used as a teen. The smell had haunted him and triggered thoughts of a youthful first love for nine years. He'd even broken off an engagement because the woman didn't smell right. He'd better not admit that to this no-nonsense, professional woman in front of him.

At the fish market, they both ordered grilled mahi, Cajun style, with French fries and coleslaw, and carried their paper plates to the picnic tables that afforded them a view of the tourists clogging the wooden pier in search of souvenirs and food.

Cade allowed Lori a minute to squeeze lemon on her fish, and take a bite of coleslaw and a sip of her soda, before he started. "Married? Children?"

Lori coughed on her drink, and her eyes watered. "No and no. You?"

He tried to contain his sigh of relief, which made it out his nose anyway and ended in a snort. "Almost and no."

She dropped her little plastic fork and dove beneath the table to retrieve it. Her muffled voice asked, "You almost had a child or you were almost married?"

"I answered in order." He cocked his head at her as she popped up, her face flushed. "You're going to use that fork?"

"Five-second rule." She polished the tines of the fork

with a napkin. "You almost got married? You didn't strand anyone at the altar, did you?"

"Me?" He aimed his own fork at his chest. "I wouldn't do something like that, but I was the one who ended things. Just didn't seem…right. How about you? Boyfriend? Any near misses?"

He held his breath as she toyed with her fish.

"A few boyfriends here and there. Ended a relationship about six months ago over work. It hadn't lasted long—nothing much has. Like you said, just didn't seem… right."

Did the guy have the wrong smell? He coughed. "Tell me about the house in Venice. A murder, really?"

Lori planted her elbows on the table, her hesitation gone now that the conversation had veered away from the personal. "You heard about the Copycat Player killings, right?"

"I did." His hand carrying his cup to his mouth jerked and the ice rattled. "Tell me one of the victims did not live in that house."

"No, it belonged to a retired LAPD detective, the one who missed the original Player twenty years ago. The Player murdered the detective in the house. I know Detective Quinn's heir, and she asked me to stay in the house. I think she's just doing me a favor. My landlord kicked me out of the duplex I was renting because she wanted her son to live there. Kyra knew I was looking for a place and offered me the house for nothing close to what she could get for rent."

"Some favor." He dragged a fry through some ketchup. "Is it safe, this house in Venice?"

"Of course. The Player is dead and gone."

He dropped the French fry, bleeding red. "When my

sister didn't show up last night at the restaurant and then didn't answer my calls, that's what I thought about—all those women The Player and his copycats killed."

Lori shifted her hand across the table, her fingers inches from his, almost touching him. "I'm sure that's not what's going on here. Does Summer have a boyfriend?"

"Not that I know of." He ran a hand through his hair, the ends curling from the damp ocean air. "I haven't been a good brother. I know nothing about her life, but I kind of hoped to remedy that with this trip."

"From what I remember about Summer, she's independent that way."

His sharp laugh startled the seagull on the alert for scraps of food, and it flapped away to the next table. "That's one way of putting it."

Lori asked, "Where does she live? Have you tried showing up on her doorstep?"

"She lives in Los Feliz. I'd just been to her place before I came to the station to file a missing persons report." He spread his hands. "Lights on, nobody answered the door, nobody home."

Lori drummed her fingers on the table. "I suppose you don't have a key to her place."

"Key?" He raised his eyebrows. "I'm lucky I got the address out of her."

Lori grabbed her cup and puckered her lips around the straw, her dark eyes glimmering as she stared over his shoulder.

"What are you thinking?" He hunched forward, splaying his hands on either side of her plate. "That's the same look you always got just before daring me to do some ridiculous stunt."

"Just came from a situation like yours." She held up

one finger as he opened his mouth. "This guy tried to report his friend missing, but just like Summer his friend
hadn't been gone for forty-eight hours yet. He took matters into his own hands and broke into the friend's place.
There were signs of a struggle, some blood stains and
poof—" she snapped her fingers "—just like that, the
police came out to investigate. Now they have probable
cause and not just a worried friend…or brother."

Cade narrowed his eyes. "Are you suggesting I break
into my sister's place?"

She stuffed a fry in her mouth and waved her hands as
she chewed. "I'm not *suggesting* anything. I'm just telling you what got the attention of the police."

"Will you go with me?"

Her head jerked up. "Me? You want me to go with you
to break into your sister's place?"

"You always were my favorite partner in crime." He
brushed his thumb across the back of her hand. "It might
help me find out where she is. Maybe I don't need to file
a report at all. She lives alone, and it's not as if Summer's
going to press charges against me for breaking into her
home. The cops didn't charge that guy for breaking into
his friend's house, right?"

"What are we talking about here? Apartment? House?
Los Feliz is kind of upscale, trendy."

"My parents wouldn't relegate Summer to an apartment. She lives in a house, definitely near the trendy
part of Los Feliz."

"I'm in."

And just like that, he had Lori Del Valle on his side
again. He smothered his smile with a hand. Didn't want
to come off as smug or triumphant, although he did feel
like he'd just won an award.

Crumpling his napkin, he said, "Let's go. It's already dark, but we don't want to leave it until midnight, when we'd be much more suspicious lurking around."

"We're not lurking." She folded her paper plate around her uneaten food. "You're checking on your sister."

They left Lori's car in the structure and took his rental to Summer's house. On the ride over, they kept things light and talked about their jobs and their families. They'd already revealed their single status to each other, but Lori wasn't offering any more details about her personal life.

He didn't want to dig too much further. She might wonder why he was asking. He had a life in New York, didn't he? He maneuvered off the freeway and squinted at the sign pointing toward Los Feliz Boulevard.

Lights from restaurants and businesses still open gave a glow to the street, lending a normalcy to this mission.

He turned off the boulevard, a sudden dread thrumming through his veins. As if sensing his anxiety, Lori tapped her fingers on his forearm.

She didn't even have to say a word. It had always been that way between them. He released a sigh and a little bit of tension with it when he turned onto Summer's block. He pulled up in front of the small house with the light still on in the front window.

Lori pointed to the empty driveway. "Does Summer have a car?"

"Yeah, but she could keep it in the garage. I've never been inside her place. I don't know her habits."

"But you know she lives alone."

"For sure." He cut the engine. "Maybe we'll get lucky and the front door will be unlocked. She was always careless about that kind of stuff."

They both exited the vehicle, and Cade stood on the

sidewalk facing the house, hands on his hips. "We should probably do our breaking and entering around the back, away from neighbors' prying eyes."

"Let's try our luck first." Lori strode up to the house, rang the bell and tried the door. "I guess Summer isn't careless anymore."

They skirted the house along the side, and Cade lifted a latch on a wooden gate. The backyard boasted a small patio with a few dead potted plants and not much more. A slider led from the house to the patio, and he tried the door. "Locked."

Lori peeked around the other side of the house and crooked her finger at him. "Let's try that window."

She pointed at a small, frosted pane of glass, open a crack.

He said, "If we're going to break a window we might as well go big and break something I can fit through."

"Who said anything about breaking? I'm from East LA, *cabron*. I may have learned a few tricks from my brother and his friends." She grabbed his arm and pulled him toward the window. "Place your hands flat on the glass and push up. If there's any wiggle room, you can create some space at the bottom of the window frame and lift it out."

Grinning at her insult in Spanish, Cade reached over her and flattened his hands against the cool glass. He shoved the entire window up and lifted it from its track. "Got it."

"Try to maneuver it out."

With a little shifting and readjusting, he cleared the window from the track, grabbed the sides and lifted it free. As he leaned it against the side of the house, he said,

"That was scarily easy." He straightened to his full height. "I hope you're not expecting me to go through that."

"Of course not. You're here for the muscle. Give me a boost."

Crouching down, he laced his fingers to create a cradle, and Lori placed one sneaker in his hands. He lifted her until her head cleared the window frame.

She said, "It's right over the tub. I'll be fine. A little higher."

He raised his hands, and she grabbed the ledge and hoisted herself through the opening. He got a good look at her backside as she wriggled through the space, and then her feet disappeared as if she'd been sucked into a time portal.

Too bad it didn't lead to a portal to the past, so he could correct all the mistakes he'd made with his first serious relationship...his first love.

"Hey!"

He started and focused on the oval of her face framed by the opening.

"I'll let you in at the front door."

He left the window propped up against the side of the house and jogged back to the front porch. Seconds later, he heard the click of the dead bolt and Lori swung open the door, her dark eyes huge in her pale face.

His heart tumbled. "What's wrong?"

"I'm not sure. I glanced into a bedroom on my way to open the door and..." she twisted her fingers in front of her "...come have a look for yourself. Maybe it's nothing."

He shut the door behind him and followed her down a short hallway, his breath coming in short spurts. Lori had been to enough crime scenes to pick up on something amiss, and her alarm jolted him.

She turned into a room off the hallway, and he stumbled in behind her, his feet suddenly feeling like he was wearing clown shoes five sizes too big.

His gaze swept the room, lit from below by a lamp on its side near the bed. The messy bed drew his attention. Summer had never been a neat freak, but the disheveled covers looked as if they'd hosted a wrestling match.

He licked his lips and met Lori's glassy eyes for a split second. Then he charged out of the room calling his sister's name. He dipped his head into the kitchen, scanning the dirty dishes in the sink…and a broken glass on the floor.

With the adrenaline pumping through his body, he charged through the rest of the house. "Summer!"

He threw open a door that led to the attached garage, his fingers clawing for the light switch to verify the fact that her car was gone. He spun around and wandered back to the living room.

"Her car's gone. Maybe she left a mess and took off before she could pick up." Before she could pick up a broken glass on the kitchen floor?

Lori didn't reassure him. In fact, she said nothing at all as she crouched beside the front door, her back to him, her shoulders stiff.

Cade wiped the back of his hand across his mouth. "What's wrong?"

She twisted her head over her shoulder and whispered, "I found a bloody fingerprint."

Chapter Three

Cade listed to one side as if he couldn't keep steady on the pitching deck of a boat. Then he squared his shoulders and came toward her. He dropped to his knees in front of the door, and she circled the air in front of the latent print left in blood on the doorjamb—just like the print left at Courtney's house.

His blue eyes clouded. "That could be her print, right? Maybe she cut her finger on the glass she broke in the kitchen and touched the door frame on her way out."

Lori nodded but averted her eyes from his. She couldn't take the pleading in their depths. "Could be."

"Too bad we don't have your car. You can take the print now, couldn't you?"

She pushed to her feet, her hand on Cade's shoulder easing her way up. "I wouldn't do that, Cade. This scene needs to be processed. It's the same as the other situation I mentioned—there's some probable cause here. Summer's been gone for over twenty-four hours. Her phone is turned off. She missed a meeting with you. If you call the police now and tell them about the overturned lamp, the messed-up bed, the glass in the kitchen—and this bloody print—they'll come."

He stood up next to her and took her hand. "I want you to do it, Lori. I want you to be on the scene."

She squeezed his hand. "I think I can arrange that. Especially because…"

She trailed off, but Cade in his current state of mind didn't notice. She'd been about to remark on how much the scene at Summer's house resembled the house they'd processed earlier. Why no real evidence of a crime except for one fingerprint in blood? It's almost as if it was placed there on purpose.

She didn't actually know what the rest of the CSI team had discovered at Courtney's house. She didn't even know what she had yet with that print.

Cade called it in, using the words she put in his mouth for maximum response. A little over an hour later, she was working with the same team that had processed Courtney's house, except Detective Marino had replaced Detective Falco.

The detective made Cade wait in his rental car, and when Marino came back inside, he rolled his eyes at Lori.

She packed up the fingerprint kit one of the CSIs had brought to the scene for her, and sidled next to the detective. "What's up?"

"Mr. Cade Larson doesn't know much about his sister, does he?" He waved one arm around the room. "The bed could be due to a restless sleep, same with the bedside lamp knocked over. She dropped a glass in the kitchen, cut her hand and left a bloody print on her way out."

"On her way out where? Urgent care? A hospital emergency room? Then why didn't she call her brother who's visiting from New York? Why didn't she cancel their dinner? Why is her phone turned off?"

Marino leveled a finger at her. "You were working

too long on that task force for The Player. You could be
a bona fide detective now."

"Are you making fun of me?" She raised an eyebrow
and tilted her chin.

"Nope. There are definitely some issues with Summer's…disappearance, but young women go missing in
this city daily. We're here at this scene because I know
the brother is your friend and—" he jerked his thumb toward the front door "—that's Cade Larson from Larson
Construction, isn't it?"

She gave Marino a stingy smile. Cade's name and connections always did and would have pull in LA. Cade's
father was tight with the mayor, even though Mr. Larson
no longer lived here. Cade probably could've thrown the
Larson name around the station earlier and gotten the
same result without breaking into his sister's house—but
she was glad it had worked out this way.

"Yes, his and Summer's father is Lars Larson from
Larson Construction."

"Then it doesn't much matter that the brother knows
nothing about his sister's habits, and that she could be on
a vacation off the grid. Money and power talk." Marino
gave a shrug of his rounded shoulders.

A flash of heat claimed Lori's chest, as she rose to
Cade's defense. "He doesn't know much about her habits
because he lives across the country and he just got into
the city. He arrived the day he and Summer were scheduled to have dinner."

Marino held out his palms. "Okay, okay. I'm just
thinking he might be overreacting because he's feeling
guilty."

Lori opened her mouth and then snapped it closed.
She knew Cade felt guilty about not monitoring Sum-

mer more in his parents' absence, but Summer was an adult. They were all adults now, responsible for their own actions.

She could give Cade a lot more to feel guilty about, but she refused to go there with him. Hopefully, his sister would turn up unharmed, they could have a nice visit and Cade could return to his own corner of the country. She had exorcised him from her mind once. She could do it again.

She'd finished her part of the CSI but didn't want to mess up the chain of evidence by taking the prints back to the station in the car with the potential victim's brother. She located Sam, the photographer, and asked, "Can I ride back to the station with you? I don't have my car."

"Sure, give me ten."

Lori went outside and ducked beneath the yellow tape to put the fingerprint case in the van. When she turned, she almost bumped into Cade.

He nodded toward his sister's house. "Did they find anything else?"

"Not yet." She tapped the side of the van. "I'm going back to the station with the rest of the CSI team. Have to make sure the prints are protected."

"I'll follow you."

Did he think he could pump her for more information? If she had it, would she give it to him? If she had known someone on the inside of her brother's case, she would've done everything in her power to get a heads-up on the evidence. She expected no less from Cade.

"It's getting late, Cade." She touched his arm. "You don't have to follow. I'll tell you everything as soon as I learn it."

"Your car's still in the parking structure in Santa Monica. How are you going to collect it? I can drive you back."

"I can take an app car."

"By yourself?" His eyes widened. "To a parking structure in the middle of the night to then drive home alone to Venice? Not happening."

A little thrill ran up her spine. As self-sufficient as she'd always been, she'd adored that protective side of Cade. He'd protected her from everything right up until the end.

"I can't guarantee how long I'm going to be at the station, and I can't invite you up to the lab."

"I'll wait as long as it takes." He placed his hands on her shoulders. "I owe you. Without your suggestion tonight, I'd be cooling my heels in my hotel room waiting for forty-eight hours to have passed. Now, we're getting somewhere."

She blinked at the intensity of his eyes. "If you insist on waiting, at least get yourself some coffee so you have something to do in the car."

"Don't worry about me." He held up his cell phone. "I can always check emails from work. Just do what you have to do, and I'll be waiting for you in the parking lot of the station when you're done."

Nobody had waited around for her in quite a while. She could get used to this…but she'd better not. That phone in his hand with the emails waiting would take Cade back to New York soon enough.

He left the scene before the CSI van pulled out. She wanted to believe Detective Marino that Summer had taken off on her own. Lots of people wanted to disconnect and tune out these days. When her supervisor, Clive Stewart, had been identified as the notorious serial killer

The Player, she'd wanted to take off and unplug for a while herself. Then there was Summer's drug use. She noticed Cade hadn't told the detective any of that. Maybe she had kicked the habit, but that didn't mean it hadn't gotten her in its clutches again.

By the time the van got to the Northeast Division, Cade's rental car was already sitting in the parking lot. Before she walked into the station, she made a detour to Cade's car and he buzzed down the window at her approach.

He stuck out a hand, clutching a coffee cup, and his head followed. "Not sure what you wanted, so I went with a straight coffee, black, and then you can add to it."

She took the cup from him, and their fingertips met. She had to grab the cup before it slipped through their hands. His touch had always caused her to quake, and nothing had changed. "Thank you. If the wait becomes too much, text me. I don't know how long I'll be. It could be minutes or it could be an hour."

He held up his coffee in one hand and a pastry bag in the other. "I'm good to go."

She left him in the parking lot and went upstairs to the lab with the prints she'd taken from Summer's house.

She hadn't gotten a response back from IAFIS on the other prints, not that she'd expected anything this soon. Only murder investigations got the rush treatment.

She got to work prepping the bloody print from Summer's place for submission to IAFIS. At a glance, that print did not look similar to the prints she'd gathered from the rest of the house—prints most likely belonging to Summer. The realization caused a flutter of fear in her chest.

The bloody print could belong to Summer's friend,

someone at the house when she'd cut her hand on the glass in the kitchen. Someone there to help, not harm.

She worked for about twenty minutes, and by the time she finished, the other techs had left. She'd felt a little creeped out in the lab alone ever since she found out about Clive, but she was never really alone at the station. Even detectives worked a graveyard shift for the LAPD, and some spent that time at their desks going over evidence, doing research, reviewing mug shots.

When she packed up to leave, she poked her head into the room that housed Robbery-Homicide in an open layout. As expected, a few detectives populated the desks and a couple of patrol officers were hanging out.

She raised a hand. "I'm taking off."

They all glanced up and one of the officers asked her if she wanted him to walk her to her car.

She snorted. "I'm at a police station. Besides, I have a ride waiting for me, but thanks."

Was he still waiting for her? Cade had let her down only once, but it had been a devastating blow to her. She swallowed and felt light-headed when she saw his car parked in the same spot, a glow coming from the interior. He hadn't been kidding about getting some work done.

Lori tapped on the driver's-side window, and Cade glanced up. The locks popped and he jerked his thumb toward the passenger seat.

As she slid into the seat beside him, she inhaled the scent of warm banana bread. She flicked the paper bag on the center console. "You really know how to make yourself at home."

"I even got some work done." He held out the crumpled bag in his palm. "There's a little piece of banana bread left. Do you want it?"

"No, thanks, but that coffee sure helped." She snapped her seat belt and studied his profile in the muted light. "You didn't have to wait."

"You said that to me once before—I took you at your word and regretted it ever since." His lips twisted into a smile.

Was that how he remembered it? To cover her awkwardness, she grabbed the bag and fished out the bread. She stuffed the whole piece in her mouth.

Cade didn't even blink. He started the car and pulled out of the lot. "I suppose you didn't discover anything yet."

She swallowed and patted the sticky crumbs on her lips. "I just prepped the prints and submitted them to the national database. I also added them to our own local database of prints—faster read, but not as comprehensive. It's not a substitute for IAFIS by any means."

She jerked her head to the side when she heard Cade huff out a breath. "What?"

A half smile curved his mouth. "I like hearing you talk shop. I'm glad you found work that inspires you."

"Don't tell me you think it's cute." She crossed her arms in case he got any ideas.

"Not at all. Just makes me happy to know you found a calling." His hands clenched the steering wheel before he flexed his fingers. "It is your calling, right? Not just another way to help Danny?"

She tightened her jaw. What if it was? "I like the work. It has nothing to do with my brother."

"Okay, good. I'd hate to hear you'd let Danny control your life like…" He stopped and bit his lower lip.

Like she used to let Danny occupy all her thoughts.

and energy? She slumped in her seat and closed her eyes. "I'm tired."

He splayed his hands on the wheel. "Got it."

Cade drove the rest of the way without talking while she pretended to doze. How had she let him get under her skin so quickly?

When he pulled next to her car in the empty parking structure, she grabbed the door handle. "Thanks for the ride, Cade, and the dinner. I'll keep you informed if anything comes up."

She gave him a quick wave and slammed the door. She needed to put this relationship back on the right track—professional only. She couldn't afford to lose her heart to Cade Larson again.

And she couldn't afford to tell him about their child.

THE FOLLOWING MORNING, Lori showered and dressed for work. She hadn't gotten rid of Cade as easily as she'd thought when she'd hightailed it out of his car and into her own in the parking garage last night. He'd followed her home to her house on the Venice Canals and waited until she'd crossed the wooden bridge, his headlights illuminating her way. When she reached her street, he flashed his lights.

Instead of giving her the warm fuzzies, his gesture had sent a wave of panic crashing through her body. The man could snap his fingers and she'd morph into a gooey puddle at his expensively shod size elevens.

She gave herself a grimace as she scraped her hair into a severe ponytail. There would be no melting if she could avoid him.

Once they found Summer crashing at a friend's place with an injured hand, Cade could return to New York, and she could return to…what? Work, worry over Danny, her mother's phone calls gushing about her grandchildren in Texas and The Hague—not about the secret grandchild Lori put up for adoption after she'd graduated from high school. The child she'd never mentioned to Cade.

It could be worse.

By the time she arrived at the Northeast Division, she'd shaken off her poor, pitiful me mood and she breezed into the lab. She hung up her jacket and purse and sidled next to Josh, working at the table in the middle of the room. "You missed some action last night—two potential crime scenes. Skiing in Big Bear?"

"I heard, and yeah, my kids wanted to catch the last of the snow up there before the pack melts." He rubbed his eyes. "But the drive home last night? Brutal. Two missing women?"

"Maybe." Lori crossed the room to her desk and booted up her computer. "Some similarities to the scenes. I processed and prepped the prints and sent them to IAFIS."

"Did you submit them to the local, too?"

"I did and—" she scooted in closer to her laptop, her breath catching in her throat "—hello. Looks like I got a hit on the local database already."

Josh grunted. "Your lucky day."

Lori brought up the report, and her eyes widened. "This can't be right."

"Don't tell me. We got The Player's prints again."

Her gaze darted between the bloody print from Courtney's house and the prints from Summer's. Her heart hammered in her chest as she stared at the irrefutable evidence.

Summer Larson had left a fingerprint in blood at Courtney Jessup's place.

Chapter Four

Cade stepped out of the shower and tucked the white hotel towel around his waist. As he brushed his teeth in front of the mirror, his phone rang on the vanity and he dropped his toothbrush in the sink as he lunged for it. His disappointment lasted less than a second when he saw Lori's name on the display instead of Summer's.

"Did they find her?" His voice echoed off the tiles of the cavernous bathroom, amplifying the sound of his fear.

"No, but…" Lori took a deep breath, which made Cade's heart rate ratchet up a few more notches. "Look, I discovered something weird this morning when I came into the station. I want to talk to you about it—in person. Lunch?"

"Yeah, yeah, lunch—" Cade slicked back his wet hair from his forehead with one unsteady hand "—but you can't leave me hanging, Lori. What did you discover?"

"Does the name Courtney Jessup mean anything to you?"

"No." The mirror had steamed up again, and he rubbed a hole in the center of it with his fist, as if that could clear the confusion in his mind. "Does she have something to do with Summer?"

Lori coughed. "Remember I told you about the other

missing woman and how her friend had broken into her place?"

"That's what gave you the idea that I should do the same at Summer's place. What about her?"

"That woman was Courtney Jessup, and I lifted a bloody fingerprint from her house just like I did at Summer's."

"Yeah?" The towel slipped from Cade's waist and dropped to the floor, pooling around his feet, but he stood frozen, hanging on every one of Lori's words.

Lori blew out a breath. "The bloody print at Courtney's place matches Summer's print. Summer was at Courtney's place."

Cade shook his head back and forth, flicking droplets of water onto the vanity. "That's not possible. Why would Summer be at the crime scene of another house? Are you implying she had something to do with Courtney's disappearance?"

"Not at all. I don't know what it means, Cade. I double-checked a few times to make sure I hadn't somehow entered the wrong print for Summer, but there it is. Summer's fingerprint was definitely at Courtney's house."

"Maybe they were abducted together." Cade grabbed the damp towel and clutched it to his chest. "Maybe Summer was injured and taken at Courtney's, and then their kidnapper returned to Summer's house to… I don't know, steal something or make her get her car and purse."

"That could be." She paused. "I turned the information over to the detective on the case, but I wanted you to know. You have a right to know, but I have to get back to work right now. Let's have lunch…near Los Feliz. Bring Summer's key. I saw you take it last night."

His grip on his phone loosened for the first time since

he picked it up. He knew what Lori had in mind, and he was game. "Give me a time and place, and I'll be there... with the key."

CADE SPENT THE morning on the phone with his assistant and working on a report for a new development, which he'd have to check for errors later. Lori's bombshell news occupied his mind, as he turned it over and over in his head.

Summer obviously knew Courtney. Perhaps the two women had been surprised together. The intruder had a weapon, but the women fought back. Maybe Summer left a bloody print at the scene as a clue. The kidnapper could've then forced Summer, or both women, back to Summer's house and another struggle ensued there.

That had to be the explanation.

He checked the time on his laptop and shut it down. He slid the computer into his bag in case he and Lori needed it for...sleuthing? He knew Lori intended to look into this on her own.

She may work for the police department, but it didn't mean she trusted the police. Her brother's run-ins with the cops had left a bad taste in her mouth, even though everyone else could see that Danny instigated the issues. You couldn't say that to Lori though. *He* couldn't say it to her. He'd tried a few times, and his efforts had ended in arguments between them.

Now Lori's distrust of the police would benefit him. He knew he could count on her to share every aspect of this investigation with him, and he planned to take advantage of that.

He should've gotten a hotel closer to Summer's house to save him the trek across LA, but he preferred staying near the coast and he had thought he'd have a couple of dinners with Summer, check on his parents' home in Malibu and head back to New York. He couldn't have been more wrong.

It took him over an hour to get to the restaurant on Los Feliz Boulevard and another fifteen minutes to find parking, but his efforts paid off. When he walked into the bustling café, Lori popped up from a table by the window and waved her hand at him. As the hostess approached him, he pointed to Lori and said, "I'm joining her."

He'd searched for Lori on social media in the past, but she didn't have much of a presence online. He didn't know what he would've done if he'd contacted her, anyway, but seeing her now made him regret not trying harder.

Over the years, he'd tried to dismiss his feelings for Lori as a shallow high school crush, but he'd never really convinced himself of that. How could something surface level seep into your pores and stay with you for almost ten years?

He threaded his way through the other tables to reach her and pulled out the chair across from her. Jerking his thumb at the window, he said, "Good spot."

"I got here a little early." With her fingernail, she pinged her glass of soda, which had to be Diet Coke. She'd been addicted to the drink. "I would've ordered you an iced tea, but I didn't want to presume. You used to drink the stuff by the gallon, the only teenage boy I knew who didn't guzzle sugary soft drinks."

"You know my father wouldn't allow that stuff in our house." He rolled his eyes and shook his finger. "No refined sugar, son."

She toyed with her straw. "I wasn't sure if you still followed your father's rules."

A flash of heat claimed his chest. "You know, old habits die hard—not that any of that health stuff our dad mandated ever had an impact on Summer."

The waitress approached, and he ordered his iced tea while they both told her they needed more time with the menu.

When the waitress spun away to her next table, Lori hunched forward. "I checked the print again, and it's a match. Summer was definitely at Courtney's place."

"What did the detective say?"

She lifted and dropped her shoulders quickly. "He's not going to tell me, is he? They'll probably investigate the contacts of the two women to find out how they might have been connected."

"Are we going to, what?" He spread his hands. "Conduct our own parallel investigation?"

"It's either that or you can wait for the police to share information with you about the case when they're good and ready." Her lips clamped around her straw and she took a sip of her drink. "Is that what you want? The police never told us about that unidentified print at Elena's house. They never told Danny or his lawyer—not until they got the confession out of Danny. Do you want to go down that road?"

"I don't want to be kept in the dark, but I don't want to get you in trouble."

Placing a hand against her chest, Lori widened her eyes and fluttered her lashes. *"Moi?"*

The waitress returned, saving him from cataloguing all the ways this could go wrong for Lori, but all she'd done so far was give him a heads-up on the print. He had a right to know that information.

After they ordered their sandwiches, Lori folded her hands on the table. "Did you bring the key to Summer's house?"

He patted the chest pocket of the flannel he'd thrown on over his T-shirt this morning when he left the hotel. "Got it right here. What's the plan? Can we get into Summer's place after the search last night, or is that off-limits?"

"Wasn't much of a crime scene to process. They're done with it, but it doesn't mean we are." She tapped a finger on the table. "Now that we know Summer knew Courtney, we have a better idea of what to look for in her house."

"What about the police? Will they be doing the same?"

"They can go a step beyond us. They can get Courtney's and Summer's phone records. There's no evidence of a murder, so they won't put a rush on those records. They can also question Courtney's friend. Of course, we can do that, too." She held up a hand as he opened his mouth. "There's no law against talking to Trey Ferrar on our own. He might open up to you more when he finds out your sister's print was at his friend's place."

"I don't know if that's a great idea. This guy, Trey, might think Summer had something to do with the disappearance of Courtney—and we know that's not true." Cade abraded his knuckles across his jaw. "I know how I'd feel if it were the other way around—if Courtney's bloody print had been found at Summer's house. That didn't happen, did it?"

Lori paused as the waitress dropped off their baskets of food. She picked up a French fry and waved it in the air. "I submitted the print from Summer's house to the national database but haven't received any match back yet and it didn't match up to anything we have locally—including Courtney's print."

Cade let out the breath he'd been holding and took a bite of his sandwich. He didn't know what Lori expected to find from searching Summer's house that the cops wouldn't uncover from her phone records, but he couldn't stand around waiting for the police to fill him in on his missing sister. Action beat inaction anytime.

Cade slurped up the tea at the bottom of his glass. "If we're going to turn Summer's house upside down, we'd better get going. You have to get back to work at some point."

"I have some time. I worked over the weekend, so I bought myself some hours off during the week."

Pushing his food away, Cade asked, "What exactly are we looking for that the police wouldn't notice?"

"The police did a forensics sweep, but we don't even know if a crime has been committed. That's a different type of search. They may get Summer's phone records, but there's no urgency...yet."

"Even after finding her prints at the other missing woman's place?"

"A lot of people go missing in LA, Cade, some even know each other. That's why you have to take matters into your own hands sometimes." Lori's lips formed a thin line, and her jaw tightened.

Did she really still believe if she'd been able to investigate the murder of Danny's girlfriend that she could've exonerated him?

He held up his hands. "You don't have to convince me.

I felt frustrated at the station yesterday when I couldn't do anything to help Summer. You changed all that."

A pink tinge touched her cheeks, and she grabbed the check. "You got dinner last night, so lunch is on me."

He gave up easily. Uncomfortable with his family's wealth, Lori had always been conscious of paying her own way, and she hadn't seemed to have changed.

Lori followed him to Summer's house, and his gaze flicked across the front as he pulled up to the curb. When Lori joined him on the sidewalk, he asked, "No crime scene tape?"

"The police are done with the search. We're not going to disturb anything." She tugged on the sleeve of his shirt. "Let's go."

Cade fished Summer's house key out of the pocket of his shirt, as he strode toward the porch. He unlocked the bottom lock. The cops hadn't had a key to lock the dead bolt when they left, so they'd left it unlocked. Pushing open the door, he held his breath. Maybe she'd just step into the room, tossing her long blond hair over her shoulder, blue eyes twinkling with mischief.

The silence that met him splashed his face with cold water.

He blinked. "She's not here."

Lori touched his shoulder. "We'll find her. You look out here and I'll check her bedroom."

"What are we looking for?" He ran a hand through his hair, his eyes darting around the room.

"Anything a little unusual." Lori held up her hand and ticked off her fingers. "Diary, for sure. Receipts, business cards, address book, even scraps of papers with names or numbers."

He shoved his hands in his pockets, his feet rooted

to the floor. Did he want to know any of Summer's private business? "If she had a diary, the police would've taken it."

"They don't even know if a crime has been committed." Lori shrugged. "Maybe we'll get lucky, but we're not going to find anything if we don't get started."

Cade felt a flush suffuse his face. She must've noticed his reluctance. His family had always looked the other way when it came to Summer's secrets, his parents covering them up to avoid embarrassment. Maybe that was why his sister had wound up missing in LA with no family members in town.

He willed his feet to move, one plodding step following the next. "I'll start with the kitchen."

Lori nodded once and headed down the hallway to Summer's bedroom.

Cade yanked open the first cabinet on his right and studied the mismatched plates and bowls, stacked into little, leaning towers. One corner of his mouth twitched. His mother would get an anxiety attack just looking at this hodgepodge...probably why Summer did it.

His other sister, Sarah, had always conformed to what Mom wanted, or maybe Sarah wanted it, too—that well-ordered existence of matching dishes and matching shoes and fake smiles that pretended that was all anyone ever needed in life to be happy.

Had he fallen into that trap, too? It hadn't been that way in high school when he'd dated Lori. She'd encouraged an aspect of his personality that he'd previously shut down, made him feel alive. Had he been living in some kind of alternate reality since then? None of the women he'd dated in New York had ever made him feel the way he'd felt about Lori.

He blinked. Staring at dishes wouldn't help Summer now. He slammed the cupboard doors and pulled open a drawer. Sifting through the jumbled mess of paper clips, pens, magnets and sticky notes, he thought that this had to be more of what Lori meant.

As he squinted at a pink square of paper stuck to his fingertip, Lori called from the bedroom, "I found something."

His heart jumped and he spun away from the open drawer, the pink sticky note still attached to his finger as he rushed to the bedroom. His gaze tracked over the rumpled bed covers and the gaping drawers and landed on Lori standing on a chair facing the closet. She'd made a lot more progress than he had.

She peered over her shoulder at him, cupping something in the palm of her hand. "I think this might be important."

He entered the room, stepping over a pillow on the floor. "What is it?"

Turning, she hopped down from the chair and stretched out her open hand. "A key."

"A key?" He tilted his head to one side and plucked the small silver key from her hand. "Why do you think this is important? It could be a key to anything, although..."

Lori cut him off. "It's important because she hid it. I could see tossing a key in a drawer, but she secreted this away in a shoebox. It was taped to the inside of the box."

"Okay." Cade chewed his bottom lip as he ran a thumb along the teeth of the key.

"Th-there's something else, Cade."

He glanced at her face, her soft lips pulled down into a frown, and his pulse quickened. Then he dropped his gaze to the shoe dangling from her other hand. "You found a shoe in a shoebox?"

"I wish that's all it was." She shoved her fingers into the toe of the shoe and pulled out a plastic bag, which crackled between her fingers. "I also found this."

He peered at the small baggie pinched between her thumb and forefinger, zeroing in on the powdery white substance inside. His jaw felt tight as he eked the word out between his lips. "Drugs."

Chapter Five

Lori curled her hand around the baggie and squeezed her fist. She hadn't wanted to tell Cade that his sister was using again, but he shouldn't run from the truth. The Larson family always ran from the truth.

His family's insistence on covering up every unpleasant blip in the road had driven a wedge between her and Cade, and it was one of the many reasons she'd never told him about her pregnancy. His parents would've gone ballistic.

He sank to the foot of the rumpled bed and braced his elbows on his knees, his head hanging down. "She told me she was clean."

"They always say that." She sat beside him and rubbed a circle on his back. The gesture took her back to their teen years when they'd console each other about their errant siblings. Now Danny was in prison for manslaughter and Summer was missing under suspicious circumstances.

Once you added drugs to the mix of a person who'd disappeared, it put a whole new twist on the situation. She flattened the baggie on her knee. "What do you think it is? What was she using?"

"According to what she told me, nothing, but this

could be anything, right? Cocaine, heroin, GHB, fentanyl, Molly."

She raised her eyebrows. "You know your street drugs."

"And how do you think I got so knowledgeable?" He clasped his hands in front of him. "Trial by fire trying to help Summer conquer her addictions."

The baggie expanded as she spread open her fingers, the white powder shifting in the creases of the plastic. "Why do you think she hid the drugs with the key? They must be connected."

"Really?" He jerked his head to the side. "Maybe she used that box to hide everything. Did you find anything else inside?"

"Just the shoes." She kicked at the suede pump on the floor, tipping it over. "If I recall correctly, that's hardly her style."

Cade hunched his shoulders. "I wouldn't really know, but I do think I know something about this key."

"Really?"

Holding it up, he said, "It looks like a safe deposit box key, doesn't it?"

"You're asking me?" She drilled a finger into her chest. "I've never had a safe deposit box in my life and wouldn't know the first thing about what a key to one should look like, although I imagine it would be on the small side…like this one."

"Exactly." He bobbled the key in the palm of his hand and it winked as it caught the light from the window. "Why would a safe deposit box be linked to drugs? She wouldn't be putting drugs in the bank. In fact, I find it hard to believe she put her stash in the toe of a shoe, in a shoebox, on a shelf in her closet. You're standing on a chair to reach it, and Summer's not much taller than you are. It's not a convenient location."

"Unless that's her backup. Maybe the person who abducted her took her drugs, too, drugs she kept closer at hand."

"That doesn't make me feel any better." Cade pushed off the bed and took a turn around the room. "And it still doesn't answer the question as to why she hid a key to a safe deposit box and a baggie of drugs in the same place."

"You're sure it's a safe deposit box and not some locker somewhere?" Lori dipped to the floor and swept up the shoe. Running her fingers across the suede, she said, "It just looks like a small key to me. It could be anything."

Cade framed the key with two fingers and held it up. "Trust me. I know safe deposit boxes, and I'm sure my parents set her up with one."

"Do you know where Summer banks?"

"I don't have a clue, but she must have some bank receipts around here. Even if she does everything online, she's gotta have some ATM receipts tucked away somewhere. It's not as if she has a great filing system." Cade tucked the key into the front pocket of his jeans. "And I know just the place to look."

Lori waved the bag of drugs in the air. "What do we do with this?"

"We're not turning it over to the police." Cade stopped at the bedroom door and gripped either side of the doorjamb.

Lori scooted off the bed, dropping the shoe to the floor, where it thunked loudly. She thought he might say something like this. "The more information the police have, the faster they can find Summer."

"You, of all people, are telling me this?" He cranked

his head over his shoulder. "Once they know she's involved with drugs, they'll lose the urgency to investigate her disappearance—not that they have much of an urgency now. You know how it is, Lori. They'll figure she's off doing drugs somewhere or ran away with her druggie friends. Let's look into this ourselves first."

She did know how he felt. Even though she worked with the police every day and respected the hell out of them, her family had been burned before by detectives who wanted the easy answer and took it.

She let out a slow breath. "Sure, we'll do it your way for now."

His shoulders slumped. "Good. Do you want to clean up in here while I claw through Summer's junk drawer in the kitchen?"

"Go for it."

When he exited the room, Lori straightened the bed and stuffed some items hanging over the drawers back inside. She perched on the edge of the bed and swept a sleep mask, a packet of condoms and a bottle of melatonin into an open drawer on Summer's nightstand. Why did Summer need melatonin to sleep on top of everything else she might be taking?

As she began to slide the drawer closed, a blue-and-green card stuck in the back corner caught her eye. She plucked it free and held it up to the light from the open blinds at the window. She read aloud from the card. "'Brighter Days Recovery Center, Reed Dufrain, Center Coordinator.'"

Pinching the card between her fingers, Lori bounced up from the bed and called out, "Cade?"

He yelled back, "I found it. I found her bank."

She joined him in the kitchen, where a drawer gaped open, revealing a jumbled mess of odds and ends.

He waved some papers in the air. "First Western Bank. Figures, since that's where my parents bank, and I still bank there due to habit. My parents probably set up the account and safe deposit box for her."

"I found something, too." She flicked the card. "Did Summer ever talk about rehab? She had this card in the drawer of her bedside table for Brighter Days Recovery Center. There's a rehab facility in Topanga Canyon and a treatment center in Hollywood."

Cade leaned in, his breath warm on her cheek. "She's been in and out of rehab, but I've never heard of this place—not that she told me much about her recovery process. I guess it didn't work out for her, or she wouldn't have had those drugs in her closet."

"That's weird, to have a card for a treatment center and a stash of drugs in your place."

"Is it?" Cade slid the drawer closed with a sharp snap. "It's not uncommon for addicts to fall off the wagon and even go back and forth. Didn't that happen to Danny?"

Tears pricked the backs of her eyes, and she ran a hand under her nose. "Danny never tried to stop using, and he certainly didn't have the money for an expensive recovery spa like this one in Topanga. His treatment center was prison."

Cade squeezed her shoulder. "I'm sorry. I didn't mean it like that."

Her sniff turned into a smile. "I know you didn't. It still might be worth checking out this Brighter Days Recovery Center and talking to—" she squinted at the card "—Reed Dufrain."

"First things first. Let's see what Summer has in her

safe deposit box that she'd keep the key hidden away with her drugs. I hope she doesn't have more drugs in there. That could be a legal problem."

"How do you plan to get into her safe deposit box? I know I said I didn't have one, but that doesn't mean I don't have some inkling of how they work. Don't you have to be an authorized user or something? Doesn't the bank have signatures on file and yours has to match?"

"You should know by now how the Larson family does things. First Western is my bank—it's my parents' bank and I'm one hundred percent sure they opened that account for my sister and they're coapplicants with her. I can also guarantee my father knows someone on the board and has done a favor for him or her in the past."

He must've noticed the sour look on her face because he spread his hands and said, "That's the way of the world. In this case, it's to our benefit."

"I know." She leveled a finger at him. "Don't think I forgot all the special treatment I got hanging out with you and the other kids at Brentwood Prep."

"At times like these—" he shoved the bank receipts in his pocket "—those connections come in handy. Speaking of connections, do you have the entire day off?"

"That doesn't have to do with connections, rich boy." She slugged his biceps, meeting rock-solid muscle. "That comes from putting in the extra work."

He glanced at his phone. "We still need to get over to the bank before it closes. Even I can't force the bank to open for my personal needs."

"I bet your dad could."

"And you'd be right."

"Are you going to tell your parents about Summer? What if they've been trying to contact her?"

"Not yet. My father would make this all about him, and they rarely call Summer. They've always taken a hands-off approach to her and her issues, or have just thrown money at them. I'll reach out to them at the appropriate time—this isn't it."

He dangled his key between them. "Ready? We can't keep following each other all over LA. Leave your car here, and I'll drive to the bank."

"Is her branch nearby?"

"I looked it up. Close enough."

They locked up Summer's house, and then Lori slid into the passenger seat of Cade's rental. Sitting next to Cade in a car like this caused the memories to come at her fast and hard. They'd spent a lot of time in Cade's car in high school. They couldn't meet at her small house in Pacoima, jam-packed with people, and she'd been uneasy around the opulence of his house, on the coast in Malibu.

She cleared her throat. "I'm still not sure how you hope to get into Summer's safe deposit box."

"We'll figure it out when we get there." He tapped his finger on her thigh. "Don't you trust me?"

Years ago, that would've been a loaded question. Today? She'd made it through her naive teenage years, and Cade had developed into a man under his own agency. Hadn't he?

"I trust the power of the Larson name. How's that?" She slid a glance to the side just in time to see his jaw harden.

Gripping the steering wheel with both hands, he said, "It has to be good enough…for now."

And the Larson name hadn't failed them, although she had to give some credit to Cade's take-charge manner that combined smooth coercion with a friendly insistence. It had taken a few phone calls and Cade's assurance that he had Summer's key, with her permission, but they'd made it to the bank's safe deposit vault alone with Summer's box in front of them.

As soon as the door closed with a whisper, on the woman who'd ushered them into the inner sanctum, Cade flipped open the lid of the long box.

Lori hovered beside him to peer into the metal container. Rolled-up papers that looked like old stock certificates nestled in the box, along with some pieces of jewelry that sparkled like fire in the low lights of the room.

She snatched one of the certificates from the box and smoothed it out on the table. "These must be old. Companies don't even issue certificates anymore."

Cade drilled his finger in the center of the paper before she let go and it rolled up again against his hand. "Pretty sure these are from our grandparents. I have a few of them myself."

"The jewelry?" Lori hooked a finger around a diamond necklace and lifted it from the box. "I'm assuming this is real or it wouldn't be here."

"It's real. Again, these are pieces from my grandmother's collection that she left to Summer and Sarah." Cade hunched over the box and sifted through the contents.

As the papers ran through his fingers, Lori spotted a familiar blue-and-green pattern. "Wait. What's that?"

"What?" Cade rested his hands on either side of the box, and Lori dipped her hand inside to retrieve the card.

Running her thumb across the embossed lettering on the front of the card, she said, "This is the same card for the Brighter Days Recovery Center I found in her nightstand drawer. Why would she put a business card for a rehab center in a safe deposit box?"

"I don't know why my sister does half the stuff she does. Maybe it wound up in here by accident."

"Because you keep a business card with heirloom jewelry and old stock certificates?" Lori bit her lip and flipped the card over.

Cade fanned through the papers in the box. "And a bunch of other papers. She could've swept it up with this stuff."

"Who are Diana, Chelsea and Karenna?" She held out the card to Cade. "All those names are on the back of this card. Is this Summer's handwriting?"

He scooted closer to her, his shoulder pressing against hers, his presence making her slightly dizzy in the small confines of the room.

"That is Summer's handwriting, and I've never heard her mention those names. That's not surprising though— I couldn't even give the police any names to contact." He ran a finger along the edge of the card. "Do you think it's important?"

"I think it's important that she felt it necessary to lock up this card with these names in a safe deposit box with priceless diamonds."

He flicked the necklace in the box. "I wouldn't say these are priceless."

"You know what I mean." Lori nudged his arm with her elbow, just to get him out of her space. Did he realize the havoc he was causing in her brain…and her body? "I think we should hang on to this card. It's the only thing in this box that doesn't make sense."

"I agree." He rubbed the back of his hand along his forehead. "I'm just happy there are no drugs in here."

"If we could get her phone records, maybe we could match up some of these first names with people in her contacts. Then we could reach out to them to find out what's going on with her." She shoved the card in her purse. "You don't have any of those golden Larson contacts with her cell provider, do you?"

"Not that I know of." He carefully rolled up the stock certificates. "Is that something the police could do?"

"They can, but like I said before, there's no evidence of a homicide. They're in no hurry on this one." She scooped up the necklace and dangled it from her fingers, watching the rainbow sparks dance across the bank of safe deposit drawers. "Are you rethinking giving them info on the drugs?"

"That's not going to give them a greater sense of urgency. In fact, the drugs are going to give them an excuse to back off. Both of us have seen this play out before." He held out his hand for the necklace. "Drug use equals throwaway person."

She dropped the heavy piece in his palm. "I hear ya. It's definitely one of the reasons why they jumped on Danny so fast."

Cade slid the box home and buzzed in the banker. Together, they secured the box and left the bank. He turned to her in the car. "Dinner later?"

Her pulse fluttered despite her best efforts to remain calm and cool. She thought her visceral response to Cade at their first meeting had been due to the time that had passed. Anyone would be excited to see a high school flame, his or her first love, the father of her only child. That was why high school reunions spelled trouble for so many people.

But the spark she'd felt when she saw him in the lobby

of the station had been growing into a full-on fire and if she didn't watch herself, she'd be in the middle of an inferno. But if she ran now, he'd see right through her.

She lifted one shoulder and dropped it quickly. "Sure, I can do dinner."

Her cheeks burned at the half smile that quirked the side of his mouth. He'd seen right through her anyway.

"Let's get your car at Summer's and we'll discuss the where and when via text later. I'm going to try to do some work."

As Cade pulled out of the bank's parking lot, Lori fished the card for Brighter Days out of her purse. "I'm going to look this up online. Maybe Summer is there for rehab, and she's not supposed to answer her phone or have contact with anyone."

"And Courtney? Why were Summer's prints at her house?"

Lori tapped the edge of the card on the dashboard. "Maybe Courtney's in the same place. They know each other and decided to get treatment together."

"We don't know if they knew each other. The detectives haven't told you that yet, right?" He slid a glance her way, as if he suspected she was holding out on him.

She'd lied to Cade only once, even though it had been a whopper.

"They haven't told me anything." She traced a line over her lips. "They keep a lot to themselves."

"What about going to the source? You told me Courtney had a friend who reported her disappearance."

"Yeah, Trey. I can track him down. We can keep it on the sly. The department wouldn't appreciate my sleuthing on my own, but they can't control everything I do on my off hours."

"Like searching Summer's place and checking out her safe deposit box? I'll never tell." Cade put his finger to his lips.

She bounced her knuckle against the window. "Just drop me off and text me about dinner. I'm going to run back to the station for an hour."

He cruised to a stop across the street from her car, then parked in front of Summer's house and left the engine running as she opened the door.

She waved her hand at him. "See you later."

She jogged across the street, feeling his eyes following her. As she approached her car, she tripped to a stop, her hand covering her mouth.

Someone had slashed all four of her tires.

Chapter Six

Cade noticed the flat tires on Lori's car before she stumbled to a halt. One flat tire he could understand, but two, possibly four? He scrambled from his car.

He reached Lori just when she dropped to a crouch near her front driver's-side wheel. She turned her head over her shoulder. "Someone slashed them, Cade, all of them."

Running a finger along the smooth gap, he swore. "That they did. Do you have any enemies? Someone who would follow you here?"

"Enemies? No, of course not." She rose to her feet and squinted at the end of the street, her nostrils flaring. "It's because I'm here, at Summer's house. Don't you get it? Nobody followed me. Someone was watching Summer's house for some reason, and wants to warn me off, warn *us* off."

Cade felt a little buzz of apprehension at the back of his neck, and slapped it with his palm. "Who would care if we were here? The police were already here."

"The same person who knows where she is. There's nothing they can do about the cops showing up. But us?" Lori folded her arms and hunched her shoulders.

He couldn't go down this risky path with her. This

might be her life, working alongside serial killers, visiting her brother in prison—but it wasn't his. "Hadn't you just convinced yourself that Summer and Courtney were in rehab?"

"That was before someone sliced my tires—two of which were brand-new."

"You need to call the cops. Does the LAPD come out for flat tires these days?"

"Not normally, but I'm one of them—sort of. They'll respond and take a report. I'll need it for the insurance anyway." She flicked her fingers in his direction. "You can head back to your hotel. I'll meet you later."

His eyebrows shot up. "Are you nuts? I'm not leaving you on this street with four slashed tires. You're going to need a tow, and then you'll be without a car. It's too late in the day for a garage to replace all your tires and get your car back to you. Call the cops, and then call your roadside service, if you have it."

"I do." She slipped her phone from her purse.

"I'll wait with you until the cops take a report and the tow truck driver hauls away your car. Then I'll drive you home. *Then* we'll have dinner."

She looked up from her phone. "What about work?"

"I think this is more important." He cocked his head at her. Did she really think he'd leave her stranded here so he could get a few hours of work in before dinner? He must've been a worse boyfriend than he'd remembered.

Lori rolled her shoulders and tapped her phone display. "Cade to the rescue."

"Is that a problem?"

She held up her finger and started talking into her cell.

Forty minutes later, a cop car and a tow truck bookended Lori's car. As the fresh-faced cop snapped her notebook shut, she said, "There's not much we can do about it, Lori, but you can have the report for insurance purposes."

"Thanks, Jen. I hope it's covered as vandalism, or something."

Jen started to follow her partner back to their patrol car and spun around. "Be careful. Takes a lot of effort to gouge four tires like that. Someone must really have a grudge against you. This is no teenage prank."

Cade shifted his stance toward Lori and placed a hand on her back. This was all she needed to fire up her imagination and paranoia…and his.

"Does your brother have ties on the outside?" Jen bit her bottom lip, maybe afraid she'd said too much.

Lori's back stiffened beneath his hand. "My brother's connections didn't have anything to do with this."

"He's a member of the Norteños, isn't he?" Jen stood her ground, her eyes meeting Lori's.

Lori's back positively vibrated, and her voice grated. "Why would you think that? He and his friends ran wild, but they weren't in a gang."

"Norteños is a prison gang, not a street gang." Jen threw her hands out to her sides and said, "Hey, everyone has to survive inside, and if they don't play by the rules…sometimes people suffer on the outside."

"If it is something like that, it's because Danny wouldn't join the gang."

"If he didn't join, he'd be dead."

"Thanks for taking the report, Jen."

Jen shrugged and ducked into the patrol car, where her partner waited. Lori watched Jen and her partner drive off through narrowed eyes.

Jen must not know Lori very well. She didn't allow anyone to question her brother.

The beeping sound as the tow truck operator lifted Lori's car onto the back of the truck cut through the silence between them.

Cade rubbed a circle on Lori's back. "Could Jen be right? Maybe your brother didn't play ball with someone, so this gang, Norteños, took it out on you."

She lurched away from him. "I'm gonna talk to the driver."

Cade slid into the driver's seat of his rental and watched Lori out the window. Danny had always had her back when they were kids, when her dad worked long hours in construction and her mom worked as a nurse's aide on the graveyard shift at the hospital. Danny had encouraged Lori's studies and had seen her safely home from the library. When the tables had turned and Danny needed Lori's help, she hadn't hesitated.

Cade always believed Danny manipulated Lori at the end, and he knew manipulation firsthand. His sister was a master. Maybe Summer was manipulating him right now.

As Lori approached his car, he curled his hands around the steering wheel. He didn't have to worry about her picking up the discussion about Danny.

As she snapped her seat belt, she said, "He's taking it to a tire shop near the station. I'm going to pick it up after work tomorrow."

"Don't worry about it. I'll give you a ride to work in the morning."

"You don't have to go through all this trouble, you know." She pinned her hands between her knees, as they bounced up and down.

"Why wouldn't I?" He covered her hands with one

of his. "You've gone above and beyond to help me find Summer. It's the least I can do. Let's not keep track of who's doing what for whom."

"Deal. So, why do you think my tires were slashed?" She dropped her gaze to her hands. "Do you really think it might have something to do with Danny?"

"Never occurred to me until Officer Jen mentioned it." He pulled away from the curb, giving Summer's house one last glance. "Do you know much about Danny's life in prison?"

"I visit him, but I'm sure he's not giving me an accurate picture of what happens behind bars. Why would he?"

"And the gang?"

Lori sighed and leaned her head against the window. "Jen's right. There are two Latino gangs that predominate in the California prison system—the Norteños and the Sudeños, and everyone knows you have a better chance of survival when you affiliate with a prison gang. They're the ones who offer protection, get you privileges, have connections with the guards. But there's always a price to pay."

"And if you don't pay it?"

She scooped her hair back from her face. "Not sure. Are you asking me if the price might be harassment of family members on the outside? Maybe. Seems strange that they nailed my car in front of Summer's house, though, doesn't it? Because of the location, it seems much more likely that this has some connection to your sister and not my brother."

"I'm not saying it doesn't." He splayed his hands on the wheel. "It's not like we found anything in her safe deposit box, or even in the house. She had a small amount of drugs, not exactly a huge stash that someone would want to collect."

"We have the card from Brighter Days. It must mean something to her if she stuck it in the bank." She folded her arms over her purse in her lap, as if protecting the cards there.

"Unless, like I said, she swept it up with other papers and put it there inadvertently. Summer doesn't exactly have a stellar system of filing...or anything else."

"We need to talk to Trey." She swiveled in her seat to face him. "Ask him about Brighter Days."

"I'm sure the police already asked him about Summer, right? I mean, her print was found at Courtney's place." He flicked on the windshield wipers to sweep away a few scattered raindrops that had shimmered in the lights on the freeway.

"Yeah, but what if Trey was protecting Courtney, like you're trying to protect Summer? Maybe Trey didn't tell the cops everything he knew about his friend, and maybe he doesn't know that Summer has a connection to Brighter Days. He'd tell us though."

"Do you know how to contact him?"

She snorted. "I can get his contact info from work. I'm the one who took his prints."

"Maybe I should talk to him—keep you out of it. My sister is missing. His friend is missing. We have a bond, and maybe he'll open up to me."

"I'd like to be there. He already knows me. I already had contact with him."

"You might get in trouble. I don't want you losing your job over this." As he merged onto the 10, he cranked his head toward her. "Lincoln or closer to Ocean? I'm not sure how to get to the canals."

"Take Lincoln, and I'll guide you in from there."

As he took the exit, Cade's gaze shifted to his side mirror. He'd been watching his back ever since they left Summer's place. If Lori's first instinct was right, someone just might be following them.

"Are you sure you're safe in this place?"

"Why wouldn't I be?" She lifted her shoulders. "The Player, Clive Stewart, is dead and so are all his copycats."

"I'm talking about the area. Venice has always been sketchy. A cluster of multimillion-dollar homes sitting on the canals doesn't change that."

"When Kyra took possession of the house, she installed a security system—cameras and sensors." She patted his thigh. "I'm safe there."

Lori directed him to a parking lot outside the canal area, and they walked past several homeless people to reach the entrance to the canals. An invisible barrier seemed to exist between the sidewalk and the path into the canals, which the riffraff of the street didn't cross.

The Venice Canals did attract a wealthy bunch because of the proximity to the beach and the home prices, but they tended to be a more artsy crowd than you'd find in Beverly Hills. Hardly seemed a suitable locale for a retired cop.

He followed her across a wooden bridge, where the brackish water slapped against the man-made barrier, the scent of salt permeating the air. A drop of rain splashed near his mouth and he licked it off with his tongue, tasting the salt that already clung to his skin from the night air.

Lori stopped in front of a red door, and Cade glanced up at the camera peeking from the eaves at the corner of the house. She hadn't been kidding.

When she unlocked the door, she pushed it open and stepped inside first. "C'mon in. Excuse the sparseness."

His gaze swept the room. She wasn't kidding about this, either. A couch faced a flat-screen TV, a small end table its only companion. A square table, with two chairs facing each other, hunched next to a sliding glass door.

"Planning to have a dance here later? Is that why you cleared the floor?"

She pushed him into the room. "Very funny. Kyra cleared the old furniture out of the house—too many memories, and I figured this was a temporary solution for me, so I didn't move all my stuff here."

He held up his hands. "No need to explain to me. It's a great spot."

"And the security? Did you check that out?" She pointed to the cameras in the corner of the room. "Kyra even installed them inside."

"You have access to the footage on your phone?"

"Yes." She tossed her purse onto the table next to the couch. "You think I need it now after the job on my tires?"

"Maybe. I'm not saying it was someone sending a warning to Danny in prison and I'm not ruling out some-one watching Summer's house, but I think we both know that wasn't a random act. Yours was the only car hit and the vandal got all four tires."

"Funny thing about that so-called warning. If they meant to put me off looking further into Summer's dis-appearance, the slashed tires had the opposite effect." She leveled a gaze at him from her big brown eyes. "You?"

"Same. I'm all in." Cade rubbed his hands together. "Let's get dinner."

"Would you be crushed if we ordered in pizza? I'm tired and stressed out…and I want to look into Brighter Days."

Cade blew out a breath. For a second, he'd thought she intended to send him home. Pizza in seemed like a reprieve. "You go do what you need to do to decompress. I'll order the pizza. Preference?"

"There's a magnet on the fridge for a pizza place on Washington that delivers. I won't be long."

When Lori disappeared down the hallway, Cade plucked the card for Mario's from the fridge, ordered a large pizza with everything, and a salad, and unearthed an unopened bottle of red wine from the small cupboard above the fridge.

When Lori emerged from the back room in a pair of tight faded jeans and a white T-shirt, Cade held up the bottle and one glass of ruby-red wine. "I hope you weren't saving this for a special occasion."

She drew closer and squinted at the label. "I didn't even realize I had that bottle. Let's kill it."

"Whoa. You *are* stressed out." He handed the glass to her and poured another for himself. "Pizza with the works and a Caesar salad. Will that do?"

"Sounds perfect." Holding her wine in one hand, she slid her laptop from the counter with her other and placed it on the small butcher-block kitchen table. "Wanna help me research Brighter Days?"

"I thought you were stressed out." He swirled the liquid in his glass and took a swig.

"Yeah, and one way to relieve that stress is by solving a few puzzles."

He could think of better ways of relieving stress. In fact, hadn't been able to think of anything else since she sashayed in here with those jeans hugging her backside, but if anything were to happen between them, any old flames rekindling, she'd have to be the one to light the match.

In the end, he'd left her to go away to college, but as he considered their breakup over the years, he'd come to the conclusion that she'd engineered the entire thing. They could've had a long-distance romance, but she dropped off the face of the earth when he went back East.

He yanked out the other chair from the table and swung it beside her. "Let's see if Brighter Days has any answers. Where did you say it was located?"

"There are a few outpatient clinics here and there, but the rehab center is in Topanga Canyon."

He tapped the side of his glass. "That tells you a lot about the place, right there."

"Such as?" Lori's fingers flew over the keyboard.

"Such as, Topanga is stuck in the '60s, so Brighter Days is probably one of those New Age, hippie places that allows you to do rehab at your own pace, in your own way." He took another pull from his glass. "Which explains what Summer was doing there."

"If she did go there for treatment. Maybe she just knows this guy…" Lori propped up the card they'd found in the safe deposit box on her laptop. "Reed Dufrain."

Cade looked over her shoulder as she entered the name of the center, followed by *Topanga Canyon*, in a search engine. Several hits came back; Lori clicked on the official website for Brighter Days Recovery Center.

As she scrolled through pictures of wooded paths, plates of fresh, organically sourced food, exercise rooms, hot tubs and a full-service spa, she whistled.

"I'd pretend an addiction just to go there and relax.

Maybe if Danny had had access to a place like this, he never would've continued his drug use and..."

"It's high-end, for sure." He jabbed his finger at the button labeled Staff. "Click this."

The thin face of a bearded man with close-cropped hair filled the screen. Lori said, "This is the center's director, Reed Dufrain. He looks the part, I guess."

"Yeah, like a typical guru." Cade scanned through Dufrain's bio, and the guy checked all the boxes of someone you'd expect in this kind of role at this kind of place. "Oh, hello."

"What?" Lori's finger hovered over the mouse.

"This is a center for women only." He circled an area of the page with his finger and read aloud. "'The center deals with the types of trauma particular to women who abuse substances, creating a safe and nonjudgmental environment.' Yeah, Summer would love that—no judgments."

"Did Summer suffer any traumas?" Lori sipped her wine, and then stared into the glass as the liquid shimmered in the low light of the computer monitor.

"If you count privilege and a surplus of clothes as trauma." He rolled his eyes, his next comment about Summer dying on his lips as he felt Lori's piercing gaze on his face. "What?"

"Talk about judgmental." She clicked on a button for photos. "The fact is, you don't really know, do you? You can never know what someone else is going through, unless they tell you or you see it with your own eyes."

"You're right. Besides, we both know my dad was a control freak who allowed his drinking to control his moods." He let the discussion die between them.

He might be too judgmental of Summer and her

choices, he'd admit that, but Lori gave Danny free rein for his choices. Maybe her brother had gotten a bum rap, but she had never faulted him for hanging with the wrong crowd or getting into fights with his girlfriend or being in possession of a stolen handgun. At least, he'd never heard an ill word of Danny drop from her lips—ever— and he never had the heart to challenge her.

She clicked through the pictures of the wooded grounds and of some gatherings—tai chi, yoga sessions, campfires. Some of the faces of the residents were blurred out and plenty of the shots didn't show close-ups, or captured only the backs of heads, but a few brave souls must've allowed themselves to be photographed for the website. Cade studied the smiling faces for his sister's image.

Lori moved the cursor to the next thumbnail photo and froze, her body jerking beside him. "Oh, my God. Here's our link."

Cade leaned in to study the women stretched out in a yoga class, none with Summer's distinctive blond hair, and said, "What do you see?"

"Her." Lori positioned the cursor beneath the head of a limber brunette. "That's the other missing girl. That's Courtney."

Chapter Seven

Cade's eye twitched as he zeroed in on the woman in the photo. "You're sure?"

"Absolutely. I saw the picture her friend Trey gave the department. We have to tell Detective Marino about this connection between Summer and Courtney. It has to mean something. That's detective work 101—find a link between the victims."

"Wait." Cade grabbed Lori's wrist. "How are you going to explain that you knew about Summer's association with Brighter Days without admitting we ransacked her place and plundered her safe deposit box?"

She raised one eyebrow in his direction. "Ransacked and plundered? We're not pirates. You're a concerned brother who looked through his sister's place to see if he could find any clues to her whereabouts. We don't even have to tell Marino about the safe deposit box. Summer had a card in her nightstand, too. We can give him the card from the bank with the names on it, and tell him we found it in the drawer of her bedside table."

"And the website?" He tipped his chin at the computer monitor. "How are you going to explain finding Courtney on the website? I've never seen a picture of Courtney."

Sighing, she folded her arms and leaned back in her

chair. "Do you think it's not allowed for family members to do a little digging on their own? You saw the card for Brighter Days, wondered if Summer had been going there and looked it up on the internet. I was with you and noticed Courtney's picture."

"I'm not concerned about how it's going to look for *me*." He swept her bangs from her eyes with one finger. "I'm worried about you."

Her eyes widened for a second, and she jumped at the sound of a knock on the door. "It's okay. I'm your… friend, and I was with you when you brought up the Brighter Days website. I'm going to get that pizza."

As she started to rise, he put a hand on her shoulder. "I'll answer the door."

By the time he paid the delivery guy and returned to the kitchen with an armful of food, Lori had taken some dishes from the cupboard and topped up their wineglasses. If he finished off that bottle, he'd have a good excuse for not driving home and spending the night here—offering to sleep on the couch, of course. She didn't have to know he usually limited his alcohol consumption to a few beers.

The slashing of her tires had left him with a tight ball of anxiety in the pit of his stomach. Whether connected to Summer's disappearance or Danny's incarceration, the destructive act was a direct threat to Lori.

He took a swig of wine, and then plopped a couple pieces of pizza onto the two plates Lori had placed on the counter. He held up the plates. "Kitchen table?"

"I don't even have a coffee table, so we'd have to balance everything on our knees if we wanted to eat in the living room." She finished scooping the salad into the bowls and grabbed some forks. "Meet you there."

He let her lead the way, the two steps to the table next to the sliding doors, and pulled out her chair. "I'll get our wine."

Cade took a long sip from his own glass before he set them both down on the table.

Eyeing his glass, Lori said, "You'd better slow down if you hope to drive back to your hotel tonight without getting pulled over."

"Maybe I should stay here tonight."

Lori choked on the bite of salad she'd just forked into her mouth. "Not as subtle as you were back in high school."

"I meant I could camp out on that uncomfortable-looking couch tonight in case there's more trouble." He could feel the heat burning in his chest and he fought to keep it from rising to his face by taking a gulp of water.

"I'll be fine, Cade. When I started working at the department, I bought a gun. One of the officers at the station took me to the range to teach me how to shoot." She formed her fingers into a gun and blew on the tip. "I'm pretty good, too, good enough to point and shoot at someone coming through my bedroom window at night."

He swallowed a bigger chunk of pizza than he'd planned and coughed. "You keep it beside your bed, loaded?"

"Doesn't do much good unloaded." She waved her fingers at him. "Don't worry. I'm not going to mistake you for an intruder if you decide to creep into my bedroom."

He snorted. "I have no intention of sneaking into your bedroom in the middle of the night, but if I did, how are you so sure you wouldn't have me pegged as a house-breaker and pull the trigger?"

"Because I'd recognize your...body anywhere." She

waved a piece of pizza at him. "I knew that was you at the front desk of the station immediately."

"I'm glad you did." Her teasing banter emboldened him, and he took her hand. "Thanks for your help in this. If not for you, I'd probably be on my way back to New York, none the wiser about Summer, waiting for... something."

She curled her fingers around his hand and squeezed. "I learned my lesson about sitting back and doing nothing. If I had fought harder for my brother when I learned about that unidentified print at the scene of Elena's murder, got him a different attorney...something, Danny might not be sitting in prison right now."

"You were young. There wasn't much you could do." He clasped her hand in both of his, and she didn't even seem to mind the pizza grease. "I hope you're not sitting around blaming yourself for that."

Hunching forward, she said, "Do you think being young is an excuse for making bad choices?"

"Excuse? I don't know if I'd use that word—more like an explanation. We all make bad choices based on our youth. Some people keep on making those bad choices even when they grow up. Look at Summer."

"Summer has an addiction. I don't know if it's much of a choice, at this point." She disentangled her hands from his and wiped them on a napkin.

"At this point, but at another point she had a choice." He tossed back the rest of his wine. "But that doesn't mean she deserves to be missing, and that's what I'm afraid the cops will think once they learn about Brighter Days. Is that Detective Marino just going to dismiss her disappearance as drug related?"

"Not sure." She shrugged and resumed eating her

pizza. "That's why I wish the case had gone to Detective Falco instead of Marino. Marino's old-school and more apt to take that view. Falco's new and a woman. She might have a different attitude."

"But you're sure we should tell this Marino about finding the card and seeing Courtney's picture on the Brighter Days website."

"They have nothing right now. That will give them a place to start, but I still think we contact Trey Ferrar on our own. It could be days before Marino gets around to checking with Trey about Courtney's association with Brighter Days. We can get to the bottom of it faster." She held up the almost empty bottle of wine. "Do you want the rest?"

"Only if you reserve the couch for me." He drummed his fingers on the side of the glass.

"I'll do you one better." She dumped the rest of the wine into his glass, where it sloshed up the sides. "This is a three-bedroom house, and I actually have a bed in one of the other rooms. It's all yours."

"I'll take it, and I promise—" he drew a cross over his heart "—no creeping around in the middle of the night."

"Okay, but you really don't have to worry about me at this house on my own. I showed you the security system, and I have my own backup. I'm fine here."

"A retired LAPD homicide detective was murdered in this house last year."

"He didn't have cameras."

"I'm sure he had a loaded gun on his bedside table."

"He did, but he knew his killer. He let him in and didn't suspect a thing."

He held up his empty glass. "Too late now, anyway.

I'm not going to drive home when I'm probably over the legal limit."

"Very convenient. Never saw you down wine like that before."

"Wine?" He collected their plates and bowls from the table. "When we were sneaking booze in high school, we weren't raiding our parents' wine cellars."

"*Your* parents' wine cellar. My parents didn't have a wine cellar."

He huffed out a breath. "You know what I mean. We were drinking cheap beer, when we could get it. I don't think I ever saw you drink wine. In fact, you didn't drink much beer in high school, either. Always the good girl."

"In some ways." She took the dishes from him and spun around toward the kitchen.

He decided to keep his mouth shut. Talking about their steamy sessions in the backseat of his BMW could only lead to trouble. She'd been keeping him at arm's length, and he didn't want to push things or take advantage. She'd helped him polish off that bottle of wine, and the alcohol had brought a flush to her cheeks and a brightness to her eyes that signaled she wasn't altogether sober.

He came up behind her at the sink, placing his hands at her waist. "I'll clean up."

She set the dishes in the sink and cranked on the water. "You do that and I'll call Trey."

"You don't waste any time." He squeezed in next to her and ran the first plate under the water.

"I'll tell Marino tomorrow at work about the connection to Brighter Days. I'm sure he won't get around to contacting Trey for a while. Courtney's case is no homicide."

"Yet." Cade scrubbed at the plate so hard, it didn't need the dishwasher.

Lori rubbed his back. "Don't think like that. It's a good thing Marino doesn't feel any urgency right now. It means he believes the women aren't in any immediate danger."

"They're both gone without a word to anyone. I'm no cop, but that has danger written all over it."

"Cops have to work within certain restrictions. If they tracked down all adults who decided they wanted a break from everyday life, there wouldn't be enough man power to do it—not to mention infringing on people's privacy rights. We do have the right to disappear if we want to." She stepped away from the sink and snatched her phone from the counter. "I'm going to place that call to Trey before it gets too late."

She rummaged through her briefcase from work while he loaded the dishes in the dishwasher, wrapped up the remaining pizza and wiped down the sink.

Perching on one of the stools at the counter, she said, "I'll put him on speakerphone."

Cade sipped from a glass of water, as Lori placed the call. She positioned the phone on the counter between them. It rang twice before a male voice answered.

"Hello?"

"Trey, this is Lori Del Valle. I printed you at the police station as part of the investigation into Courtney's disappearance."

Trey sucked in a quick breath. "Have you found her?"

"N-no. I'm not a cop. I'm calling because I have a personal connection to Courtney's case, and I want to ask you a couple of questions—and share some information with you."

"I don't get it." Trey sniffed. "You know Courtney or something?"

"No." Lori met Cade's gaze over the phone. "You're

on speakerphone and my friend Cade is with me. His sister disappeared, too. Do you know someone named Summer Larson?"

"Summer?" He clicked his tongue. "No. I would've remembered that name."

Cade spoke up. "Trey, this is Cade. Did Courtney ever mention a Summer?"

"No. How are they connected? You said you had a personal connection to Courtney. Did Summer know Court?"

"Trey, I'm going to tell you something that we discovered, but you can't tell anyone else that I told you. Don't mention it to the police." Lori braced her hands on the counter, on either side of the phone. "The bloody fingerprint we found at Courtney's place belongs to Summer."

Trey gasped. "Are you saying Summer had something to do with Court's disappearance?"

Cade's hand curled into a fist. "No. My sister is missing, too, but it might mean someone took the two women at the same time. There was a fingerprint in blood at my sister's house, too."

"This is unbelievable. How come the police haven't called me about that yet? Why haven't they told me about the print?"

"Trey, the police don't have to tell you anything about the investigation. They will probably ask you if you or Courtney knows Summer Larson, but they may not tell you why they're asking the question. That's where we come in. We can do a little extra while the cops have to cross their t's and dot their i's."

"Okay, I get it and I appreciate it because the cops won't tell me anything right now, but I've never heard of Summer before this, so I'm not sure I can be of any help."

Cade cleared his throat. "What about Brighter Days Recovery Center?"

Dead air answered them, and Lori picked up the phone from the counter. "Trey? Are you still there?"

"W-why are you asking me about Brighter Days? What do they have to do with any of this?"

Raising his eyebrows at Lori, Cade answered, "We found a card for the center among my sister's things at her house. My sister was, had been…she's had substance abuse problems, so I wasn't surprised to find the card. I mean, I thought she was clean and sober and had been for a while, so I was disappointed to see the card but not surprised. What about Courtney? Is that someplace she would've known about?"

Trey lowered his voice to a harsh whisper. "I'm not talking about Brighter Days over the phone. If you want to know more, meet me tomorrow."

Chapter Eight

After they arranged with Trey to meet up tomorrow, Lori ended the call and cupped the phone in her hands. "That was weird, wasn't it? The minute you mentioned Brighter Days, Trey clammed up, wouldn't say another word and demanded that we meet in person to continue the conversation."

"Definitely weird." Cade ran a thumb through the condensation on the outside of his water glass. "He almost sounded…scared. Or was that just my interpretation of his creepy whisper?"

"Nope." She tapped the corner of the phone on the counter. "Maybe Courtney was an addict, and he doesn't want to talk about it over the phone. Does that make sense?"

"I guess." He shrugged. "At least he wants to meet with us. Maybe he can tell us something about Brighter Days that'll help the police. Wonder why he didn't tell the cops about Brighter Days."

"Maybe for the same reason you kept quiet about Summer's issues. You said it yourself. Once the cops know a missing person has had problems with drugs in the past, they jump to conclusions and treat the disappearance differently." She waved her hand at the sink. "Thanks for cleaning up. Don't know if it's the tire slashing, the pizza or the wine, but I'm exhausted."

"Maybe it's the adrenaline, but I'm kind of wired. Then again, I could crash in ten minutes. Don't feel like you have to entertain me. I sort of invited myself over."

"Happy to have you." She finished the thought quickly so he wouldn't get the wrong impression. "I—I don't want you drinking and driving."

"And I don't want you here by yourself after that vandalism on your car."

"I'm sure I'm fine, but I really am tired. There's no TV in the guest bedroom, but you're welcome to watch in here."

"Maybe I'll do that. All I ask is for a toothbrush. Do you have an extra?"

"I use an electric, so I have tons in my closet from my dentist. Take your pick." She pushed away from the counter. "I'll leave you one in the bathroom, along with a towel."

He nodded and put his glass in the sink. "Thanks for helping me out today. You've gone above and beyond."

"What's the point of having a contact at the police station if you don't use it? Wish I'd had one when Danny was arrested and charged with murder." Lori headed down the hallway, needing to put some distance between her and Cade.

She pawed through a basket in the hall closet and grabbed a blue toothbrush, still in the package. Then she tucked a towel under her arm and carried both to the bathroom off the hallway. Thankfully, she had her own off the master suite and wouldn't have to share this one with Cade. It was distracting enough having the man in her house, sleeping in her spare bedroom.

She poked her head around the corner of the living room to find Cade slouched on her couch, clicking through the remote. He looked too comfortable, and she swallowed. "I left some things in the bathroom for you, clean sheets on the bed, even though it's just a queen."

"Thanks. That's fine. What time do you get up for work?" He'd paused the TV on some adventure reality show and twisted his head around to look at her.

"I get up around six, leave around seven. You're welcome to sleep in. I can take an Uber to the station."

"That would be one expensive ride. I want to be on that side of town, anyway. Good night, Lori." He turned back to the TV and restarted the show.

"Night."

She washed her face and brushed her teeth, then slipped into a pair of pajamas. She usually wore much less to bed, but in case there was a fire in the middle of the night, she didn't want Cade getting the wrong idea.

She giggled as she crawled between the sheets. She'd banished him to the guest room. She doubted he had any expectations of making it into her bed tonight...even though she wanted him here.

THE FOLLOWING MORNING, Lori woke up to an unusual smell in her house—breakfast cooking and coffee brewing. She rubbed her eyes and squinted at the illuminated numbers next to her bed. Her alarm hadn't even gone off yet. Cade must still be on New York time.

She turned off her alarm and planted her feet on the area rug next to her bed. She could totally get used to this.

Shuffling into the living room, she sniffed the dark, rich aroma of the coffee. That didn't come from her cupboard. Neither did the bacon sizzling in the pan.

She dug her elbows into the counter and propped up her chin with her hands. "Don't tell me you already went out for groceries this morning?"

"Had to." He jerked his thumb at her fridge. "All you had was some leftover pizza, one egg and a couple of strawberry yogurts. Do you not eat breakfast?"

"Usually I just shovel down some yogurt, but I was kinda looking forward to that cold pizza."

He scooped some scrambled eggs onto a plate next to two strips of bacon, and placed it on the counter in front of her. "Something different today. Coffee?"

"It's been so long since I used that coffee maker. Did it cough and belch steam when you cranked it up?"

"Not quite." He dipped into her fridge like he owned it. "Cream? Sugar? Sweetener? I don't even know how you take your coffee because you weren't drinking it in high school."

"Started that habit in college." She pointed to the small carton in his hand. "I'll take some cream and one packet of sweetener."

"I'll leave room in your cup for the cream." He poured her some coffee in an LAPD mug and shoved it across the counter. "You didn't steal that cup, did you?"

"It was a gift. I'm not the criminal in the family." She dumped some cream into the dark liquid and watched the vanilla swirls fan out. "Do you cook breakfast for yourself like this every morning?"

"I'm as bad as you are. I run in the morning and have a protein smoothie when I get home, usually gulping it down on my way to the office."

Inhaling the aroma of the coffee, she closed her eyes, imagining Cade's routine in New York. "Do you grab a taxi to work? Take the subway? Walk?"

He took a sip of his own coffee and turned away to dump some more eggs on a plate for himself. "I have a car and driver."

"Must be nice." She stabbed a clump of eggs with her fork and held it up. "I forgot how the other half lived."

"She says from the kitchen overlooking the Venice Canals." He clinked the plate on the counter, and positioned himself across from her.

"You'd pass out if you knew how much I was paying my friend Kyra in rent. I told you. She's doing me a big favor. She could sell this place for a few mil or rent it out for several thousand a month." She bit off the end of a piece of bacon and waved the rest at him. "I'll be looking for a crappy apartment somewhere once she decides what she wants to do with the house."

"Don't compromise too much. You need to be in a safe area, and despite the real estate prices here in Venice, this is not a safe area."

She sealed her lips, not bothering to argue with him about her safety. It felt kinda good to have someone worry about her. The cops at the station gave her tips and looked out for her sometimes, but it wasn't the same as Cade's level of concern. She'd take it for now—revel in it a little.

"I'll keep that in mind." She blew on her coffee and took another sip. "What are you going to do today while I'm at the station?"

"Finish that work I was going to look at last night… and take you to lunch." As she opened her mouth to protest, he held up his hands. "You're not going to leave me on my own here in the big city, are you?"

"This is LA. You grew up here. I'm sure you have lots of friends, but I'm happy to be your lunch date. I'll want to touch base with you anyway to let you know what Detective Marino says about that card and Brighter Days and the connection to Courtney."

"Are you going to tell him about our meeting with Trey tonight?"

She wiped her greasy fingers on the paper towel Cade had folded next to her plate. "He doesn't need to know about that. I'm sure they'll talk to Trey again about a possible connection between Courtney and Summer and their association with Brighter Days. If we get something useful from Trey, we'll turn it over to Marino."

"Won't he wonder why Trey gave you the information instead of turning it over to the police?"

"You worry too much. Let me handle that side of things. Do you want info about Summer's disappearance now, or do you want to wait a few weeks?" She crumpled the napkin and tossed it onto her empty plate. "I'm going to get ready. Do you want to shower here or…?"

"I'll just brush my teeth and then head back to the hotel after I drop you off."

"You really don't have to go out of your way. I can get a ride to the station this morning."

He swept up her plate. "Hit the shower."

"Thanks for breakfast." She hopped off the stool and rubbed her stomach. "It was yummy."

Over an hour later, Cade pulled up in front of the Northeast Division to drop her off.

Standing outside with her hand on the door, she said, "Now you have to drive all the way back to the Westside, and you don't even have your car and driver with you."

"I love LA traffic. Don't forget about our lunch date, and let me know if you have a problem with your car."

"My treat for lunch." She slammed the car door and hurried into the building.

After reporting to the lab, Lori went in search of Detective Marino, thumbing the Brighter Days card in the pocket of her jacket. She sidled into the area that housed the detectives' desks, and then made a beeline toward Marino's.

She waited until he looked up from his computer. "What is it, Del Valle?"

She plopped down on the chair next to his desk and ignored his raised eyebrows. "I have some information about the Courtney Jessup and Summer Larson missing persons cases."

"You have more information about the prints?"

"N-no." She pulled out the card with its bent corner. "You know Summer Larson's brother is an old friend of mine, and I went with him to his sister's house yesterday. He wanted to have a look around once the cops were done."

"And?" He scooted back in his chair and folded his arms over his paunch.

"He found this." She snapped the card on his desk in front of him.

Shoving a pair of glasses on his nose, he brought the card close to his face. "Brighter Days Recovery Center. Drug rehab?"

"That and other things."

"So, his sister's a druggie? That explains a lot."

Lori clasped her hands in her lap, her nails biting into her flesh. "There's more. We checked out the Brighter Days website and saw a picture of Courtney, so they both have a connection to that treatment center. It's in Topanga."

"They're both druggies."

"Well, that's not really the point, is it? They both have

ties to Brighter Days and now they're both missing, with one's prints at the other's place."

Marino's eyes narrowed beneath his heavy brows as he sized her up. "Two drug addicts missing? It kinda is the point, Del Valle."

"I thought…"

The detective cut her off and slipped the card into a file. "Thanks for this. We'll have a look."

Knots tightened in her gut, but if she got angry with Marino now, she'd be fighting a losing battle. "Okay, just thought it was something you should know about."

"Thank you." He tapped the file in a way that made her glad she'd held on to the other Brighter Days card, the one with the names.

She shot up from her chair, a little unsteady on her feet, and spun away from his desk, almost colliding with Detective McAllister.

"Where are you going in such a hurry?" He stepped back to give her space. "How's the house working out?"

"It's great. Tell Kyra I can move out whenever she makes a decision." Detective McAllister and Kyra had gotten engaged, and Kyra had given up her apartment and her newly acquired house in Venice to live with McAllister in the Hollywood Hills.

"She's busy planning our wedding." He rolled his eyes. "Don't ask. She's in no hurry to deal with the house right now, so settle in."

"Tell her thanks again."

Jake dipped his head, watching Marino saunter out of the room, and lowered his voice. "Problems with Marino?"

"Not at all. A couple of missing persons cases, and I

know the brother of one of the women. I had some info for him about my friend's sister, kind of off the record."

"Sometimes that's the best kind of information. Too bad about your friend's sister."

Lori had a strong urge to spill her guts to J-Mac, tell him everything about the two cases, and what she and Cade had discovered, but Detective McAllister wasn't on this case. He broke rules occasionally, but he wouldn't undermine another detective in the department.

"My friend is doing everything he can to help the police locate his sister. Maybe she'll just show up." Lori held up her crossed fingers.

"I hope so." McAllister jerked his head to the side. "I have to grab Captain Fields. Good to see you, Lori."

Lori marched back to the lab, irritation fizzing in her veins. She and Cade had it right—digging on their own might be the only thing to spur on this investigation.

The rest of the morning flew by with no hits from the national fingerprint database on the prints they'd collected from Summer's house and no further news on Courtney or Summer. The only prints they could identify at Courtney's place, besides her own, were Trey's...and Summer's bloody print. How did that happen?

Just because Marino didn't have any more information, he couldn't just let the cases go, could he? She swallowed as she recalled the LAPD's database of missing persons. One of the LAPD's own detectives, J-Mac's partner, Billy Crouch, had a sister in that database.

There were certain things she didn't have to tell Cade. She'd been so good about keeping his child from him, what were a few more secrets between them?

Cade needn't have worried about her car. Later that morning, the garage delivered it with four new tires—

just around the time Cade texted her about lunch. He insisted on picking her up, though, and she touched base with her coworkers in the lab before she left.

As she slid into the passenger seat of his rental, she asked, "Did you get your work done?"

"Enough. I also did a little more sleuthing. I checked Summer's social media and contacted several of her friends. Some didn't respond, but a few got back to me." He lifted his shoulders as he pulled out of the station's parking lot. "Nothing—or at least they weren't telling me anything. No new boyfriends, nobody claimed to know Courtney and they didn't admit to knowing anything about Brighter Days. Of course, if they were trying to protect Summer, they wouldn't want to mention she'd been in a treatment program. I almost called Brighter Days myself, but figured we should wait to see what Trey had to say about it first. He had a strange response when we mentioned it."

"You're really starting to think like a detective." She clapped her hands. "I've either corrupted you or introduced you to a new line of work."

The corner of his mouth quirked. "You already corrupted me in other ways."

She pinched his thigh and said, "I think you have that the other way around."

"Ouch." He rubbed his leg. "So, I did good by waiting?"

"Yeah. Let's see what Trey has to say about Brighter Days before we blunder in there, asking questions. I gave the card to Detective Marino, but he seemed underwhelmed."

"Really? I thought that was a good lead. He doesn't have anything else—at least not that we know of." He took a quick glance at her. "I'm sure they follow leads. without consulting you first, right?"

"Of course." She tapped on the window. "You can park on the street. The lot gets crowded at lunch."

He jerked the wheel to nab a spot between two large SUVs. "So, Marino might be working on something that you don't know about."

"He could be. He doesn't owe me anything. I have a better working relationship with other detectives—especially the ones who were on The Player task force—and they might've kept me in the loop, but not Marino. Our bad luck the case landed with him. He's old-school, keeps things close to the vest. He'd be more likely to tell you if he had something before he'd tell me."

"I haven't heard a word from him since the so-called investigation started. Apparently, Trey hasn't, either."

"Which might make Trey anxious to talk to us tonight." When Cade parked the car, Lori got out on the sidewalk. They crossed the full parking lot to the sandwich place and squeezed in to a table in the corner.

Cade said, "Let me know what you want, and I'll order for both of us."

Lori scanned the menu board behind the counter and gave Cade her order and two twenties. "I'm paying, remember?"

"Got it." He snatched the bills from her hand and got in line.

Five minutes later, he returned with a soda in each hand, and he took the plastic chair across from her, dwarfing it. He'd always been attractive in that lanky, athletic way, but he'd filled out into a fine-looking man. How was he still on the market?

Tapping her straw on the table to unwrap it, she blurted, "Why are you not taken?"

"Taken?" He jabbed his own straw in the plastic lid of his cup. "What do you mean?"

"Oh, c'mon." She shook the ice in her cup. "You know what I mean. Why aren't you married or engaged or cohabitating?"

"Cohabitating? I have a dog. Does that count?" He tapped on his phone's display and shoved it across the table at her. "Meet Dexter, my golden retriever."

"He's cute. Who's taking care of him?" She cocked her head. He was playing dumb.

"My friend and his wife. They have a kid who's crazy about Dexter, and Dex returns the sentiment."

"You're deflecting. Dexter, as adorable as he is, doesn't count. Where's your own wife…your own kid?" She ducked her head to sip her drink. She was on dangerous ground here for reasons he couldn't even guess.

"Would it be a cop-out to say I've been busy?"

"We're all busy, so yeah. Cop-out. Dating? Dating sites?"

"A little and yes. You?" He aimed his plastic fork at her. "I didn't notice a husband and kids at your place. You don't even have a dog."

"I did. I had to put her to sleep shortly before I moved to Venice." She put her hand over her heart. "So, Dexter? Yeah, he does count."

"Have you tried online dating?"

"I have." She held up a hand in his face. "Are you going to tell me it's dangerous?"

"It can be, but I'm sure you're not taking risks."

The guy at the counter called their number and Cade jumped up to retrieve their order, giving her a few seconds to catch her breath. She'd brought up the subject of dating. Now she wished it would go away.

Dating wasn't easy when you kept comparing every new guy you met to a high school boyfriend you hadn't seen in almost ten years. Who did that?

He set down their plates. "Do you need a refill on your soda?"

"Sure." She handed him her cup, and when he returned, she was ready to steer the conversation away from their dating habits.

"Did you find out anything more from Summer's friends?"

"Not much. They seem like a tight-lipped bunch, even when I mentioned Summer was missing." Cade held his sandwich in front of his face, studying it.

"What?" She dropped her own sandwich.

"Maybe Marino is right. Summer relapsed and she took off for parts unknown. Maybe she knows Courtney from Brighter Days, and they fell off the wagon together. The bloody prints and upended furniture could just be a bender gone wrong."

She circled his wrist with her fingers. "Maybe that's all it is and we'd be happy for it, but you still need to find your sister. Benders can get you in trouble. We're not done with our sleuthing yet. We'll talk to Trey tonight, and then give Brighter Days a call."

A man of action, Cade seemed satisfied with her words and dug into his lunch.

She hoped he and Marino were right...but her instincts told her something different.

Chapter Nine

Later that day when she got home from work, Lori changed into a pair of jeans and some boots. Most of the rain had cleared, washing the air clean with it, but the boots would protect her feet from the damp sidewalks and the errant drops that fell from the gray clouds still skittering across the sky.

She pulled on a light jacket over her T-shirt and crossed the bridge out of the canals to wait for Cade to pick her up in his rental car. Trey Ferrar lived in Hollywood, close to Courtney's place, and they'd agreed to meet him there for his convenience. They were the ones who wanted info from him, so it only seemed fair. He needed to be in the right frame of mind to spill the beans on Brighter Days.

Dropping into the seat beside Cade, she held out her phone. "Did you already put the address for the bar in your phone's GPS, or do you want me to do it?"

"You can do it. Tires okay?"

"Great. Feels like a brand-new car. The guy who slashed them did me a favor." She tapped the address she'd already saved to her phone and brought up the GPS. "Take Lincoln to the 10, and we can get the Hollywood Freeway that way."

Cade pulled away from the curb. "Did you keep an eye on your rearview mirror on the way home? You don't want the same guy doing you any more favors."

She clenched her teeth to suppress a little shiver creeping down her back. "I did watch my mirrors, and nobody followed me home. I think he…or she…delivered the message with the tires."

"Message sent but not received. You're not backing off."

"What else is this person going to do?" She adjusted her side mirror. "I work for the LAPD. He can't stop the investigation."

"That's the point. There is no real investigation, except ours. Did you find out anything new when you went back to work this afternoon?"

"Nothing." She stashed her phone in the cup holder. "In fact, Marino seemed to make a wide berth every time he saw me. He's the type of guy who resents outside interference—especially from techs."

"What about victims' families?" His hands clenched the steering wheel, and she wanted to make him feel better—but she couldn't.

"Marino doesn't consider Summer a victim, and the information about Brighter Days and her past drug use didn't help matters."

Cade's mouth tightened. "I saw that coming."

She couldn't resist any longer, so she ran her fingers lightly down his corded forearm. "We had to let him know. The police are going to be able to get more information out of Brighter Days than we are."

"You're probably right, but the Larsons still have our connections in this city. Dad even knows Mayor Wexler. Maybe it's time to pull out the big guns and tell my father what's going on." He flashed her a sideways glance. "I know you hate that influence peddling."

"Hey, whatever works to find Summer. If I'd had big guns to use to help Danny, I would've used them."

Lori sealed her lips after that. She suspected Cade thought her defense of Danny was unwarranted—most people did. But most people didn't understand, even her own family. Cade definitely didn't get it.

They'd left an hour to get to the bar, the Frolic Room on Hollywood Boulevard, and needed every minute of it.

As Cade pulled up to a valet at a lot across the street, he said, "Hope he waits for us."

"We're not that late, just a few minutes." Lori checked her cell and ended the navigation.

The parking attendant got her door and she stepped into the chilly night, pulling her jacket around her body. "When is it going to start warming up for spring?"

Cade took the ticket from the valet and shoved it into his pocket. Slinging his arm around her shoulders, he said, "I'll keep you warm."

He steered her down the sidewalk toward the signal, and they hit the curb just as the green Walk sign flashed, blurring into the neon lights around it.

The Pantages Theatre was dark tonight, its Art Deco facade sporting banners of entertainment on the horizon. The Frolic Room huddled beside it, its lighted yellow sign inviting…adventures.

Lori had never been inside the famous dive bar and had no idea why Trey had chosen it. He must live close by. Maybe he frequented the bar regularly and felt comfortable in its dark environs.

Cade opened the door for her, and she stepped into the crowded space, her eyes adjusting to the low lights. Red bar stools lined the wall, facing a mural, and she tugged on the sleeve of Cade's jacket. "Let's perch there for a minute and I'll see if he's here. If we don't grab those seats now, we'll probably lose them in about ten minutes."

They both sat on the stools, facing outward, and Lori squinted as she took in the seats at the bar. No tables dotted the room—you sat at the bar or along the wall, or stood in the space between the two when it got even more crowded than it was now.

She scanned the crowd for Trey's curly black hair and chubby form. A few guys almost had her out of her seat, but when they turned toward her, she ruled them out.

Sighing, she hitched her elbows on the bar behind her. "I hope he didn't bolt just because we were a few minutes late."

"Maybe he's later. Do you want a beer or something while we wait?" He gestured toward the bar.

"Not really, but you go ahead."

"I'm good, but we'll probably get hassled for not ordering. I'll get a couple of seltzers or soda water."

As Cade stood up, Lori smacked her purse on his stool. "I'll save your seat and give Trey a call."

Cade took a few steps toward the bar and elbowed his way in while Lori checked the door every time it opened. She pulled out her phone and brought up Trey in her contacts. She tapped his name and listened to the phone ring until it flipped over to his message. "Hey, Trey. We're here at the Frolic, sitting on the stools against the wall. Hope you didn't change your mind."

She ended the call and looked up as Cade returned with a drink in each hand and his mouth twisted into a grimace.

"What's wrong?"

He placed the drinks on the bar and plucked something from his pocket. He held up a cell phone in a tiger-print case and said, "You called?"

"What are you talking about?" She licked her dry lips and took a sip of the soda water, the tart lime bouncing against her teeth.

"This is Trey's phone. When you called, I saw it light up on the bar, displaying your number. I checked to make sure you were on the phone. It's his."

She cranked her head from side to side. "Then, where is he? Who leaves their phone at the bar and walks away?"

"That's what I'm going to find out." Cade charged back to the bar, and she followed, the sweating glass nearly slipping from her hand.

Cade hunched across the bar to get the bartender's attention. "Hey, excuse me. Did you see who left that phone?"

"No, but he or she had better come and get it before I turn it off and stash it behind the bar. It has an annoying ring."

Cade made a half turn, locking eyes with a few patrons. "Anyone else? We're supposed to meet him here."

A longhaired, rocker type held up one ringed finger. "I saw him. Young, baby-faced kid. Latino. Met up with some other dude and they went out the back door."

Lori grabbed Cade's arm. "Let's go. Maybe he was given a warning, like me."

Cade thanked the man, and grabbed Lori's hand, leading her to the back of the bar that had to let out on the alley. He pushed on the silver horizontal door release, and a smattering of raindrops hit Lori's face as she followed him outside.

The darkness enveloped them. The neon lights from

the boulevard did not permeate back here, and the light over the back door lay in shards at their feet.

Cade crept forward, and Lori hooked a finger in his belt loop. When he got past the Dumpster, he swore and stepped back, blocking her view. He made a grab for her as she stumbled out from behind him, but he wasn't fast enough.

Lori covered her mouth and choked back a scream at Trey's body splayed before her, his curls sticky with the blood from the slash across his throat.

Chapter Ten

The morning after Trey's murder, Cade hunched forward, elbows on knees, as he stared through the glass at Lori sitting across from her supervisor. He blamed himself for dragging her into their Nancy Drew investigation. He should've trusted the police to do their jobs and stayed out of it. Now Lori faced a reprimand, or worse.

They'd called 911, turned over Trey's phone and explained to the police that they'd had a meeting set up with Trey to discuss his sister and Trey's friend. They kept Brighter Days out of it—didn't want to make a bad situation worse.

One look at Lori's face told him it *was* worse.

They'd already read him the riot act about interfering in a police investigation and pointed to Trey's dead body as proof of the consequences. Did he and Lori contribute to Trey's death by involving him in their search? Trey already involved himself when he broke into Courtney's place and called the police. When people needed answers, sometimes they took matters into their own hands—but he didn't work for the LAPD.

Cade jumped from his seat when Lori and her supervisor stood up and shook hands.

Lori exited the room first, her dark eyes flashing

fire and with it a warning to him to keep quiet. "Meet me downstairs."

He nodded once and jogged downstairs to the lobby of the Northeast Division, where he'd first run into Lori. Too bad it took him this long to reconnect with her. He should've looked her up years ago, despite her tiny footprint on social media.

He paced the floor, rejecting two offers of assistance, before Lori swept down the stairs, her head held high and her shoulders pinned back, her bag hanging from her shoulder. He followed her stiff back outside, and then she spun around.

"I've been suspended from work."

Cade's stomach dropped and he reached out for her, but she shrugged him off. "Because of your side investigation?"

"Because of that..." she dashed a hand across her face "...and Trey's murder."

"They're not blaming you for Trey's death, are they?" Of course, he'd just blamed them himself less than five minutes ago.

"Not exactly, but they cautioned me that this is what happens when civilians take matters into their own hands—I think they were talking more about Trey than us, but we're painted with the same brush." She twisted her fingers in front of her. "I'm so sorry."

"Sorry? You're sorry for what?"

"We've lost our inside edge, haven't we? I can hardly keep on top of the case for you when I'm not on it."

"Let's go to my car so we can talk." Lori had driven to work herself, and he'd been called into the station for another interview regarding the murder. He happened to run into her in the hallway on her way to the meeting with her supervisor. He knew by the set look on her face that she was facing trouble.

When he slid in behind the wheel, he turned to her. "What does the suspension involve?"

"Suspended with pay for one week and when I come back to work, I'm off any crime scene that has to do with these two cases." She smacked the dashboard with her hand. "Why didn't Trey wait for us? Why did he meet someone in a back alley?"

"What did the cops tell you…before they suspended you?"

She rolled her eyes. "Not much. Cameras at the bar caught Trey talking to a man with a hat pulled over his eyes. He must've had the cameras sussed out because he avoided looking into them directly. He spoke to Trey for a few minutes, and then the two of them walked to the back of the bar. No cameras caught them going out the back door, and none caught the murder itself. They don't know if he was forced or tricked into going with the man, but he did leave his phone at the bar. Maybe he suspected something was going to go down."

Cade scratched his jaw. "What if Trey thought the man was me? Obviously, someone knew about our meeting. Some guy could've pretended to be Summer's brother, telling Trey you were on your way or waiting in the back for privacy. You told him I'd be there, but never told him what I looked like."

Lori pinned her hands between her bouncing knees. "This sounds premeditated. Another warning for us and a deadly one for Trey to back off."

"Look, I'm sorry." He placed a hand on her knee to steady it. "I'm not here a week, and I've messed up your job."

"If I don't have to apologize to you, you don't have to apologize to me. I was all in. You didn't coerce me into anything. In fact, this sleuthing around was my idea. I seem to recall your attempts to stop me."

He snorted. "Yeah, I should've known better. I suppose I'll just keep pestering Detective Marino about my sister, daily. What are you going to do with your free time?"

"Are you kidding?" She jerked her head in his direction. "Free time? Your sister is missing, Courtney is missing and Courtney's best friend was murdered just as he was about to give us some information about Brighter Days. We continue to fight."

Cade braced his hands against the steering wheel. "Loretta, your supervisor just reprimanded and suspended you. Do you want to court more trouble for yourself?"

"Loretta? You sound like my mother." She flicked her bangs from her eyes. "Actually, my supervisor was just doing what he was told to do. He never would've suspended me. Hell, I helped The Player task force get their guy because I chose to buck the rules. My supervisor loves me. It's Marino who pulled those strings."

"And he'll pull them again when he finds out you're still snooping around his case. Don't push him."

She huffed out of her nose. "You act like you don't want to find Summer."

"That's not true. I don't want you digging a hole for yourself. Tell me what to do, and I'll do it. You stay out of it." He brushed a lock of silky hair from her shoulder. "I put my family before you once before, and I won't do it again."

She pursed her lips. "But this is Summer we're talking about. This could be life-or-death. Look, every day of my life I regret not stepping up for Danny, for not fighting harder. I've been trying to rectify that for other people ever since. I'm suspended. What are they gonna do?"

"Fire you." He squeezed her shoulder. "Tell me where to start."

"We start where we left off with Trey—Brighter Days. Give them a call on the up-and-up. Your sister is missing. You know she's a reformed addict, and you found their card in her things. Do they know anything? Last time she was there?"

"It's a rehab center. They're never going to give me that information."

"She's missing. They just might, and they'll have to tell the cops if she was a patient." She bit her bottom lip. "Of course, I'm not gonna know about that."

"I should make the call right now. Put them on Speaker with you in the car."

"Do it. And…" she snapped her fingers "…I have a solution to our other problem."

"What other problem? Seems like we have several about now."

"The loss of our inside track. I'm good friends with one of the other fingerprint techs. I'm sure he'll keep me posted on the cases as much as possible."

Cade held out his hand. "Card?"

Lori fished through her purse in her lap and placed it on his palm. "Don't be confrontational."

"How far do you think I'd get in my work if I were confrontational?" He pinched the card between two fingers of one hand and entered the phone number with the other.

As the phone rang, he rested it on the dashboard. "Hello, Brighter Days Recovery Center. This is Natasha."

"Hello, Natasha. My name is Cade Larson, and I'm wondering if you can help me out."

"We will certainly do our best, Cade. That's what we do here—help people."

"Good, good. My sister Summer Larson is missing, and I found your card among her things." He put on his best persuasive voice. "Before you talk to me about confidentiality, I already know my sister has had substance abuse issues in the past. I've helped her get into several programs over the years…and financed many of her stays. I'm wondering if she checked in with you recently, or perhaps she's there now. It would ease my mind to know she was in good hands like yours."

"Oh, I'm so sorry to hear your sister is missing. Of course, everyone's stay here is confidential. What I can do for you is, if Summer is with us, I can get a message to her that you're worried and looking for her. She can call you. There are no rules about calling out."

Cade met Lori's eyes, and she nodded.

"That would be a great start, Natasha. Let her know I'm concerned and just want to hear from her. Not even mad about the relapse, and I'm proud of her for seeking treatment on her own, this time." Cade gave Natasha his cell phone number and signed off with the promise of a donation if they could put him in touch with Summer.

Lori let out a long breath when he ended the call. "That's a start. If she's there, she'll call you. If she's not there and you hear nothing from her, you call them back. Press a little harder about if she ever was there and when they last saw her."

Cade tapped the edge of his phone against his chin. "Natasha didn't say whether or not the cops already called them."

"Maybe she doesn't know. Maybe the police call went straight to..." she picked up the card he'd dropped on the console "...Reed Dufrain. My contact on the inside, Josh, can tell me if Marino called Brighter Days."

"I should bypass Natasha and reach out to Dufrain next time myself." He flicked the Brighter Days card in her hand with his fingers. "What are you going to do now?"

She slid the card back into her purse. "I have a week's paid vacation. What do you think I'm going to do? I'm gonna help you find Summer—and I've just gone rogue."

WHEN LORI GOT HOME—by herself—she threw in a load of laundry, cleaned out her fridge and surveyed her security cameras. Trey's death had rattled her more than she'd let on to Cade.

She'd had more experience looking at people who had died violently than Cade had. He'd found a homeless man dead in the park on one of his morning jogs, and one of his coworkers had had a heart attack in the office, but blood and guts? He hadn't seen that before. It affected everyone differently and Cade had been shocked but not freaked out.

She'd seen the blood and guts up front and personal at many crime scenes, but Trey's death hit close to home. He was at the Frolic Room at her behest to meet her and Cade—and he'd wound up dead. Someone had slashed her tires in front of Summer's house the other day. Did she and Trey have the same enemies?

She wished she had gotten him to reveal more about Brighter Days over the phone. Why had he been so frightened to talk to her about the treatment center? What was so scary about a rehab center?

If someone killed Trey to stop him from revealing information about Brighter Days, then Cade didn't stand a chance of getting past Natasha at the front desk. But maybe she did.

She called Josh at the lab, and he picked up on the first ring. "Hey, you're persona non grata right now. I probably shouldn't be talking to you."

"Yeah, except I saved your ass on several occasions, and you sorta owe me."

"Hang on." He came back on the line after a pause. "You caught me at a good time. I'm on a smoke break. Otherwise, I never would've answered your call, but hey, I'd have your back even if you hadn't saved my ass a few times."

"That's why I'm calling you."

"You really did step in it though. A murder? C'mon, I thought you were done with all that nosing around after we found out about Clive being The Player."

"We both talked about Clive being weird. I just happened to see more funny business than you did. This time it's personal, Josh. That missing woman, Summer Larson, is the sister of an old friend of mine. What am I supposed to do? I'm not going to leave him hanging."

Josh lowered his voice. "Especially with Marino in charge."

"I thought you were outside. You'd better not be expressing those sentiments anywhere near the station. I'm already out for a week. We can't afford you gone, too."

"Don't worry. I have a wife and kids. If I lost this job, Ginny would kill me. But…" he coughed "…if you need me on the sly, I'm your man."

"I know that. I don't need much. Just try to keep me posted on any developments on the two cases—especially prints. Also, I gave Marino some information yesterday about both women having a connection to Brighter Days Recovery Center in Topanga. See if you can find out if Marino contacted them yet."

"I think I can find out through the regular channels— you know, coffee room chitchat, bathroom breaks, smoking sessions."

"Guys gossip about work in the bathroom?"

"I hear some of the most amazing things standing at the urinal."

"Okay, TMI, but anything you can find out about Brighter Days would be great."

"Will do. What are you doing with your time off?"

"Did some laundry and cleaned the fridge. I might start on the closets next."

"Almost makes me feel glad I'm at work. I'll talk to you soon."

She'd been lying about the closets. She hadn't been in this house long enough to build up closet clutter. She trusted Josh as her inside man. She *hadn't* been lying about having his back numerous times.

She jumped when her phone rang again, and then slumped in her chair when she saw Cade's number on the display. "Thought you might be Josh calling me back already."

"You talked to him? He's in?"

"He's going to keep me posted on the cases, and he's going to try to find out if Marino called Brighter Days."

"Is it going to be hard for him to get that information?"

Lori tucked one leg beneath her. "Not really. There are a lot of loose lips around the station. It's probably how Clive Stewart was able to keep abreast of the investigation into his crimes. Any luck with Summer's friends?"

"One got back to me, but she swore Summer wasn't using." He sighed. "But most addicts are liars, so maybe the friend just didn't know."

"If Summer wasn't back on the dope, why'd she have those drugs hidden away in her closet?"

"Didn't you point out earlier that if she were really using drugs, they'd be in a more accessible place? Nightstand? Kitchen cupboard? That's a lot of trouble to go through to get a hit."

Lori rubbed her knuckles across the arm of the couch. "Yeah. But if she's not using, why does she have the card for Brighter Days?"

"Referral for a friend? Someone like Courtney? She could've been a patient there before."

"Nothing from Natasha?"

Cade answered, "Didn't expect her to call back. How are you feeling about your suspension? Is there anything I can do?"

"I know exactly what you can do." Lori sprang up from the couch, her heart rattling her ribcage. "You can come over for dinner. I don't often cook, but I have the rest of the afternoon off."

Cade paused for just a second. "Only if you make your mom's enchiladas."

Lori grinned like an idiot. He'd remembered the Sadie Hawkins dance at school. The girls had to ask the boys and pay for the dance tickets and everything else. She didn't have enough money at the time to take Cade out to eat before the dance, so she made enchiladas for him instead.

"I can do that, but don't expect my mom's Carnitas. Chicken okay?"

"Chicken is *bueno*. I'll bring the *cerveza*."

"Only if you promise not to speak Spanish with your horrible accent."

They agreed on a time, and Lori practically flew out the front door to go grocery shopping, ignoring the little warning voice in her head. She scolded the voice aloud in the car. "It's just dinner. We have to eat."

An hour later while the sauce for the enchiladas was simmering, her phone rang and this time it *was* Josh. "What do you have for me?"

"Not much. The cases don't seem to be high priority for Marino. I think he'd need a dead body across his desk before he'd take action." Josh coughed. "Sorry about that. I know it's your friend's sister we're talking about."

Lori swallowed. "Anything on Brighter Days or Trey Ferrar's murder?"

"I don't think Marino is convinced Trey's murder has anything to do with Courtney Jessup's disappearance."

"You're kidding."

"Wish I were, and Brighter Days seems to be a dead end. Police couldn't get any info over the phone, so they're going to have to schedule a follow-up with a subpoena. No estimate on that."

So, Brighter Days didn't want to cooperate with the police. Cade had no chance of getting a call back.

"You are a regular fount of information, Josh. Had I known, I would've been asking you all this time instead of peering through keyholes and putting my ear to the wall." Lori stirred the bubbling sauce, the chilies making her nose run.

"You lucked out on this one, Del Valle. One of my cop buddies is working the cases with Marino—and he's no fan of the detective's."

"I think I know who you mean, and I won't say another word about her…him."

"Anything else you wanna know?"

"I'll be in touch. I'm actually making dinner right now."

"Enjoy your vacay."

Josh's call hadn't brought good news, but Lori had an idea forming in her head, one that could get them primary access to Brighter Days—one that could be dangerous. She'd just have to convince Cade to go along with the plan—and this dinner was the first step.

There was actually one step before this one. She picked up her phone and called Brighter Days.

Chapter Eleven

When she finished the call, she took the sauce off the stove, poured some in a dish and assembled the enchiladas, burning the tips of her fingers as she rolled up the chicken in the tortillas. She started the rice and made a dash for the shower.

Showered, dressed and made-up, Lori put the finishing touches on the dinner and hit the music on her phone. She liked country, and Cade? She had no idea anymore. She selected a classical playlist and turned it low to swirl in the background.

Cade showed up on time with a six-pack of beer and a big smile on his face.

When she ushered him inside, he said, "I could smell those chilies out on the street. You're going to have every house on this side of the canals stopping by with an excuse."

"Don't forget. The last time I made these for you, I had my mom's help. This time I'm flying solo." She took the six-pack from him. "Want one?"

He slipped two from the carton and followed her to the kitchen. While she stuck the beer in the fridge, he twisted off the caps. "Glass?"

She answered, "Always tastes better from the bottle."

Cade buzzed around the stove, lifting lids and sniffing the air. "Rice, beans. I'm in heaven."

"Just a warning." She held up her finger. "This isn't as homemade as my mom's."

"Still looks great. I'll set the table." He pulled some plates out of the cupboard and carried them to the table. "How is your mom?"

Lori ladled the beans into a bowl and grabbed a couple of serving spoons. "She's doing okay. She's in Mexico now with my grandmother—her mother."

"Do you think she'll stay there?"

"Not sure. My abuela is ill. When she passes…" she shrugged "…Mom might move back here."

They squeezed past each other, as she headed toward the table and he went back to the kitchen for silverware. "I always liked your mom, but I got the impression she wasn't too impressed with me."

A smile tugged at Lori's lips, as she turned with a hand on her hip. "My mom liked you. She just wanted me to be careful around you—thought you were a little too smooth for a high school boy."

"Me?" Cade slapped his hand against his chest. "You never told her about all my awkwardness."

"That was the problem. I sang your praises so much, she warned me nobody was that perfect."

"She was right about that." Cade held up a handful of forks and knives. "Do we need spoons?"

"Just one for the salsa."

They did a little dance in the kitchen again, as she lifted the steaming pan of enchiladas from the oven with a pair of pot holders. "Let me serve you at the table, so you don't mess up my creation. They might fall apart."

"We're eating them anyway, aren't we?" He pulled out her chair and put her beer next to her plate.

She smacked him with a pot holder. "Just let me do it."

She pulled her phone from her back pocket and placed it on the table. Then she carefully scooped out two of the enchiladas and slid them onto Cade's plate. "There. Now you can pile up the rice and beans any way you like."

Cade arranged his food, and as he dumped some salsa on his plate, he asked, "Did you hear anything else from Josh this afternoon?"

She eked out a little breath. Back to business. Of course, he was here because she was helping him with Summer—and for the food. "I did hear from him. The investigation is moving about as slowly as you'd expect. Marino at least called Brighter Days but got no love. He's going to have to return with a subpoena if he wants any info from Reed Dufrain...but I have another plan."

"That's spicy." Cade fanned his mouth. "But so good. I think you're giving your mother a run for her money in the kitchen, but don't tell her I said that. She'd hate me even more."

Lori rolled her shoulders, allowing Cade to change the subject. She should probably wait until after dinner, when his stomach was full and the alcohol had relaxed him. "I'm glad you like it, but my mother doesn't hate you."

In fact, her mother had more blame for her than she did for Cade for what had happened between them and had scolded her for not telling him about the pregnancy.

Mentioning her mother again set them off on a conversation of reminiscing, a conversation they hadn't had yet. A conversation that slightly terrified Lori.

But an hour later, after eating and talking and drinking another beer, Lori couldn't have asked for a better evening. Cade hadn't changed much.

He still took care of people, but his attitude had matured into one of patience and acceptance. She believed him now when he said he had no judgment for Summer's problems.

They'd both had that in common when they were younger—a desire to fix others. She'd done so at the expense of her own well-being, and Cade had let that quality turn him into someone demanding and critical.

As an adult, he'd tempered his desire to help with a greater understanding of others' weaknesses and faults. At the end of high school, she could've told *this* Cade about the pregnancy.

"What?" She stopped scraping the foil label from her bottle when she realized Cade had spoken to her.

"I asked if you wanted another beer." He held up his own empty bottle.

"Oh, God, no, but you go ahead."

"I've hit my limit."

She swirled the rest of her beer in the bottom of the bottle. "So, you're not a big drinker?"

"You mean, like my father?"

"I didn't say that."

"But I could tell that's what you were thinking." He lightly tapped the tip of the bottle against his temple. "Seems like my father's addictive personality manifested in Summer but not in me or Sarah. I don't even like Scotch—my dad's particular poison."

"Pretty much the same with our family. Danny's the only one of us who ever had trouble with drugs or alcohol. The rest of us were turned off by Dad's drinking, but Danny went down the same path."

"Funny how that works." He collected their dishes. "You did the cooking, and I'm going to do the cleaning."

"I'll help." She hopped up from her chair and shoved her phone back in her pocket. She didn't want to miss any calls.

"You don't trust me?" He pushed back from the table as if to race her to the kitchen.

"I'm sure you can do it, but I'm also sure you have a cleaning lady. Go on. Tell me you don't have one."

He raised his hand. "Guilty, but that doesn't mean I don't know how to wash a pan or put a dish in the dishwasher. You saw me in action the other night."

As they stood side by side at the sink, Lori's heart stuttered in her chest. Wasn't this what she'd always imagined for the two of them? They might've been the silly dreams of a high school girl, but she'd felt something with Cade back then, despite their differences, and she still felt it today. She'd never been able to let go of him in her heart—maybe because she still held that secret from him. If she released the secret, told him about the baby, would that release her from the silky web she'd spun for herself? The web that tied her to Cade?

His fingers brushed her hand in the warm, soapy water. "Hey, you're someplace far away tonight. Is that place back in high school?"

She turned toward him, and her breast skimmed his arm, making her toes curl into the floor. "You made me travel down memory lane, and now it's going to be hard to come back."

"Do we have to come back?" He lifted a hand from the water and cupped her face, her hair catching the warm droplets from his fingers. "Sometimes I wish you hadn't let me go so easily. It felt like…you didn't want me."

Tears pricked the backs of her eyes and she blinked. "Oh, I did, but..."

"But you didn't want to hold me back while I was in college. Thing is..." he ran his wet thumb across her bottom lip "...I don't think I would've minded. To be held by you was the greatest joy in my life at that time."

That had to be an invitation.

As she wrapped her arms around Cade's waist, Lori asked, "Like this?"

"More like this." He pulled her close, and her head dropped against his chest, where she felt his heart thunder, mimicking her own.

He wedged a finger beneath her chin, tipping her head back. When his lips met hers, she had to hold on to him even tighter as her knees weakened. He kissed like a man now.

His fingers sifted through her hair, as he deepened the kiss. She slid one hand beneath his shirt and ran her knuckles along his smooth, warm back.

He whispered against her mouth. "Do you want this? Do you want me?"

In answer, she fitted her body against his more closely and trailed her fingers across the reddish-gold stubble on his chin. "When could I ever resist you?"

He grabbed her hand and feathered kisses across her fingertips. "We're different, we're older, but this doesn't feel any different to me. It feels like coming home."

Tugging at the hem of his shirt, she batted her eyelashes at him. "Except we have privacy now, and a bed."

"You mean we can't do it on the kitchen counter?" He tucked his fingers into the waistband of her jeans, and butterflies took flight in her belly. "I actually think we may have done that once or twice."

"Then it must've been at your house because our kitchen was too small and too crowded." She curled her hand around the material of his shirt and yanked it. "Why are you still talking? I thought a man your age would have smoother moves."

"You want smooth moves?" In one motion, he took a step back and swept her up in his arms.

She screamed and tucked her legs in to avoid kicking the beer bottles off the counter. Pointing down the hallway, she said, "This way."

When they reached the edge of her bed, she squirmed out of his arms and pulled his shirt over his head. She splayed her hands across his chest, her fingers tracing his muscles. "Mmm."

That one sentiment sent them into a flurry of activity. If she thought their first time as adults would be slow and easy, she'd sorely miscalculated Cade's impatience—and her own.

With lightning speed, they helped each other out of their clothes and left them in a heap by the side of the bed. Skin-to-skin, they sank to the mattress, and Cade pulled her into his lap. She straddled his hips and gave herself up to the kisses he rained upon her face and throat.

She moved against his erection, and he caught his breath as a shudder went through his frame.

Through gritted teeth, he said, "You're making me feel like I'm eighteen years old again, with no control."

"Control is overrated." She nibbled on his ear, and he swung her onto her back.

One thought pierced the fog of desire that had infused her body. What was she doing? They lived on opposite coasts. Were his actions tonight fueled by guilt or regret?

Then he tucked his hands beneath her bottom and

lifted her hips to meet him…and those questions dissolved into a haze of pleasure. She didn't care. She'd take this moment.

Once they'd spent their youthful enthusiasm, they lay next to each other, their limbs entwined. She drew shapes on his damp chest with her fingertip. "I'd say that was an improvement over the previous version."

He rolled his head to the side and kissed her shoulder. "That was just an appetizer—a prelude, a test run."

She did an exaggerated gulp. "You mean there's more to come?"

Running a hand along her hip, he growled. "I feel invigorated. You?"

"I feel…" Her phone rang from somewhere on the floor. "Annoyed."

"I'll get it." He reached to the floor and dragged her jeans up the bed. "You left it in your pocket."

As he removed it, he glanced at the display. "Brighter Days? Why is Brighter Days calling you?"

She snatched the phone from his hand. "Because I'm going to be one of their patients."

Chapter Twelve

Cade tried to grab the phone back from her, but she rolled away from him and answered it.

"Hello?"

Lori had at least put the phone on Speaker, and a familiar woman's voice responded. "Is this Loretta Garcia?"

"Yes, it is. This is Brighter Days?"

"It is. This is Natasha. We got your voice mail, and I'm sorry nobody was here to take your call. Are you safe now? Are you in a good place? We do have emergency services, as well, if you're not."

Lori fluffed a couple of pillows behind her and winked at him. "Yes, I'm fine. As I said in my message, I'm clean right now but I'm in danger of a relapse. I just know it. I've done this before, and I'm going to stop it before it starts this time. Someone referred me to your center, but she doesn't want me to use her name."

Natasha cooed. "Of course. We understand. We pride ourselves on being discreet. When would you like to come for a visit and discuss your options?"

Cade nudged Lori's knee and sliced a finger across his throat when her eyes met his. She was *not* doing this.

After Trey's reaction to the place and his murder, Cade didn't want Lori anywhere near Brighter Days.

She gave him the okay sign with her thumb and forefinger. "How about tomorrow?"

Cade dragged his fingers through his hair, grasping at the roots. How long had she been planning this?

"Tomorrow is fine. We can see you at eleven o'clock, if that's okay. Do you need directions?"

"Eleven is fine, and I have the address in Topanga. C-can I bring my friend with me?" She leveled a finger at him. "If I decide your center is right for me, he'll be making the deposit for my stay—in cash."

Cade let out a breath. At least he'd have the drive over to talk her out of it.

Natasha answered brightly, "Of course, but he can't take the tour—anonymity and all that. The road to our facility is a windy one, once you turn off Topanga Canyon Boulevard. Keep following it all the way to the end and you can park on the right and use that entrance."

"Thank you, Natasha."

"We'll be waiting for you, Loretta."

When Lori ended the call, she held up her hand. "Don't start. You know this is a good plan. What are we going to do, wait for Marino's subpoena? What's he going to find there?"

"What do you think *you're* going to find? Trey told us he wanted to talk about Brighter Days in person, and before he could, he was murdered. This is a dangerous move, *Loretta Garcia*."

"It'll be fine. I'll check in as an inpatient, go to a few therapy sessions, do a little yoga—and snoop around in my spare time."

He punched his fist into a pillow. "That's what I'm

worried about. What if someone catches you nosing around? Do you have a story?"

"I'll think of something." She flicked her fingers in the air. "I'm not going to do anything stupid, Cade. I just want a firsthand look at what goes on in there. Maybe I can chat up a few of the patients and see if anyone knows anything about Summer or Courtney."

"That right there is gonna get you kicked out…or worse." He swung his legs off the side of the bed and planted them on the floor. "When were you going to tell me about this? I mean, I do have to finance the scheme."

"I tried to tell you earlier, before dinner." She slid him a gaze from the side of her eye. "But I didn't want to ruin your dinner."

"Or you just wanted to get me drunk and…" he plucked up the sheet and let it drop "…sated."

She curled up her leg and wiggled her toes against his bare back. "Are you sated? You just told me five minutes ago we'd only gotten started."

"That was before I knew you'd committed yourself… and my money to Brighter Days."

She got on her knees and pressed her breasts against his back, as she wrapped her arms around him. "You're still going to finance me, aren't you? I can pay you back, but I figured you'd have a better chance of getting your hands on bundles of cash than I would on such short notice."

He took her hand that rested on his shoulder and turned it over, placing a kiss on the palm. "I'll give you the money if you promise we'll put a plan in place in case you run into something you can't handle."

"We will." She leaned forward to kiss the edge of his

chin, the ends of her hair tickling his skin. Then she whispered in his ear. "Can we take it slow and easy this time?"

Cade tumbled back onto the bed, taking her with him. He still hadn't given up on convincing her to abandon this wild scheme, but he'd save reason and sanity for the light of day.

THE FOLLOWING DAY, Cade walked out of his bank, the same one that housed Summer's safe deposit box, carrying a stack of cash in his computer bag. As he tossed the bag in the backseat, he asked Lori, "How much time is that going to buy you?"

"That'll be a deposit on one month's stay." She slammed the car door. "And if I leave early, which I will, you'll get that refunded."

"Unless you discover you like it there and wanna see out your month."

She punched his biceps. "I highly doubt I'll like it there. Sounds like a bore, but I'm hoping to get some insight into why Trey was leery of this place."

"Leery? Trey sounded more than leery." He wagged his finger at her. "Don't forget Trey is dead. The cops have no leads, except for some video of the back of the killer's head and the bartender's vague recollection of his face. *And* someone slashed your tires after you found the Brighter Days card at Summer's house and again in her safe deposit box."

"The perps who slashed my tires didn't know I found those cards."

"They figured you were going to find something they wanted to keep a secret, and that something might be Summer's connection to Brighter Days." He started the car and trailed a finger down her soft cheek. "Just remember that you may be in enemy territory while you're there."

She held up two fingers like a Boy Scout. "I'll re-member. Now, we need to find you a disguise before we drive out there."

He slammed on the brakes, and they both lurched forward against their seat belts. "Excuse me?"

"Disguise. You'll need one. Both you and Summer have those blond-blue, California-gold good looks. Some-one might recognize you. Maybe they already did some research on Summer and saw your picture. I've gotten this far, and I'm not going to jeopardize my cover."

"Your cover?" He snorted and continued to pull the car out of the parking space. "Okay, Loretta Garcia."

"I'm not searchable on the internet, like you are. My parents aren't international businesspeople and philan-thropists—unless you count the church collection plate. Garcia is a common name, if they do decide to investi-gate me. They're going to be inundated with Loretta Gar-cias if they try. Besides…" she straightened her seat belt "…I'm going to alter my appearance, too."

He raised his eyebrows and rubbed her thigh. "Not too much. I like what I see right now."

"Nothing drastic." She flipped down the visor and studied herself in the mirror. "Maybe some glasses, more and different makeup and a wig."

"Wig?" Cade laughed. "You're serious."

"Do you want me to be careful, or not? If I'm already on their radar for some reason, I want to go there in-cognito."

"Okay, you're right. Disguise it is. Where are we going to find these disguises?"

"We're a few miles away from Hollywood. If you can't

locate a costume shop here, you don't belong in Tinseltown." She pulled out her phone and tapped the display. "Found one or two."

Lori pulled up one of the stores on her GPS, and Cade followed the directions.

When they got to the Hollywood Costume Shop on Sunset, Elsa the salesperson didn't blink an eye as they shopped wigs, beards, colored contact lenses and hats.

As Cade patted the dark beard on his face, he asked her, "Do you do a lot of business?"

"This is Hollywood. People change their identities all the time." Elsa peered at him over the top of her glasses perched on the end of her nose. "You look good with a beard."

Lori turned from the mirror, a short curly wig covering her silky tresses. "What do you think?"

Picking up a hat, Cade said, "I think I like the previous version better."

"I hope so, but do I look different enough?" She pulled the hair back from her face. "Too recognizable?"

Elsa tapped her chin with one long red fingernail that matched the color of her hair. Or maybe that wasn't her hair.

She considered Lori's face. "Put on some makeup. You can go dark with the black hair. I can show you a few contouring tricks that will change the shape of your face. Throw on some glasses, and you'll look very different from the woman who walked into this store. Different enough so that even your husband won't recognize you—if that's the plan."

Lori met Cade's eyes and smothered a smile with her hand.

Elsa thought they wanted to spice up their sex lives by

changing things up in the bedroom. She couldn't be more wrong—he wouldn't change one thing in the bedroom.

Lori nodded. "That would be great. The extent of my makeup routine comprises some black eyeliner, mascara and a swipe of lipstick when I'm not eating, drinking or talking."

"That's because you're naturally beautiful." Cade came up behind her in the mirror and brushed his new beard against the back of her neck.

She shimmied. "That tickles. Watch out. I may just demand you keep that glued to your face."

Cade swept the baseball cap he'd picked up onto his head, shoved his hands in his pockets and slouched. "I'm going for hipster Hollywood director with too much money to care for fashion—or cleanliness."

Elsa smirked. "Works for me. Now, let me get my brushes."

Thirty minutes later, Elsa had transformed a fresh-faced beauty into a poster child for a "just say no" campaign. Lori stared at him from heavily lined eyes and puckered a set of ruby-red lips at him. The dark hollows beneath her eyes emphasized her cheekbones, which stood out sharply from her face. She could pass for a recovering addict easily.

She spread her arms. "What do you think? Black-on-black clothes, Elsa?"

"Absolutely—black jeans, boots, T-shirt, edgy jacket. You'd fit in at any club on the Strip."

Lori checked her phone. "We're headed somewhere else, but this will do. We'll take everything and wear it out—just to get accustomed to the disguises."

When they landed outside on the sidewalk, Cade ducked every time someone walked by. "I feel like an imposter."

"You are." Lori thumped him on the back. "But if you're going to play the hipster director, you'd better own that persona and stop hunching every time someone looks at you."

"This is exactly why I never did theater arts in school."

"You didn't do theater arts in school because you thought those kids were nerds, and you were the hotshot athlete."

He tugged on the scratchy beard. "Was I that insufferable?"

"Sometimes, but you were always kind to everyone... even the little Latina from East LA. Once I had your attention, no one ever dared to bully me."

"Nobody was going to bully you anyway. The boys thought you were hot as hell, and the girls saw you as a project."

She drilled him in the back with her knuckle. "Now you're my project, so you'd better play the part—a good, rich friend concerned about his friend relapsing, needing anonymity and putting cash down as a deposit."

"What am I supposed to do while you're taking the tour?"

"Smile and drink your green smoothie."

He said, "Then I'll head to the bathroom, get lost and do a little reconnaissance on my own."

"I wonder if they can take me as soon as tomorrow. I do have to get back to work in a week."

He took her arm and led her to the car parked down the street. "You hope so. If the LAPD finds out about this stunt, you may not have a job to go back to."

AFTER THEY CHANGED into appropriate clothes to match their disguises, Cade drove his rental along the Pacific

Coast Highway. As they cruised past Malibu, Lori asked, "Do your parents still own the house?"

His gaze flicked toward the azure sea to his left. He'd spent much of his childhood in that water. He missed it. He'd given up too much in his quest for independence from his father. He shot Lori a look from the side of his eye. Maybe it was time to get it back.

Flexing his fingers on the steering wheel, he answered her. "They still own it. They rent it out. Do you remember where it is?"

"Of course. I'll never forget that house—the ocean views from every room, the pool looking almost seamless with the ocean, that kitchen. How come Summer doesn't stay there?"

He lifted his shoulders. "Too big for her. That's a family home. Too far away from the city and the things she likes to do—the things that got her into trouble."

"At least we're doing something to find her instead of sitting around waiting for Marino."

His stomach dipped just like it did every time he thought of Lori trapped at Brighter Days. What had Trey been so afraid of? Had he paid with his life because of what he knew about the treatment center?

"If we don't like the look of the place or the people running it, all bets are off. I'll take my bag of money and go. This is just a tour. You don't have to commit to anything."

"Okay, we'll see how it goes." She tapped the window. "Topanga Canyon Boulevard is coming up at the next light."

Cade made the turn and maneuvered the car along the winding, two-lane road that cut through canyons and forests. Wildfire season could hit this area hard. He remembered watching a few times from his house in Malibu as an orange haze hung over the mountains here.

He took the turnoff toward Brighter Days, but the facility hadn't bothered to put out a sign. If you needed a sign to find Brighter Days, you didn't belong there. Lori didn't belong there, either.

"This is off the beaten track, isn't it? No wonder they have such great views to show off on the website." She fluffed her black curls and smacked her lips to moisten her lipstick. "Natasha said veer to the right and we'll see parking and an entrance."

Cade rolled past a delivery truck from a high-end natural food grocery chain and spotted a handful of parking spaces. "At least you'll be eating well while you're here—if they don't kick you out first—or worse."

"Stop worrying." She squeezed his arm. "I'm going to make a few discreet inquiries and see if I can access any computers."

He jerked the car to a stop. "Wait, what? You never mentioned computers before."

"How else am I supposed to get any info on patients? Do you think they keep filing cabinets stuffed with patient details?"

"You know about computers, too?" He narrowed his eyes. He could still make out Lori under the disguise. He'd know her anywhere, although he wouldn't have noticed her at the Northeast Division the night that he went in to report Summer missing if she hadn't noticed him first. That night made him believe in luck…or maybe it was fate.

"I'm not a hacker, but I know a little about computers. We have a kick-ass tech guy, Brandon Nguyen, who taught me a few tricks. I can get past a password or two."

"You just heightened my anxiety, tenfold." He cut the engine and took a deep breath. "All right. Let's get this over with. Remember, you can walk away from it all."

"Got it." She winked and cranked open the car door.

They walked up a gravel path that led to a side entrance. A bubbling fountain greeted and soothed them at the door and Cade tried to open it. While his hand still rested on the handle, he heard a muted buzz and a soft click. It turned beneath the pressure of his hand.

As soon as they stepped onto the cool tile of the foyer, an attractive woman with dark hair pulled into a bun floated toward them, hands outstretched. "Loretta, here for the tour?"

"Y-yes. Are you Natasha?" Lori knotted her fingers in front of her, looking as nervous as he felt.

"I am." Natasha reached out and captured Lori's hand with both of hers, expensive-looking rings sparkling on her long fingers. Cade had been around jewelry long enough to know the real thing. The rehab business must be booming.

"And you are?" Natasha turned her dark, inquisitive gaze on Cade in a way that made him want to tug down his cap.

"Her friend."

Natasha threw up her hands. "I get it. Well, friend, I did mention to Loretta on the phone that we give tours only to prospective patients, so you'll have to wait in our lounge while I show her around."

"Understood." The fewer words he said, the better. He didn't think she'd recognize his voice from one phone call, but let her think he was afraid she'd out him as someone famous who didn't want to be seen at a treatment center.

"Good. Then we all understand each other." She reached past them and pressed a button on the wall. "Ready, Loretta?"

Cade half expected the button to release a trap door, dropping them into the bowels of this bucolic retreat, but it only summoned a short dark woman in some kind of green tunic that looked like a nurse's uniform.

"Ella, please see this gentleman to the lounge and offer him refreshment." Natasha waved her slim hand in the air. "We have smoothies, organic coffee, herbal teas, whatever you like."

Lori made a little move beside him, and he had to clench his teeth to trap his laugh.

"Thanks." He turned toward Ella without another glance at Lori. Some instinct told him Brighter Days preferred clients who didn't have a lot of outside support. He could be wrong, but he didn't think so.

He'd figured that was the reason why Lori had identified him as a friend to Natasha over the phone instead of a husband. A husband or boyfriend could be bothersome. At least, that was his story, and he was sticking to it. It couldn't be that Lori didn't like the idea of calling him Husband.

He followed Ella into a beautiful room with two glass walls, the nature outside clambering all over them to get inside. The room seemed like an extension of the outdoors, and he sank into a teak chair with green floral cushions, facing the riotous growth.

"Can I get you something, sir?"

"How about a green smoothie? Something healthy." He suppressed a smile. Lori had nailed this place. He just hoped he was wrong about the rest of it and that Brighter

Days wasn't complicit in Trey's death. Because where would that leave Lori?

"Of course, sir. Any allergies or restrictions?"

"None. Thanks for asking." They really wanted his money. This just might be the most expensive green smoothie he'd ever had. When Ella left, he glanced at the tables littered with books on meditation, yoga, veganism. He didn't see any informational pamphlets about the center. Business must come via word of mouth among the wealthy and connected.

Mom had spent a month in a place like this for her prescription pill addiction. How Mom and Dad could read Summer the riot act about her drug use was the epitome of irony, given their own addictions. They had to figure they'd turn out one child with issues.

His sister Sarah had different issues—control issues. She left nothing to chance. She even organized her kids' birthday parties down to the last balloon.

Who was he kidding? He'd had the same type of predilections. He'd worked hard to overcome them. His business went smoother when he allowed his top executives to have a say in the direction of the company. So far, so good. He'd outearned his father last year for the first time—not that that was his primary goal.

"Your smoothie, sir." Ella sailed into the room with a tall glass filled with green mush on a silver tray.

She set it in front of him on the table and he unwrapped the straw and stuck it in the sludge. She hovered while he took the first sip. He closed his eyes and said, "Perfect."

"Let me know if you need anything else, sir." Her shoes whispered on the tile, as she left him to his glass of health.

He took another sip and smacked his lips. To break the silence that hung over the room, he said aloud, "Not bad."

They should probably have music. No sooner had the thought left his brain, than some Peruvian flute music floated from the hidden speakers. Maybe they could read minds here, too.

The sound of heels on the tile echoed from the other room and once again, he heard the buzz and the click of the door. Another prospective patient? Did they get their times mixed up? What happened to Brighter Days' famed discretion?

He pushed up from the chair, drink in hand, and wandered to the arched entry to the foyer. Natasha ushered in two men in suits, who didn't look like prospective patients to him.

As the taller guy in the gray suit turned to glance at him, Cade almost choked on his green smoothie.

He knew they weren't prospective patients—because the man in the gray suit was Detective Marino.

Chapter Thirteen

Lori gazed at the view from the patio, staring past the outdoor yoga lesson. The circuitous coastline etched in blue with a white edge twisted its way up to Ventura County, the rugged Santa Monica Mountains almost meeting the sand. She could get used to a place like this.

Cade's childhood home had just such a view, although from a lower elevation. She'd loved that house. The beach off the house's back deck wasn't private, but it was far enough away from public parking and the primo surf spots of Topanga Beach and Surfrider that not many people ventured down to the sand.

She and Cade had made love on that beach—stupid, foolish, teenage sex—not thinking about the consequences.

She jumped when Natasha came up behind her. "I'm sorry, Loretta. I have a few more areas to show you, but I have to deal with a situation right now. I can have Ella continue the tour, if you like."

"I've seen enough, Natasha. It looks like the perfect setting for me. I'm determined to stay clean this time."

"We can certainly help with this first, rough period of sobriety." She slipped a folded piece of paper into Lori's hand. "The payment options. Ella can assist you with the deposit and schedule for your stay."

She was in. "D-do you think I can start tomorrow? I'm on shaky ground right now, and my friend out front, the one financing this, has kind of had it with me. He has work in Canada and will be out of town."

"Tomorrow is fine." Natasha patted her back. "Ella will give you all the details."

She followed Natasha across the patio, back inside the airy building. What possible evil could take place behind the walls of such a place? Maybe she and Cade had it all wrong. Maybe Trey had it all wrong.

They stepped into the lobby area, and Lori nearly tripped to a stop. Positioned by the side door, arms folded over his belly, loomed Detective Marino.

Her knees quaked as they walked past him and his partner, Detective Suarez. Both detectives discreetly averted their eyes from her, as she dropped her head, letting the curls from her wig hide her face.

Natasha left her at the small ornate desk in the corner, clutching its edge, as she turned toward the cops. "Gentlemen, come this way and tell me what you'd like to see."

As the two suits lumbered toward Natasha's office, Lori let out short little breaths and placed her hand against her heart. She cracked her stiff face into a smile when Ella joined her at the desk.

"I'll take care of you, Loretta. You're joining us tomorrow?"

"Yes."

Cade sauntered in, clutching a glass with green residue stuck to the inside. "You're going ahead with it?"

"I am. Now you can go to Canada with a clear conscience. I'll be here." As she faced him, away from Ella, she brushed her fingers across her forehead, indicating she'd had a close call. Had he seen the detectives?

They settled their business with Ella, and Cade handed over the cash for the deposit. He requested a generic receipt for the money, and Ella scurried from the desk, cash in an envelope.

Cade whispered. "Did Marino see you?"

"Yes, but no hint of recognition from him or Suarez. I'm safe." She sealed her lips as Ella emerged from the office, waving a white slip of paper in the air. "Here you are, sir. Do you need anything else?"

"I think we're set." He placed the empty glass on the desk. "And thanks for the delicious smoothie."

Lori waited until they were in the car before turning toward him. "You really ordered a green smoothie?"

"It was good, although I nearly upchucked all of it when I saw Marino walk in. So, he got his subpoena faster than we thought he would. Maybe he's taking this seriously, after all."

"Who knows? Maybe Reed Dufrain decided it would be a better look for him to open his doors to the LAPD than force them to issue that subpoena. They'd have had time to hide whatever needed to be hidden."

He eased the car back onto Topanga Canyon Boulevard and some semblance of civilization. "If there's anything to be hidden. I didn't have a chance to get lost after the detectives showed up. What did you see on the tour? Anything nefarious? Looks like your typical high-end rehab center to me."

"I'll get a better look tomorrow, won't I?" She cracked the window and sniffed the air. "Smells so good up here."

"Do you want to stop by my old house on the way back? I've been handling the rental for my parents, and the tenants indicated they wanted to move out at the end of their lease. I told them I'd drop by on this visit to discuss some terms with them."

"I'd love to see the old house." She grabbed a handful of curls. "Are we going like this?"

Cade chuckled. "I got so comfortable with the beard and dark wig, I forgot I had them on." He tapped his phone sitting in a holder on the dashboard. "I'll call the tenants to see if it's okay that we drop by. The husband works at home. He writes scripts for a few very popular TV shows, and his wife stars on one of the shows. If it's a go, we can stop for lunch at the Reel Inn and shed our costumes."

She tapped her forehead. "Aren't you glad I insisted on them? Marino would've made you in two seconds, and both he and Suarez would've hauled my sorry behind back to the station."

He clicked his tongue. "Your behind is anything but sorry—and I know that for a fact."

She gazed out the window with a stupid smile on her face. She wasn't sure yet how this was all going to work out between them, but she'd enjoy the ride for as long as possible.

She covered her mouth. That didn't mean she was happy Summer had gone missing, and was still missing. She'd have given up running into Cade again if both Summer and Courtney could come home safely. Wouldn't she?

Cade spoke to the man on the other line for a minute or two. The tenant had agreed to meet Cade in an hour.

"Lunch and a change of clothes."

Lori's heart skipped a beat for a second, as she glanced

in her side mirror. "Nobody followed us from Brighter Days, right?"

"I've been keeping an eye on the rearview. Kinda hard to tell when you've got a two-lane road most of the way—one end spilling out on the coast highway, the other end onto Ventura Boulevard. But I haven't noticed one car behind us the whole way. Do you want me to pull over for a few minutes in case we have a distant tail?"

"Would you mind? I don't know why it didn't occur to me before. We had the disguises and the cash-only payment, but Natasha could get suspicious and have us followed. Maybe it's even protocol for them."

"Okay, hang on." Cade wheeled the car into a small dirt parking lot in front of a marijuana dispensary. As he backed up to face the road, he said, "I'm sure this store does a booming business up here."

"Charlie Manson stayed in Topanga for a while before relocating to Spahn Movie Ranch due north and across the valley."

"Yeah, don't remind me. That's just another reason for you to abandon this scheme."

"Charlie Manson is dead and gone." She brushed her hands together.

"Plenty more devious minds out there, and we both know Topanga isn't all peace and love." Cade hunched forward over the steering wheel for several minutes, watching the traffic cruise past. "I don't see any familiar cars. I think we're good to go."

He peeled out of the parking lot, kicking up dust and gravel with his back wheels. Several miles later, they stopped at the bottom of the boulevard to make a left turn at the light, an expanse of the Pacific Ocean gleaming in front of them. Less than a mile away, Cade turned onto a street bordering the Reel Inn, a casual seafood restaurant with barrels of peanuts for appetizers and shells on the floor.

As he parked the car, he said, "I can do my quick-change act out here." He pulled down the visor and carefully peeled the beard and moustache from his face, leaving a ruddy color behind on his skin.

He patted his face. "Almost there."

He tossed the baseball cap in the backseat of the car and pulled the dark wig from his head. He tousled his blond hair with one hand. "What do you think?"

She leaned over and kissed his clean-shaven cheek. "Much better. Now, it's my turn."

She removed her own wig and shook out her hair. She'd already ditched her glasses and wiped off the lipstick. "I'll wash my face in the restaurant. This disguise was good enough to fool Marino and Suarez, so that makes me feel better. I just need to re-create that makeup every day at the center."

"Hopefully, you won't be there long enough to perfect it. You're going to have a sudden change of heart or a family emergency once you find what you want, or realize there's nothing there to learn." Cade scratched his beardless face. "If the subpoena doesn't turn up anything, maybe you should cancel. I can eat the deposit."

Squeezing his hard biceps, she said, "Stop trying to talk me out of it. I can uncover things a subpoena can't. Marino and Suarez aren't going to be talking to the patients."

Self-conscious about her heavy makeup, Lori kept her head down when they entered the restaurant and made a beeline for the restrooms. She'd already given Cade her order and by the time she emerged from the ladies' room fresh-faced and hungry, Cade had snagged a table on the patio and had filled a basket with peanuts.

She slid into her chair and took a gulp of her iced tea. "Better?"

"It's all good to me. You could wear a bag over your head, and I'd be happy to sit across from you. No, wait. The bag would have to have cutouts for your eyes, so that I could gaze into their depths."

She snorted and took another slug of her tea, even though she couldn't quiet her singing heart. "Have you been watching romance movies? You already got into my bed—you can relax now."

He tossed a peanut shell on the ground and grabbed her hand, lacing his fingers through hers. "That's not what it's about between us. It never was. You don't believe that, do you?"

She studied his blue eyes, sparkling with intensity. That intensity made her shy. There was so much between them, so many unspoken words—at least on her part.

She traced the seams where their fingers interlocked. "There was always more, but what now? You live in New York. You're here to find Summer, and I'm helping you. When we find her, and I know we will, you'll go back to your life and I'll go back to mine."

He released her hand and stirred his tea with his straw. "Don't you think there's a reason neither of us is married or even dating exclusively?"

Beyond the reason that she compared every man to her first love? "You thought about me so much over the years, you never once contacted me."

"I can take a hint, Lori. You broke it off with me. You were supposed to join me that summer in Boston before we started college. You were going to look into transferring. Yeah, I know I could've chosen a college in California, but I wasn't strong enough then to stand up to my father. He wanted me to go to Harvard, so that's where I went."

"I didn't blame you for that." She blamed him for not fighting harder for her. She blamed him for not asking more questions. She blamed herself for so many things.

Sweeping some shells to the floor, she said, "It's not about the past anymore. It's the future that concerns me. If I wouldn't move across country then, I'm not going to do it now and I don't expect you to give up your life in New York, and everything you built there."

"I can achieve that kind of success in any big city—even here."

The waiter saved her from answering, as he dropped off their fish tacos and refilled their tea.

When he left, she asked Cade, "Is the first step looking at the Malibu house?"

"Maybe it is."

Despite her doubts, a fish taco never tasted so good.

Forty minutes later, they were cruising down the Pacific Coast Highway once more before turning down a road that led to the ocean and the mansions perched along its coastline.

Cade rolled up to the security gate and buzzed down the window. He waved his hand outside. "They're expecting me, Raoul."

"Nice to see you again, Mr. Cade."

"You, too. How's the family?"

Raoul gave him a thumbs-up and a big smile as he raised the parking arm.

Cade drove onto the small road that curved along the edge of the houses, most of which you couldn't see behind the large gates. He pulled up to the familiar Mediterranean-style house with the red-tile roof and soaring arches. When Lori first saw this house, she thought it was a palace and Cade was surely her Prince Charming.

She swallowed against her dry throat. "Looks the same."

"Feels different." Cade jumped out of the car, and he steered her up the long walkway to the front door, which opened before they could knock.

A tall, lean man with glasses shoved to the top of his head stepped onto the porch. "Saw you coming. How are you doing, Cade?"

Cade introduced her to Jerry Wise, who invited her to relax on the patio while he and Cade discussed business.

As she sauntered toward the pocket door that opened onto the deck and a crisp, salty sea breeze, Jerry asked her if she wanted anything to drink.

"Lemonade, wine, champagne, Bloody Mary. Whatever you like."

"Lemonade is fine."

"Go on out." He shooed her with his bony fingers that she could imagine toiling over a computer keyboard, churning out scripts for hit shows. "I'll have my assistant, Gretchen, bring you a drink."

Lori stood at the railing, leaning over to watch a mom and her two small kids building sandcastles. She turned when she heard scuffling steps behind her.

A young blonde woman with her hair in a chignon held up a tray with a pitcher, a glass of ice and a bowl of tropical fruit. "Jerry said you wanted some lemonade and insisted I include some food. For as skinny as the guy is, he's constantly eating and thinks everyone else should be, too."

"It looks lovely. Thanks." Lori peered at the jug of pale yellow liquid still rippling from a vigorous stirring. "This isn't hard lemonade, is it?"

"No." Gretchen's laugh was like the trill of a bird. "He thinks everyone in Hollywood drinks in the middle of the day, so he always offers alcohol. I can spike it if you like."

"Oh, God, no." Lori grabbed the handle of the glass pitcher before Gretchen could. She didn't know how often this young woman's duties involved serving food and drink to Jerry's guests, but Lori didn't want to waste her time.

The glass tinkled as she filled it. Holding up the pitcher, she asked, "Do you want to join me?"

"Would love to, but I have a Diet Coke at my desk that includes a pile of work."

"Then I won't keep you. I don't need anything else, thanks."

Gretchen tipped her head toward the view. "I'll miss this when the Wises go back to New York."

"You're not going with them?"

Gretchen shook her head so hard, her bun slipped. "I'm an LA girl, born and bred. There's something about this place that seeps into your blood, isn't there?"

"I agree." Lori raised her glass to the ocean and took a sip, the tart lemonade spiking her tongue. She whispered as Gretchen turned away, "Especially when you have this view."

As she drained her second glass of lemonade, Cade and Jerry joined her on the deck.

Jerry inspected the tray with the half-eaten bowl of fruit. "Do you want anything else?"

"I'm fine. Thank you so much for the refreshments, and thank Gretchen again for me."

"I have a request." Cade jerked his thumb toward the beach. "Okay if we have a walk down to the beach?"

"You know as well as I do, it isn't private." Jerry unlatched the gate that led to a path to the sand.

"Yeah, but I also know we'll have to come back this way to get to our car, unless we walk around the rocks."

"It's your house, Cade, or it will be in a few months." Jerry lifted his hand as they squeezed through the gate.

"I'm going to take off these boots." At the bottom of the steps, Lori sat down. "What did he mean the house was yours? Isn't it your parents'?"

"Actually, no. My parents signed the house over to me. It's mine." He scuffed the toe of his tennis shoe in the sand. "Let's go."

They slogged through the dry sand until they hit the shore. Lori's bare feet slapped along the wet sand, her shoulder bumping Cade's awkwardly until he put his arm around her and they moved as one.

"Why didn't you tell me you owned the house?"

He stopped and squinted at the horizon. "I don't know. It was in the works before I came out here. It was part of the reason for my visit. The place is already calling me back, and you just might be the siren's call I can't resist."

He turned her toward him and bent his head to touch his lips to hers. As his kiss brushed her mouth, her phone rang.

She pulled it out of her pocket. "It's Josh."

She cleared her throat. "Hey, Josh. What's up?"

"This is just some weird stuff, Lori."

Her heart jumped and she clutched the phone. "What? What happened?"

"You know Summer Larson's print was at Courtney's?"

"Yes?" A thrumming dread pounded against her eardrums and Cade was poking her and making hand gestures. "I'm putting this on Speaker for Summer's brother. Go on, Josh."

"We got a report of another missing woman. Roommate came home to an empty, disheveled house. A bloody print was found on the doorjamb, just like the other two scenes."

Cade grabbed her arm, and she answered Josh. "That's unusual, I guess. A coincidence."

"It's more than that, Lori. The bloody print belongs to Courtney Jessup."

Chapter Fourteen

When Lori ended the call, she sank to the sand and he dropped next to her. "What is going on, Lori?"

"I have no idea. What or who is tying these women together? Where are they? Are the prints part of some sick joke?" She gouged the sand with a stick. "Now I regret my suspension. I should've been the one to discover that."

"When can Josh confirm the name of the latest missing woman? You still have Summer's Brighter Days card with the names on it, right? You didn't give that one to Marino."

"I still have it. As soon as Josh contacts me with her name, I'll check it out. I'm also going to memorize those names for my stint at the center—in case I run across any of them."

"If we can get a picture of her, we can check the website again to see if she shows up like Courtney did, although there are more blurred faces than clear ones on the site."

Lori bunched her hands in the sand. "The one silver lining here is if the women's prints are at other crime scenes, it means they're not dead."

"I've been thinking ever since you mentioned Manson." Cade juggled a couple of broken shells from one hand to the other. "What if this situation is something like a cult? What if these women are involved in the kidnapping of other women?"

She cocked her head at him. "Do you think Summer would participate in something like that? She had her issues, but she was always so gentle and sweet, too sweet."

"Exactly—too sweet, easily manipulated. How do you think she got into the whole drug scene? It was because of some idiot boyfriend of hers. The guy left her with an addiction and a baby."

"A baby?" Lori's fingers curled into the wet sand, and a pulse throbbed against her temple. "Wh-what happened to the baby?"

"My mom made her get an abortion." The line of Cade's jaw hardened. "She never told anyone, not even the guy. He didn't deserve to know, anyway…loser."

Lori hopped to her feet and dusted the sand from her palms. "We should get going. I have a big day tomorrow. I still want to do some shopping for Loretta. I figure at a retreat like that, she might wear black leggings and rock and roll T-shirts."

"As long as I don't have to dress up like the anonymous money man again." He stood up next to her and brushed off the back of his jeans. "Why did you let it slip to Ella that I was going to be out of the country?"

"It was just a feeling. Courtney had no family here—no husband, no boyfriend. Summer was on her own." She touched his arm. "At least as far as Brighter Days knew. I thought I'd be a more appealing prospect for anything that might be going down there if I presented as adrift from my friends and family, too."

"That's interesting because I had the same feeling

when I was there." He picked some debris from her hair and let it fly away in the wind. "That's why I turned away from you when you embarked on the tour, and didn't show an interest in your treatment. I hope we're both wrong."

"Why?"

"Because if Brighter Days prefers patients who are on their own, there is something nefarious going on there—and you're going to be right in the middle of it."

CADE DROPPED HER off at her house and returned to his hotel to squeeze in some work. He also planned to call Marino to see if he could find out anything about the search warrant at the treatment center.

Lori spent the rest of the day picking up some clothes for her stay at Brighter Days and some makeup to keep up her disguise while she was there.

The packet Ella had handed her indicated that she should bring clothes for the week, and that the support staff would be doing the laundry weekly. She didn't intend to be there for laundry day.

As she packed her bag, she replayed her conversation with Cade in her head. Would he really give up everything in New York to move back to LA? To her? The fact that the transfer of the Malibu house had occurred before he even came out here and before he ran into her made her feel a little better. At least he wouldn't be making the move solely for her. She'd be unable to stand that pressure—especially once he found out about the baby…and she'd have to tell him. But not tonight.

He was taking her out to dinner in Santa Monica for a last meal before her dive into Brighter Days Recovery. She wanted to meet Reed Dufrain. She hadn't asked Natasha about him because she didn't want to show any undue interest in or knowledge about the center. Just another lost girl looking for a place to land.

As she watered her plants—just in case she spent more than a few days at the rehab center—her phone rang and she crossed the room to pick it up. Her heart fluttered when she saw Cade's name. Not much had changed since high school.

"It's still a little early for dinner. What's up?"

"Get on your laptop and access the Brighter Days website." His voice had an edge to it, which caused her heart to flutter *and* flip-flop at the same time.

"Okay, what's the problem?" She spun her laptop around on the counter to face her and woke it up.

"You'll see in a minute. Should be obvious."

She brought up the Brighter Days website. "I'm here. Looks the same to me. I thought maybe they'd added my name and photo or something."

"It's not what they added. Go to the images and click through, like we did before."

She clicked the icon for the photos and scanned through them. Then she caught her breath. "There's no picture of Courtney."

"Exactly. Marino finally got back to me and said he hadn't needed to get a search warrant for the center because Reed Dufrain, himself, invited him back. I asked if they'd found anything connecting Summer and Courtney to the center, and he said they hadn't."

"The picture, I told Marino about the picture on the website. Did he show Natasha?"

"I asked him about that and he replied that he looked at the photos on the site and nobody looked like Courtney. I went back to the website and nobody looks like Courtney because they removed that picture."

Lori flattened a hand against her stomach. "That proves something suspicious is going on."

"Ah, you didn't screen capture that picture, did you?"

"I guess I don't know as much about computers as I thought I did. It didn't occur to me to do that. I suppose you didn't, either."

"Nope. You need to reconsider your stay, Lori."

"Don't be ridiculous. It's more important now than ever. We know something's up with that place. Dufrain invited the cops in because they'd had time to sanitize everything."

"Then we have another item on the agenda at dinner tonight."

"Which is?"

"We have to establish a way that I can communicate with you while you're there. I need to know you're okay."

She tried to reassure him. "I even bought a burner phone to bring with me in case they let me keep it or want to search it, but my guess is they'll take it from me. In fact, I think that's in the pamphlet Ella gave me."

"You'd better not bring it at all. They'll wonder why you have a basic phone instead of one with all your contacts, apps and pictures on it."

"I can hide it."

"I don't think I wanna know where you plan to hide a phone."

"I have a compartment in my suitcase. They won't find it. It's not a maximum-security prison. Even inmates where Danny is smuggle in cell phones. They're not going to rip my bag apart."

"Hide it before I get there, and I'll see if I can find it. If I can, leave it. We'll think of something else."

By the time Cade picked her up, she'd finished packing, secured her phone in the lining of her bag and had her clothes laid out for tomorrow.

When he showed up on her doorstep, he made a beeline for the suitcase. Crouching down, he tipped it on its side and unzipped it. He spent the next ten minutes mauling her carefully packed clothing.

Finally, he sat back on his heels. "You stumped me. I can't find it."

She practically skipped toward him and showed him the area behind the lining where the top and bottom of the suitcase met, creating a space. "It's in there. I'll be fine."

"Okay, that's step one. We're going to map out a meeting place or escape route for you."

"Escape route? Do you think it'll get to that point?"

"Both Summer and Courtney are connected to Brighter Days in some way, they're both gone, Trey was murdered when he was about to tell us something about the center and they scrubbed Courtney from their website. You need an escape route." He rubbed his hands together. "Are you up for burgers on the way?"

"Burgers on the way?" She assessed his faded jeans and dark T-shirt through narrowed eyes. "I thought you were dressed a little too casually for dinner out—even in Santa Monica."

"We need to find a way in and out of that place before I'm gonna let you walk into the lion's den."

She widened her eyes and blinked. "Tonight?"

"Yeah, burgers on the way?"

"Give me a minute to change. I'm not wearing my

good jeans, silk blouse and heels to crawl through the underbrush in Topanga Canyon."

FOR THE SECOND time that day, they wound their way up Topanga Canyon Boulevard, but this time they parked on a turn-off road near the entrance to the road that led to the Brighter Days Recovery Center. Cade had studied maps of the area while they ate their dinner in the car, and had discovered a hiking trail near the center.

He turned on the dome light and spread the map between them. Poking his finger in the middle of the forest, he said, "We should be able to see Brighter Days from this trail and figure out a path between the trail and the center—unless they encourage you to hike. Didn't we see hiking as an activity on the website?"

"We saw a lot of things on that website." Lori chewed on her lower lip. "I can join the hiking group, and we can figure out a way for me to get lost to meet up with you somewhere off the trail."

"Let's check it out." Cade refolded the map and they exited the car.

They walked up the road for several feet, Cade's backpack bouncing on his back, and ducked into an opening that started the trail called Skull Rock Loop.

Lori whispered, "I hope we don't find any actual skulls on the loop."

"I think it refers to the view you get of a rock shaped like a skull. We're not going that far, so don't worry about it."

Cade had come prepared and whipped out a flashlight that he directed to the ground. "Watch this part. It drops down, but we should be okay in the dark. There are no cliffs or waterfalls."

"Or skulls." She traipsed down the trail, sticking close to Cade and his beam of light.

After hiking for about fifteen minutes, Cade grabbed her arm and pointed through the trees to their left. "There it is. Those are the lights of Brighter Days."

Lori ducked as if someone could look out those windows and see them. "What do you think? About a mile?"

"Not more than that." He canvassed the ground with his flashlight. "I don't see a branch-off path though. Maybe the residents of Brighter Days go up to the road to access this trail—like we did."

"They're so close out here, there has to be a way, even if it's not official."

Cade reached out to a bush and fingered the branches. "These are pushed back and broken."

They shimmied through the foliage, and although nobody had officially cleared the way, there was a definite path heading toward Brighter Days.

Cade said, "This is it. Single file, follow me."

They crunched and crackled down the path, sending a few night creatures skittering out of their way. When Cade stopped, Lori bumped into him, as she'd been so focused on her feet and not tripping over a root or stump.

He pulled her beside him and put his mouth to her ear. "We don't have to go any farther. Someone from Brighter Days must use this path. You took the tour. Can you tell where this ends at the center?"

"I think off the back lawn and patio, which run right up against the trees. It makes sense. Do a little yoga and stretching, maybe a little tai chi, and then hit the trail."

"You need to contact me tomorrow and let me know what's going on. If you're in trouble or you need to get away, we'll meet here." He jerked his thumb toward two trees, a dark hollow between them. "I'm going to tie some yarn on the branch, so you can find it. Duck between these two trees, and you'll have some cover. I'll meet you and I'll get you out of here."

Cade tied the yarn on the branch and they turned and hiked back to the road, keeping silent most of the way. When they got to the car, Lori said, "Seems a bit elaborate to me. They're not going to suspect anything about me. I'll do a little snooping, and they'll be none the wiser."

"I always feel better with a backup plan." He reversed out of the turnout, and they started the descent back to the coast. "Now, let's get you home for a good night's sleep."

She rubbed his thigh. "I had something else in mind. You're not gonna leave a girl alone the night before she enters rehab, are you?"

"In that case..." He quirked his eyebrows up and down.

By the time they reached her house, she had Cade's backup plan memorized because he kept reciting it to her over and over. She had also memorized his cell phone number, so she could call him from the burner if she needed to.

Cade tossed his backpack in the corner of the room. "I'm going to drop you off at the Reel Inn, and you can take a car from there so it won't cost so much."

Lori sucked in her bottom lip. "If I take an app car, they're going to figure I have a phone with me."

"They're not going to know where your ride originated. You ordered a car from home and then left your phone there." He stepped toward her and squeezed her shoulders. "You don't have to do this."

"I have to do it more than ever now—Marino found

nothing there and they scrubbed their website. We know something's up with that place." Hunching her shoulder, she twisted her head to the side and kissed his hand. "It'll be fine. I have my escape plan, and I know you have my back."

He reached around her and pulled her laptop toward the edge of the counter. "I was thinking—we should screenshot the rest of the photos on the Brighter Days website, just in case."

"Probably a good idea, or I can just take pics with my phone of each page."

He spun the laptop toward her so that she could enter her password. Then he accessed the website. He held out his hand. "You want me to do it?"

"I'll do it." She pulled out her phone, and as Cade clicked through each image, she snapped a photo with her phone.

"Can you send those to me? Looks like we can't have too many copies of this stuff."

"I will." She placed her phone facedown on the counter. "Let me wash my hands and face first."

She shrugged out of her hoodie on the way to the bathroom and splashed some water on her face, after washing the dirt and grime from the trail off her hands.

"Okay, I feel halfway human now." She traipsed back into the living room and stopped short.

Cade looked up from her phone in his hands, his head cocked to one side, a furrow between his eyebrows. "Whose baby is this?"

Lori swallowed the lump in her throat and curled her fingers around the hem of her T-shirt. "What baby?"

He waved the phone in the air and his voice rose.

"There's a picture on your phone of you and a baby—a very small baby, looks newborn."

"Why are you looking at the pictures on my phone?" As soon as the words left her mouth, she knew it was the wrong thing to say.

Cade's blue eyes got a little wild, and his cheeks flushed. "I was sending myself the website photos. Why are you holding a baby in what looks like a hospital gown with a tube in your arm?"

She'd wanted to tell him, but not now, not this way.

Cade brought the phone to his face, his nose practically touching the screen. "Whose baby is this? Is this your baby?"

Lori expelled a long breath, her shoulders slumping with the effort. "It's ours."

Chapter Fifteen

The picture of a young, teary-eyed Lori cuddling a new-born baby with a thatch of brown hair on its head blurred before his eyes. The room tilted and Cade dropped down to the stool, the phone still clutched in his hand. "When? Where?"

Lori folded her hands in front of her, looking like the picture of innocence—but now he knew better. "We had a baby girl. I gave her up for adoption."

"We?" The word came out flat, barely above a whisper. Cade cleared his throat. "*We* had nothing to do with this because you neglected to tell me anything about it."

"How could I, Cade?" The folded hands knotted and she twisted her fingers. "Realistically, how could I have told you? You had your whole life mapped out in front of you—Harvard undergrad, Wharton business school. A teenage bride and a baby hardly fit that plan."

"Where did you get off making decisions about my life for me? Those plans weren't even mine. Those were my father's dreams for me."

"But they became your dreams. You were looking for any excuse at the time to rebel against your dad. I would've handed you the perfect package. You would've jumped on it and then regretted me forever after."

"Package? Is that what a baby is?" He covered his face with his hands, so much of Lori's behavior that summer suddenly making sense. He should've known, should've seen something different. "Where is she?"

"She's with a good family in San Diego. Her parents are teachers, and she has a younger adopted brother."

"A-are you in touch with them?"

"No. It's a closed adoption until she's eighteen, when and if she chooses to track me...us down." She crossed her arms over her body in a protective move. "I pulled some strings to find out where she went, but I'd never disrupt her life. It was the right thing to do."

"And you made that determination all on your own."

"Of course, my parents advised me. They helped me. Sent me to an aunt in San Diego to have the baby. I came back here after I gave birth and started the winter quarter at UCLA."

Dragging a hand through his hair, he said, "Your mother counseled you not to tell me?"

She dropped her lashes over her eyes. "She wanted me to tell you."

"You didn't take her advice about that." He smacked the counter with the flat of his hand and relished the sting that traveled up his arm. "Were you ever going to tell me?"

"Believe it or not, I was planning to tell you before you went back to New York. I realized..." She lifted her shoulders.

"You realized you'd kept something from me that I had every right to know about." He jumped from the stool, knocking it to the ground. "You lied to me back then. You've been lying to me on this trip."

"I was trying to protect you. I didn't want to ruin your

life." She shoved her hands in her pockets, looking small and vulnerable, and another wave of sorrow crashed over him when he thought about her on her own in San Diego, pregnant, delaying college, giving birth without him by her side, having someone take that sad photo of her and the baby she'd have to give up.

"That was up to me, Lori. Who says you didn't ruin my life by not telling me about my daughter?" He hooked his hand around the back of the stool and righted it.

He wanted to ask her a million questions about their daughter, but he could barely look at her.

Instead, he swooped down to snag his backpack. "Look, I gotta go."

"What about tomorrow?"

"I'll pick you up at noon, just like we discussed." He stepped outside and clicked the door softly behind him. Closing his eyes, he took a deep breath of the salty air.

By the time he got back to his hotel, the shock had subsided, leaving him with a dull ache in the pit of his stomach. How could Lori justify what she'd done?

He stripped off his clothes and showered, scrubbing his skin so hard it stung. He didn't know what he was trying to wash away—the memories of that time, how he'd shrugged off Lori's changed behavior, how he'd embraced his father's plans for him, or Lori's deception.

As he climbed into bed, his cell phone on the nightstand pinged. He reached for it and opened the text from Lori. She'd texted him the picture of her and their baby girl.

He fell asleep clutching the phone to his heart.

THE NEXT DAY, Lori wiped her damp palms against the thighs of her black jeans before opening the front door to Cade. Sleep had escaped her the night before, but at least the dark circles beneath her eyes matched her persona of the struggling addict.

She stepped outside, dragging her suitcase behind her, and mumbled a barely-there greeting.

Reaching past her for the handle of her bag, he said, "I'll get this."

She followed his stiff back out to his car, resisting the urge to throw herself at him and apologize profusely. Reviewing the dramatic scene in her head last night, she realized she'd never told him she was sorry for withholding the truth from him. Was it too late now?

As she slid into the passenger seat, he hauled the suitcase into the trunk of his rental. He sat behind the wheel, and she spun toward him. "I'm sorry, Cade. I'm sorry I didn't tell you about my pregnancy or tell you about the baby later. I was scared, stupid and had too much pride to use a pregnancy to snag you. Your parents would've hated me—even more than they already did, and half of my family would've disowned me for getting pregnant before marriage. It seemed like the best plan at the time."

He held up his hand to stop the flow of words. "I understand why you didn't tell me."

She studied his white knuckles on the wheel of the car. Was that an acceptance of her apology? Not quite. "D-did you get the photo I sent you?"

"I did, thanks. Do you have any more?"

"No." She clasped her hands between her knees, accepting the needling pain at the old wound as payment for her deceit. "Although I have a general idea where she lives, I wanted to honor her privacy and her parents' wishes. I've never looked her up or even tried to catch a glimpse of her at play or school."

"She'd be..."

"Nine. She's nine years old now." Lori held her breath waiting for other questions, questions she knew he must have.

"She's healthy?" He relaxed his grip on the wheel and started driving.

"She was a healthy, full-term baby and weighed seven pounds, eight ounces at birth. Sh-she was beautiful." Her nose stung and she blinked her eyes, as she turned her head and stared at the traffic.

"Was your mother with you?"

"She was there. It killed her almost as much as it did me when we left the hospital without the baby. I met her parents, and they were wonderful. I'm sure she has a great life."

Cade let out a long ragged breath. "It must've been hard on you. That's what cuts me the most—the thought of you in San Diego, going through this pregnancy on your own while I was at college going to frat parties and football games."

"It wasn't easy." She sniffed and squared her shoulders. "But soon enough, I was at college going to frat parties and basketball games—secure in the knowledge that I'd done the right thing for our baby, that she'd have two mature parents who wanted to raise her with no regrets. She deserved that."

"Are you going to make contact with her when she turns eighteen?"

"I'm going to leave it up to her. Her parents may have already told her by now that they adopted her. If she's interested in finding me, I'm open to that discovery. I'm open to a relationship, if she wants that. I'm also okay if she doesn't." She traced a pattern on the window. "What do you think you would've done if I'd told you back then?"

Cade accelerated onto the freeway with a burst of speed. "I would've married you."

Lori didn't have much to say after that proclamation, and Cade had retreated into a morose silence, not even emerging to go over her escape plan from Brighter Days, if that became necessary. At this point, he probably didn't care if she stayed at Brighter Days forever.

Finally, he pulled onto the street beside the Reel Inn and parked the car. "It's probably not a good idea for me to come inside with you. Order your car from your regular phone now, and then leave it with me. Don't worry. I won't do any more snooping. I don't even know your password. I saw the photo of the baby because I picked up the phone as soon as you put it down—just to send the Brighter Days pictures to myself."

"You don't have to explain yourself. I know you weren't going through my phone." She slid her cell out of her purse and pulled up the car app. "You don't have to be on call for me. Nothing is going to happen. I'll have a look around and decide the place isn't for me after a few days."

"Don't be obstinate. You don't always know what's best, and I'd appreciate it if you'd stop trying to control my actions."

"Whatever." She lifted her eyebrows and blew out a breath, as she scheduled a pickup in forty-five minutes. "I'm going to eat some lunch first. I'll try to contact you tonight. Keep on Marino…if you want."

"I plan to." He popped the trunk and exited the car.

Sighing, she dropped her phone in the cup holder and joined him, her boots crunching the gravel beneath them.

"Thanks for helping out with all this. I'm hopeful I'll find something."

He landed a hard kiss on her mouth. "Just be careful."

She wheeled her suitcase up to the door of the restaurant and watched Cade drive off with tears in her eyes. She'd really messed up, but she felt stronger about the decision she'd made nine years ago than ever before.

If she'd told Cade about the pregnancy, he would've done the honorable thing and married her. His parents probably would have cut him off. Neither of them could've afforded college right away. He would've resented her for his missed opportunities. She would've resented him for resenting her, and they would've taken it out on each other and ended up getting divorced.

He couldn't see that now through the haze of hurt, but maybe one day he'd come around—maybe not soon enough to repair their relationship on this visit and maybe they'd never have another chance.

Right now, she had to focus on playing this role to help his sister, Courtney and the other nameless woman who'd gone missing. Josh hadn't gotten back to her yet with an identity for the third victim but as the police had found Courtney's prints at this woman's place, the connection between the three of them was undeniable.

Lori ordered a bowl of clam chowder and toyed with it as she waited for her ride. When she saw her car arrive outside, she left a half-full bowl of soup and dragged her suitcase outside.

The driver helped her load it into the trunk, and they took off on the now familiar drive to Brighter Days. She had to direct the driver down the final road, as his GPS was giving him confusing signals to the bucolic center tucked away in the canyon.

He pulled around to the side where she and Cade had parked before. As she wheeled her suitcase toward the side door, it opened, and a thin man of medium height with close-cropped hair and a full beard stepped onto the stone walkway.

Lori recognized him from the website as Reed Dufrain, and her heart skipped a beat. He didn't offer to help her, nor did he talk or greet her in any way. He watched.

She swallowed as she approached him, her eyes behind her sunglasses studying the still face before her. He didn't move one muscle, but his light-colored eyes seemed to probe her very soul as she approached. She'd have to be careful with this one.

She clattered to a stop before him, and stuck out her hand. "I'm Loretta Garcia. I'm checking in today."

"I'm Reed Dufrain, the center's director." He had some kind of accent she couldn't readily identify, and she jumped when he suddenly snapped his fingers, ignoring her outstretched hand.

As if hovering nearby awaiting his command, a young man, dressed all in white, appeared next to Dufrain and smiled at Lori, his teeth bright against his brown skin. "I'm Peron. I'll take your bag and show you to your room."

She dropped her hand awkwardly and handed off her bag to Peron. She shoved her sunglasses to the top of her head as she walked past Dufrain, meeting his eyes directly for the first time. An instant chill dripped down her spine.

The man had no lashes or very light lashes that seemed at odds with his brown beard. Coupled with his light blue eyes, it gave him an otherworldly quality. He probably played that up to the patients to make them think he was on some different plane.

Dufrain turned to cup her elbow in his hand, a scent of sandalwood wafting over her. "I'll accompany you to your room, Loretta, and we'll discuss your program. You're off all substances now?"

"That's right. I quit cold turkey with some help from Narcotics Anonymous, but my main support person is out of town right now for an extended period and I feel shaky."

"Understandable." His fingers pinched her flesh through her jacket, as if he feared she'd take flight at any moment.

Should she?

She cleared her throat. "Where's Natasha?"

"She's busy in the office. You won't see much of her during your stay, as she handles the business end of the center and isn't involved in the treatment programs."

As the heels of her boots clattered on the wooden floors, she realized Dufrain was barefoot beneath his wide-legged trousers. His footsteps whispered next to hers, and he moved as silently and gracefully as a cat.

He glided down a hallway of closed doors, propelling her along until he threw open a door to the right. Light flooded a sparsely but beautifully furnished room. "This is yours. It's quiet right now because most of the guests are at an after-lunch yoga and meditation session. You still have time to join, if you'd like."

"I'd very much like that. Where should I go once I change?"

Dufrain flicked his fingers in the air, toward a button on the wall beside the door. "You can summon Peron or one of our other attendants to show you the way when you're ready. I'll leave a copy of your schedule on your bed and you can peruse that at your leisure and let me know if you have any questions."

Lori pointed to the call button. "Do I contact you the same way?"

"That's for the attendants…or in an emergency, but the attendants can always reach me."

"Emergency?" She tilted her head.

"Our guests are in different stages of recovery, Loretta. I'm sure you recall the discomfort of detoxing."

"Oh, I do. Nice to know Brighter Days is equipped to handle anything."

Dufrain put his hands together as if in prayer and dipped his head. "I'll leave you to change now. I hope you find everything you're looking for here."

So did she.

Dufrain stopped at the door. "Who did you say referred you to us?"

She crouched beside her suitcase where Peron had left it on the floor and unzipped it. Without looking up, she said, "A friend who wishes to remain anonymous. It obviously worked for her, or she wouldn't have referred me."

The soft click of the door was the only signal that he'd left. Lori fell back on her heels and huffed out a breath. The man put her on edge. It must just be because she was here under false pretenses, and he seemed so…all knowing.

She dug through her clothes for a pair of black yoga pants and a long T-shirt. As she tugged off her jeans, she leaned over the bed to read the schedule Dufrain had left there.

She could choose from several activities each hour, but the center expected you to choose something. You couldn't sit around in your room all day—unless you were ill—and he had a few nurses on staff.

She'd do this yoga, get the lay of the land, do a survey of some of the other patients—guests, he'd called them—and do a little snooping around when she could.

Forty-five minutes later, stretched out and refreshed, Lori lounged by the pool with several other women who'd been doing yoga with her. They had a free hour or so before the next set of activities started, so a few of them dangled their feet in the water while others reclined on the lounges with their eyes closed. She wasn't going to get anything out of them, so she turned to the woman sitting next to her at the pool, a tall, thin blonde with alabaster skin.

"I'm Loretta. I just arrived."

"I figured that since I haven't seen you here before. I'm Lucy." The woman lifted her hand where she'd been trailing it in the water and offered it to Lori.

Lori clicked through the names in her head from the Brighter Days business card, but Lucy wasn't one of them. Strike one. Lori shook her hand, water and all. "Nice to meet you, Lucy. How long have you been here?"

"Too long." She wrinkled her slightly turned-up nose. "My husband made me come here, and is making me stay for the full month as a condition to continue our marriage. We have a little girl."

"That's nice." Cupping some water in her hand and dumping it on the pool deck, Lori asked, "Is it working for you?"

"I'm clean and sober." Lucy held up her hand as if to testify. "I suppose it works—at least here. Hope it holds for the real world, or I might lose my girl."

"And Reed Dufrain?" Lori twisted her head over her

shoulder, pretending to investigate a sound by the door, but really making sure Dufrain wasn't tiptoeing around the pool. "Is he as good as they say?"

Lucy flattened her hands on her thighs. "His program is effective, but he does have his favorites."

"He has favorites?" Lori's pulse quickened.

Lucy lifted her sunglasses and studied Lori with her green eyes. "Don't hold your breath. You're not gonna be one of his faves."

"Not that I want to be, but why do you say that?"

"You're not messed up enough. Dufrain seems to gravitate toward the worst cases. He isolates them from the rest of us once he makes his picks. I've seen it happen a couple times since I've been here." Lucy lifted her shoulders. "Maybe he just figures they need more help than the rest of us. The yoga, meditation, cooking sessions, hikes—those seem to work for those of us who are already off the substances."

Lori turned her head to survey the women stretched out on chaise lounges under umbrellas and whispered, "Any of those his favorites?"

Dismissing them with a wave of her hand, Lucy said, "His pets wouldn't be out here. They mostly stay cooped up in their rooms and have private sessions with Reed. They're probably doing some other kind of intensive treatment program. Hey, let's be happy we're not in that boat."

"Amen to that."

She continued chatting with Lucy about their own particular vices and Lucy's daughter, until it was time to select the next activity. Lucy was participating in the group therapy session, so Lori decided to follow her there.

Had Summer been one of Dufrain's favorites? Why

did she have his card in a safe deposit box? Had she been messed up when she'd arrived here?

After the group session, she walked with Lucy back to their rooms. When they were clear of the other women, Lori asked, "Did you know someone named Summer here, or Courtney? It would've been earlier in your stay."

Lucy twisted up her mouth to one side. "Don't think so."

They turned a corner in the hallway and Lucy jerked her thumb to the side, indicating a smaller hallway off the main one. She lowered her voice. "You asked about the pets? They usually bunk down there. Reed spends a lot of his time in this area."

Nodding, Lori said, "They must need that extra help."

The guests were supposed to use this time to shower and change from their daytime activities to meet in the kitchen for some cooking lessons on preparing healthy food. With everyone in their rooms, this might give Lori an opportunity to check out Dufrain's favorite guests. She already knew the doors wouldn't be locked, as locks weren't allowed.

When Lucy turned into her own room, Lori sailed into hers and made a quick change of clothes. Then she poked her head out her door and looked both ways down the hallway.

On bare feet as quiet as Dufrain himself, Lori crept back to the smaller hallway, where two doors faced each other. She tried the first door, easing it open onto a clearly empty room. She padded to the next door and inched it open, peeking inside.

A dark-haired woman lay prone on the bed in the darkened room, her eyes half-closed. Lori glanced over her shoulder quickly before slipping inside the room and softly closing the door behind her.

She tiptoed to the bedside and crouched beside the woman. "Hello? Are you all right?"

The woman's slack mouth moved slightly, and Lori bent her head closer to her lips and repeated. "Are you all right? Should I call someone?"

The woman's hand curled around Lori's wrist in a tight grip that startled her, and she jerked back. Rasping words came from the woman's mouth, and Lori leaned in again. "What did you say?"

The woman licked her cracked lips and widened her dilated eyes. "Not Reed. Please don't call Reed."

Chapter Sixteen

With her heart pounding, Lori dropped to her knees. Wasn't this woman supposed to be one of Reed's favorites? "Why not? Why not call Reed?"

Lori heard a bump outside the door followed by Reed Dufrain's voice, and her gaze darted wildly around the Spartan room for a place to hide. The doorknob turned as he continued to talk, and Lori collapsed to the floor and scooted beneath the bed. She twitched the bed skirt into place seconds before she heard Dufrain's footsteps in the room.

He snapped the door behind him, and Lori released a tiny breath from her nose, stirring a fine film of dust on the floor. If she sneezed now, it would be all over.

In the small space that existed between the hem of the bed skirt and the hardwood floor, Lori spied Dufrain's bare toes as he stood next to the bed. The blood roared in her ears so loudly, she could barely hear his words.

"How are you today, Karenna? I think you should be up and about soon, and then you'll get to leave. You'll like that, won't you?"

Karenna made a gurgling noise, and Lori squeezed her eyes closed. Karenna, Karenna. That was one of the names on Summer's card. This couldn't be a coincidence.

She hoped Karenna didn't think Lori had summoned Dufrain to her bedside. She was obviously terrified of him…and Lori should be, too.

"Just a few more…" something clinked on a metal tray as Dufrain paused "…shots of this and you won't be able to live without it."

Lori clenched her jaw. Wasn't he supposed to be curing addictions instead of introducing them? What was he doing to Karenna?

Karenna thrashed in the bed, shifting the covers, creating a bigger space between the bed skirt and the floor. Lori noticed a strand of her black wig very close to Dufrain's foot, but she feared the slightest movement would alert Dufrain to her presence.

"Not to worry." Skin slapped against skin, and Lori curled her nails into the hard wood. "I have enough of this magic potion to keep you well supplied and feeling good for as long as I need you. I'll lessen the dose today, and you'll be walking and talking within days. But make no mistake about it, Karenna, you'll need it and only I can give it to you."

Karenna made a muffled cry, and Lori smashed her nose into the floor to keep quiet.

Dufrain spent several seconds more hovering over Karenna on the bed before his footsteps whispered across the room, and then the door snapped shut.

Lori lay still for another minute and then shimmied out from beneath the bed. She loomed over Karenna, but the drug had sedated the woman again. She lifted Karenna's limp arm, squinting at the needle tracks on the inside of her elbow, some old and one very fresh. Her stomach turned. Dufrain had shot her up with something.

She slipped out of the room and scurried back to her

own. When she closed the door behind her, she fell across her bed. Dufrain was some kind of monster. He was taking vulnerable women, and under the pretense of helping them overcome one addiction, he was addicting them to something else. What was it? Heroin? Some kind of opioid?

She and Cade had left the powder they'd found at Summer's place in that shoebox. Now she wanted to get her hands on it and have it tested. Was that what Dufrain had injected into Karenna? Had Summer and Courtney been addicted to the same substance?

She needed to reach Cade tonight and tell him to get that drug from Summer's. She had a friend who could test it for her—no questions asked.

What had she stumbled onto? Whatever it was, she knew it was serious enough to get her killed.

LATER THAT NIGHT after a healthy dinner of brown rice, stir-fried vegetables and soy curls, Lori crouched before her suitcase and unzipped the compartment where she'd stashed her burner phone.

Peron had dumped out her purse to search it and then did a cursory search of her suitcase. He'd never thought to unzip the lining of the bag.

Lori rolled the phone into a towel and padded to the patio in the back to join some of the other women in the hot tub. They obviously had no idea what was going on in those other rooms. Did Dufrain have someone in addition to Karenna captive in that hallway? Were Diana and Chelsea, the other names on the card, here, too?

She shoved her towel next to a bush and slid into the hot bubbly water next to Shannon, her cooking buddy.

Shannon handed her a flute with fizzing golden liquid. "Don't get too excited. It's sparkling apple cider, not champagne."

"I'll take it, thanks." Lori sipped the chilled, tart liquid and maneuvered until a jet of bubbles hit her lower back. "That feels good."

One of the other women, Jessica, submerged her shoulders beneath the water until just her head bobbed on the surface. "Yeah, this place would be great if they added weed and wine to the nightly activities."

A few of the women laughed, but some didn't appreciate her humor and a couple of them used the opportunity to get out.

"Bye-bye." Jessica waved at their backs. "How do they think they're going to cope in the real world when someone does more than just talk about it?"

Lori cupped some water in her hand and sprinkled it on the deck. "It's not easy."

"Oh, right. You were clean when you came in here." Jessica wrapped one of her dark curls around her finger. "If I was able to get clean on my own without rehab, I'd stay far, far away from places like this. Despite its obvious comforts, it's still a prison. What made you come here?"

A prison? Karenna would have to agree.

Lori draped her arms across the edge of the hot tub and lightly paddled her feet. "I had a friend helping me out, and he had to leave for work out of the country. I'm still wavering on the edge, and didn't think I could make it without his support. So far, so good, but I didn't realize the center took people in the throes of their addiction…like Karenna."

The other women met her words with dead silence. She studied their faces. "What? What did I say wrong?"

"Nothing." Shannon took a swig of apple juice as if it were booze. "It's just that we don't talk about guests like Karenna…or Diana."

Lori gulped. Another name from the card. She asked, "Diana?"

"She's like Karenna—on the Cocaine Corridor or Heroin Hallway, if you prefer." Jessica gave a short hiccup of a laugh.

Lori looked from Shannon to Jessica. "What does that mean? They're still addicted?"

"Aren't we all?" Shannon smoothed her hands over the surface of the choppy water.

"The thing with those women…" Jessica leaned forward, her chin skimming the water "…they came in like the rest of us—some still high as kites, some one day clean and a few like you, but the difference between us and them is that we're all taking the steps to get better and those two don't seem to be getting any better. Reed doesn't like it when we talk about them."

Shannon said, "He doesn't want us to dwell on the negative."

Jessica snorted. "He doesn't want us to dwell on his failures."

Lori swirled the remainder of her apple juice in her glass, where it caught the lights around the pool and sparkled. Was that the story Reed spread? The women had relapsed or couldn't get with the program? He had to isolate them and offer special treatment?

She asked, "Why doesn't he just discharge them?"

"He wants to help everyone." Shannon scrunched her eyebrows over her nose. "He doesn't want to give up on anyone."

He wants to take advantage of them.

Jessica seemed all talked out, and as she placed her glass on the tray, she said, "I'm going to bed, ladies. If you see a hot guy wandering around, send him my way."

Shannon winked at Lori. "There's always Peron."

"A hot, *straight* guy." Jessica rose from the water and it sluiced from her body in steaming rivulets. "You two coming? Curfew in less than thirty."

"I am." Shannon stood up to join her, the water lapping around her knees. "Loretta?"

"I'm going to spend a few more minutes in here." She placed her glass on the tray and tipped in a little more juice. "Don't worry about the tray. I'll take it in."

The tray would also give her an excuse for being outside on her own. She said good-night to the other women and sipped her juice for a few minutes. When she spied more lights in the main building going out, she staggered from the hot tub and grabbed her towel.

She jogged across the sprawling lawn toward the tree line. The entrance to the path that met up with the Skull Rock Loop nestled just beyond those trees. If she had any sense at all, she'd make a beeline for that trail and never look back.

She could call Marino and let him make sense of this, but then she'd have to explain how she knew all about Karenna and Diana.

Instead, she reached for the phone buried in the towel and ducked between some bushes, twigs stabbing the bottoms of her feet. She punched in Cade's phone number, and he didn't even wait for the first ring to end.

"Hello?" Cade's voice sounded businesslike. He must still be fuming about her pregnancy.

"That's it? Hello? Who did you expect from this number?"

He let out a breath across the line. "Just in case it wasn't you, I didn't want to use your name."

"You're really getting into this."

He cut her off. "Stop, Lori. Are you all right? Are you ready to leave?"

"I found something out today, Cade, and it's bad."

"Summer. Did you find out what happened to Summer?"

"Not yet, but Reed Dufrain is a messed-up guy. He's evil. He's singling out a few of the women who come through these doors, and he's…he's making them worse."

"What does that mean?"

She didn't intend to tell Cade about her close call with Dufrain in Karenna's room. She didn't want to freak him out any more than he already was.

"He's drugging some of these women, addicting them to some substance. I have no idea why, and I don't know what he's using." She glanced over her shoulder. "There's something else."

"What?"

"The two women he's targeting for special treatment are Karenna and Diana—two of the names from the card."

Cade whistled through his teeth. "I've got more bad news for you. The third missing woman, where Courtney's prints were found? Her name is Chelsea Kim. We've identified all three names on that card, and they're all in trouble."

"Karenna and Diana are here, but where are Summer, Courtney and Chelsea?"

Cade swore. "Lori, get out of there, and we'll call the police. We'll tell Marino."

She hissed over the phone. "Are you kidding? I have

no proof. Dufrain will clean things up again before Marino comes out here. Just give me another day or two to figure this out."

"Does anyone suspect you of anything?"

"No. The other clients here know about those women Dufrain is dosing, but they just think they relapsed and Dufrain is treating them." She growled into the phone. "He's treating them, all right."

"I don't like this, Lori. The man is dangerous."

"I've got something to keep you busy and your mind off…everything." She sucked in her bottom lip. "You need to get those drugs from Summer's closet and deliver them to a guy I know. I want to find out what she has."

"A guy? The police?"

"Yeah, he is a cop, but he'll do this off the record if I ask him. If you ask him."

"Great, I'll be running around LA with illegal drugs in my possession, meeting a dirty cop."

"He's not dirty. He worked undercover vice for years and he knows people, discreet people. You don't want the cops knowing Summer had those drugs, do you?"

"Okay, give me his name and number."

"His name is Trevor Jansen. I don't have his number on me, but you can get it from my cell phone. My passcode is the year of my birth. Just mention my name, tell him as little as you like—oh, hell, you know what to do."

"Be careful, for God's sake. And Lori?"

"Yeah?"

"Just so you know, I hired a private investigator to find our daughter."

Lori's knees wobbled and she almost sank to the ground. "Don't do this, Cade."

"Don't worry. I'm not going to interfere in her life. I

just want to know more about her parents, her family. Give me that, will you?"

She knew Cade had to wrest back some kind of control over this situation. "I understand, as long as you don't contact her. We have to think of her first. And no sending her anonymous donations of money, or anything."

"I'm not going to do anything like that."

She loosened her grip on the phone. "Okay, thanks for giving me a heads-up."

"You'd better get back before you're missed. I'll retrieve the drugs from Summer's and contact this guy, Trevor. Stay out of trouble. Don't draw attention to yourself...and don't take any strange vitamins."

As soon as Lori ended the call, she deleted it from the phone and rolled the burner back up in her towel. She ducked out of the underbrush and squelched across the damp lawn. When she reached the deck, she almost slipped, as a dark figure rose from a lounge chair.

Peron had changed from his all-white ensemble to an all-black one. "Loretta, right?"

"Th-that's right." She put a hand to her throat. "You scared me."

His mouth widened into a smile. "I can say the same thing. I thought that maybe a mountain lion had crossed onto the grounds. It's happened before."

"Oh, no. If I had known that, I wouldn't have gone over to the bushes to investigate the noise I heard." She swept an arm toward the tray of empty glasses on one of the tables. "I came back to get the tray, heard a noise and skipped over there to investigate. I hope it wasn't a mountain lion."

"Maybe you scared him." Peron tapped his wrist. "It's past curfew."

"Is it?" She sidled to the table and lifted the tray. "Didn't realize it was so late."

"I'll take that. We wouldn't want Reed to catch you out after curfew."

"Why? What's the punishment for that? Extra yoga sessions or an extra helping of soy curls?" She forced a laugh that sounded hollow.

The whites of Peron's eyes shone in the darkness, and he put a finger to his lips. "I won't tell on you."

With her mouth dry, Lori spun away from him and strode toward the building. "Good night."

She hurried along the corridor and slipped into her room. Gripping the handle behind her, she pressed her back against the door, her heart racing. She couldn't tell if Peron believed her or not, or if he'd tell Reed about her nocturnal sojourn, despite his assurance.

Then her gaze stumbled across her suitcase in the corner, and she froze. Someone had been in her room tonight and had moved her bag. Whether Peron told Reed about finding her out after curfew or not didn't seem to matter anymore.

Somehow, someway, she'd gotten onto Reed Dufrain's radar—and that was a very bad development.

Chapter Seventeen

Cade sat under the umbrella at the hot dog stand with a bag of drugs in his pocket and a sheen of sweat on his forehead. Only Lori could get him into a situation like this. Although to be fair to her, he put the blame for this squarely on Summer.

A motorcycle roared up to the curb, and a lean, dark man hopped off, pulling a helmet from his head. Trevor said he'd be arriving on a bike, and he even sort of looked like a cop despite the black jeans and motorcycle boots. He'd told Cade he didn't work undercover anymore.

He stopped at the table and put his helmet on the attached seat. "I'm gonna grab a dog. You want something?"

Cade raised his soda. "I'm good."

Several minutes later, Trevor returned with a hot dog, dripping chili, in one hand and a drink in the other. He stepped over the bench with a long stride and sat straddling the bench, facing Cade. "Where's Lori? I heard she was suspended from the job."

"She was. She's taking some time away."

Trevor shook his head as he bit into the hot dog. He wiped his mouth with a napkin and crumpled it in his fist. "She's good at her job, but sometimes she rubs people the wrong way because she's a little too overzealous. You know what I mean?"

Trevor had no idea how overzealous Lori had gotten. "She always feels like she has to right an injustice. You know about her brother."

"I do." Trevor licked some chili from his fingers and grabbed another napkin. "Between you and me, Danny Del Valle is guilty as hell, unidentified print or not."

"I think so, too, but..." Cade ran a finger along the seam of his lips "...I don't tell her that."

"I tried that once, and she nearly bit my head off. I guess it's hard to face the fact that your brother is a killer."

Cade toyed with the plastic bag of drugs in his jacket pocket and said, "You always want to believe the best about the people you love."

"I get that, but Danny's arrest and conviction have colored Lori's life. Like you said—she hates to see an injustice, and it drives her to do stupid things sometimes."

Cade figured he'd better break off the direction of this conversation before he presented Trevor with the drugs and Lori's new scheme.

Lifting his shoulders, he said, "We all have our weaknesses."

"That's for sure." Trevor washed down another bite of his hot dog with a sip from his cup. "What can I do for you...or Lori?"

"It's really a favor to me. Lori just said you might be able to help without forcing me to go through regular channels."

"Happy to help. I owe Lori. My girlfriend's a PI, and Lori has come through for her a few times running prints for her." Trevor wedged his hands on his knees. "Whad-dya got?"

Cade pinched the plastic baggie of drugs between his fingers and drew it out of his pocket. "My sister is missing, and I found this white powder hidden away in her closet. She's had substance abuse problems in the past, so this isn't a surprise to me, but Lori couldn't tell me what type of drug this was. She said you had some connections."

Trevor held out his hand and Cade dropped the packet in his palm. He whistled through his teeth. "This looks like some of that wicked China Girl we've been seeing on the street. You see the pink tint? Highly addictive, less deadly than some of the other strains."

"China Girl?"

"One of the many street names for fentanyl." He jiggled the baggie. "This is a new product that's hit the street just in the past year. We don't know where it's coming from yet. You said your sister had it?"

"Yeah, and she's missing."

"Is your sister a dealer?"

"What?" Cade wiped a hand across his mouth. "No. She doesn't need money. There wouldn't be any reason for her to be selling drugs."

"Unless she's addicted and is getting her fix as a reward for selling." Trevor waved the packet in the air, and Cade looked around.

Good thing he was with a cop.

"This looks like it's packaged to sell. It's about the right amount, and it has a number stamped in the corner of the baggie, as if it's one of many."

Knots twisted in Cade's gut. Was this what Summer had been doing? Was that why she was missing now?

"Can you tell for sure? Lori said you had a way to test it."

"I can't, but I know someone who can." Trevor pocketed the plastic bag, and Cade relaxed his muscles for the first time since retrieving the drugs from Summer's house.

Trevor picked up the last bite of his dog. "Can I ask why you're not going to the police with this?"

"My sister's missing, she's an addict and I found drugs at her house." Cade spread his hands. "Why do you think?"

"You got a point." Trevor popped the hot dog in his mouth. "I'll take care of this, and I'll contact Lori when I have some info. If your sister has any shady acquaintances, I'd appreciate a name. We know this pink China Girl is coming from a particular source, and we want to nail it down."

Cade didn't want to mention Reed Dufrain until Lori had left Brighter Days. If he thought she'd ID'd him and she was still under his control there, there was no telling what he might do. He obviously had henchmen on the outside. There's no way he slashed Lori's tires or killed Trey himself.

Trevor cleared his throat. "You got a name?"

"Can't think of anyone." Cade shook his head.

"I'll get this done." Trevor smacked the table as he got up, and a minute later, he zoomed off on his bike.

Cade rattled the ice in his empty drink, and then lobbed it into the nearby trash can. If Reed Dufrain had facilitated Summer's addiction to this China Girl stuff during her stay at Brighter Days and Summer was selling it for him to maintain her supply, that meant Lori was in grave danger at that place.

And he was going to get her out of there.

THE DAY AFTER her run-in with Peron, Lori kept her head down and participated in as many activities as she could squeeze into her day. She didn't want to stand out to Reed or anyone else. She didn't even know if she could trust those women in the hot tub last night. Jessica had seemed too chatty for her own good, and Shannon had seemed pretty dedicated to Reed. What if one of them was a plant to draw out the new girl?

She avoided both Jessica and Shannon…and Peron. She'd seen him once today, and he'd given her that slightly sinister grin that she didn't like one bit.

She wanted to get back into Karenna's room to make sure the woman was okay, but if anyone caught her there, she'd have a hard time dancing her way out of it.

She'd seen Reed around a few times, floating through the compound in his baggy cotton pants and tunic, but he'd barely given her a nod. Maybe the staff routinely searched all the rooms at night for any contraband. She'd signed off on staying in a facility that didn't lock the rooms, so she couldn't complain now.

Peron knew animals haunted the wilderness around them, so her story had probably made sense to him. She was fitting in just like any other guest. Maybe her paranoia wasn't as justified as she imagined.

Her next goal was to snag a sample of whatever Reed was giving Karenna. If she had something solid to take to Marino, he could make a move. Of course, she'd have to explain her presence at Brighter Days and she couldn't admit to an addiction, not in her line of work.

Lori gritted her teeth through the last activity of the day—art therapy—and then returned to her room during the quiet time. She knew she had several minutes to visit Karenna before Reed showed up with her potion, and this time she took her burner phone with her. It might be basic, but it still had a camera.

Wearing her paint-spattered smock from earlier, she crept down the hallway to Karenna's room. She pressed her ear to the door with her fingers around the handle. She turned the handle and bumped the door with her hip.

Unlike her own airy room, all the shades in this room were pulled down and the room itself faced north. Through the dim light from a few slats in the blinds, Lori could make out Karenna's form on top of the bed.

She tiptoed toward her and crouched beside the bed. "Karenna?"

Karenna's dark lashes fluttered and she held up her hands as if to ward off an attack.

Lori put her finger to her lips. "I'm not going to hurt you. Why is Reed doing this? Do you know what he wants?"

Karenna worked her mouth and a line of drool dribbled from the corner.

Lori plucked a tissue from the box on the nightstand and dabbed at the moisture. "I'm here to help you, but I need to know what's going on. Why is Reed drugging you?"

Karenna tried again, firming her lips into a line. "Drugs."

"I know he has you on drugs, but why?"

"Control." The word proved too much for Karenna, and she closed her eyes.

"Why does he want to control you, Karenna? What does he want you to do? Where are the others?"

Karenna's lids flew open. "Below. Go."

"Below where?"

"Go." Karenna's eyes darted to the door.

She obviously knew Reed's schedule, too.

Lori patted Karenna's dry hand. "I'll be back. Don't worry. The police are going to put a stop to this."

She crept back to the door and cracked it open. Her gaze shifted back and forth and she slipped into the hallway. As she made her way to the main corridor, she heard Reed's voice and the trundling wheels of a cart.

She'd left it too long. She spun around and tried the door to the empty room, but someone had locked it—not all the rooms were on the honor system.

As the voices and wheels grew louder, Lori raced down the hallway to the door at the end. She shoved the metal bar to exit and stumbled outside, facing a bank of trees. The door beeped behind her and with panic flooding her veins, she pulled it closed and dived into the tree line. She ducked behind a bush and peered through the leaves at the building.

Several seconds later, the door swung open and Peron stepped onto the landing. He cranked his head from side to side and said something over his shoulder.

How long would he stand there—waiting, watching?

A minute later, he retreated inside, but Lori didn't trust that he'd stay there. Hunching over, she traipsed through the wooded area, the twigs and pebbles biting into her feet. She circled around and came out where she was last night.

The other women must still be getting ready for dinner, as she faced an empty lawn and pool area. She ran across the grass and let herself in a side door. One of the cleaning crew looked up as she sailed past her, giving her a slight nod. She doubted the janitorial staff would report wayward guests to Reed Dufrain—but who knew?

Slightly out of breath, she shrugged out of her smock and leggings and pulled on a dress. Noticing scratches on her arms from the branches, she threw on a sweater and shoved her battered feet into a pair of flip-flops.

When she joined the others in the large, commercial-sized kitchen, she put on a smile and started dicing veggies. Nobody seemed to notice anything amiss about her appearance except for Shannon, who plucked a leaf from Lori's hair.

"The hike's not until tomorrow. Did you get an early start?"

"Just thought I heard an animal creeping around and stuck my head out there to scare him away. Peron told me there were mountain lions."

Nobody seemed to be interested in catching her out in any way and the cooking and eating of dinner passed without a hitch. But Reed and Peron had to know someone had exited that door at the end of the hallway. Security doors like that didn't just open and close on their own. They'd be on the lookout, and Peron already had her on his radar.

As Lori prepared for another hot tub session with apple cider, someone knocked on her door. "Just a second."

She rolled up her phone in her towel again and tucked it under her arm. "Come in."

Peron walked into the room, and she caught her breath. The last time she'd seen him had been when he'd been scanning the trees, looking for whoever had set off the alarm on the security door.

"Excuse me, Loretta. Reed would like to see you in his office."

Her heart slammed against her rib cage, and her hand clutched at the material of her swimsuit cover-up. "Now?"

"Yes, please. It won't take long, and then you can join the others for your swim."

"Okay." She squeezed her arm against her body, securing her towel as she followed Peron out the door and down the hallway.

He turned to the right, down a small light-filled space that contained Natasha's small office. They moved through her office to a door beyond, and Reed stood up from behind a large mahogany desk lined with computer monitors.

Lori crossed her arms over her chest and her towel, digging her fingers into her biceps. Did those monitors display images from cameras stationed throughout the center? Every move she made could've been projected back to Reed in this office.

She lifted her stiff lips into a smile. "Hello, Reed. You wanted to see me?"

"Welcome to my inner sanctum, Loretta." He tipped his head toward a comfy-looking chair on the other side of his desk. "Take a seat."

She perched on the edge of the deep armchair, afraid if she sank into it, she'd never be able to get up—or wouldn't be allowed to. She scanned the array of books behind him to avoid meeting his pale eyes.

"How are you settling in, Loretta?" He steepled his fingers and watched her above the tips.

"Fine. Great. I feel so much stronger after just a few days here. This is a wonderful program." Her hands had formed claws around the arms of the chair.

"That's nice to hear, but…" a deep furrow formed between his eyebrows "…one of our therapists believes you're closer to the edge than you think."

Lori swallowed. Where was this leading? She blinked. "Oh?"

Reed reached for a drawer and slid it open on a whisper. He pulled something from the drawer and cupped it between his hands. "We're experimenting with some vitamins here at Brighter Days that we believe are beneficial during the recovery period."

Lori licked her lips as her gaze dropped to Reed's surprisingly strong-looking fingers. "Like a weaning type of drug? I don't need that."

Reed smiled through his beard and shook the bottle of pills. "This isn't a drug at all, Loretta. It's a combination of vitamins—our own formula."

This was ridiculous. He couldn't force her to take a pill, vitamin or not, that she didn't want to take. This was a voluntary treatment center, not some court-ordered detox lockup. Peron shifted his stance to her right, moving closer to her chair.

She could take a stand right now, make a fuss, leave. What could they do at this point? They weren't going to assault her here in Reed's elegantly appointed office.

She peeled her hands from the arms of the chair and folded them in her lap. "I really don't think I need a vitamin, Reed. I feel good, strong. I'm not sure what the therapist heard from me."

Stroking his beard, Reed almost whispered, "Panic, fear, loneliness—a woman at a crossroads."

Lori locked eyes with him for a second and a shock reverberated through her body. She let her gaze wander to the bank of books behind him. If she flat-out refused, he'd probably kick her out and she'd leave with very little for her efforts. If she continued to demur and then accepted it, he'd be suspicious. If she swallowed it, she might wind up like Karenna. Even Cade might not be able to help her.

"I'm not denying I'm at a crossroads." She tilted forward slightly in her chair, resting her forearms on his desk. "What's in it?"

Reed's eyes flickered. "A combination of B, C, D, zinc, biotin, L-carnitine and a few other natural ingredients. We've had some amazing success with it."

Like Karenna and Diana? She wiped her hand on the thin cotton of her beach cover-up and thrust it out, palm up. "I'll give it a try. I'm committed to this process, and I want to continue on this path."

"Excellent. Of course, we can't force you to take anything here, and we wouldn't want to do that." He shook a white pill into his hand and dropped it into her palm. The light gave it a pink tint.

"All that in this little pill." Was this the same drug Summer had in powder form in her closet? Lori popped the pill into her mouth. "It's so small, I don't even need water."

Reed rubbed his hands together. "Excellent. I'll have Peron put a supply of these in your room. Take another one before you turn in tonight and another in the morning. You won't feel the effects right away—it's just a vitamin, after all—but by the end of your stay with us, you'll feel like a new woman."

"Thanks, Reed. Thank you for thinking of me." She rose from the chair. "I'm going to join the other ladies at the hot tub."

"Sweet dreams, Loretta."

She nodded to Peron and forced her steps to slow down as she left the lion's den. She sailed through Natasha's office and when she pushed through the doors that led to the patio, she shoved her finger in her mouth and scooped the pill from beneath her tongue.

She carefully tucked the damp pill into her towel and spit out the bitter residue on the ground. Reed suspected her of something, and now she'd have to watch her back like never before. But he'd given her a gift. She had one of his drugs and there would be more by her bedside tonight.

Now just might be the time to make her move and get out of here. If she didn't, she might end up one of Reed's zombies—or worse.

As she soaked in the Jacuzzi with the other women and played nice, she didn't mention Reed's special vitamin. Any one of these people could be his spy. She didn't believe for one minute either of the therapists she'd seen in group or individually had reported her *instability* to Reed. She'd barely said two words in those sessions.

She didn't trust the apple cider, either. She didn't want to eat any of the food here. He could be spiking all of it. She said her good-nights and pulled her cover-up over her wet one-piece suit. She grabbed her towel and held it in a tight roll to keep both the phone and now the pill tucked inside.

She padded to her room and closed the door, her gaze immediately traveling to her nightstand containing a bottle. Sitting on the edge of her bed, she picked it up between two fingers and opened the lid. True to his word, Reed had left her several of the pills.

She shook her phone from her towel and snapped a picture of the bottle and the pills. Then she wrapped the phone and the bottle back up and snuck outside. The

women had left the hot tub and steam rose from the water
and curled away into the night.

Lori ducked back onto the path through the trees and
punched in Cade's number.

The first words out of his mouth made her feel warmer
than the Jacuzzi. "I'm worried about you. Is everything
okay?"

"I'm fine." *For now.* She ran a fingertip around the
bottle cap.

"I'm here, Lori."

"I know you are, Cade, and I appreciate it, especially
after I threw you for a loop the other night."

"No, I mean I'm *here*, in Topanga."

"Why? Where are you?"

"Listen, I met with your friend Trevor Jansen. He had
the drug analyzed today and called you back with the results. I answered your phone. Summer had a powerful
synthetic drug in the fentanyl family. He said they've
been seeing it on the street in the past nine months. They
don't know where it's coming from and just when they
get a line on a dealer, that dealer disappears. And, get
this. The dealers are primarily young women."

Lori put her hand over her mouth. "It's Reed Dufrain. If he's not manufacturing the drug somewhere,
he's the one distributing it. He must be using women
from Brighter Days to do his dirty work. I have the drug,
Cade, right in my hot little hands."

"Why? How do you have the drug, Lori? Did you steal
it? You need to get out of there before they catch you."

"Dufrain gave it to me—to take. He called it a special vitamin."

"God, Lori. He knows you're up to something. Leave

now. Take that trail and meet me at the turnout on Topanga Canyon. I'll be waiting."

"Cade, I…" She glanced down at her cover-up, damp
where it lay against her wet swimsuit. She hadn't planned
on running tonight.

A twig snapping to her left sent a wave of adrenaline
rushing through her body. When she heard a whisper,
she cut off the call.

The recognizable voice rose, and while she wanted
to run, her feet seemed rooted to the ground. "Shut up,
Peron. I know she's out here. Loretta! Come out, come
out, wherever you are. I have some more vitamins for
you—and this time you're going to take them."

Chapter Eighteen

Lori dropped to the ground and crawled into a hollowed-out area between a fallen log and a bush. She dragged the gauzy cotton of her cover-up around her, tucking in the edges, and peered between the leaves.

A beam of light swung along the path, right over her hiding place, gliding across the bush. She held her breath.

Dufrain came crashing down the trail, not even attempting to be stealthy, his flowing clothes replaced by dark jeans and a hoodie. "Get out here, Loretta. I'm going to make your wildest dreams come true. You can stay high all the time and earn a ton of cash. Not a bad deal."

She clutched her hands together, digging her nails into her palms, hoping that Cade wouldn't call her back.

"Start moving, Peron. You need to find her. I have work to do. She can't stay out here all night."

Dufrain and Peron moved into her line of vision, and her muscles ached with the tension of keeping still.

Peron scrabbled in the dirt and leaves, and then bent over and yanked something. A lid? A manhole in the forest? He cleared a path and Dufrain stepped to the edge of the clearing.

"Come back for me in two hours."

Dufrain descended into the ground, as Lori clasped both hands over her mouth. Where the hell was he going? Or maybe he was descending into hell, where he belonged.

When he disappeared, Peron covered the space with the leaves and twigs and turned to peer into the darkness. Would he continue looking for her as Dufrain ordered?

He finally moved toward the light and warmth of the center. Dufrain obviously didn't think she was too much of a threat if he'd abandoned his search for her. He probably thought she had no way out, no way of contacting anyone. He hadn't been watching her as closely as she thought he was.

She waited another ten minutes. She had no hope of following Dufrain into his underground bunker—and she didn't want to do it alone.

She didn't have to. She had Cade.

CADE SAT IN his car tapping the phone against the steering wheel. If Lori didn't show up soon, he'd dive in there and look for her. She'd cut off the call so abruptly, he figured she was in trouble but was hoping for a call back.

As he snatched the keys from the ignition and grabbed the door handle, a vision appeared out the window—a vision in a short white dress, bare legs and sandals.

He shot out of the car and engulfed her in a hug. "Thank God you're out of there. Did you get the pills?"

The pills clattered as she shook a bottle. "I have them, but we have to go back."

"You just escaped. You're not going back in there."

"Cade, Dufrain has an underground bunker. I saw

him go into it. Summer might be there. Courtney. We have to follow him."

His head jerked up. "You think he's keeping them somewhere?"

"It's a possibility. He's drugging women with this synthetic concoction, turning them into zombies and then forcing them to sell this stuff on the street. When things get too hot—it's like Trevor told you—he yanks them off the street and replaces them with new dealers so that the product doesn't get traced back to him." She grabbed his shirt. "When I was talking to one of his drugged-out disciples, she told me the other women were *below*. I didn't know what she meant at the time, but I do now. We have to go back. I can show you where it is. Dufrain is coming back up in two hours. We can surprise him."

"We can't do this alone, Lori, even with your gun in my backpack. We have to call the police."

"And tell them what? There are women on drugs in a drug treatment center and the director has an underground bunker? They can't move in on that information. They'll even have to test the pills I give them. If I've learned anything working with the LAPD, it's that they have a process they need to follow, or the DA will throw out the whole case. They have to collect evidence and get a judge to sign off on a search warrant. If they don't, nothing they find in an illegal search is worth anything. We started this on our own, and we're gonna have to finish it on our own."

"You're right. We can't wait any longer. I brought a backpack just in case I had to go in and rescue you from that place." He reached behind him for the car door. "Let me get that. Do you want a sweatshirt? Why are you wearing a bathing suit under that thing?"

"It's a long story. I'll take the sweatshirt…and the gun."

"I'm not going to sit here and have an argument with you about who handles a gun better, but since it's yours, you take it. If Dufrain has Summer down there, I'm not going to need a gun to take care of him." He hoisted the backpack over his shoulders and they moved down the road to the trailhead.

They followed Cade's flashlight along the same path they'd gone a few days before until Lori held out an arm to stop him. "This is where we veer to the left. We need to be on the lookout for Peron. He's Dufrain's henchman."

Animals scurried out of their way as they plowed through the underbrush. Cade stalled when he saw the lights from the center. "Do you think he has cameras out here?"

Lori answered, "I'm not sure, but it's not like he has a security team patrolling the place. I wouldn't think he'd want his comings and goings recorded for posterity, either."

Cade dropped back as Lori led the way to an area that looked as if it had been disturbed already tonight. "It's here. There must be some kind of lever or something."

He dropped to his knees beside her, and together they pushed aside the natural debris of the forest, which formed a thin layer over a hard, square cover with a heavy ring on it.

"The handle." Lori lifted it. "If Peron could pull this open alone, you shouldn't have any trouble."

From a crouching position, Cade grasped the ring with both hands and braced his feet against the ground. One hard yank cracked the doorway, and he lifted it wide enough for Lori to shimmy through the gap.

She called up, "There are steps."

Cade held the lid open until he slid through, and then he lowered it into place. He immediately covered his nose against the sickly, sweet smell that permeated the air. He gagged. "What is that?"

"I have no idea." Lori pulled the neck of her sweatshirt over her mouth and nose.

"Keep that sweatshirt in place." Cade tugged a ski mask from his backpack and covered the lower half of his face. He then pulled his phone from his pocket and in a muffled voice said, "I'm sharing my location with Jansen for as long as I can. I'm sure service will be cut off soon."

They descended until they reached a flat, dirt surface. Cade hopped off the last step, cocking his head. He whispered, "Do you hear that?"

"Metal scraping against metal?" Lori pulled out her gun, and Cade gripped a short club in his hand and killed his flashlight. They didn't need to announce their arrival.

Hugging the damp walls, they crept down the passage until the clinking and clanking sound grew louder and the smell more noxious. They rounded a bend and froze as a clearing opened in front of them.

A small underground lab appeared like some kind of drug dealer's mirage. What made the scene more surreal were the lab workers in white hazmat suits moving from station to station sliding along chains suspended from the ceiling and connected to belts around their waists.

Dufrain had enslaved these people to manufacture his drugs. Were these all women? Dufrain's clients? Summer?

Cade stiffened, and Lori placed a hand on his arm. One of the suited-up workers had to be Dufrain himself. Lori had seen him come down here.

Lori took a few steps back and put her mouth close to his ear. "We can't stay here. The fumes are going to overwhelm us."

"We can't leave them here. What if one of those automatons is Summer? I can't abandon her, Lori. What made Dufrain think he could do this to Summer? He must've believed she was utterly alone. *She* must've believed that."

"I understand, Cade. Really, I do, but if we don't get into a hazmat suit and join the fun or get out of here, we're going to pass out."

He didn't know if it was Lori's suggestion or if the chemicals really were affecting him, but Cade felt a wave of nausea course through him. "Okay, but we get Jansen, and the whole sheriff's department to swarm this place once we're out. I don't care what it takes. I'll report a dead body down here if I have to."

She held up the cell phone he'd returned to her. "Once they see a picture of this, we won't need a dead body."

She ducked around the corner once more and then seconds later joined him again, stuffing the phone in her pocket. "Let's go."

They reached the stairs and Cade stepped aside. "You first."

"If we're not waiting for Peron to show up, you'd better go first. I'm not sure I can lift that lid."

He swung himself onto the ladder and said, "Stay close."

About halfway to the top, Lori yelped behind him. He twisted around to see someone coming up the step behind her. Cade roared. "Move!"

He took another step but almost missed it when Lori cried out, "He's got my ankle."

"Where's your gun?"

"In my pocket. Go, Cade. Get help, or we'll both die here."

A voice boomed below Lori. "I'm not going to kill you, Loretta. You're coming to work for me."

A white, hot anger pounded through Cade and he descended another step.

Dufrain, his beard wildly sticking out from a bandanna around the lower half of his face, had a hand wrapped around one of Lori's ankles. "In fact, I could use both of you in my stable."

Lori looked up at Cade with her big brown eyes set in a determined glare. "Get out, Cade. You can come back for this piece of garbage."

Dufrain clicked his tongue. "I'm one step ahead of you, junkie scum. When I spotted you in here, I radioed ahead to Peron. He and another one of my orderlies will be waiting on the other side of the doorway with some weapons—and theirs will be in their hand, not uselessly stuck in their pockets."

Lori kicked out with her other foot but Dufrain ducked the blow.

"In fact, your training is going to start right now, Loretta." He wrapped his other arm around the ladder and secured Lori's leg with that hand and then reached into his pocket, emerging with a needle. "The pill I gave you earlier, which you probably didn't even swallow, was just a starter dose. The drug in this syringe will make you mine in a matter of seconds."

With both of Dufrain's hands occupied, Cade took his chance. He lowered himself, coiled his leg and stomped on Dufrain's head.

Dufrain gasped, and he released his hold on Lori to claw for one of the rungs.

Lori kicked the hand holding the needle and Dufrain flailed for a second or two before plunging backward off the ladder with a scream.

Chapter Nineteen

Lori leaned against the ladder, breathing hard, her head swimming. "Cade, we have to get out of here. I'm going to pass out. If Peron is on the other side, you can use my gun on him."

"Can you hold on to my leg? I'll get you out."

As she circled her fingers around Cade's ankle, a square opened above them, and bright light flooded the area.

"Stop right there. Don't make another move. LAPD."

Lori had never been happier to hear that announcement. "Trevor? It's Lori and Cade, and we just found you a drug lab."

"That's what it smells like. Get out of there before you succumb to the fumes."

As Cade clambered out, he said, "There are people in chains down there. We have to get them out."

Trevor's jaw dropped. "Are you telling me he's forcing people to work for him?"

Cade turned around to help Lori out of the hole in the ground, and she collapsed on the dirt, gulping in the fresh air. When Lori's head rolled to the side, she saw Peron and another man she hadn't seen before, handcuffed and sitting by a tree.

"Yeah, he has them chained up to some apparatus so that they can move about, and one of those people might be my sister. I'm going back down with you."

"Stay here. A few of the guys went down already. They'll bring everyone out."

A head popped up from the entrance to the bunker. "Jansen, you're not gonna believe what's been going on down here."

"I just heard. Bring those people up. I have an ambulance on the way, and I'll call for more. Lori said there are women inside the center in distress, and we need to question everyone who worked there to find out if and how they were involved in Dufrain's sick business. Do you have Reed Dufrain in custody?"

The other cop shrugged. "Easy. He was out cold when we found him."

"The fumes?"

Cade said, "Ah, that would be us. He came after Lori, and I kicked him down the ladder. Too bad he's still alive."

Trevor narrowed his eyes. "No, that's a good thing for you, Larson."

Minutes later, Lori watched, as if in a dream, woman after woman emerging from the bunker in a hazmat suit, pulling the headpiece off and staggering toward an officer or sinking to the ground. How Trevor had gotten all these cops from the LA County Sheriff's Department to show up, she didn't know, but they were needed.

As a tall woman peeled off her headgear and shook out her blond hair, Cade shouted and bounded to his feet.

He grabbed his sister and pulled her into a hug, hazmat suit and all.

Lori rested her head back on the ground, a smile spreading across her face.

Epilogue

A few days after the raid, Lori had invited Summer and Cade to her house to compare notes.

Summer scooped her hair back from her face and curled one leg beneath her. "Do you think Reed knew who you were when you went to Brighter Days?"

Lori eyed Cade on his phone, pacing the back patio. "He didn't know, or he never would've allowed me to go there."

"But what about your slashed tires and…and Trey Ferrar's murder?" Summer cupped a mug of tea in her hands, her color back in her cheeks and a sheen creeping back into her blond tresses.

"Reed's guys weren't following me. They were watching your place, saw my car there and slashed the tires as a warning. Same with Trey. He started calling Brighter Days when Courtney went missing, as she'd done a stint there a few months earlier. He didn't like the answers they were giving him." Lori gave an involuntary shiver. "Reed was having Trey followed. They scared him off enough that he didn't mention it to the police but when Cade and I approached him, he was ready to talk."

"So, they took their opportunity when Trey went to

the bar." Summer sniffed and rubbed her nose with the back of her hand. "Courtney's all messed up about that."

"I'm sure she is." Lori watched Cade waving one arm in the air. If that was a work call, something must need his attention. "You and Courtney weren't friends before?"

"We met after becoming Reed's lackeys."

"And you two and the other woman, Chelsea, all cleverly decided to leave your fingerprints at each other's places to send a message to the cops, linking you all together."

"We messed up our places, also. We figured people would be looking for us once Reed took us. I knew Cade was expecting me, so I was sure he'd find my disappearance suspicious. We just didn't know how else to get a message out. Reed and his minions controlled our actions, supplied us with pink China Girl and made us sell it for him." She held her hands. "I never would've sold that stuff for him, but he got us hooked. When things got too hot on the street, he sent his henchmen to grab us and imprison us in the drug bunker. We didn't want to disappear without a trace so we left our prints…and you did figure it out."

"It wasn't quite enough for the police though."

Summer's gaze wandered to the patio. "I knew it would be enough for Cade. I knew he wouldn't let me down. He never lets anyone down—not even you, Lori. If he'd known about the baby, he would've stayed."

"I know that."

Cade opened the sliding door and stepped into the kitchen, wrinkling his nose at their cups. "Hot tea? The sun's starting to come out, you know."

"Finally." Summer stretched her legs out like a cat,

and then crossed them. "What was that phone call all about? You weren't talking to Mom and Dad, were you?"

"Not yet, but we'll have to tell them, and Sarah, too." He clamped a hand on his sister's shoulder. "Don't worry. They're not going to blame you, Summer. It's not your fault."

"If I hadn't gone back on the drugs, I never would've had to check myself in to Brighter Days. Reed never would've targeted me to become one of his drug pushers."

"How are the other women?" Lori pressed a hand over her heart. "How are Karenna and Diana? I never even saw Diana there."

"Reed already had Diana on the street selling. He'd groom us to sell, send us back out into the city and if anyone started sniffing around, he'd drag us to the drug lab to cook. That way, he had a rotating group of pushers. We never escaped because he had us addicted and he threatened to turn us in—or worse. I don't think he would've hesitated to kill any one of us."

"And the rest?"

"We're all recovering. Some are in worse shape than others, but one of the therapists at Brighter Days is forming a recovery-support group."

Cade growled. "You'd trust someone from that place?"

"Hannah felt terrible that she was part of Brighter Days and that Reed was committing those atrocities, literally right beneath her. She knew nothing about it. Most of the women knew nothing about it. He operated a legit treatment center in addition to his drug trade. The police have already questioned and exonerated Hannah—Natasha, too, although she suspected something wasn't right.

Anyway, Hannah reached out to all of us, and is offering her services for free."

"And you?" Lori took Summer's pale hand. "Are you okay now?"

"I'm not gonna lie. That China Girl that we were manufacturing was some primo stuff—smooth high and completely addictive. My doc has me on some tranquilizers to ease the transition, but I'm going to be okay under his supervision and I'm going back to NA. That program works for me." She squeezed Lori's hand and patted her brother's still resting on her shoulder. "I swear."

Lori swirled her tea in the bottom of her cup. "What was that phone call out there? You're not doing any more digging around in our daughter's life, are you?"

"That's done. I have the PI's report and I can share it with you when you're ready, but it's nothing you don't already know. She's in a good home with loving parents, she adores her little brother, she does well in school and she's well-adjusted. She's living the life you gave her, the one you made possible by your unselfish act."

A pool of tears formed in Lori's eyes. "Thanks for that…and your forgiveness."

Shaking her head, Summer pushed back from her chair. "You two were always made for each other. Have you figured that out yet?"

Lori's eyes met Cade's, and his lips twisted up on one side. "I think I'm figuring it out."

"I think I'm going to leave you two to come to your senses. I'm having lunch with Courtney today. She's having a tough time with Trey's death, and I'm going to be there for her."

When Summer left the house, Lori turned to Cade. "When are you going back to New York? My suspension is up, and I'm returning to work tomorrow. No more Nancy Drew. I'm also on probation for my latest stunt, so I have to watch myself."

"I'm leaving later in the week, but you should visit me before I move."

Lori's heart jumped. "You're leaving New York?"

"I've got a perfectly good house in Malibu—if you've figured out the same thing I've figured out."

Curling her arms around Cade's neck, she said, "I think I knew it all along."

"Great. Let's get going, or we'll miss it."

"Miss what?" She flattened her hands against his chest.

"Visiting hours."

"At the correctional institution? You're coming with me to visit Danny?"

"You helped me find my sister, and now I'm going to help you find your brother."

Cade wouldn't give her any more information than that, not even on the long drive out to Tehachapi. He joined her in the visiting room and had a brief conversation with Danny before leaving them together.

Danny smiled when he left. "The two of you are getting back together? You and the rich kid."

"As soon as he moves back here from New York, we're going to see how it goes."

"You told him about the kid?"

"I did. He forgives me."

"People need forgiveness." Danny ran a tattooed hand across his buzz cut. "Cade's a good guy, always was. Cares about you."

"I know that." She tilted her head. "What is it, Danny?"

"Yeah, I have something to tell you, Lori."

TWENTY MINUTES LATER Lori walked into the sunshine, blinking. Cade rose from the bench beneath the looming oak and wrapped his arms around her. "Did he tell you?"

She pressed her wet face against Cade's chest. "He told me he killed Elena—a fit of passion, he said. D-did you ask him to tell me?"

"I did. I told him he needed to release you, release you from that fantasy you wove around him. How do you feel?"

"Disappointed. Deflated, in a way. Free."

"Did you tell him you forgave him?"

"It's not for me to forgive him, is it? That's for Elena's family to work out."

"You need to forgive him for holding you captive all this time, for lying to you, for perpetuating a fraud against you."

She pulled away from Cade and held his hands. "I forgave him for that. I'm visiting him in a few weeks. I won't abandon him, even though there's a part of him that's a monster. I still need time to reconcile that piece of him with the sweet, gentle Danny I know. I suppose I should tell Mom and the rest of the family."

He cupped her face with one hand. "Your mother knows. They've all known for years."

"You're right." She wiped the back of her hand across her damp cheek. "Was this a condition of your moving back here? Of seeing me again?"

"My love for you has no conditions, but I wanted you to move on from the lie you were telling yourself." He stroked the side of her face with his thumb. "Can you do that now?"

"I think I'm moving away from a lot of lies." She captured his hand and kissed his palm. "As long as I have you by my side, I think I can do anything."

"Then you can do anything, Loretta Maria Del Valle, because I'm not going anywhere."

And as he held her there outside the prison walls, she felt free to love him with all her heart.

* * * * *

THE SPY SWITCH

KAREN WHIDDON

To all my amazing rescue peeps. Saving dogs and finding happy homes for them brings so much joy!

Chapter One

Situational awareness. When Jennifer Glass had taken a basic self-defense class for women, those two words had been her single biggest takeaway. The instructor had drummed that into the entire group: *the best defense is prevention and being attuned to what's going on around you can help you prevent trouble before it even begins.*

If Jennifer, along with several hundred other eager shoppers, hadn't been so enthralled by the amazing sale going on at Mountain Rocks Sporting Goods Company, she might have noticed the big man with dark sunglasses staring at her. She might have also been aware of another man hovering right behind her, almost as if he was trying to protect her.

Instead, she'd been so intent on finding her size in an insanely good, sale-priced pair of the hiking boots she'd been coveting for months, that she jumped when the man behind her grabbed her arm. She tried to jostle into position to elbow him or knee him or something, but he'd pressed her up against the display and held her tightly enough that she couldn't move.

"Whatever you do, just play along," he murmured,

his mouth right against her ear. "I'll explain later, Jennifer Glass."

How did he know her name? Jennifer stiffened. Though her first instinct was to twist out of his grip and move away, she'd just gotten her hands on the last remaining box of size-seven boots in the color she wanted. They were in a crowded space as well, which meant whatever nefarious plans he might have wouldn't go down easily.

Turning, she forced herself to relax, letting her body go limp. It would be much easier to get away if her assailant wasn't expecting her to flee.

She looked up, into the bluest pair of eyes she'd ever seen, bright enough to make her blink in surprise. "Please," he said, his deep voice pleasant. "Just follow my lead."

"Let me go," she insisted. "Right now, before I—"

"Lania!" A huge, hulking brute of a man stepped in front of her, smiling. He wore mirrored sunglasses and skinny jeans. "And Mike, of course." A quick nod at the blond man still holding her arm. "Great to see you two here. I think half of Denver is shopping today." He pointed to Jennifer's hiking boots. "Of course, these deals are phenomenal, aren't they?"

Jennifer stared, trying to figure out why this man thought he knew her. And *Mike*, who clearly must be the blond man.

"You know it," Mike said cheerfully. "Lania's been waiting for this sale all week, haven't you, honey?" A syrupy, fake smile accompanied the questions.

Play along, he'd said. Curious now, and still not feeling any real danger, she decided to do exactly that.

"I have," she agreed, her voice equally bright. "These hiking boots are almost sixty percent off."

"Hiking boots?" Removing his sunglasses to reveal cold brown eyes, he eyed her with a quizzical expression. "I can't picture you, with your high-fashion designer clothes and high heels, wanting to climb around rocks in the wilderness."

"She's considering taking up a new hobby," Mike interjected before she could respond. "We both are. Together."

Sliding his sunglasses back on, the stranger laughed, a hard, cold sound without a trace of humor. "Let me know how that goes. I'll be seeing you two tomorrow night, correct?"

"Tomorrow night?" she started to ask. Mike squeezed her arm, a clear warning.

"Of course," he responded. "Lania and I wouldn't miss it for the world."

"Perfect." With a quick dip of his chin, the other man turned and walked away, the crowd of people appearing to magically part for him. Struck dumb, Jennifer could only stare after him, trying to figure out what the heck had just happened.

Finally, the man named Mike let go of her arm. Glaring at him, she rubbed the red spots where his fingers had gripped her.

"Mind telling me what all that was about?" she asked, stepping away from him with her boxed boots held close to her chest. "Or do I need to call for store security?"

He shook his head, dragging one hand through his

short blond hair. "Please don't. It's a long story. How about we go for coffee so I can explain?"

"I'm not going anywhere with you." Staring at him with mounting disbelief, Jennifer started backing away carefully.

"Wait." He held up one hand. "You have an identical twin sister," he said. "You and she were adopted separately, and the records were sealed. I know your sister very well. That man who called you Lania? He thinks you are her."

This stopped her in her tracks, as no doubt Mike intended. First, he was correct in that Jennifer had been adopted and knew absolutely nothing about her past. For all her life she'd had dreams of a sister, though she'd never known for sure she had one. But a twin? That would explain the sense she had sometimes of experiencing someone else's emotions.

But how did she know he was telling the truth? He was a total stranger, so why think she'd believe him? Then again, how would he know she'd been adopted? No way she could chalk that up to a lucky guess.

"Please." He must have noticed her prevaricating. He flashed her what under any other circumstances would have been a devastatingly charming smile. "We need to go somewhere else and talk. I can't risk being overheard."

Somewhere else. Torn, she almost put the boots back, but common sense prevailed. "Let me pay for these." Glancing around, belatedly using her situational awareness, she noticed the other man, the one who'd called her Lania, lingering over by the kayaks. Reaching a quick decision, she nodded. "There's a coffee shop two blocks west of here. Java Jones. I'll meet you there."

"Okay." He, too, glanced at the other man. "Please don't stand me up. This is too important. Your sister's life could be at risk."

Now he definitely had her attention, as he'd no doubt intended. "I'll be there," she finally said, in shock but deciding to believe him for now. A sister? Not just any sister, but an identical twin? All this was news to her. "But first, tell me my sister's name."

"Laney," he answered promptly. "I'll explain the Lania part later."

"Sounds good." Turning to make her way toward the cash register, she frowned when he went along with her. "What are you doing?"

"I can't leave you alone as long as he's here," he explained. "He's not only dangerous, but it's important that he believe we're a couple."

"Are you?" she asked, stepping into line while still trying to process that he'd used the word *dangerous*. "Are you and my sister together?"

"Not in the way you think."

Since she didn't want to ask too many questions and risk being overheard, she simply nodded. Once she'd made her purchase and headed toward the door, with him still right there by her side, she panicked. "I'm not comfortable with you walking outside with me."

"The parking lot is just as crowded as the store," he said, gesturing. "I promise you have nothing to worry about from me."

Even though he was right about the crowds, she still didn't like it. In fact, the more she thought about it, the more tempted she was to get in her car and drive away, washing her hands of this entire thing.

Except…what if he was telling the truth? What if she really did have a twin sister?

"You go in front of me," she said. "Stay at least six feet away and I'll follow you. Don't look back. I'll get in my car and drive to the coffee shop, and you can do the same."

"That will work, as long as he doesn't follow us outside. If he does, we've got to go in the same car."

Ignoring the certainty in his bright blue eyes, she shook her head. "Then you'd better hope he doesn't come out. Because there's no way you're getting in my car with me."

Outside, the parking lot teemed with cars and shoppers, all eager to check out the huge semiannual sale. Mike stayed close to her as she wove her way toward her car. She couldn't help but glance over her shoulder toward the exit, just to see if they'd been followed.

"I don't see him," she said, reaching her Mazda and hesitating before using her key fob to unlock her doors. "I'll see you at the coffee shop." She slid into her car, quickly locking the doors after her. Though she started the engine, she didn't back out until he'd walked away.

Then, heart pounding, she took a deep breath and drove to Java Jones.

At this time of the day, the popular coffee shop had a few open parking spots. Jennifer pulled into one and sat for a moment, trying to calm herself down. She vacillated between feeling foolish, a bit worried and also a sort of eager anticipation. Did she truly have a twin sister? How did this man Mike even know about this while Jennifer knew absolutely nothing? She'd been told her adoption records had been sealed, and despite numerous attempts, she hadn't been able to unearth anything about her past.

Taking a deep breath, she got out of her car. Looking around, she kept her keys in one hand as a potential weapon in case she needed it. She walked inside the coffee shop, the blast of cold air a welcome respite from the summer heat. She found an empty table near the front window and took it, watching the door.

When Mike strode in, the instant his blue eyes found hers, a shiver snaked down her spine. Every female eye in the place was on him—tall and broad shouldered, with his short blond hair and chiseled features. Jennifer couldn't blame them. She might as well admit to herself that she found him attractive. Far more than she actually should, considering.

Smiling, he walked over to her table. Her traitorous body sizzled at the power of that smile. "What would you like to drink?" he asked. "My treat."

"Just a coffee," she replied, some of her tension easing at the utter normalcy of the conversation. They weren't alone, just a couple among many in a busy coffee shop. "Two creams and one sweetener."

He nodded and went to the counter to place the order, returning a few minutes later with both their drinks, which he placed on the table. "Here you go."

Dropping into the chair across from her, he cocked his head and studied her. "It's amazing how much you two look alike," he said. "Uncanny, even."

Nodding, she sipped her coffee and watched him. "I'm still trying to decide if I can trust you."

The sounds of the busy coffee shop were all around them, effectively keeping the atmosphere both private and impersonal.

"Here." Reaching into his pocket, he pulled out a plastic badge with the letters *ATF* emblazoned on top and slid it across the table.

She picked it up. "Special Agent Micah Spokane," she read out loud, turning it over in her hands before handing it back to him. "Why don't you tell me what's really going on?"

Slowly, he nodded. "Your sister's name is Laney Peterson. She and I are part of the same undercover operation, involving that guy you met back at Mountain Rocks. She and I are pretending to be married business partners."

"Which is why that man thought he knew me."

"Exactly. The thing is, Laney is pregnant, and she's had some complications. Her doctor has ordered complete bed rest. We've been trying to figure out how to handle this without blowing anyone's cover."

Pregnant. "I take it you're not her husband?"

"No." Again, that flash of a smile. "Not in real life." He took another sip of his coffee, leaning forward. "There's a party tomorrow night she and I were supposed to attend. All the big players in Igor's ring will be there. Obviously, that's not happening now." He eyed her, his expression intent. "I was planning to attend alone and make up some excuse about Lania." He took a deep breath. "I have a better idea. How about you fill in?"

What the what? She fought back a sudden urge to push back her chair and scramble for the exit. Instead, she forced herself to stay planted in her seat. She took a drink of her coffee and shook her head. "I don't think so. I'm a teacher. Since it's summer break, I'm taking it easy."

"A teacher?" he repeated. "What grade?"

"Fifth." Exhaling, she gathered up the courage to ask what she so badly wanted to know. "I'd like to meet my sister. Where is she? I'm guessing she knows about me, since you knew my name."

Slowly, he nodded. "She does. Though the adoption records were sealed, the agency took a look at them as part of her vetting process. She was allowed to know the results."

Each word felt like a knife into her heart. "That's not fair. I know nothing, but she knows…everything." She pressed her hand to her chest, willing away that familiar ache. "Why hasn't she ever contacted me?"

He held her gaze, his own steady. "She said she thought long and hard about doing so, but in the end she decided she didn't want to disrupt your life."

Disrupt her life? Unexpectedly, her eyes filled with tears. Her twin mustn't be very much like her if she thought meeting your long-lost sister would be anything but joyful.

She pushed away the hurt. "What about our parents? Why were we given up for adoption, and more importantly, who would split up twins?"

Instead of immediately answering, he continued to drink his coffee. "I understand you have a lot of questions. I can tell you that your birth mother is deceased, but other than that, you need to talk to Laney."

Practically vibrating from nerves, Jennifer nodded. "Sounds good. When can I do that?"

He studied her, clearly considering. "After you do this favor for me. I want you to substitute for your sister. Not for very long—only until the operation is complete. We're nearly there. I'd like you to go undercover with me and assume her identity."

So many emotions in such a short time. She'd gone from shock to joy to hurt. Now, anger. She could hardly believe what she was hearing. "Go undercover? That's ridiculous. I'm not a spy." Her voice rose. "Are you blackmailing me? Because that's what it sounds like to me."

"No, not blackmail. I'm only asking for your help. Think about it," he urged. "I could give you a quick training course, plus brief you on everything you need to know."

Stunned and still peeved, she sat back, unable to keep from glaring at him.

"I wouldn't ask if I had any other choice," he continued. "Now that Igor has seen you, I can't show up at his party without you. He wouldn't like that."

Igor? "Who cares?" she shot back.

Mike—Micah—actually rolled his eyes. "Come on, Jen. Live a little. If your sister can do it, so can you. Think of how impressed she'll be with you."

His phone pinged, causing him to pull it out and glance at it. "I need to take this," he said. "Please excuse me, I'll be right back." He smiled. "While I'm gone, please think about it. Two weeks, three tops. I wouldn't involve you if I had any other choice. I really need your help."

MICAH ANSWERED AS he stepped outside. The caller, Carlos, was another member of Igor's group of gun smugglers. In this business, it was every man for himself, though everyone took care to stay on Igor's good side. If they didn't, they were likely to end up dead. Carlos constantly tried to make deals outside Igor's group. Either he had a death wish, or Micah was being tested. Micah had been fending this guy off for months now, refusing his offers while pretending to lead him on. It was nerve-racking balancing on a precarious edge.

From what he could tell, Carlos had the same sort of ruthless cruelty as Igor, though on a less powerful scale. So far, Carlos hadn't gotten brave enough to try an actual coup against Igor, though he did a lot of posturing.

Saying as little as possible, Micah listened to Carlos rant. The gist of his gripe was that he felt he could make better deals than Igor did, thus bringing in more money. Finally, he ended the call, promising to talk more at the party tomorrow night.

Tomorrow night. Micah's stomach turned. He'd acted impulsively, asking Laney's twin to help him out. This was a hell of a nightmare job even for seasoned undercover operatives like him and Laney. He could imagine a hundred ways a nervous and innocent newbie could mess things up.

Yet his gut told him having Jennifer step in was the right move. As long as he could manage to ignore the unexpected flash of attraction he felt toward her, this could work. *Would* work. He'd long ago made it a practice to trust his gut instincts. Igor was in the middle of arranging the biggest illegal arms trade of his career. It wouldn't be long before everything went down and the ATF swooped in and arrested them all. They were after bigger fish than even Igor, and from the sounds of things, they'd soon have them all. Micah knew he'd particularly relish walking Igor out in cuffs. Maybe then he could finally wash off the unrelenting stench of the other man's amoral wickedness.

Shaking his head as if he could shake off the evil, Micah turned to make his way back inside the coffee shop. When he spotted the lovely Jennifer still sipping her coffee, he heaved a sigh of relief. Gut instincts aside, he still wasn't sure he was doing the right thing, asking a civilian to fill in for a fully trained ATF operative. Certainly, were his superiors to get wind of it, he'd find himself in a hell of a lot of trouble.

But hey, these days trouble was his middle name. Though he'd dedicated his life to his job, this under-cover assignment had been the worst one ever. Part of him felt as if some of the evil he spent time with every day had leached inside him, into his blood. He'd spent years getting close to a lot of awful people. Some nights he took two showers, as if he could wash the taint off his skin.

"Well," he said brightly as he approached Jennifer. As she raised her big brown eyes to his, he felt a jolt of attraction so strong he sucked in his breath. What the hell? He and Laney had worked together for years, and there'd never been even the faintest spark between them.

Ignoring it, he sat down. "Have you thought about it? I wouldn't ask if I didn't really need your help."

"I know you wouldn't," she said softly, as if she knew something he didn't. "If my sister trusts you, then so will I. So yes, I'm in. Tell me what I need to do."

He should have felt guilt, he knew. Laney would have his hide if she found out about this. Which she would, eventually. But not until the entire operation had been wrapped up and Igor and his cohorts had been arrested.

"Perfect." Picking up his cup, he drained the last of his coffee before pulling out his phone. "What's your number?"

Typing it in as she gave it to him, he created a new contact. Then he called her so she could do the same. "Go on home, pack a suitcase with essentials and call me. You won't need a lot of clothes. You and Laney appear to be the same size, and she left an extensive wardrobe at the apartment. I'll come and pick you up in, say, two hours?"

"Okay." She got to her feet, eyeing him. "Would you like my address?"

"That's okay, I have it."

Her eyes widened, but she only nodded.

"Whatever you do, don't tell your friends and family where you are. Say you're going on vacation or something. Can you do that?"

"Of course." Drawing herself up to her full height, she looked him straight in the face. "Before I go, do you happen to have any pictures of my sister that you can share?"

Stomach clenching, he nodded and scrolled past photos on his phone. "Here," he said. "This was the two of us at one of Igor's parties." Laney wore a formfitting, shimmery dress and sky-high heels. She wore her long, dark hair in a sophisticated chignon, and even though she and Jennifer had the same features and slender figures, something about the way Laney carried herself spoke of sophistication and elegance. Jennifer, on the other hand, appeared more down-to-earth and easygoing. He found her natural beauty a hundred times more appealing than he should have.

"She's stunning," Jennifer breathed, her eyes wide.

He shrugged. "She looks just like you," he said. If she heard the compliment, she didn't comment, only continued staring at the photo of her twin.

"Would you text that to me?" she asked. "I'd like to keep it, if you don't mind."

He did as she'd requested. Her phone chimed and she nodded, then flashed him a smile so brilliant it took his breath away. "Thank you."

"I'll pick you up in two hours," he reminded her, still puzzling over the way she affected him.

"Okay." Back straight, she turned and walked away.

He watched her go, enjoying the casual yet sensual grace with which she walked. Though she and Laney looked identical, there were enough subtle differences between them to make someone who knew Laney well notice. Luckily, Laney's undercover persona would be easy to imitate, and Micah felt confident that her twin sister would be up to the task.

Still watching, he waited until she'd climbed into her small SUV and driven away. Then he tossed his coffee cup into the trash and walked outside to the black Corvette he'd been assigned as part of his cover. He drove back to the luxury apartment the ATF had rented for him and Laney to use.

Two hours later, he pulled up in front of the town house in Longmont where Jennifer lived. Parking, he headed up the sidewalk. The front door opened, and Jennifer stepped out.

"You really did know where I live," she said. "I wasn't sure I believed you."

Smiling, he kept his voice casual. "Are you ready to go? I'll be happy to carry your luggage to the car." Even though she hadn't brought any out with her.

She eyed his 'Vette. "Like luggage will fit in that thing."

"You'd be surprised."

"Maybe so." Her gaze slid from his car to his face. "I'm not sure this is a good idea."

"You have a point." He decided he might as well level with her. "I'm not sure it is, either. Truthfully, after having Igor spot you at the sporting goods store, the story Laney and I cooked up to explain her sudden disappearance would no longer fly."

Arms crossed, Jennifer waited to hear more.

Micah sighed. "Look, I considered it a huge stroke of good luck that I happened to have been there at the same time as you. I shudder to imagine what might have happened if Igor had approached you and you'd brushed him off as inconsequential."

"Who is he?" she asked. "And why are you so worried about what he thinks?"

"He's the head of an extremely violent group of domestic terrorists," he told her, bracing himself for her reaction. She deserved nothing but the truth, even if that same truth might make her change her mind about helping.

"Domestic terrorists?" Her eyes had gone huge. "Like with bombs?"

"Guns, mostly. He's a dangerous guy. That's why I had to step in when he thought you were Lania. In all the time I've spent getting to know Igor, the one thing certain to send him into a rage is being treated as if he was unimportant. And that's what he would have thought you were doing had you claimed not to know him."

Despite the summer afternoon heat, Jennifer shivered. "That's…terrifying."

"Yes." Micah nodded. "I actually went to the store because I was following Igor. I saw the expression on his face when he spotted you." It had made his stomach churn—raw lust combined with the laser-focused stare of a hunter about to take down smaller prey.

Jennifer frowned, her confusion plain. "Expression? What do you mean?"

"Igor has never made any secret of his desire for Lania. Your sister walked a careful tightrope, managing to discourage him while still doing business with him. She and I had even amped up our supposed relationship, and I made it clear that I felt extremely possessive of my business partner–slash–lover."

Silence as Jennifer took this all in.

"Were you and my sister lovers?" she asked.

The question shouldn't have startled him, but it did. Even though he couldn't blame her for asking. "Hell, no. We're partners, that's all. Laney is happily married to a buddy of mine, Tanner Green."

Shifting her weight from one foot to the other, she sighed. "I assume my sister lives close to here, then? In Colorado, maybe even the Denver metro area?"

"She does."

"But she never reached out, so I'm guessing she didn't want to be found." Pain faintly tinged the edge of her voice.

"I can't speak for Laney. I'm not sure how long she's known about you, even. All I can say is that for the past two years, she and I have been deep undercover working this case."

"Two years?" Up went her brows. "Isn't that unusual?"

"It depends on the case," he replied. "But yes, two years is a long time for anyone to stay undercover. Laney and I managed, though most nights Laney snuck off to spend with her real-life husband." He smiled. "We even had a plan in case she was discovered. Her persona proved she was a powerful, tough woman, with many appetites."

To his amusement, Jennifer blushed. "I see," she said, her voice faint. "Let me get my bags."

She disappeared inside. A moment later, she returned with a single overnight bag. "Perfect," he said, trying to take it from her. Instead, she hung on.

"I'll keep it with me, if you don't mind," she said.

Once she had gotten settled in the passenger seat with her bag on her lap, she eyed the instrument panel. "Since when do ATF agents get expensive sports cars to drive?"

Her question made him grin. "It's my undercover persona. Mike—that's me—is a hard-drinking, heavy-partying, rich SOB who lives life in the fast lane."

"I see." She sat up straight in her seat, her lush mouth set in almost prim lines. "What kind of car does my sister drive?"

"A Mercedes-Benz."

She shook her head. "That's nice. A bit over-the-top, but nice."

"Not over-the-top at all, not for the role you're going to be playing. Luckily, we've got time to give you a crash course before the party tomorrow. We'll start small today, and we'll do a bit more intensive training starting tomorrow. How handy are you with a firearm?"

"A gun?" She looked askance at him. "I've never shot one. I don't like them. Why?"

Though he kept his gaze on the road, he grimaced. "Well, for this job, you've got to become more than passing comfortable with a pistol. Your life could very well depend on it. Mine, too."

She didn't argue, which he appreciated. The drive back into Denver wasn't a long one—less than an hour, depending on traffic. Again, he thought of her sister, his partner, and how pissed she'd be once she learned he'd involved Jennifer.

Laney hadn't wanted to back out, not at such a crucial stage. They could work her pregnancy in, she'd insisted, vetoing the protests from her husband, Tanner. After all, they just needed a few more weeks. She'd be fine. They were at too crucial a stage for her absence to put the entire thing at risk.

But her doctor had overridden her. If she didn't go on complete bed rest, the probability of her losing her baby would be high.

"I'm guessing since you're a teacher, you are off for the summer?" he asked Jennifer. "That's how you're able to take time off with such short notice?"

"That's right," she replied. "Since we're on summer break, time off isn't an issue."

"What about your family?" he pressed, all too aware they could leave nothing to chance. "And your friends. What did you tell them?"

When she didn't immediately reply, he glanced at her. "Let me guess. You haven't."

"Not yet. I was in too big of a rush to pack. Now that it's all finally sinking in, I realize I have to come up with something plausible." She shrugged. "I was thinking of telling everyone I took off on a journey of self-discovery. Kind of like an *Eat, Pray, Love*–type thing."

Careful to remain neutral, he nodded. "Would that be something you would actually do?"

"I don't know. But my parents are artsy types, and they'd be thrilled. My mom is ill, so leaving her worries me some, but I think she'll be all right." She stared straight ahead, twisting a beaded bracelet over and over on her wrist. "I'll need my best friend to take my cat. She's got a key to my house, so that won't be a problem."

"Yet you still sound worried," he pointed out.

She sighed. "I'm not sure what I'm going to tell my boyfriend."

Micah shouldn't have felt that prickle of jealousy, but he did. Even though he told himself it was ridiculous to think someone as lovely as Jennifer wouldn't be taken. Especially since they would only be work colleagues, nothing more.

Besides, he couldn't get involved with anyone, not now. He'd learned the hard way not to allow any distractions of the sexual kind to interfere with his concentration while undercover.

They were almost at the condo. "I'm sure you'll figure something out," he said. "Let's get you settled in, and then we need to talk about what you can expect at that party."

The look she gave him might have been totally innocent, but his body stirred. Even that simple sentence, spoken as matter-of-factly as he could make it, now felt laden with sexual innuendo.

Furious at himself, he knew he needed to shut this down immediately. Or there'd be nothing but trouble for both of them, further down the road.

Chapter Two

"One Lincoln Park?" she asked, dazed and wondering why he suddenly seemed angry. "Sounds fancy."

"It is," he replied. "But even better is the location. It's close to Uptown, LoDo, Five Points and Curtis Park. Our condo is one of the smaller ones, but it's perfect for what we needed. Two bedrooms, two baths and a great patio with a view. If I could, I'd live here in real life."

In real life. That was what felt surreal. No part of this adventure was even remotely based in reality.

"Two bedrooms." With her head beginning to ache, she latched on to that. "I'll have my own room, then."

"Of course." Parking, he killed the ignition and turned to look at her. "Inside, everything was decorated by an interior designer. None of it is personal, or a reflection on Laney or me. Instead, it's what our undercover personas would have liked."

She shouldn't have understood that, but she did. She was also beginning to get the sense that Micah didn't particularly like the person he was pretending to be.

The quietly elegant lobby reminded her of a luxury hotel. With Micah carrying her overnight bag, they quietly rode the elevator up to the ninth floor.

"The entire building has been remodeled," he said as they stepped off. "Personally, I think it was very well-done."

"Way above my pay grade," she said, her tone joking, though she really wasn't.

"Mine, too." Stopping, he unlocked the door and stepped back so she could precede him.

"Wow." The first thing she noticed were the floor-to-ceiling windows with their stunning views of Denver. They filled the room with light. A modern fireplace took up one wall, and the furniture had been arranged to take advantage of it and the view. A small kitchen with granite countertops and stainless-steel appliances sat next to the dining area. The entire main living area had an open, airy feel.

"Come see the balcony," Micah said, sounding as proud as if the condo really belonged to him. "It's huge."

Stepping outside, she looked around in wonder. "It really is. I've never really been a city person, but this is truly amazing."

Grinning, he let her absorb the outdoor view for a few minutes. Then he motioned for her to step back inside. "I'll show you your room. Unpack, relax for a bit and we'll talk about the party later."

Slowly, she nodded. "I need to make a few phone calls," she said. "But if you talk to my sister, tell her I'm really looking forward to meeting her."

Micah laughed, a hearty, masculine sound. "Oh, I'm not going to be talking to her. If she found out I had you here, she'd kill me."

This made Jennifer pause. "She's not on board with your plan?"

"She doesn't even know about it," he admitted. "Actually, no one but you and I do. This plan was born out of desperation."

"That means if something happens to me, I'm on my own?"

"No. You're not on your own," he replied. "I'll make damn sure you stay safe, no matter what I have to do."

His fierce tone sent an answering shiver up her spine. For just one second, one absolutely insane moment in time, she yearned to have him haul her up against him and kiss her. Not sure where the heck that had come from, she shook her head. "But what if something happens to *you*?"

Expression dark, he eyed her. "Then you run away as fast as you can."

Not sure what to make of such a stark statement, she stared right back. While super attractive, this man seemed dark. Deep. And intense. So much so that being around him made her nervous. No doubt her sister knew him well enough to figure out what made him tick, but she didn't. *Her sister.* She still struggled with that concept, too.

"But don't worry," he added. "Nothing's going to happen. I've been involved with Igor and his group for two years now. As long as you don't blow your cover, we'll be fine."

Blow her cover. "Nothing like putting the pressure on," she said, only half joking.

"I'm sorry. But this is serious. And important. Have you ever done any acting?"

Slowly, she nodded. "Yes. Both in high school and in

college. I've even considered auditioning for parts with a local group, though I've never done it."

"Good." He smiled. "That will help you a lot. Look at this as a part, an acting role. Lania is a ruthless, sexy, cunning woman. She's willing to do whatever is necessary to get what she wants the most—power and money, in that order. She has expensive tastes in everything, from her designer clothing to the alcohol she drinks."

"I don't really drink," Jennifer said faintly.

"That's actually good," he responded. "Laney mastered the art of nursing one single drink all night long. You can't afford to allow alcohol to make you let down your guard."

Pushing down her rising panic, Jennifer sighed. "Do you mind showing me my room?"

"Of course not. Follow me." He led her toward what had to be the master bedroom. "This is yours."

"Wow." Blinking, she slowly turned and took in the large room. It even had its own door to the balcony. "For some reason, I assumed you'd get the master."

He laughed again. "Lania needed the larger closet. I'm glad you and Laney appear to wear the same size. If you like clothes, you're going to be really happy."

Jennifer didn't tell him that her fashion style leaned more toward whatever felt comfortable. As a teacher, she spent school days on her feet a lot, so high heels were out. In fact, she only owned one pair, and even those were wedge heels.

"Come look," he urged, clearly anticipating her reaction. "There's a huge walk-in closet full of clothes."

She wouldn't be human if she didn't feel a tiny thrill of anticipation. Slowly, she walked in the direction he'd pointed. When she reached the closet, she gasped. Not only was it packed with what appeared to be expensive clothing, but everything had been organized by type and color.

One entire wall appeared to be entirely full of dresses, ranging from shorter, cocktail-type frocks to long, slinky evening gowns. Jennifer owned a lot of dresses, but she'd never seen anything like this.

In addition to the dresses, there were slacks and jackets, power suits and more casual suits. Even jeans, along with high-end sneakers and numerous silky tops. On the top shelf were the purses, every size and shape and color, all designer, most so far out of Jennifer's price range she had to wonder if she'd be afraid to carry them. She shook her head.

"I told you," Micah said, leaning against the doorjamb and watching her. "She has shoes that match everything, too." He pointed to shelves of footwear, mostly heels, again coordinated by color.

"This is too much." Turning again to take it all in, she struggled to express how out of her depth all this made her feel.

"Hey," he said, his voice soft. "If you can teach kids all day plus deal with their parents, you can do this."

Stunned, she could only stare up at him. "Was I that obvious?"

"A little. That's one thing you need to work on—making sure every emotion doesn't show on your face. Of course, I know you're not acting yet."

"Right." She nodded, panic rising like bile in her throat. "But you know what? I think I made a huge mistake agreeing to do this. I don't know how to wear clothes like this, and I'm not sure I can act well enough to pull off all the character traits you mentioned."

"You got this." His reassuring tone did nothing to reassure her. "Remember, you'll be meeting your sister in the end."

Now, the carrot dangling in front of her nose. Exhaling, she tried to focus. "Maybe you'd better tell me a bit more of what all is involved. I'm sure there's more than going to parties and dressing up in designer clothes."

"There is," he readily agreed. "Though most of it is done behind the scenes, so no one will be scrutinizing you. Since we're business partners, I can guide you."

Though she could feel her resolve weakening, she still had more questions. "How long do you think this will take?"

"A few weeks," he answered. "Three, tops. We've been working hard at negotiating a huge shipment of weapons. Once that is set in stone, teams will be in place to take them down."

Looking around the room, she shivered. "Maybe I've seen too many crime shows, but how do you know they don't have this place bugged?"

"Because we have it swept often. First up, no one comes in here without our consent, not even cleaning services. We have hidden cameras mounted all through the condo, which makes it easy to monitor." He grimaced. "I promise you, we know what we're doing. Laney would still be doing this, even though she's pregnant, but her doctor ordered her to do complete bed rest."

If her pregnant twin could hack this, then surely Jennifer could manage.

"All right," she said, squaring her shoulders. "I'm in. What do we need to do next?"

"Training." His smile told her he'd never doubted her. It also started heat humming low in her body. "We'll get started on that right away."

"Sounds good, but I don't want to learn how to shoot," she told him, trying hard to focus on something else but the strong tug of attraction he made her feel. "So there's no point in trying to teach me."

He paused, considering. "You might surprise yourself. Anything can become comfortable with practice."

Again, her mind went in a direction it shouldn't. She had to force herself back to the subject at hand, which shouldn't have been so difficult, since she had strong feelings about it.

"You're not hearing me. I'm not a gun person. I don't like them. I have a healthy respect for them and, to be honest, a whole heck of a lot of fear. But in my mind, I'd be more of a danger to myself—and possibly you— than anyone else. No gun for me."

He opened his mouth as if he meant to try and argue, but then closed it and nodded instead. "Suit yourself. How about we work on some self-defense moves, then?"

"I'm good," she said proudly. "I took a class."

Her response made him grin. "You did? All right, then. Show me what you've got."

Without waiting for her to agree, he rushed at her. Though she had about two seconds to get prepared, this was exactly the scenario her instructor had made them practice, over and over and over. She spun, tucked her shoulder to catch him in the chest and swung her leg, hitting him right at the kneecap.

He went down with a grunt of surprise, which made her laugh.

"I was top of my class," she told him. "Get up and we can try another move."

Slowly, he climbed to his feet. This time when he approached her, he moved much more cautiously. "I'm going to grab you from behind in a choke hold," he warned.

She knew that one, too. Elbow to the gut, spin, knee up, though she stopped just short of following all the way through.

In fact, Micah seemed familiar with all the moves she'd been trained on. She demonstrated them all flawlessly, using the same amount of restraint as she had in class. "My instructor said not to hold back if I ever found myself in one of these situations in real life."

Grimacing, he dusted himself off as he got back to his feet. "Kudos to him, whoever he was. He did a damn good job teaching you."

"Ex-military," she replied. "Really a kindhearted man. He's also the one who helped train us teachers for active-shooter scenarios."

This made him wince. "Okay, then. Sounds like you got this part down. Now let's talk about your role."

Her role. Slowly, she nodded, shoving back her dread and uncertainty. She told herself she needed to think of this as a play, and that Micah was about to give her information on the character she was to play.

"Cold-blooded and ruthless. Lania lives for money and fine things and has no use for people unless they can help her get something she wants. And sex," he added, almost as an afterthought. "She revels in her sexuality and isn't above using it to get what she wants."

Lania, she reminded herself. Not Laney. This role her sister—and now she—played. Despite that, she felt hot all over at the thought of her and this man, this gorgeous, masculine specimen, pretending to be lovers.

"I need to make a few phone calls," she said, jumping to her feet. "I can't just up and disappear. Plus, my cat is going to want to be fed tonight."

His expression revealed nothing, though she thought she saw a spark of humor in his eyes. "Go right ahead. We can talk more later. Plus, you might want to try on some of the clothes and shoes and make sure everything fits."

They would, she had no doubt. If she and Laney were identical twins, she had to think they were the same size. What she would need to do would be to practice walking in some of those sky-high stilettos.

Once she'd escaped to the sanctuary of her spacious bedroom, she sat down on the edge of her bed and tried to think of what she might say. Her parents wouldn't doubt her, she knew. She'd never given them any reason to, and even now, the thought of lying to them made her feel queasy.

Still, she'd committed to this wild plan, and she'd follow through. One thing all Jennifer's friends knew was that she always honored her word.

Her mother took the news exactly as Jennifer had guessed she would. "I'm so thrilled for you, honey! It's about time you did something for yourself."

Jennifer agreed, explaining she wouldn't be using

her phone while she was on her "retreat," since she was trying to learn more of her inner being.

"Like that book, *Eat, Pray, Love*," her mother exclaimed. "You are going to have so much fun. I'm so happy you decided to do something for yourself."

Another twinge of guilt, a bit stronger. Somehow, Jennifer managed to power through it. Mainly because she knew the truth was even stranger.

They spent a few more minutes on casual chitchat. Jennifer promised to let her mother know the moment she returned home and ended the call.

Next up, she needed to call her boyfriend, Caville. Now you'd think with a name like that, he'd be a muscular athlete, excelling in some sport. Or a patrician academic, with multiple degrees and a bookshelf full of esoteric tomes. In fact, he was none of these. Jennifer had met him at one of her school district's weekend team-building retreats, and they'd bonded over the fact that they both despised any sort of fake, over-the-top team-building activity. Like her, Caville worked as an educator, though he taught high school social studies and history.

Though they'd both agreed to keep things casual between them since they were both off for the summer, Jennifer had honestly figured they'd spend more time together. Caville clearly hadn't gotten that memo. If anything, she saw him less than she did during the school year.

He answered on the third ring, sounding annoyed. Jennifer wasn't sure exactly how to explain a sudden absence to him, though honestly she had to wonder if he'd even notice. She went with the same story she'd told her mother—that she was going on a journey of self-discovery and would be completely unplugged for the next several weeks.

He listened, not commenting. When she finished, she held her breath, reasonably certain that he knew her well enough to know she'd have to be forced at gunpoint to do anything like that. Instead, he told her he was glad to see her doing something for herself. "I'll see you when you get back," he said, sounding not bothered in the least. "Have fun."

So much for even remotely missing her—or expressing the slightest bit of concern that a woman who had always been a big fan of routine and schedules had apparently decided to throw caution to the wind and take off on some harebrained, wild adventure.

Maybe Caville didn't know her as well as she thought he did. Clearly, their relationship wasn't serious at all.

MICAH PACED, QUESTIONING his decision over and over. Despite the identical appearance, Jennifer appeared to be nothing like her sister. Laney thrived on danger, and there'd never been a challenge she wasn't ready to meet head-on. She'd volunteered for this undercover assignment, knowing how dangerous it might be. In that, Micah and she were a lot alike.

Jennifer seemed more delicate. Softer. And, if he was completely honest with himself, sexy as hell. Where he'd thought of Laney as kind of his sister, every single time he looked at Jennifer he imagined her naked underneath him.

Which would only cause trouble. He needed to be focused on the complicated role he played, not on how badly he wanted to get into his new partner's panties. He'd made that mistake once, as a rookie agent, and his libido had nearly cost the ATF the mission. He wouldn't allow that to happen again. He knew if he let down his guard, he'd start making mistakes. They were too close to the end for him to mess it up now.

Right now, he figured she was making phone calls. He wondered how her boyfriend would react to the news that she'd be virtually dropping off the face of the earth for a couple of weeks. Micah couldn't imagine it would be good. He could only hope Jennifer wasn't too upset, because they had a lot to go over between now and the big party tomorrow night.

When she emerged from her room with two spots of color high up on her cheeks, he knew he'd been right.

"He didn't take it well?" he asked, resisting the urge to comfort her.

Lips pressed together, she met his gaze. "Oh, he took it just fine. In fact, he couldn't care less that he won't be seeing me for a few weeks."

"Then he's a total idiot," Micah growled. "Don't worry about him. Maybe by the time this operation is over and you return home, he'll have realized what he's been missing."

Instead of brightening at the prospect, she shook her head. "I'm thinking he might just have to keep on missing me. If he even will. He almost seemed happy to get rid of me for a while."

Since she didn't appear to be looking for sympathy, he didn't offer any. "His loss," he said, meaning it.

"How do you know?" she countered. "You barely

know me. I could be the girlfriend from hell, making the poor guy's life miserable."

The wry twist of her mouth and flash of humor in her big brown eyes captivated him. Not good. "I've got some photographs I'd like you to look at," he said, focusing back on business.

"Okay," she nodded.

"And heads up. Once we change into our clothes that we're wearing to the party tomorrow night, we also change into our undercover personas. No slipping in and out."

"But what if I have questions?" she asked.

He shrugged, hating to be so rough on her but well aware he had no choice. "Just follow my lead and do the best you can."

Slowly, she nodded. "Fair enough. I don't plan on talking much, so I hope that won't be an issue. The way I'm looking at it is to observe as much as possible."

They sat down at the gleaming granite bar, where he showed her the dossier the ATF had compiled on Igor and his band of thugs and killers. She studied each photo and listened intently while he explained who they were and what each person's part was in the organization. Laney would have been fidgeting. She had a notoriously short attention span.

When he got to the women, Jennifer made a small sound of surprise. "Wow," she said. "I had no idea so many women were involved with criminal organizations."

"There are a few." He pointed. "Those two run their own group under Igor's blanket. The rest are mostly wives or girlfriends. Some of them can be, as Laney put it, mean girls. Will you be able to handle that?"

She laughed. "You should see some of the parents I deal with during the school year. *Mean* is a pretty good description. So yes, I'm sure I can deal with them."

"I like your confidence." The compliment slipped out, making him wince inwardly. "You're going to want to hang on to that. It's an integral part of Lania."

"Thanks." She swallowed, drawing his attention to her slender throat. "What are we doing about food? Can we order takeout or something? I haven't eaten since breakfast, and I'm really hungry."

"Laney and I took turns cooking," he said. "Let me see if I can rustle something up."

"Wait." She touched his arm, sending a shock of awareness through him. "Before you go through all that trouble, you should know I'm vegetarian."

He should have been surprised, but he actually wasn't. "So is Laney. I'm not, but I'm used to it. Weird coincidence, huh?"

For a moment she only looked at him, clearly at a loss for words. Then, she simply nodded. "You know, one time I remember reading a study about twins who'd been raised apart and how they turned out to have similar habits and likes and dislikes. So I guess it's not unusual that both Laney and I are vegetarians." She took a deep breath. "If you don't mind, over dinner I'd love to hear a lot more about my sister."

"No problem." Checking his watch, he smiled. "I should be able to have something to eat in about thirty minutes. How about I call you when it's ready?"

"Is there anything I can do to help?"

He had to remind himself once again that she wasn't Laney. One of the rules he and Laney had agreed on was when one of them was cooking, the other didn't interfere. While they were good partners and friends, entering into any kind of domestic relationship could lead to dangerous territory, so they simply didn't. Neither had been even the slightest bit attracted to the other.

Laney had always kept tofu in the fridge, and she'd shown him how to prepare it. He made one of their staple meals, a teriyaki tofu stir-fry on jasmine rice.

"I'm impressed," Jennifer said, eyeing the meal. "Did my sister teach you how to cook?"

"No," he said. "I already knew, though she had to teach me about tofu. It took some time to get used to eating that."

"I imagine. Caville won't even try it."

"Caville?" He wondered if that was her cat.

"My boyfriend," she explained. "I know, he has an unusual name."

He decided not to tell her the immediate picture he'd formed of the guy simply based on the name.

"Please tell me about my sister," she asked. "I have so many questions."

"I imagine you do." He kept his tone gentle. "But right now, with so much else going on, I'd rather you focused on Lania. Once this is finished, you'll have all the time in the world to learn about Laney."

If she found it odd that he spoke as if they were two separate individuals, she didn't say. But the defeated expression on her face made him feel bad, even though he knew he was only doing what was necessary to help her survive.

Again, the twinge of guilt, making him wonder if he should send her home and try to brazen out the last few weeks on his own. Bitter experience had taught him that the slightest change in plans could have a domino effect and take down years of carefully calculated work.

He was doing the right thing, even if it seemed risky.

"Are you sure you won't reconsider a trip to the shooting range?" he asked, keeping his voice casual. "I'd sure feel a lot better about your safety if you knew how to handle a pistol."

"I'm sure," she replied. "After all, I'm sure none of the other women will be carrying a gun."

Her naivete would have been humorous if it weren't such a serious situation. "Oh, I can guarantee you that every single woman in that room will be packing. In fact, you'll be the oddity if they notice you aren't."

"Can't I just say I forgot my weapon?"

Somehow, he kept from cracking a smile. "One does not simply forget a weapon." He shook his head. "Especially around people this dangerous. When you carry on a regular basis, it's as much a habit as putting on your belt or your shoes. Being able to easily access your pistol can be a matter of life and death."

Watching him, she considered his words. "Do you honestly think I'll need a gun?"

"Yes."

"How about I carry one with no bullets? Will that work?"

"Are you serious?" he asked. When she nodded, he took a deep breath. "What good would that do?"

"You just said I'd be the only woman not carrying one. Since I don't want to stand out, just give me a small one and I'll wear it in a holster or something. I don't actually have to know how to use it."

In a twisted way, that made sense. "Except if it has no bullets, you won't be able to use it as protection," he pointed out. "That would defeat the point of being armed."

"Fine." She gave in with an exasperated huff. "I'll go with you to the shooting range. Just don't expect me to like it or to be any good."

At the shooting range the next morning, it turned out she was a natural. Once he showed her how to handle a gun, the safety, where to load it and never to point it at anyone unless she meant to shoot them, he took her to shoot at the paper targets. He didn't expect a whole lot of accuracy, not until she got the hang of shooting a pistol. For her, he'd chosen a Glock 26, 9 mm. Once he showed her how to shoot with a two-handed grip, he stayed close behind her in the booth, ready to help if needed.

With her long hair in a neat ponytail and the ear protection on, her dead-serious, intent expression made him proud.

And then she shot. Again and again, hitting the target almost dead center every time. When she needed to reload, she waved him away and did it herself with a quiet kind of competence.

He stepped back, watching and waiting until she finally decided she'd finished. He pressed the button to send the paper target toward them, wondering if she'd realize how unusually brilliant her shooting ability had been.

Once he unhooked it, he handed it to her. "Good job," he told her. "You've got a gift for this."

To his surprise, she grinned. "I didn't expect it to be so loud, and to smell so strongly of gunpowder. Despite the sensory overload, once I got past that, I could focus. I faced my fear. And weirdly, I like it more than I thought I would." Her smile faded. "But then, shooting at targets is a lot different than shooting at people."

"True." He squeezed her shoulder. "Which is why it should only be done when absolutely necessary. I'm not planning on you having to shoot anyone. Now you know how to use the pistol, keep the safety on and carry it with you. For the party, you can keep it in your purse, or you can wear a garter/thigh holster. I'm thinking that's what Laney did."

"The name is intriguing," she told him, as they walked out. "A garter/thigh holster. I assume that won't show when I wear a dress?"

He swallowed, pulling his thoughts away from her inner thigh, where they had no business drifting. "Laney's never did."

Chapter Three

Walking out of the shooting range, Jennifer almost didn't recognize herself, especially on the inside. She felt charged up and powerful, as if being a talented shot gave her some sort of superpower.

She'd shot a gun. And done it well. Something that should have terrified her. While she'd told Micah she didn't like guns—which was the truth—it wasn't the entire truth. The reason she'd taken that self-defense class in the first place had been because she'd been assaulted at gunpoint several years ago. She would have been raped, too, if two college students hadn't run to her rescue. She'd been walking out of a convenience store late at night and a man had rushed at her, put a gun to her temple and forced her around back to the dumpster. When she was backed up against the dirty metal with the putrid scent of trash filling her nose, the man had been so intent on what he was about to do to her that the college boys were able to disarm him, take him down and hold him until the police arrived.

She hadn't been able to stop shaking. Other than the police, she'd told no one, not even her parents. She'd felt ashamed, as if what had happened had been her fault.

Not until she'd signed up for the self-defense class and heard some of the other women's stories had she realized how wrong her guilt had been. As she'd learned to defend herself, not only had her confidence grown, but she'd begun to heal.

Despite that, even now, five years later, the awful memory made her choke up and freeze. When Micah had first brought up the idea of teaching her how to handle a weapon, she'd actually broken into a cold sweat. But then, something one of the other women in her self-defense class had said came back to her. *Face your fear.*

Now she had. Even better, this had given her something better to associate with a gun.

And she'd actually been good at shooting! Who knew? While she felt quite confident about hitting a paper target, she wasn't sure she could actually shoot a human being. But then she remembered how she'd felt pressed up against that dumpster and realized she would have shot her assailant if she could have in order to get away.

If she was careful, she saw no reason she couldn't use her newfound proficiency as yet another tool in her self-defense kit. She'd need to get a concealed carry permit, of course, but from what she'd read, getting a concealed handgun permit was a simple process.

"You did well," Micah said, his voice as warm as his gaze. "Did you surprise yourself?"

"Yes," she replied. "But I'd really like to practice as often as possible. I think the more hands-on I am, the more comfortable I'll feel handling this gun." After double-checking to make sure the safety was on, she went to hand the pistol back to him, handle first.

"Keep it, it's yours," he said, surprising her. "Seriously, that's just like the gun your sister used. And yes, we'll go the range often. I find spending a few hours hitting targets does wonders for stress."

Unsure if he was kidding, she nodded.

While Micah skillfully navigated Denver traffic, he kept up a running stream of small talk, which mostly required her to listen. Her exhilaration began to fade, and her earlier doubts crept back in. Shooting at a gun range was one thing. Using that pistol to defend herself was something completely different. Still, she swore to herself that she would continue to practice. The more she handled the gun, the more comfortable she'd be.

"Are you all right?" Micah asked. "You seem awfully quiet."

Glancing up at him and seeing the concern in his blue eyes, she decided to be honest. "I'm just thinking. I was actually terrified of guns, and now I've learned not only to shoot one, but how to load and unload it. You've been really patient with me, and I appreciate that."

He shook his head and laughed, the warm, masculine sound making her smile. "How could I be otherwise, considering the huge favor you're doing for me?"

"You have a point." Smiling, she relaxed in her seat. She couldn't help but wonder what else she might learn from this little adventure. Maybe if she continued to think of it that way, she might be a little less nervous.

When they got back to the condo, she excused herself and closed the door to her bedroom. Though she'd intended to try and nap, she found herself inside the closet, staring at all the beautiful, expensive clothes.

While she did okay on her teacher's salary, she certainly couldn't afford to buy designer things like these.

Surveying the rack of cocktail dresses, she decided to try some on. After all, she needed to choose something to wear to the party.

The first dress she tried on, while a perfect fit, felt way too revealing. As a teacher, Jennifer tended to dress conservatively, going more for comfort and value than anything else. Never in her entire life had she worn anything like this.

The second dress fit better. While equally sexy, it seemed more elegant. She moved that to one of her possibilities.

She tried every single cocktail dress on. They were every color of the rainbow, though Laney—like Jennifer—appeared to have a penchant for blue. There were two gold dresses, one silver and a bronze-colored one that fit like a dream.

Once she'd narrowed her choices down to four, she decided to take a look at the shoes. After all, she'd need to see how the entire outfit came together.

Eyeing the shoes, she immediately decided against any that had heels over four inches. While of course she'd worn heels before, she wasn't comfortable in them. Teetering around in shoes too tall for her would be a dead giveaway that she wasn't whom she was supposed to be.

Her sister had arranged the shoes not only by color but by heel height. Luckily, there were numerous pairs of midrange heels. Jennifer tried a few pairs on, relieved to learn she could walk in them. Like the dresses, they were a perfect fit.

Since doing this—all of this—would be way outside her comfort zone, in the end, Jennifer chose a red dress. She rarely wore red, except maybe during the holidays.

But this dress…something about it said *power*. In it, she felt like Lania, the ruthless criminal who wore a gun strapped to her thigh. Red shoes that appeared to have been made to go with the dress and a matching evening bag. Now all she needed to complete the look was jewelry.

She hadn't thought to bring anything, and even if she had, all her cute costume pieces would look completely out of place with designer clothes. She assumed Laney had a safe somewhere. She'd have to ask Micah about that.

Then she checked out the makeup. There was a lot of it, numerous high-end brands unopened. Though Jennifer had brought her own foundation, she could hardly wait to try some of these. Especially since she knew they'd all go with her skin tone, since her twin had purchased them.

Her twin. The news had blindsided her, and she still wasn't sure she'd actually absorbed the impact of realizing she had a flesh-and-blood sister.

Her stomach grumbled, reminding her she hadn't eaten lunch.

She headed into the kitchen to see what she could rustle up to make a meal.

"Hey," she said, spotting Micah sitting in a chair, checking his phone.

"We need to practice," he said, getting up when she entered the room. "Being in character for the party tonight."

She eyed him. He moved with an easy sort of grace,

unusual in such a large man. But then again, maybe not. While he had broad shoulders and a muscular chest and arms, his narrow waist and lean hips gave him an athletic appearance. "Do you play sports?" she asked, coloring as she realized she'd blurted out the question.

"When I'm not undercover, yes," he answered, as if her random thought process wasn't the slightest bit unusual. "I play in a softball league—or I used to. And I also belong to a bicycling club, though they haven't seen much of me in the last couple of years."

"I see." Now she felt like a slug. "What do you do to keep fit these days, since you had to let those things go?"

"This building has a pretty awesome gym. I work out there just about every day. You're welcome to join me, if you'd like."

She thought about claiming she had no workout clothes but then realized Laney probably had some around here, too. "Did my sister use the gym?" she asked. "My gym experience at home is limited to taking fitness classes. I'm really into yoga."

"Laney lifts weights," he answered. "And she uses the treadmill and elliptical for cardio."

"I do those, too." She looked around the condo, still amazed at how luxurious it was. "You say we need to practice, and I agree. But before we do, do you mind if we eat lunch?"

Checking his watch, he appeared surprised at the time. "I can make us a few sandwiches," he said. "Your sister keeps those veggie burger things in the freezer. Will that work for you?"

"Sure. But I don't need bread. I can heat it up while you make your sandwich."

They worked in companionable silence. She made a small salad to go with her veggie burger, and he took some of the lettuce for his sandwich. Then they both sat down at the table and ate. She waited until they'd finished and then stood. "Before we start practicing, I have a few questions."

Expression inscrutable, he nodded. "Go ahead and ask."

"This undercover operation. How often are you actually in your role? I'm wondering, because you speak of it like it's a split personality. I'd think it'd just be easier—and safer—to stay in the role you're playing 24/7. That way there'd be less chance of slipping up."

"I couldn't do that. I'd go insane." He blanched as he realized what'd he'd said. Swallowing, he gestured for her to sit down. "I guess I need to explain."

Heart pounding, she took a seat. "I think you do."

"Of necessity, the person I am when I'm undercover as Mike is my polar opposite." He watched her, his gaze narrow. "To play the role properly, I've had to go deep undercover. Which means I sometimes have to do things or say things that make me sick."

"Like commit crimes?"

To her surprise, her question made him flash one of those incredibly sexy smiles. "I try not to if I can help it. But often I have to make it appear as if I have."

"I don't understand." Again, she wondered if she'd gotten in too far over her head.

He thought for a moment before replying. "You're going to be playing a role. Some of the things your character, Lania, believes and thinks and says might be against everything you know to be right, deep down in your soul. But you'll do them anyway, because when you're with these people, you *are* Lania, not Jennifer."

"I get that," she said. "But inside I'll know that this is just a role."

"Probably," he admitted. "Because you'll only be Lania for a couple weeks. I've been Mike for almost two years now. I don't like myself much when I'm him. That's why it's so vital that I get downtime here at home."

That made sense.

"Do they never come here?" she asked. "The bad guys?"

"They've been. There's a reason why the ATF spent all this money to make us look like we really are who we say. Lania purposely made it clear she had a predatory nature and would take partners when and where she chose. Laney's husband, Tanner, has done some undercover work during this operation, and she made it seem like they were having a secret affair that I know nothing about. Igor enjoys knowing, because he thinks he has something to hold over me if necessary."

"When in reality, she was using that as an excuse to spend time with her husband," Jennifer said. "Clever."

"It was," he agreed. "Until she got pregnant. They weren't even trying, but they were both thrilled. Tanner was over-the-top with excitement."

"Will I be meeting Tanner?" she asked. "Laney's husband? Since you said he was working undercover as well."

"No. He's decided to stay out along with Laney. Which is a good thing. I can imagine how he'd react if he caught sight of you." He grimaced. "It wouldn't be good."

"You're taking a risk doing this, aren't you?" she asked. "I'm guessing that your boss wouldn't approve?"

"No, he wouldn't." Again that flash of teeth, though this time it was more of a grimace than a smile. "But my instinct tells me this is the right thing to do."

"And you always trust your instinct?"

"Yes. That's why I'm so good at what I do."

Everything about him, from his unabashed masculinity to his rough-hewn good looks, attracted her. Though she doubted she affected him the same way, he made her think of raw and primal sex, the kind without words of explanation. Her entire body went hot and then cold as she pictured him shoving her up against that wall and having his way with her.

"Are you all right?" he asked, clearly concerned. "You looked kind of funny there for a hot second."

Glad he couldn't read her mind, she swallowed and forced a smile. "I'm fine. Just feeling a bit overwhelmed by everything."

"Don't be." He leaned over and patted her hand. "That's why we're going to practice a few things. I don't want you to feel uncomfortable, especially because it'll show."

"Uncomfortable?"

He took a deep breath. "Lania is a very…handsy woman. She hangs all over me when we're out in public. She's independent and very, er, sexual. She does whatever the hell she wants."

Again, hot and cold. "You want me to hang on you? Like drape myself over you?" She wanted to fan herself.

"It's a role, remember. You're playing a role. As am I. Neither of us takes this seriously. And the people we're playing would sell each other out in a heartbeat if it would benefit them in any way."

"I see." But she didn't, not really. She was a fifth-grade teacher from Longmont, Colorado. Anything she knew about criminals or terrorists came from reading thrillers or watching crime dramas on TV. "Let me go freshen up for a second, and then we'll practice." Without waiting for a response, she rushed off, escaping to her room.

THE INSTANT MICAH heard Jennifer close her door, he dropped back into the chair. He hadn't expected to want her; after all, he'd spent two years with her identical twin sister and never felt even the slightest hint of desire. Yet twenty-four hours with Jennifer and he couldn't stop thinking about how she'd taste if he were to kiss her or how she'd feel pressed up against him.

How the hell was this role-playing thing going to work? Lania as played by Laney was an out-and-out sexual tease who used her body as a weapon to distract and disarm her opponents. He wasn't even sure Jennifer could do that, but if she could, just thinking about it played havoc with his libido.

Maybe it had something to do with her innocence. So fresh, so attractive to a man who'd spent far too much time living among the dregs of society. The schoolteacher-turned-seductress carried its own kind of unique appeal, and in fact— No. Not going to go there.

He shook his head. This kind of thinking could get a man killed. He couldn't afford even the slightest distraction, never mind a constant haze of sexual lust. He'd already jeopardized both his career and the mission by bringing in a civilian. He needed to keep his focus laser sharp on the end goal—catching the bad guys.

Jennifer's bedroom door opened. He looked up—and lost the ability to speak. He swallowed, watching as she strolled into the room wearing one of Lania's sexy short black dresses and a pair of sky-high heels.

"I'm ready to practice," she purred, her seductive voice hitting him hard.

Hard. Oh yes, he was. He shifted his weight and hoped she wouldn't notice.

"Well?" she demanded, turning slowly and giving him a view of her amazing body. "Do you think this looks okay?"

Belatedly realizing he needed to say something, he nodded. "Looks great," he forced out, his voice rough. "I see you're already in character."

She lifted one bare shoulder in a graceful shrug. "You wanted to practice. Then let's get to it."

This was exactly the reminder he needed to get back on track. He forced himself to look away, setting his jaw and turning into Mike without too much effort.

"Sexy," he drawled, noting her instant flush. "You'll have them all drooling over you if that's what you're wearing tonight."

Though she visibly wavered, she managed to hang on to her character, raising one perfectly shaped brow and flashing a half smile. He almost clapped, but he didn't want to startle her.

"I don't know what I'm wearing yet," she responded, gracefully taking a seat on one of the bar stools and crossing her incredibly long legs. "I just thought I'd try this one out on you and see your reaction."

Dangerous territory. But she needed to get used to the kind of people they'd be running with. "You look hot," he said, keeping it blunt. "Sexy as hell. Igor will be falling all over himself trying to get you into his bed. Most of the other women will be jealous. They might get together and try to make snide comments. But you're Lania, and you care nothing for their petty concerns. You'll walk around like you own the place, and I'll try to act as if I own you. Of course, you'll laugh in my face. I'll get mad, and then you'll switch direction and have me eating out of your hand."

Eyes wide, she stared at him. "Why? What's the point of all that?"

"It's what we do," he answered. "It amuses Igor, and that is always good. He's much easier to get along with if he's happy."

Sliding off the bar stool, she adjusted her skirt and turned to go. "I'll be right back," she told him. "I think we've practiced enough for now." She turned and went back to her room, closing the door with a decisive click.

When she emerged a few minutes later, she wore jeans and an oversize T-shirt that somehow managed to cling to her figure like a second skin. His immediate reaction startled him.

"I'm really nervous," she said. "Honestly, I'm not sure I can do this."

"You'll be fine." Keeping his voice confident, he smiled. "All you have to do is play your role."

She nodded, though the worried look never left her big brown eyes. "You'll be around, right?"

"I'll try not to leave your side."

Her arch look told him what she thought of that. *"Try?"*

The stiff set of her shoulders spoke to her tension. Eyeing her, he made a quick decision. "We've got hours until that party. How about we change and hit the gym? We can work off some of that nervousness."

Though she looked at him as if she thought he might have lost his mind, she finally nodded. "Sounds good. I'll just need five minutes to change."

He went to his room and put on his workout clothes. When he came out, he saw that Jennifer had made it to the living room before him.

"There were even workout clothes in the dresser," she said, smiling. "And just like everything else my sister owned, they fit perfectly."

They rode the elevator to the gym on the ground floor. Inside the mostly empty room were rows of gleaming, top-of-the-line fitness equipment.

"This is nice," Jennifer breathed. "I might not lift weights, but I do like to run." With a casual wave, she headed for the treadmill.

He stood still and watched her go, wondering how she managed to affect him so strongly. Then, because he needed to sweat it out, he also headed for a treadmill. A pulse-pounding run might just be what he needed to help clear his head.

Turned out he needed more than a run. He did some heavy lifting, and then after, he got on the stair-climber.

Sweaty and feeling much, much better, he walked with Jennifer back toward the elevator. She seemed even quieter than usual.

"Good thing we have plenty of time for a shower," he mused just as they stepped inside.

"True." She looked up at him, smiling. "Thanks for the good idea. That was exactly what I needed."

She glowed. She freaking glowed. He'd never seen a woman look so damn attractive after exercise. Quickly, he looked away.

Back at the condo, after heading into the kitchen to grab bottles of water, they each went their separate ways.

A few minutes later, he heard the shower turn on in the master bathroom. And of course, his mind immediately went to picturing her naked, water running off her impossibly smooth skin.

What the actual hell? Shaking his head at himself, he hurried off to take his own shower, well aware it'd be a cold one.

Later, Micah put on his power suit and the Italian leather shoes that cost more than his first car. He had to admit they were comfortable, but the first few times he'd worn them, he'd been overly worried about damaging their perfect sheen. Never mind that he had three more pairs just like them in the closet.

He kept picturing Jennifer in that sexy little dress and battling the edge of arousal. He'd never reacted that way to Laney, which he now considered a blessing.

If he'd thought the black dress was hot, the red was scorching. The first sight of her robbed him of the ability to think, never mind speak. He still hadn't gotten used to the constant state of semi-arousal that came from being around her, but right now his fully turned-on body had his blood pounding.

"Well?" she asked, frowning slightly at his lack of reaction. "I take it you don't like red?"

Staring at her, he desperately struggled to put his fragmented thoughts into something coherent. "The red looks even better than the black," he managed. "And I wouldn't have believed that would be possible." Cracking a smile, he hoped he didn't appear as shell-shocked as he felt.

At his words, her frown disappeared. "Good. Because I'm not used to dressing like this. I have no idea if I'm doing it right."

"You are." Though he knew he sounded curt, he tried to soften it with another smile. She clearly had no clue how she affected him. Her combination of innocence and sexy as all get-out would be his downfall if he wasn't careful.

Somehow, he managed to clear his head. "I'll be right back," he said. "You just need a couple more things to complete the look."

Once he reached his bedroom, he closed the door behind him and went to open the safe in his closet. As he worked the combination, he was stunned to realize his hands were shaking. *Damn.* He hadn't been this rattled since he'd been a teenager. One thing for sure—he needed to get himself under control or he'd likely mess something up. At this stage in the game, that was the absolute last thing he needed.

Chapter Four

Cherry Creek. Of course. Why Jennifer would have thought Igor would reside anywhere else, she couldn't say. Following a snaking line of luxury vehicles, they pulled up into a circular drive, in front of a stone-and-brick mansion complete with valet parking and manicured yard. She couldn't help but wonder if Igor's neighbors had any idea that a criminal resided in their tony zip code.

Mike tossed the keys to one of the kids manning the valet station and went around to the other side while another kid helped Lania out. In character, she flashed her long legs, laughing as this movement drew Mike's gaze.

Arm in arm, they followed another group of people up the sidewalk. A profusion of well-tended flowers of every color lined the path. Inside, lights cast a welcoming yellow glow.

Though entering a room full of glittering strangers made her heart stutter in her chest, Jennifer kept her head high and her shoulders back as she sauntered inside. The stilettos weren't as wobbly as she'd feared, probably because they were a hundred times better made (and more expensive) than any pair of shoes she'd ever owned. In fact, wearing them made her feel as if she truly could be Lania.

Her confidence grew as she and Micah worked the room. She'd practiced her ruthless smile in front of the mirror until it felt natural and here she flashed it periodically. Micah—no, *Mike*—seemed a different person, too, which she actually liked, as that helped her to stay in character.

She'd been right about the jewelry, too. Once she'd appeared in the living room in the red dress, Micah had excused himself. He'd returned a few minutes later with a glittering diamond necklace, earrings and a ring so large she'd wondered if it might be cubic zirconia.

But Micah had assured her everything was real. "These kinds of people would spot a fake from a mile away," he'd said. "Since all of this comes from seized property, it belongs to the ATF, so be careful with it."

Never in her life had she worn anything even half as expensive as this. Between the jewelry, the dress, the shoes and the clutch purse she carried, she estimated she wore close to an entire year's worth of her salary.

This made her nervous, but she pushed the thought away and assumed her character. Her acting training came in handy with this. Because as Lania, she *deserved* to wear only the finest.

Her only concern, and one she didn't allow herself to think about, was while all these faceless people were strangers to her, they *knew* her from before. Luckily, she had a gift for remembering names, since that was a necessary skill as a teacher. Hopefully that would enable her to bluff.

Mike had just handed her a glass of champagne when

she spotted Igor making a beeline for her. He reminded her of a charging bull, intent and focused.

When he reached her, she flashed that same cool smile. "Igor," she purred. "So good to see you again."

"Is it?" He looked her up and down, his gaze hooded. "Have you had a chance to try out those hiking boots yet?"

"Not yet," she shot back. "Soon, I think. And you? Did you find what you were looking for in that huge sale?"

"Oh, I did." His smile turned savage. "Unfortunately, you were not alone."

Next to her, Mike stiffened. Tossing her hair back, she leaned into him, trailing her fingers up one arm. "I'm never alone," she said, speaking to Igor. "Actually, I prefer it that way."

Igor snorted. "I imagine you do." He turned his attention to Mike. "I have a job for you," he said. "I need a moment of your time."

"Not without me," Lania put in, her voice as smooth as silk. "You know Mike and I are partners."

This must have been the correct response, as neither Igor nor Mike appeared surprised.

"Of course, darling," Igor said, holding out his arm as if he expected her to take it. "We'll talk later. Now, I believe it's time for us to eat."

Unsure what to do, she held tight to Mike's arm. From what she'd been told, it was best to tread carefully around Igor, but she also knew Lania would have taken pains to never be alone with him. Men with too much power were more than dangerous.

"I need to freshen up first," she said, batting her eyelashes. "Please don't wait for me. Mike and I will join you in just a few."

Though she thought she saw anger flash in Igor's dark eyes, he nodded and moved away. Only once he'd disappeared from sight did she release a breath she hadn't even known she was holding.

"You did good," Mike murmured. "The restroom is this way. I'll wait outside the door for you."

Nodding, she looked up at him and then, since she was Lania, not quiet, proper Jennifer, she did what she'd been fantasizing about doing ever since she'd seen him in that dark, tailored suit. She grabbed hold of his lapels, stood on the tips of her toes and kissed him, pulling him as close to her as decency allowed.

An instant inferno flared. Seeming startled—but not really—he kissed her back, mouth open, deep and full of tongue and passion. His arousal felt huge against her.

"Get a room," someone said, passing them. "Come on, you two."

At the words, Lania gasped for air, jerking away. "Whoa," she murmured, her face flaming and her mouth seductively swollen. "I should have seen that coming."

Mouth tight, Mike stared at her. Her first thought, that he was angry, proved wrong when he gave a bitter-sounding laugh. "Good job," he said, his mouth tight. "That's exactly the kind of thing you like to do. You've always been great at keeping people off balance."

Not sure how to respond, she nodded. She'd actually meant of course she'd act differently, dressed up, playing a role, on the arm of the sexiest man she'd ever known. She wanted to tell him she'd made a mistake, but since she knew Lania would never admit such a thing, she couldn't.

"Come on." He held out his arm. "Let's get you freshened up so we can eat. I don't know about you, but I'm starving."

After she made a quick stop in an elegantly appointed bathroom, she and Mike made their way to the room where a buffet had been set up. Several round tables occupied the space that seemed to be about the size of a small hotel ballroom. An open bar sat in one corner, with people lined up to get drinks.

"That smells great," Mike said, sniffing the air appreciatively. "Let's get in line for the buffet."

She'd never seen such an array of food choices. Igor had definitely taken everyone into consideration, because she had numerous vegetarian choices. So many, in fact, she had to take small bits of each to taste. Next to her, Mike loaded up his plate with a wide variety of food.

Like everything else about the party, the food choices were over-the-top, so luxuriously rich and decadent and delicious they might have been eating in a five-star restaurant. She wondered if he had these parties catered or if he actually employed a staff of cooks and chefs. She wanted to ask, but since that seemed like something Lania would already know, she didn't.

Sitting next to Mike, who made no secret of how much he was enjoying the meal, she couldn't stop thinking about the kiss. While it had come out of nowhere, she hadn't expected the sheer combustion of heat to erupt between them. She couldn't help but wonder if he'd been as strongly affected as she.

Pushing the thought away, she tried to focus on the conversation going on at their table. Typical small talk, like at any other cocktail party.

No one discussed business. Unlike in other, legal occupations, apparently talking about work at the table was taboo. Her father had always told her more deals were made over drinks and dinner and on the golf course than in corporate meetings.

Apparently, that wasn't the case here. But then again, other than the vague information Mike had given her about supplying weapons to terrorist organizations, she had no idea what most of these people truly did. Nor did she really want to know. She suspected the less involved she was, the better off she'd be.

Next to her, Mike appeared relaxed and at ease. He cleaned his plate, eating with gusto, and then offered to go get them both dessert. Laughing, Lania shook her head and told him she was too full to possibly eat another bite.

Mike took himself off, returning with two plates and a selection of desserts. She eyed the decadent chocolate cake and the rich, cherry-topped cheesecake and shook her head. "Seriously, I can't."

He grinned, so darn devastatingly sexy she nearly groaned out loud. "More for me," he replied cheerfully. Despite that, he carefully cut off bite-size pieces of each dessert, placed them on a separate plate and slid it over to her. "Just in case you want a taste."

How could she resist? Laughing, she shook her head and rolled her eyes. "Charm will get me every time," she said. When she realized the double entendre, she blushed but managed to keep her expression steady. Of course, it helped to bend her head and pretend to concentrate on sampling the food.

A band started playing in the backyard. People began drifting out there while staff started to clear out the food.

"Looks like there will be dancing," Mike said. "Just FYI, you and I are accomplished dance partners."

By which he was indirectly asking her if she knew how to dance. "Acting and dancing," she murmured. "Two of my favorite hobbies. I hope you can keep up with me."

The flash of amusement in his blue eyes made a hum start low in her belly. "Once again, you've managed to surprise me," he said, the warmth in his voice making her smile. "Come on." He held out his arm. "Let's go dance."

Heart racing, she nodded. Arm in arm, they walked outside into the cooling night air. The band started playing an old classic rock ballad, and Lania glided into Mike's arms. As they moved together, chest to chest, she realized this might be a different type of torture. Her breasts tingled, aching for his hands or his mouth on them. Her hips swayed, pressed against him, making her want more than a sensual dance.

And then she realized Mike had become just as aroused—she felt the strength of it pressing against her. A thrill shuddered through her, and she realized with a toss of her head that as Lania, she quite enjoyed having such power over him. It was actually a heady aphrodisiac.

The song ended, and the band began playing a faster-paced song. Lania went to move out of Mike's arms, but he tightened his grip and held her close. "Not yet," he managed. "Give me a sec."

This made her laugh. Not a Jennifer laugh, no. But a toss of the hair, head back, deep-throated Lania laugh.

Staring at her, Mike narrowed his eyes. "Finding this funny, are you?"

"Yes," she admitted, still chuckling. "I'd think it'd be easier for both of us if we stopped moving."

Both of us. The flash of awareness in Mike's eyes showed he'd caught her inadvertent revelation. One corner of his sensual mouth curled upward in the beginning of a smile. "Really?" he drawled. Then he bent his head just enough to let his mouth graze her ear. "I'm guessing this is also a bad idea."

Unable to suppress a shudder of desire, she stared up at him. "Is that a dare?" she asked with a Lania smirk. "Because I can promise you that if you push me, I'll really make you suffer."

As they locked eyes, she swore she could see the heat rising like steam from their skin.

Jennifer might not know much about being a seductress, but Lania sure did. And Mike knew it.

"Don't," he muttered. "If you do, this will end badly."

Somehow without her realizing it, they'd moved away from the dance area and stood near the edge of the garden, partially secluded from the others by a large, flowering bush.

Emboldened, Lania raised her head. "You know me, Mike. I never, ever pass up a challenge."

Eyes glittering, Mike bent his head to kiss her, apparently ready to match her dare for dare.

"There you are." Igor's voice.

When Lania went to push away from Mike, he used his arm to keep her in place, tucked into him. "Igor." Not a hint of friendliness in Mike's gruff voice. "What can I do for you?"

Clearly amused, Igor shook his head. "Quit monopolizing the most beautiful woman at my party."

Lania preened, smirking over her shoulder at the other man. "I appreciate the flattery, but I'm kind of busy right now."

Mike stiffened, making her wonder if she'd gone too far.

But Igor only laughed. "You always were a sassy one," he said. "Both of you come see me when you've got yourselves under control."

With that order, he spun around and strode away.

As soon as he'd left, Mike released her. "That did it," he muttered. "Damn, you're on fire tonight."

Not sure whether to take that as a compliment or not, Lania shrugged. "At least I'm never bored."

Mike shook his head. "That's the truth, for sure." He held out his hand. "Let's go find Igor and see what he needs. Most likely he has a job for us to do."

Which was a good thing, she thought, taking his hand. From what Mike had told her, the more information they had, the sooner they'd be able to take the operation down.

IGOR WASN'T USED to being kept waiting, so Mike hustled Lania along, though he made sure to keep his distinctive swagger while Lania did her normal catwalk stroll. Once inside, he saw that Igor waited for them by the bar, a glass of no doubt expensive scotch in his hand. He jerked his head in a nod and motioned for them to follow.

They left the party, traveling down a short hallway to a room marked by a highly polished double door. Igor opened it, turning slightly to allow Lania to precede him. She did, twisting herself to avoid physical contact. Mike followed right behind, doing his best not to scowl at Igor.

"Sit, sit," Igor ordered, motioning to a set of plush chairs in front of a large, gleaming mahogany desk.

They sat, Lania gracefully crossing her legs in a way that made her skirt ride up just enough to attract Igor's attention. Mike felt a flash of uncustomary possessiveness, which he ignored, since it wouldn't be helpful at all right now.

As usual, Igor wasted no time beating around the bush. "I need you both to help me broker a new deal. Arms smuggling pays," he said. "As long as we continue to mix legal arms deals with the illegal ones."

Mike nodded, as usual pretending he'd never heard Igor dispense this particular platitude before. What Igor did was common practice, and a way to get around legalities. Usually, there would be someone who was a straw purchaser, who was legally able to buy the bulk firearms as a front for someone else who was not. This operation so far had spent an inordinate amount of time dealing with Africa and Mexico, but as of yet they'd been unable to determine who worked on the inside of the gun manufacturing companies. As best as they could tell, via a complicated rerouting process, someone or a group of people inside the manufacturers tampered with legitimate orders, adding an extra hundred here, two hundred there. Once those surplus weapons had been produced, they were diverted to Igor and the purchase order changed back to what it had been originally.

For a good while, no one had noticed the discrepancy, likely due to a bookkeeper being in on the scam. Two years Mike and Lania had been undercover, working hard to gain Igor's trust. Now, it appeared they finally had it. Igor trusting them to broker a deal on his behalf was huge. Mike knew it was a test. If this deal went well, they'd be in for bigger and better things. Like the major deal Igor had in the works that everyone hoped would finally bring the operation to a close. They were so close Mike could taste it.

Right now, keeping Igor happy was their main goal. Attentive and taking care not to appear too eager, Mike listened as Igor rambled on about the people they were to meet. They apparently ran a legitimate shipping company, at least on the surface. They kept a small office in Denver, though it seemed likely they'd opened that to facilitate Igor's business. As far as legitimate, that remained to be seen. In Mike's experience, some of these were fronts, easily set up and, after doing their job, quickly dissolved. Ships would go off course, never arriving in their listed port and eventually showing up in a country run by militants or terrorists. By the time any regulatory agencies caught up, not only had the cargo of guns disappeared, but the ship and crew as well.

"We'll get it handled," Mike said once Igor had finished talking and shared the contact phone number.

"Good. Because if these people do a good job on this, hint around to them that I might be able to use them for something larger. Much larger."

Mike managed to give a cool nod, though inside he'd gone on high alert. This shipping company might become his in on that larger operation. If so, it could be the break he'd been waiting for.

"You are quiet, Lania," Igor commented, his tone softer, though his flinty gaze missed nothing. "Like you were yesterday. In fact, after seeing you two yesterday, I actually wondered if you'd still be attending."

Mike arranged his expression into one of calculated watchfulness. Igor frequently took delight in playing head games and it helped to stay a few steps ahead of him. "Why would you think that?" he countered. "I told you we'd be here."

Igor flashed a wolfish smile at Mike, though he locked his gaze on Lania. "I'm speaking to her," he said. "The most beautiful woman at my party."

Expression cold, she flashed him an indifferent smile. "I wouldn't have missed this for the world."

"Really? Because you truly didn't seem like yourself," Igor told her, blatantly undressing her with his gaze. "I assumed you were not feeling well, from the way you acted."

Inside, Mike froze. He kept his posture relaxed, slouching a little, and pasted an amused half smile on his face. Hopefully, Lania wouldn't stutter here.

He needn't have worried.

Narrowing her eyes, Lania lifted one ivory shoulder in a graceful shrug. "Shopping is like hunting to me," she purred, clearly choosing to ignore his leering. "When I shop, I focus on little else."

This made Igor chuckle. "I see," he replied. "Though I still can't picture you wearing those ugly hiking boots."

If this was Igor attempting to flirt, Mike almost felt sorry for the other man.

"Ugly?" Lania regarded Igor coolly. "Beauty is in the eye of the beholder. I wouldn't call them ugly. They're just different. And I'm always open to trying something new."

Though she no doubt hadn't meant to, the innuendo behind that last sentence brought a gleam to Igor's dark gaze. Beside him, Mike felt Lania tense as she noticed it, too.

"Come," she said, pushing gracefully to her feet. She gestured to Mike to come with her, tapping one foot impatiently until he rose. "I believe we're finished here, correct?"

Slowly, Igor nodded, his expression bemused.

"I thought so." She took Mike's arm, gazing adoringly up at him. "Darling, let's make one final round before we go. Good to see you again, Igor. And no worries, we'll carry off that job spectacularly."

With difficulty, Mike suppressed a grin. She'd just summarily dismissed not only the host of the party, but the most powerful man in the house.

Leading her away, Mike made sure not to glance back at Igor. This—the way Lania always made her self-involvement take precedence over anything else—was part of the reason Igor appeared drawn to her. Unlike the vast majority of other women in his orbit, Lania didn't fawn over him. Such a novelty could only pique Igor's interest.

Of course, she used Mike as a buffer. For her own protection.

"Too much?" Lania murmured, leaning into him as they stepped back into the crowded room.

"Exactly right," he replied, grinning his approval.

They made a quick circle of the room, stopping here and there to exchange banal pleasantries with people he knew would just as soon stab them in the back.

Finally, he judged it time to make their escape. "Are you ready?" he asked.

Exhaling, Lania nodded. "Definitely." She cut her eyes to one side of the room. "Don't look now, but Igor is watching us."

"Really?" Raising one brow, Mike pulled her in for a long, slow kiss. By the time they'd finished, his knees were weak and his body fully aroused. *Damn it.* Discreetly, he tried to adjust his pants.

And then he looked at Lania again. Really looked.

Like him, she was breathing heavily, and her color seemed a bit high. Her eyes were bright, and she smoothed down her silky blond hair with a graceful move of her hand. Despite her swollen mouth, she appeared unbothered and definitely not as turned on as him.

She smiled and even managed to remember to take a look behind them. "That did it," she said with some satisfaction. She held out her hand. "Come on, let's get out of here."

Hand in hand, they walked out the front door.

Once he'd exited the house, Micah could feel some of the tension leave his spine. As the evening had gone on, Lania had gotten progressively quieter. They'd danced, so close he'd been unable to conceal his arousal. In fact, the more they'd moved together, the worse it had gotten. If he hadn't known better, he could have thought she enjoyed tormenting him. Which made a sort of convoluted sense, because even though Lania was Mike's partner, this version of her clearly didn't possess the professional detachment her sister had. Of course, there had been zero sexual tension between him and Laney, either.

At the valet station, they waited while one of the teenagers brought around his Corvette. Jennifer leaned into him, and it felt like the most natural thing in the world to put his arm around her. His relationship with her sister had been completely different, more like siblings than anything else. An only child, he'd always wanted a brother or a sister, so he'd embraced the relationship gladly.

The sports car rumbled up, and the kid handed over the keys with some reluctance. Micah slipped him a twenty, which helped.

Once they were settled inside the car, Micah pulled away. He waited until they'd left the Cherry Creek area before allowing himself to speak to her as himself rather than his alter ego Mike.

"You did well," he offered. "You're a really good actress. Your Lania was great. There were a few small differences from the one Laney played, but not enough to matter."

"Do you miss her?" Jennifer asked, almost as if she'd known his earlier thoughts. "My sister? Since you worked together for so long, it must be difficult dealing with a poorly trained substitute like me."

"You're doing great," he reiterated. "And yes, I miss her. We were partners. But in all honesty, I'm really glad she got out. She promised she'll stick to less dangerous work now that she's about to become a mother."

"A mother." Jennifer sighed, letting her head loll back against the headrest. "How wonderful. Do you think she'll continue to work for the ATF?"

Damn, it felt good to get out of Mike's skin and let himself be Micah again. The longer this assignment went on, the less he liked remaining in his undercover persona.

"Or do you think she'll stay at home with her baby?" Jennifer continued.

"Who knows?" Giving in to the urge to touch her, he lightly squeezed her bare shoulder. Her soft skin felt like silk. The kiss they'd shared earlier wouldn't leave his thoughts, nor would the feel of her body pressed against his as they danced. "She did tell me that she and her husband were discussing the possibility of her becoming a stay-at-home mom."

Jennifer nodded. "I don't blame her. Quite honestly, those people were scary as heck."

Pulling into the parking garage, out of reflex he checked behind him to make sure they hadn't been followed. Seeing no other vehicles, he cruised up to the third level to find his spot. Though he tried to change things up every couple of days, he'd parked in this one all week. Realizing this, and since he knew there was danger in routine, he made a snap decision and turned a sharp right to go up to the next level.

A black sedan came around the corner, traveling way too fast for inside a garage. Micah slammed on the brakes, missing the other car by inches. He bit back a few choice curse words.

"Dang, that was close," Jennifer exclaimed.

"It was." He stared after the vehicle. Either unaware or uncaring, the driver continued on, disappearing fast. "Damn fool."

"I agree," she responded.

"You never swear, do you?"

"I'm a teacher," she replied. "It's kind of frowned upon to swear around children. So, I've trained myself not to do it at all. That way I don't have to worry about slipping up."

"More acting?"

"Maybe." She shrugged. "But honestly, I think it's just who I am."

He parked, once again doing a quick perimeter check. The out-of-control car hadn't returned, so perhaps his feeling of unease had been unwarranted. Still, he'd learned not to take chances.

"Come on," he told her. "We'll go inside at this level and then take the elevator up to our floor."

She got out, again with a flash of her long, perfect legs. He held out his hand and she took it, lacing her fingers through his. He tugged her along with him, wordlessly urging her to pick up the pace.

"Hey," she protested. "I'm in heels. No way I can run in these shoes."

Slowing, he apologized. "Maybe I'm overreacting. I just can't shake the feeling that there was something about that car…"

Eyes wide, she stared at him. "Oh. I didn't realize."

She bent over and slipped off her shoes. Once she had them in hand, she grinned. "Race you to the elevator!" And she took off running, laughing as she went.

Chapter Five

Back at the door to the condo, Jennifer took a look at the bottom of her feet and gasped. She hadn't thought and now her soles were black. Micah, having just unlocked the dead bolt, turned to look over his shoulder. "What's wrong?"

"I can't go in," she explained, lifting one foot to show him. "At least not yet. Would you mind bringing me a wet, soapy washcloth and a dry towel? There's no way I'm tracking this inside the house."

Though he appeared puzzled, he nodded. "Sure. But at least come in and stand in the foyer. It's not going to hurt the tile."

When she still hesitated, he took her arm. "Please."

Which meant he either didn't want the neighbors to see or he felt her standing out in the hall wasn't safe. Either way, he was right. She could always mop the ceramic tile afterward.

Stepping inside, she took a seat on the long marble-and-wood bench just inside the front door. A moment later, Micah returned, carrying a bowl of soapy water, a washcloth and a clean towel. He knelt down on the floor in front of her, motioning her away when she went to try and take the washcloth from him. "Let me," he said, the husky note to his voice sending a shiver down her spine.

Surprised, she nodded. Any other time, with any other man, Jennifer would have been the first person to deny that having her feet washed would be so intimate, so sensual. Yet when Micah took her left foot in his big hands and slowly lowered it into the warm water, she shivered. His touch was gentle, tender even, as he used the washcloth to clean the bottom of her foot, his blue eyes never leaving hers.

What on earth? A bolt of pure desire lanced through her, so strong that she closed her eyes. The sensations of the warm water, his hand on her skin… For a moment the world spun and she couldn't catch her breath.

Micah took his time, gently cleaning the one foot, dipping it in the water and finally drying it off and placing it on the floor. He did the same with her other foot while she melted into a puddle of desire. By the time he'd finished, she wasn't even sure she could stand. Or speak. Or keep from stripping off her clothes and throwing herself at him.

As if he had no idea what his touch had done to her, Micah flashed a smile before he pushed to his feet. Gathering up his supplies, he carried everything off. "I'll see you in a little bit," he called back as he went, sounding perfectly normal. "I want out of this suit."

A moment later she heard his bedroom door close. Stunned, her knees weak, she managed to struggle up. She took a moment to regain her equilibrium, trying to figure out what the heck was wrong with her. Her entire body throbbed. Throbbed! From something that

Micah had clearly not meant to be sexual. Which meant she was obviously a lost cause.

Shoes in hand, she made her way to her room, shutting her own door before sinking down on the edge of her bed.

What the heck was it about this man? Jennifer had been in her fair share of relationships in her twenty-nine years. Some had been completely lighthearted, just for fun, while others had felt more serious. But none of them, not one single man, including Caville, had been able to make her crave him with a simple touch of his hands or a direct glance from his blue eyes.

She couldn't help but wonder how her sister had managed. Had the same spark existed between Laney and Micah? Ignoring the spark of jealousy such speculation caused, she remembered Micah had said her twin had a husband she loved.

Fighting a sudden urge to call Caville, even though her so-called boyfriend had made it clear he wasn't actually going to miss her, she pushed herself up and walked into the amazing closet. She unzipped the red dress and hung it back on its hanger and pulled on a pair of comfy shorts and one of her own T-shirts. Sliding her feet into a pair of flip-flops, she went into her bathroom with the intention of scrubbing the makeup off her face.

At the sink, she stared. The woman in the mirror didn't even look like her. She'd never been one to use much makeup, but the framed photo of herself that Laney kept near the makeup vanity had let Jennifer know she needed to up her game—false eyelashes, bright lipstick, the works. She wasn't sure if all this made her look older or younger, but as she'd gotten ready for the party, she'd believed she saw a sophistication and elegance she'd never possessed before. Luckily, just before she'd met Micah, she'd had a manicure and pedicure, which was her one concession to vanity.

Time to go back to her regular self. In short work, she'd removed the false eyelashes and washed her face. Bare skinned, she looked like herself again. Even better, she *felt* like herself again. The fog of sexual arousal had dissipated. Thank goodness.

At least Micah hadn't noticed. Even with the spark between them, she'd be mortified if he learned how strongly he affected her. Bad enough that she was a complete rookie when it came to helping him in this undercover operation, but to have her melting into a puddle of desire every time he touched her... Well, that would be downright embarrassing.

She needed to do better. She *had* to. With resolve straightening her spine, she turned around and marched back to the kitchen for a glass of water, determined to get everything back on track. Though it was late, she needed some time to unwind before she'd be ready to fall asleep.

Micah had apparently had the same idea. She froze when she realized he was in the kitchen, his back to her, allowing her a moment to take in his broad shoulders and narrow waist. Her mouth went dry.

Turning, he smiled when he caught sight of her. "Here," he said, sliding a glass of ice water across the bar toward her. "I figured you might be thirsty, too. I was just about to turn on the TV and catch a late-night talk show or something. Would you like to join me?"

Perfectly normal. Clearly, she had issues. Fine. She'd deal with them, starting now.

"Sure." She could do this. Simply sit on the opposite end of the couch and prove to herself that she could regain her self-control around him. She had to. She would.

Certain, she took a seat on one end of the couch, absurdly grateful when he sat on the opposite end, nowhere near her. Despite the distance, she still felt overly aware of him.

Instead of turning on the television, he eyed her. "Tell me about your boyfriend. Caville, I think you said was his name?"

Her boyfriend. Oddly enough, the question helped her feel more grounded. "There's not a whole lot to tell," she replied, wondering why he wanted to know. "He's a teacher, though he teaches high school. He's divorced, with no children."

Micah nodded and took a sip of his water, his watchful gaze never leaving hers. "He really didn't mind you taking off for a couple of weeks with no notice?"

Lifting her head, she refused to allow herself to feel ashamed. "We don't have that kind of relationship."

Despite her best efforts, something must have shown in her voice. Micah's expression softened. "He's a damn fool," he said. "Believe me."

Though she wasn't entirely sure what he meant by that, something in his voice had turned her on again. Darned if she knew why everything about this man managed to arouse her, but she knew she needed to make it stop. Somehow, some way.

"What about you?" she asked, deliberately casual. "Do you have anyone special in your life?"

"I do not." He gave a wry smile. "For the last several years, I have considered myself married to my career. I didn't want to spend the time or the energy to keep up a relationship."

"Wow, that stinks," she said, meaning it. "I mean, to each his own, but that sounds kind of lonely." And then she blushed. "I'm sorry. I shouldn't have said that."

"It's okay, I'm used to it. Laney didn't like my life-style, either. She's always trying to set me up with her friends, even when I refuse." He grimaced. "She's very pigheaded, your sister. When she gets an idea in her head, she won't let it go."

Interesting. Curious, she nodded. "Have you known her very long?"

"Not really. Only a couple of years. We met when we got paired up for this undercover assignment."

"So you didn't know her before this assignment. Is this usual, being undercover that long?"

"Not really." He took a sip of his water. "Nobody expected it to take this long. In fact, at one point, they were thinking about pulling us."

Two years. It boggled her mind. "Did you and my sister ever date?" she asked, not sure she really wanted to know.

For some reason, this question made him laugh. "Me and Laney?" He shook his head. "She's like my kid sister. We're partners and friends, but nothing more. If such a crazy thought ever entered my head, which it didn't, her husband would have my head."

"Was Laney already married to Tanner when she became your partner?"

Expression still amused, he nodded. "She was. I

mean, she's gorgeous, but that kind of entanglement is a career killer."

A career killer. As if she needed any more reason to stay away from this man. However, she couldn't help but note that if Micah found Laney gorgeous, since they were identical twins, that might also go for her.

Nope. Not going to ask. Not even going to go there.

Forcing her mind back on track, Jennifer managed a smile. "Tell me more about my sister. You can't imagine what it's like to learn you have a twin. Being adopted, it's hard enough not knowing your birth parents or if you have aunts and uncles or cousins. But a sibling?"

Compassion darkened his blue eyes. "Laney was the same way when she learned about you. It came up in her background check, but she didn't know for years."

"Really? How'd she find out?"

"She was shot. Wait." He held up a hand. "She's fine now. It was a few years ago, before I even knew her. She told me the doctors thought she might need a kidney transplant. Because she has a rare blood type—"

"AB negative," she murmured. "The same as me."

"Right. Because of that, the ATF made the decision to tell her about you. Until then, she had no idea of your existence."

Her head spun. She couldn't imagine learning about her twin sister and being asked to donate a kidney at the same time. Of course, she would have done so, without hesitation. "But I'm guessing she pulled through, since I never got a phone call."

"She did. She's a tough one, that Laney."

"I'm glad." Jennifer eyed him. Even sitting quietly

on the opposite end of the sofa, he exuded masculine energy. Briefly, she realized how badly she wanted to crawl up on top of him and kiss him until they were both senseless.

This shocked her. She'd never been the take-charge type in romantic relationships. But then again, she'd never met a man who made her crave him the way she craved Micah.

A career killer, he'd said. She'd keep those words close and use them whenever she got too tempted by him.

Like now.

Desperately, she gathered up her wayward thoughts and ordered herself to calm down. Her sister. They'd been discussing Laney.

"Would you have given her a kidney?" Micah asked. "If it had come down to that?"

She didn't even hesitate. "Of course I would. Just like I'd like to think she'd do the same for me."

"She would," he told her. "She always thinks of others before she thinks of herself."

Jennifer nodded. He'd told her once that Laney hadn't contacted her because Laney hadn't wanted to disrupt Jennifer's life. While that still stung, she knew that would be one thing it would be best to ask her sister about in person.

"You'd like her," he said. "Everyone does. She has this way of putting people at ease."

"I have so many questions for her," she mused. "I can't wait to meet her in person."

"Hopefully soon," he responded, and then he picked up the remote and turned on the TV.

MICAH HAD NEVER washed a woman's feet before. He hadn't expected the entire thing to be so sensual, either. By the time he'd finished, he'd been so turned on he could barely walk.

Luckily, innocent that she was, Jennifer never suspected. He'd gathered up the supplies and managed to sound normal, he thought. He'd gone to his room to change and had ended up needing a quick, cold shower.

Damn, but she got to him. And she didn't even seem to understand how sexy she was. Which he had to admit might be part of her appeal.

A career killer, he'd told her, needing to remind himself as much as he'd needed to clue her in. Allowing himself to think with the wrong head could not only jeopardize the entire operation, but cost lives. He'd witnessed this firsthand when a fellow undercover agent had fallen for one of their targets. That had nearly cost not only the mission, but their lives.

He needed to get a grip. The cold shower and dressing in his oldest, most comfortable clothes brought him back to a more normal frame of mind.

In the kitchen, he got them both a glass of water. He'd known the instant she walked in, with that supercharged awareness of her that he'd been experiencing. He'd turned and managed to keep things friendly, ignoring the way he had to constantly stop his thoughts from veering off track.

He'd turned on the television and located a late-night talk show. She'd watched for twenty minutes before excusing herself to go to bed.

Once he heard her door close, he exhaled and

switched off the TV. Now maybe he could get out his laptop and work.

Micah functioned best when he was well prepared. He'd planned to get on the secured computer and re-search the people Igor wanted him to meet with. The more he knew about them, the greater advantage he'd have in the negotiations. This focus on preparation had been one of the reasons he'd been so successful with every job that Igor tasked him with.

Yet instead of burying himself in research, he'd taken one look at sweet, sexy Jennifer and abandoned his plan. She'd scrubbed all the glamorous makeup from her face, and her dewy skin glowed in the soft lamplight. She wore her hair long and straight, and the shapeless T-shirt she wore only served to accentuate her curves. She had no idea she was beautiful, which both astounded and aroused him.

And she had no idea how much danger he'd placed her in.

The thought sobered him, exactly as he'd known it would. Laney would kick his ass when she learned what he'd done. Hell, he'd be lucky if he wasn't fired when the higher-ups found out he'd roped a civilian into helping him.

He'd acted impulsively, he admitted, which wasn't like him at all. But he knew that if he hadn't been there when Igor had confronted her, Jennifer would have found herself in grave danger. If she'd brushed Igor off or, worse, tried to alert store security, Igor would have followed her home. Her life, not to mention the entire operation, would have been placed in jeopardy.

So he'd done the only thing he could. Now he'd have to live with the consequences.

He opened his computer and got to work researching the shipping company Igor wanted him to meet with. As he'd expected, the company was newly formed and owned by what was most likely a shell company out of the Bahamas. They operated out of two ports, one in Galveston, Texas, and the other in New Orleans. He could find absolutely nothing on the men whose names he'd been given as contacts, but with this knowledge, he felt confident that this would be one of those weapons shipments that were legal on paper when the ship left the port. After that, who knew where the ship and its cargo of weapons would end up.

His job—and Lania's—would be to negotiate the rates. The weapons had already been sold, and Micah would be working undercover to find out to whom.

Regrets, a little too late, would keep him up at night if he let them. He never should have involved sweet, innocent Jennifer in something like this. Not only was she inexperienced, but the wrong move could get them both killed. If his higher-ups found out, he'd likely not only be reprimanded, but possibly fired.

So much at stake here. He'd acted impulsively, and he had no choice now but to go with the flow and try to keep them both alive.

Looking up from his computer, he was surprised to realize that over an hour had passed. Time to get to bed. Tomorrow was another day.

The next morning, he woke up before sunrise, his body so hard that even moving was painful. Resigning himself to yet another cold shower, he trudged into the bathroom before deciding to turn the water to a comfortable warmth and take care of the issue himself. He knew he'd function a hell of a lot better once he took the edge off.

Later, clean and dry and more relaxed than he'd been in days, he headed into the kitchen for a much-needed cup of coffee. The sun had crept over the horizon, and the clean brightness of the early-morning light promised a hot summer day.

He made himself his coffee and carried it to the bar to drink. As usual, the first sip tasted like ambrosia. He checked his phone, a bit surprised to realize he already had received a text message.

When he realized it was from Samir and Ernie, the two shipping company reps with whom he'd requested a meeting, he frowned.

"Morning!" Jennifer chirped as she wandered into the kitchen. Barefoot, wearing an oversize T-shirt that kept slipping off her shoulder and with her long hair pulled back into a messy ponytail, she looked so damn sexy.

"I just got a text from the shipping company reps," he told her.

"You definitely don't sound happy about that." She pulled a mug from the cabinet, went to the coffee maker and began pouring her usual creamer and sugar in preparation for her morning cup of joe.

"I'm not. They want to meet for lunch," he said, slightly annoyed. "Which is wasting our time. This is the kind of short meeting that can be done in their office—in and out once the terms are agreed upon and the paperwork is signed."

Jennifer smiled at him over her ridiculously huge mug of coffee. "Maybe they're hungry." She noticed him eyeing her mug and held it up. "I brought it with me. It's my favorite."

Find the Joy was emblazoned on one side in hot pink. If anything, that phrase summed up the Jennifer he was getting to know. "I bet you're a good teacher," he said.

She narrowed her eyes. "Why do you say that?"

"Because you have a good attitude. I bet the kids love you."

His answer made her relax somewhat. "Sorry I got a bit defensive," she said, taking another sip of her coffee. "I *am* a good teacher. But Caville always tries to give me tips on how to be better, even when I don't need them or even agree with them. I guess I thought that's what you were going to do."

"Me?" He shook his head. "I wouldn't even begin to presume. I could never do what you do."

This clearly tickled her. "Don't say *never*," she chided. "A week ago, I would have said I could never do this." She waved her hand. "And now look at me."

They sat there grinning at each other like a pair of fools before he collected himself and told her they had to go.

THE BURGER JOINT where they were to meet Samir and Ernie was off I-25 in an area of North Denver called Jefferson Park. They could see the old amusement park Elitch Gardens from the parking lot, which contained only a few cars. The two men waited for them inside, texting that they were in a booth near the back.

The smells of frying grease and meat filled their

noses the instant they walked inside. Lania glanced at him but kept her expression cool and collected. Mike spotted the two men and headed over. He and Lania sat opposite the other two, which meant their backs were to the door, a position Mike preferred never to be in. This time, he clearly had no choice.

Introductions were performed. Samir had dark skin and a full head of hair, while Ernie was pale and bald. Both men openly ogled Lania. After she sat, at first she pretended not to notice. Then, when Samir mumbled something to her without lifting his gaze from her breasts, she snapped her fingers in front of him. "Look at me," she ordered. "My face. This is a business dealing, so you can at least do me the courtesy of acting professional."

Samir glanced at Ernie, then back at her, smirking. "But it's so much more fun to look at you. You're a beautiful woman."

"That's it." Lania pushed to her feet. "We're done. Come on, Mike. We'll just tell Igor that we can't work with these people."

Mike stood, too. While he knew full well that they'd do no such thing, since that would mean they'd blown this assignment, he also wanted to see how these men reacted. Respect in these circles had to be earned. Right now, Lania was demanding they respect her as a professional.

They made it halfway to the door before Ernie caught up with them. "Wait," he said from behind them. "Please."

Lania turned, her brows arched. "What?"

"Samir is a fool. We cannot afford to lose this contract. I apologize."

Inclining her head in such a quick nod that her earrings swung, she glanced back toward the table. "Accepted. But he'd better not act that way again."

Ernie glanced at Mike, who remained motionless. "He will not. Now, please, will you come back to the table?"

Relieved that she hadn't demanded that Samir apologize also, Mike took her arm. "We will," he said. "Come, my dear."

Once they'd gotten settled, Samir kept his face hidden behind the menu. Which was probably a good thing, Mike thought. Because if he so much as smirked at Lania, things would go south fast.

A waitress came to take their order. Everyone ordered a burger and fries except for Lania. Though there didn't appear to be any vegetarian options on the menu, she asked for a salad with a side of onion rings. The combination made Mike laugh.

"What?" she asked, smiling back. "Onion rings are my weakness."

After bringing a round of iced teas, the waitress disappeared, and Mike got down to business. He'd made a list of questions all about their shipping experience. While he knew, and they knew, all of it was bogus and most likely the company had been created specifically to get this shipment of weapons where it needed to go. If things went as planned, the ATF would show up in time to intercept it.

The food arrived, the meaty scent of the burgers making Lania wrinkle her nose. But she managed like a trouper, biting into a crispy onion ring with gusto. Samir eyed her, rapidly returning his attention to his food the second she looked up.

The burgers were good, juicy and perfectly cooked. While Lania picked at her salad and ate her onion rings, Mike polished his off quickly. Somehow, he resisted the urge to check his watch. He had the contract in his briefcase, along with the initial payment—a sealed envelope full of cash, no doubt. Since Igor had given it to him sealed, he hadn't dared to open it. One thing he could say about Igor—the man was thorough in his business dealings. He ran a large illegal operation but took great pains to make everything appear to be legit on the surface. This was one of the reasons he was so successful, though if the ATF had their way, that would all be about to change.

Finally, everyone finished their meal. The waitress brought the check, and Mike paid. Once the dishes had been cleared away, he placed his briefcase on the table and opened it. Withdrawing the manila folder containing the contract that Igor had prepared, he eyed the two men sitting across from him. "Gentlemen, are you ready to do business?"

Samir looked up, his expression stone-cold. "We were promised the woman," he said, enunciating each word. Next to him, Ernie slowly nodded his agreement.

Lania stiffened. She opened her mouth and then closed it.

Mike's blood ran cold. If they were telling the truth, the only reason Igor would do something like that would be as a test.

"I am not for sale," Lania said, her voice dripping

ice. "Not to you, not to anyone." The flash of fury in her brown eyes warned anyone to contradict her.

Neither Samir nor Ernie acknowledged her. They both kept their gazes locked on Mike. "If you want to close this deal, you'll honor your boss's promise," Samir said, a slight sneer on his face.

"No deal." Shoving the folder back into his briefcase, Mike pushed to his feet. Next to him, Lania did the same. "Let's go."

Backs straight, they marched out of the restaurant. Mike kept his right hand close to his holstered pistol, just in case Samir and Ernie got any crazy ideas.

Back inside the Corvette, Mike wasted no time starting the engine and backing out of the parking spot. He fought the urge to floor it, to let the powerful car race down I-25, weaving in and out of traffic, until he'd cleared his head. Damn, he wanted to, but there were two reasons he couldn't—one, attracting attention would be bad for his cover, and two, he didn't want to scare the hell out of Lania.

"That ticks me off," she finally said, the tight set of her jaw matching her rigid shoulders. "I'm thinking about calling Igor and hashing this out."

"I'm not sure that's a good idea," he began, but then he realized such a reaction was most likely what Igor had hoped for. Why else would he have said such a thing?

His phone rang. Glancing at it, he handed it to Lania. "It's Igor," he told her.

"Thank you." Snatching it out of his hand, she took a deep breath, and then she pressed the icon to decline the call. "He can leave a voice mail," she said and handed the phone back to him. "I need to cool off before I speak to him."

"I agree." He took the exit that would bring them to the condo. "I still haven't figured out what he's trying to pull."

"I think he's trying to get my attention," she said. "It's the sort of thing my students would do. Act out to make sure they get noticed. Igor seems to find it personally insulting that I don't fawn all over him."

"You have a point." Turning into the covered parking garage, he pulled into one of his usual chosen spots and parked. When Lania went to open her door, he motioned at her to wait.

"What's wrong?" she asked, her eyes wide.

"Nothing, yet." Every instinct he possessed was screaming a warning. "However, I think we need to drive around for a bit longer."

Shifting into Reverse, he backed out, executed a quick turn and headed for the exit. Just as he rounded the first corner, gunshots rang out, shattering his back window.

Chapter Six

Jennifer screamed, jolted out of her Lania persona by sheer terror.

"Get down," Micah ordered, maneuvering the Corvette skillfully. "I can't believe they shot up this damn car."

She bent over in her seat, frozen in shock.

A few seconds later, they raced out of the parking garage, Micah barely slowing to check for traffic before taking the street.

Slowly, Jennifer sat back up and refastened her seat belt with shaking hands. *Not hit*, she told herself. Neither she nor Micah had been hit, thank goodness, though the back windshield was a mess. She took several deep breaths, trying to regain her equilibrium. Her heart still pounding in her chest. This was real. Someone had actually shot at them, using a real gun with actual bullets. While Micah had mentioned this could be dangerous, it had never really registered until now.

Despite how badly she wanted to meet her sister, she might have gotten in over her head.

Micah glanced at her. Something in his gaze—sympathy, perhaps—told her he had a pretty good idea of her thoughts. "Are you all right?" he asked.

Not sure how to answer, she settled on a quick nod. She figured they both knew she wasn't telling the entire truth. Maybe she wasn't okay yet, but she would be. She just needed to catch her breath.

"No injuries?"

She had to double-check to make sure. Despite glass shards everywhere, she didn't see any blood. "No," she finally answered.

"Good."

"What was that?" Jennifer asked, relieved to note that her voice only sounded a little shaky. "More importantly, *who* was that?"

"I don't know." Grim faced, Micah concentrated on his driving. "It might have been Samir and Ernie's buddies. Or an enemy of Igor. It could even have been someone in Igor's organization who's pissed that we got that last job."

"The one that didn't work out."

Micah's cell rang again. This time, he answered it. He didn't speak much at first, only listened. "Thanks," he finally said. "But too late. Someone was waiting for us in our building's parking garage. They shot up my car. My damn Corvette!"

Again, he went silent while the other person spoke. "Thanks, Igor. No, neither of us was hit. If you have any idea who this might have been, I'd like to know so I can settle with them."

He listened again, pulling into a convenience store parking lot. "Yeah, I know it fell through. It wasn't our fault. Mind telling me what was the deal with Samir and Ernie? They said you promised them Lania. Obviously, that didn't sit well with me. She's my woman."

Back in character, Lania snorted, hopefully loud enough for Igor to hear through the phone.

"I see." Micah grimaced. "Send me the info and I'll get everything handled."

After ending the call, he shoved the phone back into his pocket. "That first call that we didn't take was him. Igor was trying to warn us. He'd already heard from Samir and Ernie. They were furious about losing the contract, among other things."

"What about Igor? Is he angry with us?"

"He didn't sound like it," Micah replied. "And believe me, if he was upset, he'd let me know. Anyway, Igor thinks they might have sent someone to help them get a little revenge."

Slowly, she nodded. "That is logical." For a television crime drama or a suspense novel. Sometimes she could hardly believe that this kind of thing was actually her real life right now, even if only temporarily. "But why did Igor tell those two men that they could have me? Why would he treat me like some hooker to be pimped out?"

Micah exhaled. "That's the problem. He said he didn't. But someone must have. Those two sure as hell believed what they were saying. Igor said he'd be looking into it."

"What about your car?" Turning, she eyed the shattered back windshield. "I feel like I have glass all over me."

"You probably do," he admitted. "We both are lucky we weren't hurt. I'll skip the insurance company and get the back windshield replaced myself." He gave a rueful smile. "Hopefully they didn't hit the car. If so, that will require more extensive bodywork."

"Now what do we do?" she asked. "Clearly, they know where we live. Are we going to be dodging bullets whenever we go home from now on?"

"No." He turned to face her. "I need to go on the offensive and hunt down whoever did this. That's the only way I'm going to stop it."

Fascinated and more than a little afraid, she stared at him. "But…"

"I don't have a choice, Lania," he said, his expression going dark. "Unless Igor takes care of it for me."

Since he'd called her Lania, she understood he was speaking as Mike. "I understand," she told him, even though she actually didn't. "In the meantime, are we able to go home?"

"Of course." He pulled out of the parking lot. "Not only is our unit equipped with an alarm, but we have quite a cache of weapons there. Now aren't you glad you learned how to handle a gun?"

His half smile told her he might be kidding. Sort of. Again, she felt like a fish out of water. For an instant she longed to be back in her town house with her cat and her plants, living a life of boring normalcy.

But only for an instant. Because while she had her job and her parents, she'd also been dating a man without realizing the relationship was going nowhere. She hadn't known anything about her past, nothing at all, and now she'd learned she had a twin sister. Even better, she'd soon be meeting her and hopefully becoming part of each other's families.

This thing she was doing, while dangerous, was also the most exciting adventure she'd ever been on. Definitely far outside her comfort zone. She felt…different. More alive. Sexier. Of course, she'd be lying if she said that didn't have anything to do with the rugged man who was her partner.

"Are you going to be all right alone for a few hours?" Mike asked her as he swung the car around to the front of the building instead of the parking garage.

"Alone?" Despite her best intentions, she balked at that. "Why can't I just go with you?"

"Not this time." His hard voice told her there wasn't any room for discussion. "I don't want you involved." He pulled into a smaller lot that charged for parking by the hour. "Come on, I'll walk you up and make sure everything is secure."

Heart in her throat, she got out of the car. She didn't want him to go. For one thing, it sounded incredibly dangerous, and for another, whatever he intended to do had to be outside the law.

Side by side, they entered the building and rode the elevator up to the ninth floor. When they arrived, neither spoke until they reached their unit.

"Just a second," Micah said, motioning for her to wait while he unlocked the door. The chimes and the alarm system's robotic voice asking them to disarm was reassuring. It meant no one had been inside since they'd set the alarm.

Once inside, Micah began to prowl around the room. "Stay away from the window," he told her, closing the blinds. "I know we're pretty high up, but I don't want you to take any chances."

"I don't like this," she said.

"I'll fix it," he promised. "No one is going to make us feel unsafe in our own home."

"That's not what I meant." Hesitating, aware she didn't have the right to offer advice, she felt she had to try anyway. "I don't think you should become a murderer."

"Murderer? Who said anything about murder?"

Now confused, she eyed him. "You did. You said you were going to hunt down whoever shot at us."

"I'm not going to kill him. I promise. Just put the fear of death into him, so he never even thinks of trying something like this again."

Once more, she had the uncomfortable feeling she'd gotten in over her head. "Do you really feel like that's something you have to do?"

"It's something *Mike* has to do," he said, his voice as fierce as his expression. "Believe me. It's difficult gaining these people's respect. Letting something like this slide would definitely cause my standing to go way down. I don't have a choice."

She nodded, trying not to let her worries show on her face.

But something must have, because he crossed the distance between them and took her chin in his big hand. Then, when she opened her mouth to ask him how long he'd be gone, he kissed her.

He must have meant it to be a quick, hard press of his lips to hers, for reassurance, maybe. But the instant their mouths connected, everything changed. A slow burn ignited low in her belly as she kissed him back.

She had no idea where this thing between them might be going, but she'd joyfully go along for the ride.

Which, again, wasn't like her. She'd always been a planner, a list maker and a scheduler. She didn't do spontaneous, at all. Since she'd met Micah a mere three days ago, she'd done a complete about-face. In fact, she didn't really recognize the person she'd abruptly become. True, most of it was playacting, playing a role, but it had been Jennifer herself who'd agreed to do this impetuous thing. And now she was living in a luxury condo with the sexiest man she'd ever met while both of them pretended to be criminals. If she'd been a writer, she'd definitely write this in a book. She could only imagine what would happen when she went back to work teaching after the summer was over and someone asked her if she'd done anything interesting over the break. Because she'd have one heck of a story to tell, even if it seemed so over-the-top that most people would never believe her.

AROUSED AGAIN, MICAH managed to break the kiss off. He didn't want to, especially with Jennifer staring at him with her big eyes, her lush mouth slightly swollen. What he really wanted to do had nothing to do with his job and everything to do with the way he felt around her.

"We've really got to stop doing that," he said, more to himself than to her.

She laughed. The light, feminine sound tied his insides up in even more knots.

"*We've?*" she asked. "I think you're the one who kissed me."

Uncomfortably aware that she was right, he nodded. "My apologies. It won't—"

"Stop." She held up her hand, interrupting him. "Don't make promises you might not be able to keep."

This shocked him, as it wasn't like the Jennifer he'd begun to get to know. But then, as he eyed her, he realized she might be right. "Maybe not," he answered quietly. "But I think I ought to at least try. I'm attracted to you, Jennifer, as you can no doubt tell. But what we're doing is dangerous. I can't afford to get distracted. We can't afford to make mistakes."

Her smile faded at his words, making him feel like he'd just crushed a butterfly under his shoe. He actually almost reached for her to offer comfort but managed to stop himself in time.

"I'm going to go now," he said. "Stay inside and keep the alarm activated. I'll be back as soon as I can."

"Okay." She nodded, her expression more vulnerable than he'd ever seen it. "Stay safe."

"You, too." Turning away, he left before he did anything else he would regret. Like grab her and kiss her and promise to always protect her.

Despite the mess of broken glass, the Corvette fired right up with the rumbling roar he'd been getting attached to. After he took care of his first problem, he'd see about getting that rear windshield repaired. *Focus on the task at hand*, he reminded himself. Not on the beautiful and frightened woman he should have been shielding from all this.

Driving to North Denver, he knew exactly where to look for Samir and Ernie. Igor had initially given him their address before they'd decided they wanted to meet for lunch. He drove to a neighborhood of run-down warehouses near the burger place, trying to formulate a plan. They might be expecting him, all too aware that what they'd done could not go unpunished.

His phone rang. Checking it, he saw Igor was calling. Almost as if he knew exactly where Mike was. Before he answered, he made a mental note to have the Corvette swept for a tracking device.

"It's been taken care of," Igor said after Mike answered. "Samir and Ernie are here with me, and they have come to greatly regret what they did."

"I just pulled up to their warehouse," Mike replied. "I figured I'd take care of this personally."

"You work for me. By attacking you, they have personally insulted me," Igor declared, his voice steel. "You know as well as I do that this sort of thing cannot be allowed."

Aware he couldn't show his relief, Mike swallowed hard and forced himself to thank Igor. No doubt whatever punishment Igor had come up with was far, far worse than anything Mike would have conceived.

Which meant his hands would remain clean.

"What about the shipment?" Mike asked.

"I'm making other arrangements for that," Igor replied. "I'll let you know if I need you to do anything."

Not good. Damn it. Mike wanted to pound the steering wheel. Instead, he thanked Igor again and ended the call. What the hell had just happened? He had no idea. But his intuition told him it wasn't very good.

He started the car and used his phone to find the nearest place that repaired windshields. Though he didn't have an appointment, he hoped that once they took a look at his car, they'd find a way to work him in. He definitely wouldn't be working with the insurance company, as he couldn't afford to draw attention to himself.

When he pulled up at the windshield place, both of the twentysomething workers came out to look at his Corvette. "Who'd you tick off?" one asked. The other whistled, shaking his head as he inspected the damage.

"Do you have any technicians here who could fix this?" Micah asked.

"We're kind of backed up. We normally ask that you set up an appointment in advance."

Since he'd been expecting this, Micah reached into his pocket and pulled out a wad of bills. "I'll pay an extra hundred dollars if you can get this taken care of right away," he said.

The two kids glanced at each other. "Give us a minute," the first one said. "Wait here."

They walked inside while Micah parked himself on the hood of his car and waited. A few minutes later, the first one returned. "Great news," he said, smiling broadly. "Our technician can squeeze you in."

Micah went inside to wait while they took his car back. He'd been given a quote, pleased to realize they'd also vacuum out all the glass shards from the inside of the car.

When they brought the 'Vette out, looking as good as new, he paid, refusing to wince at the price. He also slipped the extra hundred-dollar bill to the kid, thanking him.

As he got into his car, he started to call Jennifer and then decided he'd simply surprise her. Feeling pretty good about how the rest of the afternoon had gone, he stopped off at a farmers market and picked up a bouquet of flowers. Then, whistling to himself, he drove to the condo.

Entering the parking garage, he caught himself tensing up, even though this time his instincts weren't screaming any silent warnings. Once he'd pulled into his slot, he exited the car and headed for the elevator. After an uneventful ride to the ninth floor, he walked down the hallway toward his unit.

Still hanging on to the brightly colored flowers, he managed to get his key into the lock and pushed the door open. The room seemed quiet—too quiet. About to call for Jennifer, he moved into the living area.

And then he saw her, sound asleep on the couch. His heart stuttered in his chest.

He stood and looked at her for longer than he should have. Even in sleep, she was lovely. He didn't understand how he could react so differently to her and her sister—if he put them side by side, most people wouldn't be able to tell a difference. But he knew he could. The differences were subtle, but they were there. Jennifer was softer, more innocent. Laney had always had a quick wit, but she had a sharp edge that hinted at past trauma. When he'd asked her about it once, she'd shut him down quickly, letting him know she didn't want to discuss it.

With Laney, Micah felt like a big brother. They'd made a great team, and he considered them to be actual friends as well as coworkers. He knew even if Laney left the ATF, the two of them would stay in touch.

Her sister, on the other hand…

He hadn't known Jennifer very long. He didn't know what made her tick, nor did he think they'd be working this operation too much longer, so he likely wouldn't have time to learn.

Yet he couldn't stop thinking about her. Every time they were in any sort of close proximity, he had to fight the urge to touch her. If he was honest, he had to admit that he wanted to be her lover.

Damn. Turning, he knew he'd best shut down that line of thought. Again. Kissing her earlier had been a mistake and one he shouldn't repeat again.

Leaving her asleep on the sofa, he made his way quietly to his room. He closed the door behind him and sat down on the edge of the bed. The entire deal with Samir and Ernie had gone south, so the big shipment either would be going off without him knowing about it—which could mean his cover had been blown—or Igor was testing him.

Without thinking too much about it, he grabbed his phone and called Laney. She'd been working this case as long as he had, and right now, he needed to get her perspective.

She picked up on the second ring. "Hey there, stranger," she drawled. "How's it going?"

"You sound damn good for someone on complete bed rest," he countered back, releasing some of the tension inside him.

This made her laugh. "Tanner is spoiling the hell out of me. But I want to hear an update from you. What's new on the case?"

He felt a flash of guilt, which he shoved aside. He couldn't tell her about her twin sister taking her place.

He knew Laney well, and not only would she be furious, but she'd likely inform the upper brass and have all hell rain down on him. Which would definitely jeopardize the operation.

So no, he wouldn't be relaying that bit of information. Instead, he told her an edited version of what had happened with Samir and Ernie.

"They got pissed off about what?" she asked. "That makes no sense."

"Apparently they believed Igor had offered you to them," he said. "He claims he never said that. They said he did. And then when I got home, they shot out the back windshield in the 'Vette. It could have been worse."

"Yeah, they could have gotten you right in your big head," she replied, her tone both stern and amused. "That still makes zero sense."

"I agree. And then when I went to find them to settle up the score, Igor called me and let me know he'd already taken care of it. He also said he was making other arrangements for the shipment but didn't elaborate. Just said he'd let me know if he needed me for anything."

Laney swore. "That's bad. Can you think of anything that might have changed?"

Oh, he could, he definitely could. Unfortunately, he'd have to keep that bit of information to himself. "Other than you? Not really," he replied, glad he didn't have to lie outright to his former partner.

"That must be why," she agreed. "Everything is off balance without me there."

She had that right, he thought. In ways he would never in a million years reveal to her.

They talked a little bit longer about her health, Tanner and the baby-to-be.

"Micah?" Jennifer knocked on his closed bedroom door. "Are you back?"

"Yes," he called out. "I'm back. I'll be out in a second."

"Okay," she replied.

Meanwhile, Laney chuckled. "You have a woman there? My, my. Did Igor set that up?"

"No." Again, he stuck close to the truth. "This is all on me. Listen, I'm going to let you go. We'll talk again soon."

"Yes, we will." The humor remained in her voice. "And Micah, you deserve to have a little fun. Just remember what's important, okay? The operation comes first."

"Agreed," he replied and ended the call.

When he went back out into the living room, Jennifer was sitting on the couch, her gaze still a bit sleepy and unfocused from her nap. She'd used her fingers to comb through her long, blond hair, though it had a tousled appearance that made him think of how she'd look after making love.

He sat down and told her everything that had happened after he'd left, ending with getting his back windshield replaced.

After listening, she nodded. "Is the fact that Igor wanted to handle it a good thing or bad?"

"I don't know." Hesitating, he decided to tell her the truth. "Actually, it's bad. Since he told me that he'd let me know if he needed me, it feels like I'm being cut out of the next deal."

She considered. "Can't you talk to him about that? Like call him and ask?"

"One doesn't actually question Igor's decisions. It's more like what he says goes." He thought for a moment. "Though you could call him. He has a soft spot for you."

Watching him, she shuddered. "Soft spot? Then why would he tell those two men they could have me?"

"He said he didn't. They seemed to honestly believe he did."

The expression that crossed her face seemed a combination of fear and distaste. "I'd rather not have any private interaction with Igor. It's difficult enough learning how to pretend to be Lania. I don't want to take a chance on making too big a misstep."

She had a point. "Well, until he decides to contact us, we're out of the loop," he said. "So how about we do something fun tonight? Maybe go out to dinner and for drinks?"

Cross-legged on the sofa, she tilted her head. "Why?"

Why indeed. Her response shouldn't have stung, but it did. "Because you're working really hard to help me out. Think of it as a bit of a repayment. Between friends," he clarified, just to make sure she didn't get the wrong idea.

"Friends," she echoed. "I like that. Sure, I'll go. As long as we can be ourselves and not Lania and Mike."

"Agreed." He suddenly felt lighthearted. "I know a great Thai restaurant that has an extensive vegetarian menu."

This made her beam. "Perfect. Can we wear normal clothes? I really don't want to wear any of that fancy stuff unless I have to."

"Fancy stuff." He grinned. "You do realize that most women would kill to have access to those high-end fashions?"

"I'm not most women."

He stared. Damn, she was beautiful when she was serious. "I'm glad," he finally replied. "And yes, wear your regular clothes." He didn't tell her how much he'd miss seeing her in one of those sexy-as-hell outfits. That would kind of negate the idea that they were going out as friends.

Still, he found himself actually looking forward to taking a break from Mike and Lania. These days, it wasn't something he got to do often.

Micah spent the next several hours working on his laptop, reading the latest intel about Igor's operation on a highly secured connection. He made sure not to download anything. Instead, he read the reports in an internal cloud group that had built-in safeguards. As soon as he closed out each session, everything he'd viewed automatically deleted.

Jennifer took her e-reader and went out to sit on the patio and enjoy the cloudy day. Unable to keep from glancing over at her, Micah wondered why this all felt so comfortable and domesticated. It shouldn't. He'd never felt this way when he and Laney had been stuck in the condo. Though when he thought about it, that had been a rare occurrence. Laney preferred to spend her free time shopping.

Since the sun set late in the summer, it was still daylight when they left the condo. Though he tried not to be too obvious, Micah did a thorough scan of the parking garage as they walked to his car.

He eyed her Mercedes. He couldn't remember the last time it had been driven. It had to have been at least a week—sometime before Laney went on medical leave. "Maybe we should take that," he said, pointing toward the sedan.

Jennifer made a face. "That's boring. I much prefer your car."

This made him laugh. "Me, too," he admitted. "We'll take the Benz another time."

"Sounds good."

He laughed again and unlocked the doors.

"Wow," Jennifer said as she got into the Corvette. "This is amazing. You couldn't even tell it was covered in glass."

They arrived at the Thai restaurant shortly after seven. Though the place was packed, Micah had called ahead and made reservations. They were seated almost immediately.

Once they had their menus, Jennifer made sounds of delight as she perused all the vegetarian choices.

They had a quiet meal, and Micah felt himself relaxing for what felt like the first time in months. Jennifer seemed to be enjoying herself, too. The food was fresh and delicious, and she exclaimed over her meal, eating every bite.

He held the door open for her as they left. As they'd walked through the restaurant to go, he couldn't help but notice how every other man in the place watched her pass. The same thing had happened with Laney, but unlike her sister, Jennifer appeared to be completely unaware of her appeal.

Outside, the night air felt refreshing. "Where do you

want to go next?" he asked as they walked toward his car. "We can go to LoDo if you want." LoDo was short for Lower Downtown, an area of Denver packed with restaurants, clubs, galleries and shops.

"I'd like that," she replied, smiling up at him. "I've never been."

"Mike Fisher," a deep voice said from behind them, using Micah's undercover name. Micah spun around, his hand going to his holster. Two men stood behind them, both wearing long black coats. One brandished a large pistol, keeping it mostly concealed. "And Lania Trevoy. Igor requests you come with us."

Igor. Micah resisted the urge to curse out loud. Jennifer reached for his hand, squeezing it tightly. Deep breath. He was Mike now.

"We'll follow you," he said, gesturing toward his 'Vette. "Just lead the way."

Neither of the men moved. "No. Igor wishes you to come with us. Now."

A black panel van pulled up, and one of the men opened the back door. "Inside."

Mike didn't like this. At all. But one did not ignore an order from Igor. Ever. Holding fast to Lania's hand, Mike nodded. "Come on, Lania. We'll get those drinks later."

With her brave face on, she flipped her hair over her shoulder and allowed him to help her up into the back of the van. Surprisingly, there were several large wooden crates there, which could act as impromptu chairs. Glad they wore jeans, he helped Lania get settled. One of the men climbed up front with the driver, and the other man got in back with them.

With dusk fast approaching and the lack of windows in the back, Mike found it difficult to get a read on their captors. On the one hand, no one had bothered to disarm him or Lania. On the other, what the hell was Igor up to? He didn't treat his loyal subordinates this way. Had Mike's cover been blown? If so, he and Lania were in awful danger. But then again, if that were the case, these thugs would have made sure neither of them was armed.

Finally, they pulled up to what looked to be a warehouse loading dock. The van's back doors opened, and Mike and Lania were ordered out and hustled inside the warehouse.

Blinking in the much brighter light, Mike looked around. He still didn't understand what was going on, but as long as he still had his weapon, he stood a fighting chance if things went south. That was, as long as he could keep Lania safe. While she might have brought her own pistol, he doubted she'd be able to use it in a pinch.

Chapter Seven

Lania might be new to all this, but even she could tell that this situation was not good. Following Mike's lead, she made an effort to appear relaxed and confident.

"You," one of the men said, pointing at Lania. "Igor wants to see you first. Alone."

Next to her, she felt Mike stiffen. "It's all good, darling," she drawled, playing her role to the hilt. "I'll be right back, and maybe we can pick up our evening before we were so rudely interrupted."

Mike shot her a warning look, but she kept her head high and strode confidently with her two escorts. She did have her pistol in her purse, but she honestly doubted she could use it, even to save her own life. Shooting at a person was very different than shooting at a paper target, and she'd only even done that one time.

Igor waited in a small office, surrounded by old metal file cabinets and a matching desk covered in papers and file folders. Not at all what she would have expected from a wealthy criminal. Maybe that was the point.

"There you are, my dear," he said, holding out his arms as if he expected her to walk over and hug him.

Instead, she kept her distance. She took his hands and air-kissed both sides of his face, European-style. "Why all the theatrics?" she asked, releasing him and moving away. "Mike and I were having a quiet evening out when your men practically kidnapped us."

He was already frowning; his eyes narrowed, and she thought she might have gone too far. But then he leaned back in his chair and laughed, an honestly amused guffaw. "You know me, Lania. I'm not above putting on a show when I need to."

Nodding, she eyed him. "A show for whom?"

He parked himself on one corner of the desk. "Remember Samir and Ernie?"

"Yes." She made a face.

"I need their ship. But I no longer want to work with either of them. I set up a meeting with their boss."

Her heart began to pound. This might just be the break Mike had been hoping for. Except there must be something more, some reason why Igor had wanted to talk to her alone.

"Please tell me you're not offering me as some kind of added incentive," she drawled. "Once was bad enough. Doing that again that would be going a bit too far, even for you."

Just like that, his expression closed down. Gaze hard, he crossed his arms and glared at her. "You work for me."

"But not as a prostitute." Despite her inner terror and pounding heart, she lifted her chin and met his gaze directly. "Surely you have other women for such tasks. I am far too valuable and powerful to be used in such a way."

His face cleared. A ghost of a smile twitched at the corner of his mouth. "That you are, my dear. And gutsy, too."

Not sure how to respond, she settled for dipping her chin in a curt nod.

"Samir and Ernie work for a woman," he continued. "I'm sure you'll be meeting her soon."

A woman? Lania considered. "I didn't see that one coming," she admitted.

"Yes. She heads up several business operations, from drugs to human trafficking. In her own sphere, she is almost as powerful as me."

Now *this* was interesting. She couldn't wait to tell Mike about this.

Igor watched her, his intent gaze making her uncomfortable. "Why are you telling me all this?" she finally asked.

"Because I have made no secret of my interest in you," he answered. "There are many women who would do much to have a spot close to me." He rolled back his chair, patting one plump leg. "Come, sit here and I'll show you what I mean."

Nausea clawed at her stomach. Wildly, she tried to figure out how to react. Should she pretend not to understand? Act flattered but claim to be exclusive to Mike?

Her hesitation must have been answer enough.

"I see," Igor muttered, his expression thunderous. "For your information, beautiful Lania, women chase me. I do not run after them." He raked his gaze over her, his upper lip curling. "Perhaps you don't understand what I am offering, so let me spell it out for you. I offer you a partnership, like you have now with Mike. Only you would be my partner instead of his."

She swallowed, aware she was treading on dangerous ground.

Apparently taking her silence to mean she was considering, Igor continued, "I can't stress to you enough how rare this is. You should be flattered. As you know, I'm the most powerful man in the Rocky Mountain region and one of the wealthiest. Your power and your wealth would only increase with our alliance. I know how valuable both are to you."

She sucked in her breath, trying to process. Then she said the only thing she could think of. "But what about Mike?"

"What about him?" Igor shrugged. "I know about your other dalliances. It seems clear that he means nothing to you."

Other dalliances. He must mean her sister with Tanner. "I wouldn't say *nothing*," she protested weakly. "Mike and I have been together a long time. We've worked hard to get where we are."

Snorting, Igor made a dismissive hand motion. "He is nothing, a minor player. You deserve better."

Mouth dry, she managed to grimace. "I don't know," she began.

"I will not make this offer again," he said. "Do not take too long to decide. I might lose interest, and then where would you be? Especially if something bad were to happen to your Mike. It might just happen to you, too."

A threat. An honest-to-heaven threat. She suppressed a flash of anger, underscored with fear. Did this man really think threatening her would persuade her? What kind of win would that be for anyone? Neither person could ever fully trust the other.

"I understand," she said softly, hoping this noncommittal response would be enough.

Evidently, it was. Igor nodded and then gestured at the man standing guard by the office door. "Go get Mike for me."

The man immediately spun around and left. Igor continued to stare at her, no doubt as an intimidation tactic. "You are so beautiful," he crooned, the words turning his gaze into a leer.

Refusing to let him see how much he'd rattled her, Lania pretended to study her nails, trying to calm herself. At least she hadn't blown it. Still, what on earth had *that* been about? Another test? Pushing her to see how far she'd go? In her full-on character assessment of Lania, she suspected if Lania was a real person, she might have allowed Igor to seduce her, just for the heck of it. Maybe even agreed to his offer of partnership, betraying Mike for the lure of more power and money.

But then again, Lania would understand that for Igor, all the thrill was in the chase. If she allowed herself to be caught, in his mind she'd be just like all the others. He'd soon become bored with her and find someone else to replace her.

Either way, there were only so many things she'd do to play a role. Sleeping with Igor wasn't one of them.

A moment later, Mike entered the room, his stride confident but his expression guarded. He took great pains not to look at her, so she kept her gaze trained on Igor, too.

"Sit," Igor ordered, gesturing to both Mike and Lania. "Both of you."

Lania sat. A moment later, Mike did the same. Lania resisted the urge to reach for his hand, sensing right now wasn't the time.

"Why the theatrics?" Mike asked. "All you had to do was call and we would have been here instantly."

Igor's slow smile sent a chill down her spine. "That wouldn't have been any fun. Since you caused me a slight delay, I decided to amuse myself. Plus, there was someone I needed to send a message to."

Mike's jaw tightened, but he didn't comment.

"I have renegotiated the shipping contract," Igor announced, letting his gaze sweep over first Mike, then Lania. "Instead of dealing with him, I'm now working with his boss. Once she and I finish our negotiations, I'm sure it will go off without a hitch. I believe we will be ready to go within a week."

Mike nodded. "Since you said *she*, I assume this time you did not offer Lania as a bonus incentive?"

Sitting up straighter, Lania watched Igor, half dreading his reaction. But once again, he surprised her by laughing, though this time the sound had a mean edge to it.

"I did not," he said, locking his gaze on Lania. "And I will never do so again. Lania and I have an agreement."

An agreement? Just because she'd said she'd have to think about his offer? Was he so egotistical that he believed it was already a done deal?

And he'd said he'd never do so *again*. Did that mean he was actually admitting to having done so the first time? No matter what, Lania knew this was something she didn't need to press him on. She'd already taken enough risks for one day.

Mike seemed to have similar thoughts. "What matters is that we move forward."

"True, so true." Igor reached over to a pile of paperwork on his desk. He handed one sheet of paper to Mike and another to Lania, which surprised her.

"These are the details of the shipment. The contract has just about been finalized. I want you two to oversee the transfer of cargo. You will meet the trucking company that will be transporting it to the dock in shipping containers. I want you to inspect each container against that master list. Once you've confirmed the contacts are as they're supposed to be, you will seal the container and sign off on it for transport."

Mike nodded. "How many trucks?"

"There will be seven. Each with one container full."

Lania knew nothing about shipping containers, but even to her, that sounded like a lot.

"That's a large shipment," Mike said, confirming her suspicions. "I'm honored by your trust."

Eyeing him, Igor bared his teeth in what he no doubt meant to be a smile but that looked more like a grimace. "So far, you have been quite valuable to me. Enough that I'm choosing you over others to make sure everything goes smoothly. Don't mess it up, understand? If you do, you're a dead man. If you don't, it will be well worth your while. This deal is worth millions."

Millions. Of dollars in guns. Going to terrorists and enemies of the United States. Lania managed to keep her face expressionless, but inside her thoughts were racing. This had to be the one, the big one the ATF had been waiting for. Which would mean the end to this undercover thing. Once it was over, she'd be able to meet her twin sister.

As long as they survived.

Paper in hand, Mike pushed to his feet. "Igor, I give you my word. I will make sure everything goes exactly the way it's supposed to."

Lania nodded and also stood. She couldn't help but notice how careful Mike was with his verbiage. *Exactly the way it's supposed to* could mean different things, depending on which side of the law you were on. If things went according to plan, the ATF would take down one of the largest illegal gun shipments in history.

All she had to do was keep her mouth shut and play along. And, she reminded herself, keep her hands—and mouth—off Mike and away from Igor. Far, far away.

"I'm counting on it." Igor made a hand gesture, indicating they were dismissed.

At the doorway, Mike turned. "I assume you'll have your people take us back to where we were?"

"Of course." Igor looked at Lania. "Do not take too long to make up your mind," he said.

All she could do was nod.

They rode back to the restaurant the same way they'd come—in the back of the panel van, though this time their only escort was the driver. Lania stayed quiet, still trying to process everything. Mike, on the other hand, appeared energized. She imagined he couldn't wait to make his report.

Once they were dropped off in the restaurant parking lot, they stood side by side, silently watching the van drive away.

"Why did Igor want to see you alone first?" Micah asked.

Exhaling, she told him. "I was afraid to out and out turn him down, especially when he threatened you."

Micah frowned. "I don't understand. Igor is first and foremost a businessman. This is an important shipment. Why the hell would he jeopardize it right now? As far as he knows, you aren't going anywhere. What's the rush?"

"I don't know." She thought for a moment. "He mentioned the possibility of forming a new partnership with some woman, the one Samir works for. Maybe that's what's making him rush."

"Maybe so, but stall him as long as possible. We need to get this shipment on the way so the arrests can happen."

"I will," she promised.

"Good. Now, are you ready to finally go and get that drink?" Micah asked, scratching his head.

Jennifer stared up at him. "Do you still want to? I would have thought all that drama kind of ruined the night."

"Only if we let it," he responded. "Actually, I'd definitely say we have something to celebrate."

He meant the huge shipment, of course. Maybe he had a point. Even though everything that had transpired since they'd had dinner had left her exhausted, she didn't want to ruin his night any more.

"Okay. I'm in," she said. His grin felt like a reward. They climbed into his car and took off.

"Finally," Micah mused. "After two freaking years, it's actually going to happen."

"This is pretty big, isn't it?" she asked.

"It is." He drummed his fingers on the steering wheel, clearly energized. "It's what I—and your sister—have spent the past twenty-four months working toward."

Maybe she wouldn't tell him about Igor's offer to cut him out. At least not until after he'd had a chance to celebrate a little. He deserved that. She'd fill him in later.

"What are you in the mood for?" he asked. "I know a place that has great martinis. Or would you rather we go to a wine bar?"

Since she didn't drink much, she wasn't sure. "I really like a good margarita," she said. "I've heard good things about a place called House of Tequila or something."

Her response made him chuckle. "Tequila it is."

WATCHING JENNIFER SIP her margarita, Micah wished they'd gone to a place that had live music. More than anything, he wanted to take her in his arms out on the dance floor. Actually, he simply wanted her body up next to his.

Restless, he drank his beer and tried to tamp down some of the energy buzzing through his blood. But he couldn't, not with the end finally in sight.

The meeting with Igor and overseeing the major illegal shipment of weapons to known terrorists would lead to the culmination of the undercover mission, and once the arrests had been made and the weapons seized, Micah would be free. Free to take some time off, to try and forget the personality he'd become as Mike.

He couldn't wait. He'd been planning the vacation for months. It involved sun and sand and drinks with umbrellas delivered by pretty senoritas. No reason to think, nothing but waves and water and heat.

Now, though, the vacation for some reason no longer held its prior appeal. Actually, he knew why, but since the reason was sitting across from him, looking innocently sexier than any woman had a right to, he pushed the thought away. He knew better—he'd always vowed to keep his relationships casual so no one would get hurt. He'd seen far too many law enforcement spouses suffer due to their husband's career. He'd sworn never to do that to any woman, especially one as special as Jennifer.

He pushed away such heavy thoughts. Tonight, he wanted to celebrate. He'd make his report in the morning so the others could get their teams in place.

"You're awfully quiet," he finally said.

She looked up, her expression pensive. "All of this has been exhausting. I'm sorry, I know it's a good thing for you. I'm just not used to it."

Immediately contrite, he reached across the table and took her hand. "Do you want to go back to the condo?"

"Yes." She didn't bother to hide her relief. "You don't have to stay. If you'd rather go out and celebrate some more, I understand."

He stared at her, feeling almost as if she spoke a foreign language. She didn't seem to understand that it wouldn't be any kind of celebration without her.

Draining the last of his beer, he gestured toward her half-full glass. "Do you want to finish that?"

Taking another small sip, she shook her head. "It's

delicious, but I'm not much of a drinker. And this is a huge margarita."

"Then let's get out of here." He held out his hand, and she took it. He refused to acknowledge how good he felt with her small fingers intertwined with his.

Back at the condo, as they walked toward the front door, he considered changing and heading down to the gym. Some weight lifting and a good run on the treadmill might help take his energy down a notch.

After locking the door, he turned and found Jennifer standing way too close. She appeared uncertain, shifting her weight from one foot to the other. He reached out, intending to steady her so he could brush on past her, but he ended up pulling her into his arms instead.

One kiss. Just one. The instant his mouth touched hers, his reason shattered, making him realize that was a lie. Their open mouths met, a caressing of tongues so deep, so drugging, that his hunger for her obliterated all his previous reservations. Equally fierce, she held nothing back, acting as desperate for him as he was for her. Her kiss demanded, tantalized and made him crave more.

All of her. He thought he might die if he couldn't bury himself deep inside her.

This feeling shocked him enough to try and put the brakes on things. He broke away, breathing ragged, the temptation of her swollen mouth and hooded gaze more than he could stand.

Gaze locked with his, she slowly pulled her T-shirt up over her head and tossed it to the floor. Her full breasts filled the white lace cups of her bra, and when she stepped out of her sandals and shimmied out of her jeans, standing before him in her matching panties, he couldn't help but groan. Talk about a sexy schoolteacher.

More aroused than he'd ever been, he fumbled with his belt, trying like hell to ease his jeans past his massive arousal. Somehow, he managed, kicking the jeans to the side. She reached for him, easing him out of his boxers, cradling him in her small hands so tenderly he almost lost it right then.

"Are you sure?" he managed, giving her the opportunity to call this off before it was too late.

"Yes," she said softly before pulling him close for another kiss.

Somehow, they made it to the couch, locked together, his hard-on pressing against her soft belly. Together, they sank down onto the cushions. "Slow," he muttered, a request he made both to her and to himself. As for him, he couldn't get enough, which made it more difficult for him to rein himself in. Everything about her, from her warmth and her softness to the fierce way she caressed him, intoxicated him.

He let himself explore her, the curve of her hip, the swell of her breasts. He put his lips to her nipples, yearning to taste her. As his mouth closed over her, she arched her back and let out a strangled moan even as she reached for him to guide him to her.

"Wait." Moving away, the air cold against his heated skin, he grabbed his jeans and removed his wallet, locating one of the condoms he had there. With shaking hands, he managed to put it on, returning to her with his heart pounding in his chest.

"Come here," she murmured, holding her arms out to him.

Gently, though his blood continued to roar in his veins, he eased her back so that she lay under him. Pressing the swollen tip of himself against her, he entered her, overwhelmed at how tightly she sheathed him in her warm honey.

Though he intended to move slowly, he somehow lost his mind. Nothing would do but a raw, primal possession. Clearly, she felt the same, since she urged him on, matching him stroke for pounding stroke. When she came apart in his arms, her body shuddering around his, he finally allowed himself to give in, too. Pure, explosive pleasure ripped through him in waves, so strong he could hardly catch a breath.

After, they held on to each other tightly. When she stirred under him, he belatedly realized he might be crushing her and moved away just enough to be able to gather her closer to him.

Holding her felt good, and right. The thought floored him, making him realize he didn't need to go there. Not now. Especially not now.

"Micah? There's something I need to tell you," she said, her voice hesitant. "I meant to let you know earlier this evening, but you seemed so happy that I didn't want to ruin your night."

Content, almost dozing, he smiled at her. "What's up?"

"Remember when Igor made me come back to his office without you?"

Fully awake now, he nodded.

"Well, he wanted to offer me a partnership. With him. He asked me to ditch you and go with him."

Micah stiffened, which caused Jennifer to squirm

out of his arms. "I'm sorry," she offered. "But I thought you should know."

"I'm not surprised," Micah said slowly, trying to figure out Igor's angle. "I'm alarmed at his timing, but he's been hinting around about that for a good while now."

Pushing to his feet, he grabbed his boxer shorts and pulled them on. Then he shoved his hand through his hair and began pacing between the sofa and the kitchen bar. "This makes no sense. The biggest deal of his tenure is about to go down, and he's talking about stealing my woman? He knows that would cause an out-and-out war with me. And he's asked me to oversee the operation? What the hell is he thinking?"

She shrugged. "I don't know. But I thought you should know."

"Thanks." He stopped his pacing and dropped back onto the couch next to her. Still naked and appearing completely at ease, she looked beautiful and vulnerable and sexy as hell. He swallowed hard and forced his thoughts back on track. "How did you answer him?"

"I was vague and hesitant. When I reminded him that I was with you, he told me he could tell I was a woman who liked power and money and reminded me how much more of both I could have with him. When I mentioned I'd been with you a long time, he said he knew about my other dalliance. I'm assuming he meant Tanner. He ended it by letting me know I'd better not take too long to decide, because he's a man of little patience."

Gut twisting, Mike whistled. "Damn. It sure sounds like he's trying to cut me out."

"What are you going to do?" she asked, the anxiety in her voice matching her expression.

He leaned over and kissed her on the cheek. "I don't know. I'm thinking it wouldn't be a good thing to confront him. Too much is riding on this."

"I'm sorry."

This brought him up short. "Don't apologize. None of this is your fault. Igor makes his own rules."

"Oh, I know." She waved her hand vaguely. "I meant I was sorry about this. You and me."

"You are?" *Sorry* was the last thing he wanted to hear from her.

"Not really. Well, maybe just a little." Raising her head to look at him, she offered a wry smile. "I guess we broke the rules, didn't we?"

Still speechless, he could only reach out to push a strand of hair away from her beautiful face.

"This doesn't have to change anything," she continued. "But I do want you to know I'm not usually a one-night-stand kind of gal."

He couldn't help but love that she used the word *gal*. "I guessed that," he replied, wishing he could say the same. Unfortunately, for the past two years, he'd been deep undercover. All he'd been able to have were one-night stands. That had actually suited him just fine, as things were less messy that way.

Then the rest of her words registered. *It doesn't have to change anything.* Which was how it had to be, with the conclusion of this operation nearly upon them. Messy emotional entanglements would only complicate things.

Yet he already wanted her again. Not good. Not good at all.

"Would you like me to promise you it won't happen

again?" he asked. "Because if that's what you want, I'll make sure of it."

Eyeing him, she made a face. "Why would I want that? We're both consenting adults. Since we're stuck together for the duration, why shouldn't we enjoy ourselves?"

Stunned, he wasn't sure what to say at first. Then, as he collected his thoughts, he knew he had to speak the truth. "I don't want anyone to get hurt. We're at the tail end of a very deep undercover operation, and things will get a bit…intense."

Leaning forward, she brushed a light kiss on his cheek, sending a shudder of wanting through him. "I'm a big girl, Micah. I don't have any expectations, I promise. But if you're saying you can't handle us having a noncommitted relationship, that's okay. I get it. I don't want you to get hurt, either."

For a second, he stared. Then, when he realized how she'd turned the tables on him, he laughed. She might not realize it, but he'd swear she was channeling Lania at this very moment.

"Fair enough," he replied. "No expectations, okay. Just two single people, enjoying each other."

"Perfect." Totally, unabashedly naked, she got up from the couch, grabbed her discarded clothing and strode off to the bathroom.

He couldn't tear his eyes from her. *Damn.* He was in big trouble now. Because he knew deep inside that she wasn't a one-night-stand kind of woman. He'd finally found a true distraction from his work.

Chapter Eight

Closing the bathroom door behind her, Jennifer exhaled. As she looked down at her hands, she was unsurprised to realize they were shaking. She'd definitely become one heck of an actress. With that performance, pretending to be some sort of sexual adventurer, she'd almost managed to fool herself.

Except deep down she knew she was messing with fire. She wasn't the kind to give her body freely or to let passion override reason, even though she'd done both after only knowing Micah a few days. She couldn't seem to help herself when it came to him. Even though she knew when this case ended, he'd likely break her heart.

This entire thing felt like she might have bitten off more than she could chew. She'd assumed she'd simply be playing a minor role, maybe as some sort of arm candy for Micah. Having the head of the criminal organization offer her a partnership felt as if it had come out of left field. Of course, maybe Laney might have been able to see it coming. After all, she'd been playing Lania for almost two years.

Thinking about her sister brought a wave of yearning. For her entire life, she'd felt as if part of her had been missing. Now she knew why. Her twin. She couldn't wait to meet her.

Stepping into the shower, Jennifer turned the water on hot. The lovemaking with Micah had been surreal, unlike anything she'd ever experienced before. She had to consider that maybe it was because she'd been playing a role, which allowed her a freedom she'd never had.

One thing she knew for sure. She didn't want to give it up. As long as she could keep her heart from getting tangled up, she'd be fine. Or at least that's what she chose to believe.

When she emerged from the bathroom, her hair wrapped in a huge, soft towel, Micah was nowhere in sight. She wandered into the kitchen and grabbed a bottled water, then took a peek down the hall to see if he'd closed his bedroom door. He hadn't, but he wasn't in his room. Instead, she heard the shower in the other bathroom start up. Which meant they'd both washed all traces of each other off their skin.

The thought shouldn't have made her sad, but it did. Suddenly, she wished she could call her sister and ask her advice. Somehow she knew Laney would know just what to do. After all, she'd been undercover with Micah for a long time.

However, that option wasn't on the table. She went back to the bathroom and began to comb out her hair. Tomorrow would be another day. And true to what she'd told Micah, she was determined not to let their lovemaking change anything between them.

That night, she slept deeply, and she woke in the morning refreshed yet slightly sore. Her entire body heated as she remembered what she and Micah had shared, but she resolutely put that out of her mind so she could focus on the day ahead. Otherwise, she might do something foolish, like try to seduce him so they could make love again. The thought made her roll her eyes at herself in the mirror. *Who are you?* she mouthed to herself. *A sex-starved nymphomaniac?* The ridiculousness of the thought made her grin. The other teachers on her team teased her and called her Ms. Prim and Proper. They wouldn't believe it if they saw her now.

Micah was already in the kitchen when she arrived for coffee, sitting at the table with his laptop open in front of him. He looked handsome and sexy and dangerous. Just seeing him had her heart rate increasing.

He looked up as she approached, his blue eyes warm. "Good morning," he said, smiling. "You look really young in those braids."

That smile sent a twinge of lust through her like a lightning bolt. Reminding herself that she needed coffee, she managed to smile back and touched her hair. "I forgot I'd done them. Sometimes I like to have my hair wavy."

She could have sworn his gaze darkened at her words. Something passed between them, unspoken. She felt it in the tightening of her throat and a heaviness in her lower body.

Not going there. Not now, at any rate.

Once she'd filled her mug, she took a seat across from him at the kitchen table. "What's on the agenda for today?" she asked.

Though he didn't move, his entire posture changed from relaxed and casual to alert and tense. She could practically see Mike taking over Micah in the space of a heartbeat.

"We need to do the preliminary work," he said, his curt tone matching the coldness in his gaze. "I want to inspect the trucking company and oversee the loading of the containers. First, I'll need to nail down some dates."

"Igor didn't give you a timeline?"

He frowned. "He did, but it's really loose. I want to tighten it up. Too many things can go wrong on a shipment of this size."

Which made sense. "What do you know about the trucking company? Is it reputable?"

Glancing at his screen, he shrugged. "Seems to be. They were incorporated two years ago, have a decent accident record, and all their interstate filings are current. They're insured by a large, A-rated insurance company and carry five million dollars in liability insurance."

"Have you set up a meeting yet?"

"Not yet. I didn't want to call before 8:00 a.m. Igor gave me the owner's name and number. Once I nail things down there, I'll need to get with the shipping company. This will require a couple of meetings with Samir and his people, assuming they're still in the game."

Though the thought of seeing either Samir or his partner again repulsed her, she managed to appear indifferent. "Sounds good." Darn if she wasn't getting good at this role-playing stuff.

"You don't have to go if you don't want to," Micah continued, almost as if he knew.

Allowing a slow smile to curve her lips, she eyed him. "Oh, I definitely want to go. I can't wait to face that weasel again." Another Lania thing. She was beginning to see how being undercover for such a long time could seriously mess with one's mind.

"We've also got another dress-up thing tonight," he said. "Charity event with a bunch of rich movers and shakers. Some of them are crooked. Igor wants us to mingle, listen and report anything unusual back to him."

"That ought to be fun." She made a face. "I get to pick another amazing outfit to wear. I need to make you take some pics with my phone. My coworkers will never believe it when I tell this story without proof."

The reminder of her other life had his smile fading. He nodded, his expression serious.

"I admire your courage." The sincerity in Micah's voice made an ache start in the back of her throat. "You're really brave."

"Not really. I'm just keeping my eye on the prize. Meeting my sister will be worth all of this."

Something—maybe guilt—crossed his handsome face. "I'll make sure Laney knows. After she finishes killing me, I'm sure she'll feel the same way."

Fascinated, she waited for him to elaborate. Instead, he closed the laptop and pushed to his feet. "I'm going to shower and then start making phone calls. If I can set up any meetings today, I'll let you know."

"Did you already have breakfast?" she asked and then inwardly winced at how domesticated she sounded.

"I picked up some pastries." Pointing to a white cardboard box on the counter, he nodded. "Help yourself."

He left. A moment later, she heard his shower start up.

Although she usually liked to start her day with protein along with carbs, she opened the box to see what he'd gotten. Inside, instead of the doughnuts she'd expected, there was a colorful array of fruit-filled pastries, cinnamon rolls and a huge bear claw. She took a cinnamon roll and a raspberry-filled one and carried them back over to the table to enjoy with her coffee.

Once she'd finished, she made herself a second cup of coffee and headed back to her room to get ready to start the day. She'd just finished doing her makeup when Micah tapped on her door.

"We're touring the trucking company facilities at noon." Micah stood in the doorway, wearing jeans, his feet bare and his hair still damp from his shower. For one second, all she could think of was how badly she wanted to jump his bones.

"We are?" she managed, reminding herself internally that she needed to get this lust thing under control. "I'm assuming we can wear regular clothes." As opposed to expensive designer dresses.

"Of course." He gestured at her jeans. "What you've got on now will be fine. Can you be ready to leave around eleven?"

"I can."

Getting dressed seemed a lot easier when she got to wear jeans and a T-shirt, along with comfy, rubber-soled shoes. She met Micah in the kitchen shortly before ten forty-five to find him similarly attired.

He smiled when he saw her. She felt the warmth of his smile all the way into her heart. "Ready?"

"Yes."

When he held out a hand, she barely hesitated before slipping her fingers through his.

The trucking company looked exactly like she'd imagined such a place would. A smiling receptionist welcomed them, showing them back to the owner's office. A balding, rotund man with glasses, he shook hands and handed them off to one of his employees for a tour of the facilities.

Several large trucks were parked out back, gleaming in the summer sun. They were shown the truck wash area, and finally, Mike was invited to inspect one of the trucks.

This part Lania found fascinating. Not only were the vehicles huge, but inside she saw what was termed the sleeper area, a small bedroom where the truck driver could rest.

Mike seemed satisfied by what he saw. He thanked the employee, a rail-thin, bearded man named Ned, and he and Lania walked inside to say goodbye to the owner before they left.

"They seem legitimate," Micah said once they were headed back to the condo. "I have a feeling the owner doesn't have any idea what Igor is shipping. Or if he does, he's been told it's a legal shipment."

"Is it on him to find this out?" Jennifer asked. "Or is it considered okay if he takes the shipper's word for it?"

"That would be for the court to decide. As it is, when we do the roundup, the owner and the drivers will be taken in."

She exhaled. "Now that we've done that, do we have any other tasks to complete before the party? If not, I plan to take a nap before getting ready."

"A nap sounds great." His impish grin told her he'd like to do more than sleep. "And no, all that's left is the shindig tonight."

When they got back to the condo, she told him she'd see him later and closed the door to her bedroom. The headache that had been lurking all day had finally surfaced strong. She figured a nice, quiet nap and then a shower would help.

A couple of hours later, she woke. Momentarily regretting not inviting Micah to join her, she stretched. The headache had gone. Now all she needed was a long, hot shower and she should be on her A game for Igor's little soiree.

Since there were at least twelve black cocktail dresses in the closet, Jennifer decided to go with one of them for the shindig tonight. They all fit perfectly, so she chose one at random, found a pair of black heels that she could walk in and used the flat iron to make even more casual waves in her long hair. The evening bag hung from a long, silver chain. Inside she put the fake driver's license Micah had given her, lipstick and some cash.

Now all she needed was jewelry. Slipping on her high heels, she walked into the living room, looking for Micah. He wasn't in the living room or kitchen, so she walked toward his bedroom. He turned as she entered, making her stop short, her chest tight.

"You're wearing a tux?" He looked like a movie star and an outlaw, all in one. "Do I need to change to an evening gown?"

He laughed. "Nope. You look amazing. Let me get

you some diamonds to go with that outfit. You can choose if you'd like."

Intrigued, she followed him into his closet. He moved aside some hangers with shirts, revealing a medium-size wall safe. After punching in the code, he opened it. "Earrings or necklace first?"

"Earrings," she answered promptly. "I want something big and blingy. Then I'll need a subtle, understated necklace."

"Understated?" Turning, he eyed her, one brow raised. "These people don't understand subtlety. If you're going to be flashy, you need to go all out."

"I'm going for elegance," she told him. "If I wear big earrings, I need a smaller necklace. I promise you, I know what I'm talking about." She smiled, remembering. "My mom always told me to put all my jewelry on and once I had, remove one piece. For whatever reason, that stuck with me."

Shrugging, he pulled out a black velvet box. "These are the largest earrings. They're worth a fortune, so be careful not to lose them."

Slowly, she opened the box. Nestled inside was a pair of diamond teardrop earrings. "They're beautiful," she breathed. After choosing an understated necklace, she asked him to help her put it on. Lifting her hair, she turned her back to him.

His fingers felt cool on her skin. She barely suppressed a shiver. Instead of caressing her as she'd secretly hoped he would, he made efficient work of fastening the necklace and stepped away.

"There you go," he said. "Are you about ready?"

Careful to hide her disappointment, she nodded. "Are we going to Igor's house again?"

"Nope. Not this time. We'll be at the home of one of his high-ranking associates."

This was the part of this job that she hated the most. Jennifer had always been more of an introverted person. She wasn't a partier or even very social. Of course, spending all day, every weekday with twenty-five children, and dealing with their parents, tended to make her all peopled out.

Her lack of desire to socialize had been one of the things she and Caville had disagreed on. As soon as school let out on Friday, all Jennifer wanted to do was go home, put her feet up and crack open a good book. Caville, on the other hand, often wanted to hit up a raucous sports bar, have a couple of beers and watch whatever game happened to be on at the moment. Sometimes Jennifer forced herself to go with him, though she always ended up with a pounding headache and regrets.

"Are you all right?" Micah asked.

Blinking, she collected her thoughts. "Yes. Sorry. I got lost in my thoughts. I'm not much of an extrovert, and I'm definitely not high society. So all this is definitely out of character for me."

He squeezed her shoulder. "I get it, believe me."

For the first time, she realized she knew little about him. She'd ask, but later, maybe after the party. No sense in making it more difficult to get into character.

Despite the different location, when they arrived at the huge house and parked, Jennifer—now Lania—got a sense of déjà vu. There were valets waiting to park the cars, possibly even the same ones Igor had hired.

She wondered if inside would be the same group of people. Probably so, since she'd think these people ran in tight circles.

As they approached the front door, a uniformed servant opened it for them. Stepping into the foyer, Lania's heels clicked on what she guessed was Italian marble, polished to a high sheen. An enormous crystal chandelier hung overhead, and well-dressed people mingled in the huge room ahead of them.

"Same story, different night," she muttered.

Mike glanced down at her in surprise but then grinned. "Yes, it is," he replied. "How about I get us both a drink?"

About to ask for a glass of water, she decided to go with wine instead. "White wine, please. Something sweet."

"You got it. Wait right here." Still smiling, he disappeared into the crowd.

Lania forced herself to move a bit farther into the room.

An elegant older woman with her hair in an elaborate bun walked over to her, looking her up and down. "I saw you at Igor's get-together. You work for Igor, I believe?" she asked.

Lania deliberately let her gaze travel over her new companion, raising one brow as if she found the other woman lacking. "I do. And you are?"

"My name is Carmen. I am working to secure a new contract with numerous partners. Igor is one of them." She paused, again raking her gaze over Lania. "I need someone to help oversee my operations. He suggested that you might be a good candidate."

This was the woman Igor had mentioned. Every instinct she possessed told her she needed to be careful.

"A good candidate to partner with you?" she asked. "I understood you were partnering with Igor."

Carmen laughed. "That man has an ego the size of Texas. He knows I prefer women to men."

"I see." Good gravy, what the heck was going on now? Igor had claimed he wasn't offering Lania out. He'd also stated his intention to make Lania a partner with him. Clearly, he'd told this Carmen woman something else completely.

If she let herself, Lania could easily panic. Bad enough she and Mike were supposed to be in charge of a huge weapons shipment. Now Igor was playing more bizarre games?

Maybe this was another test. Either way, it was exhausting.

"I'm afraid I'm very busy." Lania flashed a completely insincere smile. "But I do appreciate you thinking of me."

"I don't think you understand." Clutching Lania's arm, her long, bloodred nails like talons, the woman put her face far too close. "This is a major opportunity for you to make a name for yourself. I think you'd do well with these girls. They'd look up to someone like you."

These girls. Alert now, Lania took pains not to reveal her thoughts. "What do you mean?" she asked, practically purring. "What girls?"

"Come to my warehouse tomorrow and see." From inside a tiny yet expensive purse, the woman extracted a card and handed it over. "Igor will vouch for me. After all, he's considering becoming one of my partners."

Watching as the woman sailed off, Lania dropped the card into her own purse. Saying Igor would vouch for her didn't mean much, at least in Lania's mind. Still, she needed to tell Mike about the girls. If there was a possibility of human trafficking, these people needed to be stopped.

Maybe the ATF could run two operations at once.

Mulling it over, she turned to find Mike, but Igor appeared instead. "I saw you were talking to Carmen Montenegro," he said. "She has a huge opportunity that I'm considering. You do remember my invitation to become my partner?"

"As if I could forget." Smooth smile, light, flirtatious touch on his arm. "I'm still trying to figure out a way to have my cake and eat it, too."

His eyes darkened. "Like Mike, I do not share my women. If you agree to become mine, then you will be exclusive."

"Interesting, since Carmen just made me a similar offer."

Igor laughed. "I already told her you wouldn't take it. I give her props for trying."

Unsure how to react to this, she spotted Mike making his way toward them, two glasses in his hand.

Following the direction of her gaze, Igor grimaced. "Don't take too long to consider my offer," he said. "I am not a patient man." With that, he disappeared into the crowd. Staring after him, she realized he'd just made a subtle threat.

MIKE'S HEART SKIPPED a beat when he realized Igor had cornered Lania. So far, she'd been able to do an amazing job handling the criminal leader, but the way Igor appeared to be pressing his case was worrisome. A man as powerful as him wouldn't be willing to wait forever. Yet another reason why he wanted this damn assignment over with.

Reaching Lania, he handed her the glass of wine and took a sip from his whiskey. "Are you okay?" he asked.

Slowly, she nodded. "So far, so good. But Igor's getting impatient."

"I suspected as much."

"I'm not sure what to do," she admitted. "He pretty much told me he's running out of patience. He hinted that wouldn't be a good thing."

"It won't. I'm hoping we can wrap this up before that happens."

She took a sip of wine. "Me, too."

"Who was that older woman?"

His question made her grimace. "She's an associate of Igor's. She had another business proposition for me. I'll tell you about it later."

For whatever reason, it sounded as if Igor was casting an ever-widening net around Lania. And, in doing so, attempting to cut Mike out. Which wouldn't bode well for a successful completion of this mission.

Not to mention the possibility that Igor might decide to do more than end his association with Mike. He could decide to end Mike's life.

From experience, Mike knew focusing on the negative possibilities wouldn't do him any good.

Somehow, they managed to make it through the rest of the evening, which involved a lot of fake smiling and glad-handing, even though every time Mike caught Igor watching Lania, his skin crawled.

Finally, people started taking their leave. Lania nudged him, slipping her arm around his waist. "Do you think we can go?" she asked, her gaze imploring.

Damned if he didn't want to kiss her. Spotting Igor staring, he decided to do exactly that.

She met him halfway, as if she knew his intentions. All sense of reason flew out the window the instant their mouths connected.

Luckily, she had enough common sense for the two of them. "I can't wait to get you home," she purred, just loud enough to be heard by anyone standing close. Which he figured meant someone was.

When he lifted his head, attempting to blink away the haze of arousal, he realized Igor had walked over. He stood, fists clenched, less than ten feet away, glaring at them.

Keeping his arm around Lania, Mike flashed what would hopefully be his last fake smile of the evening. "Great seeing you again, Igor. I hope to have a complete report for you by the end of the day Monday."

Igor nodded, his narrowed gaze deadly as he focused on Lania. "Tick tock," he said before turning and striding away.

"Whoa." Lania leaned on Mike, hard. "Please get me the heck out of here."

So he did.

On the drive back to the condo, she told him what Carmen had said. "Selling weapons to terrorists is bad enough, but human trafficking? Even thinking about it makes me feel sick. Please call someone in your office and make them investigate this."

"I'll definitely report it," Micah replied. "But I believe that type of thing would be the Department of Homeland Security's jurisdiction."

They pulled into the garage and parked before she spoke again. "I'm going to take the meeting."

Surprised, he glanced at her. "You're brave, but you're already doing enough. I don't want you getting involved in any of that. Those human traffickers are ruthless, as much or more so than Igor and his bunch."

"She said Igor might become a partner." Expression troubled, Jennifer swallowed. "This entire thing has become a lot more involved and frightening than I thought it would be."

"Stay steady." He got out of the car, crossing over to the passenger side to open her door for her. Once he'd helped her out, he pulled her close for a quick hug. "Focus on our case. You don't need to get involved with this Carmen woman. It's too dangerous. I'll have someone in my office alert DHS, and they can investigate."

Arm in arm, they started toward the elevator. He could tell from her pensive expression that she was still mulling things over.

Once inside the condo, instead of going directly to her room so she could change, Jennifer began pacing, her long strides in her sky-high heels eating up the floor.

He watched her, bemused but equally aroused. Shy, quiet Jennifer looked quite fierce when something had her riled.

"Are you still worried about that woman?" he asked.

"If it will make you feel better, I can put in the call to my handler now and you can listen in."

Stopping, she stared at him. "That'd be good, but not good enough. I'm worried about the girls. I can't stop thinking about how terrified they must be, how helpless they must feel. From what Carmen said, I'd be in a unique position to get good, inside information." She swallowed hard. "I almost can't believe I'm saying this, but I think I should try."

Equal parts impressed and concerned, Micah eyed her, one brow raised. "You sure are ballsy, I'll say that."

This made her laugh. "No, Lania is ballsy, not me. And before you think I've lost my grip on reality, I haven't. I'm going to take a wild guess that you've faced similar situations before and wondered, *what would Mike do*."

Since he couldn't deny that, he nodded. "I have, but I'm a trained federal agent. You're not. I didn't ask you to step in here to put you in more danger. Please, let's just focus on our case so we can close it. Other people, other agencies, can deal with the rest."

Instead of backing down, she crossed her arms. "Please. I've seen enough crime drama shows to know once the bust goes down, all the others will scatter to the wind. Even if the other agents try to locate the human traffickers, they won't be able to find even a trace. Those girls will be lost."

He wanted to point out that this was real life, not a TV show, but she did have a valid point. Once the ATF swooped in and arrests were made, anyone not caught directly in the net would vanish without a trace.

"Also," she continued, "if Igor really is involved,

that's one more crime he can be tried for. I've seen documentaries about human trafficking, and it's awful. They're primarily runaway teenage girls, many of them with families who are still desperately searching for them."

"I admire your compassion," he said, meaning it. "But don't you think you have enough on your plate?" He ached to reach for her, to distract her the only way he knew how, yet he also wanted her to know he respected her courage. "You're new at all of this. Igor is trying to split us up, we have a huge weapons deal about to go down after two years of hard work undercover, and now this? I think you'd definitely lose focus."

"Maybe so," she admitted. "While you might be right, I wouldn't be able to live with myself if I didn't at least try."

"Damn it." He loosened his tie. "I was afraid you were going to say that."

"I just need to make the one initial visit. After I see what's really going on there, I can back out. Then you can notify the proper authorities and I won't be involved."

When she looked at him like that, with her big eyes so guileless and her expression pleading, he wondered how he could possibly deny her anything. But then he thought about her getting hurt, or worse, and his blood ran cold. He couldn't lose her. He never should have endangered her to begin with.

His regret had come too late. He hadn't expected Igor to step up his pursuit or for this other operation to try and draw Lania in. He'd been so laser-focused on his own operation that he must have overlooked the signs.

If he'd seen them, he'd never have gotten Jennifer involved. The double-edged sword—but then he would never have gotten to know her.

"Let me think about it," he finally said.

"Okay." She crossed the room to him and put her arms around him.

His heart skipped an actual beat. *Damn.*

Though he shook his head, when he nuzzled her neck, she shivered. "I'd much rather be doing something else right now," he murmured. "How about we talk more about this tomorrow?"

"Wait." Expression pensive, she pulled back. "While I too can think of something else I'd rather be doing, I just realized I know almost nothing about you, while you know everything about me. Tell me about yourself."

"Like what?" He frowned, realizing he'd never had to have this discussion with Laney, because she'd read his official file, just as he'd read hers. Plus, they'd only been coworkers, not lovers.

Lovers. He could see he was setting himself up for a world of hurt. Even so, he had no desire to take a giant step back, like anyone with common sense would.

"Where'd you grow up?" Jennifer asked, completely unaware of his internal turmoil. "Do your parents live nearby? Do you have any brothers or sisters? Regular stuff like that."

He relaxed. He could do this. "I grew up in Oklahoma. Only child. My dad left when I was ten, and my mom raised me on her own." This made him smile slightly. "She wasn't really on her own. We had a large extended family. My grandmother and grandfather, my aunts and uncles, and six cousins. It was a good childhood. My grandparents are gone now, and the last time I saw my cousins was at my mother's funeral, twelve years ago."

Even now, he was surprised how he could still hurt.

"How'd you decide to get into law enforcement?" Jennifer asked.

"Ah, the million-dollar question. When I was in my freshman year at college, someone robbed a convenience store when my mother was inside buying her weekly lottery tickets. She was shot and killed."

"I'm so sorry." Clearly taken aback, Jennifer reached out and touched his arm.

He shook his head. "Thanks. I still miss her. Anyway, the police caught the guy who'd killed her and he went to prison. But I developed an interest in law enforcement. When I graduated with my degree in criminal justice, I applied with both the ATF and the FBI."

"Let me guess." Her genuine smile was guileless. He felt it like a punch in the gut. "You got into both."

"I did," he agreed. "And I decided I wanted to work for the ATF more. So here I am." Removing his jacket, he draped it over a chair and motioned to the couch. "Come sit."

Immediately she did, crossing her long legs and revealing a flash of thigh. "Thanks. Those heels were killing my feet."

He sat down next to her, leaning back into the cushions, intent on keeping this casual. "What about you?" he asked. "While I might know the facts on the surface, that's all I know. When did you decide that you wanted to be a teacher?"

The question appeared to surprise her. "No one has

ever asked me that," she admitted. "My parents and friends said they could always tell teaching was my calling. Kind of like you said you felt about law enforcement."

He squeezed her bare shoulder, unable to resist trailing his fingers down her arm. She shivered and smiled at him.

"You were saying?" he encouraged. "You were going to tell me when you decided you wanted to become an educator."

"I like that you chose to call me that—an educator. A lot of people think of us as glorified babysitters. Anyway, I've always enjoyed working with children. When I was in high school, in the summers I worked at a day care."

"You must have a lot of patience," he began. "And you're definitely brave. Not to mention kindhearted and sexy…"

She kissed him then, and those were the last words either of them said for quite a while.

Chapter Nine

The next morning, Jennifer woke up with a man in her bed. Of course, Micah wasn't just any man. Even though she hadn't known him long, this felt…right. They were partners, however short the duration. Stretching, she felt like a languid cat. Sated and…content. Happy, even.

She glanced over at him, her heart full. He slept on his side, with one arm around her. Letting her gaze drift over him, she drank in the sight of him. Lean and muscular, with chiseled features and thick, golden hair. She hadn't realized his lashes were so long. She'd never met a man so masculine, so rugged and yet so darn beautiful. *Beautiful.* She almost snorted, because that wasn't a word she'd ever thought would apply to any man. In Micah's case, it did, though she suspected he'd be appalled if he knew.

They'd made love, this time slow and leisurely, and he'd brought her to orgasm over and over before allowing himself to experience his own release. After, he'd held her close. They'd snuggled and talked for hours before finally dozing off in each other's arms, only to wake up and do it all over again.

His touch had been both gentle and rough, his body

both pliant and hard. Everything about him excited her, including the way he acted as if he felt the same about her.

In her entire life, she'd never had a night like this, with a man like this one. Which definitely said a lot about her poor choice in men. The thought made her grimace. Before Micah, she hadn't known such closeness was even possible. Now, she knew she could never settle for anything less ever again.

Trying to figure out if she could manage to squirm out from under his arm without waking him, she glanced at the clock on the nightstand. "Eight o'clock!" she said, shocked. "Micah, wake up. We have meetings this morning."

She had to give him credit for his rapid comprehension. He went from sound asleep to wide-awake in an instant, jumping from her bed fully naked and rushing off for his own bathroom. A moment later, she heard his shower start.

As she swung her legs over the side of the bed to go do the same, his phone pinged. She realized he'd left it on the nightstand. She shouldn't look, she knew, but she reached for it anyway.

The text was from someone designated by an initial rather than name. *L.* Which had to be her sister, Laney.

Call me when you can, it said. I have some news.

Heart pounding, she set the phone back on the nightstand and rushed off to take her own shower. It wasn't until she stood under the water shampooing her hair that she realized she should have jotted down the phone number.

Racing through her shower in record time, she

wrapped a towel around herself and another around her hair and rushed back into her bedroom. The phone was gone. Clearly, he'd already retrieved it. Which was probably all for the best.

Disgusted with herself, she marched back into her bathroom and began blow-drying her hair. She got ready in record time, only using mascara and a smidgen of pale pink lip gloss. In the still-empty kitchen, she made herself a cup of coffee and helped herself to one of the pastries, which still tasted surprisingly fresh for being a day old.

Micah hadn't told her he kept in touch with her twin, though it made sense that he would. After all, they'd been partners for two years. She couldn't help but wonder if he'd told Laney about her at all and, if he had, how her sister had reacted.

"Ready to go?" Micah sauntered into the kitchen wearing jeans and an unbuttoned shirt. Jolted out of her thoughts, she jumped and then tried to cover it with a quick smile.

"I am," she responded. He looked sexy as heck, and her entire body melted.

"Good." He made a cup of coffee in a stainless-steel travel mug and eyed her over the rim as he took a sip. "We'll grab something to eat on the way," he said. "I need to get a little caffeinated first."

She gestured toward the box of pastries. "They're still good, if you pop them in the microwave. I had one with coffee a few minutes ago."

"Thanks." He did the same, chowing down while still standing at the counter. "How'd you beat me out here? I'm assuming you showered."

"I did. I'm an expert on getting ready quickly. I can shower, do my hair and makeup, and get dressed in under thirty minutes."

He flashed a smile. "Good to know." Finishing off his bear claw, he drained the last of his coffee and then washed his hands at the kitchen sink. "Let's do this."

Suddenly apprehensive, she pushed her nerves back inside. "I can't wait to see Samir's face when we arrive."

When they pulled up in front of the warehouse, two armed men escorted them inside. Instead of Samir and Ernie, they were greeted by Carmen, the woman who'd approached Lania at the party. She wore a bright purple pantsuit with a nipped-in waist. She managed to look both stylish and intimidating.

Shocked, Lania stopped short. Every nerve prickled a warning. Next to her, Mike did the same.

No one spoke at first.

Clearly noting their unease, Carmen flashed a cold smile, her gaze raking over Lania first, then Mike. "Follow me," she said, leading the way to a small office in the back of the warehouse. "Sit," she ordered, gesturing at two chairs across from her desk.

Lania glanced over her shoulder. The two armed men blocked the doorway. It looked like they weren't being given much of a choice.

Still, neither she nor Mike made any move toward the chairs.

"What's going on here?" Mike asked, his tone as icy as Carmen's smile. "Igor sent me here to nail down the details of an important transaction. Who are you and why are you here?"

"Igor and I have become partners." She glanced at

Mike, but her attention remained focused on Lania. "Samir and Ernie work for me. I have already handled this transaction and Igor has been filled in." Her gaze narrowed. "Now sit. Please."

Lania didn't have to have any special training to understand that this wasn't good. At all.

Mike muttered something under his breath. Lania touched his arm, intending to soothe him.

Lania sat. A moment later, Mike did the same.

"Igor hasn't mentioned anything to me about having you take care of this," Mike said, his tone suspicious. He got out his phone. "I'm going to give him a quick call and make sure he's aware of what's going on here."

Taking her own seat behind the desk, Carmen inclined her head. "You go right ahead and do that. I'll wait."

Expression savage, Mike punched in a number. He listened for a moment and then ended the call without speaking. "It went to voice mail. As I'm sure you knew it would."

Carmen shook her head. "Now, how would I know that?" she asked, her voice silky smooth. "I don't keep tabs on the man. That would be asking for more trouble than even I am prepared to deal with."

"What do you want?" Mike asked flatly. "I hope you know that Igor will not take it well if you mess up his transaction."

Ignoring him, Carmen looked directly at Lania. "Have you given my proposition any thought?"

"Some," Lania replied, well aware she had to be careful.

"What proposition?" Defensive again, Mike sat forward, looking from Lania to Carmen and back. "What are you talking about?"

"I haven't had time to tell you," Lania said, even though she had. "Carmen asked me to assist her with a new venture."

"We work for Igor." Mike's tone was as flat as the expression in his blue eyes. "Together. We don't even know who this woman is."

Lania started to nod but thought better of it. She needed to play this carefully until they knew what exactly was going on.

Again, Carmen ignored Mike, her attention completely focused on Lania. "I believe I mentioned to you last night that Igor was considering becoming part of my operation. He has now agreed, and we've combined forces. From everything he's told me about you, I believe you'd be a valuable asset."

Dang, dang, dang. Aware she had to choose her words carefully, Lania nodded. "I need more time to consider your offer. As I told you, Mike and I are a package, a team. In addition, I would like to complete this deal before taking on anything new."

"Come on, now," Carmen purred. "I recognize some of myself in you. I know you are able to multitask. Likely much better than the man you have with you."

Lania stiffened. "The *man*—Mike—is my partner. In more ways than one. If you knew me at all, you'd know that I am extremely loyal. If you're thinking about cutting Mike out, you'd better think again. We work together or not at all."

From the way the other woman's perfectly arched eyebrows rose, Lania had surprised her.

"You do not have the right to make that choice, I believe. You both work for Igor. You will do what he says."

Which meant Carmen was aware that Igor had been trying to get Lania to get rid of Mike. "We are partners," Lania repeated. "We work together or not at all."

Carmen sat back in her chair, frowning. "Igor is not aware of this, is he? I don't believe this decision will work out well for either of you."

"We'll take our chances," Mike said, pushing to his feet. He held out his hand to Lania. "Let's go."

Regarding him coolly, Lania didn't move. "I'd like to have a word with Carmen privately."

Expression thunderous, Mike shook his head. "Don't do this," he warned. "You're playing with fire."

Though Lania knew what he meant, she allowed herself a faint smile. "Don't worry, Mike. I've got this under control. Now, please, wait for me in the other room."

When Mike didn't move, Carmen gestured to her two men standing near the door. "Please escort this gentleman out into the warehouse. Once there, please watch him to make sure he does not return here until we've concluded our business."

Clearly aware he couldn't win this one, Mike spun on his heel and stalked toward the door. Carmen's men fell into place alongside him, closing the door behind them.

"Now we may speak freely," Carmen said, leaning back in her chair, hands behind her head.

"Yes, we may." Lania bit her lip, nervous. "I'm willing to be part of your organization, but it must be done on my terms or not at all. Men do not control women like us. That's why I refuse to let Igor dictate who I choose to partner with—or take to my bed."

Carmen caught on immediately. "I agree with you, but Igor is a dangerous man to refuse. Have you truly thought this through?"

Deciding to be direct, Lania made a face. "Seriously. Would you sleep with that man?"

This made Carmen laugh. "I will be honest with you. Once, I might have, if I thought doing so would help my career. Now I am powerful enough that I don't have to make that kind of choice."

Lania squared her shoulders. "I want to be that powerful, too. Tell me what you want me to do. I need more information before I make a decision."

MIKE HAD NEVER been as worried as he was while waiting outside for Lania to talk with this Carmen woman. If Laney had been the one sitting in the small office, he would have been able to relax, since Laney completely knew what she was doing. Over the two years they'd been undercover, they'd both dealt with numerous people like Carmen. Laney knew exactly what buttons not to push. Her twin, however, would be winging it. Even now he suspected his new partner had no idea how dangerous this situation could be. The thought of her inadvertently messing up made him break out in a cold sweat.

They were nearly at the successful completion of a two-year-long mission. And now it appeared Igor wanted Mike out. Normally, something like that might mean his cover had been blown, but this time he believed that wasn't the case. Igor's obsession with Lania had grown, so much so that Igor appeared willing to get rid of Mike if that meant he could have her. Never mind that Mike had worked diligently to prove his loyalty or that he'd made himself a valuable asset to Igor's organization. There truly was no honor among thieves.

Then where did this Carmen woman come in? Mike had no doubt that Igor believed he would use her, discarding her once he was done. Likely, Carmen had her own plan. All these people were only out for themselves. They wouldn't hesitate to stab even their closest friends in the back if it would benefit them.

While Mike wasn't Igor's friend, he'd worked himself up to a position of trust, with Lania right by his side. Igor had come to rely on the pair more and more, trusting them with several lucrative deals, which they'd handled perfectly. In fact, until Jennifer had replaced her twin, Igor had merely done some casual flirting with Lania. It almost seemed he, like Mike, sensed the difference in the two women and, like Mike, felt an irresistible pull to the second Lania. So much so that he was apparently willing to shunt Mike aside in his quest to possess her.

The question was, what should he do about it? He couldn't let Igor's lust destroy the ATF's chance to take down one of the largest illegal weapons smuggling operations in history.

Damn. He forced himself to appear unconcerned and glared at the two goons blocking the doorway to Carmen's office. He decided to take the bull by the horns and pulled out his phone, dialing Igor's number again.

This time, Igor picked up immediately. Mike outlined the situation, stating that he believed this Carmen person was up to no good. "In fact, she's meeting privately with Lania right now."

"Why?" Igor asked, sounding only mildly curious.

Mike glanced around and lowered his voice. "Honestly? I think she's planning to take over your operation. She's trying to get Lania to join her and cut us both out." Unless, of course, Igor had engineered all this. Which would mean Mike was wasting his breath.

He waited for Igor's reaction. Nothing but silence on the other end of the phone. Igor hadn't exhibited any surprise, or anger, which meant he truly had partnered with Carmen, even if temporarily.

Mike decided to take a chance, well aware it could go either way. "I know you want my woman," he said, his tone fierce. "As of right now, she's still mine. But if she forms an alliance with this Carmen woman, neither of us will have her."

Igor laughed, apparently finding that statement humorous. "Carmen might like women," Igor drawled. "But Lania prefers men—I can tell. She will not be so easily swayed. Not only that, but she is loyal to you. If she wouldn't choose me over you, why would she want Carmen?"

Relieved, Mike exhaled. Apparently, his bluff had paid off. Or, at least, he hadn't managed to infuriate Igor.

"I have not lost yet," Igor continued. "Women like Lania go where the power is. I have power. You do not. She will come around eventually. It's quite clear what her choice will be."

"Is it?" Mike asked. "Because as far as I can see, she's done nothing to indicate she wants to leave me for you. Especially after you offered her to Samir and Ernie like she was for sale."

Igor chuckled. "That was a test. She knows that. And the reason Lania hasn't left you yet is because she has a mistaken sense of loyalty. She told me so."

Mike forced himself to unclench his jaw. This could still go either way. Best-case scenario, Igor would be suspicious of Carmen, maybe even sever his alliance with her and reinstate Mike. Worst-case scenario, it could all blow up in his face. Either way, he had to take a chance. There was no way he could risk this entire operation imploding.

"I thought you wanted me to meet with Samir and Ernie. Instead, they are nowhere to be found, and it appears Carmen has taken over their office."

"They are doing work that I ordered them to do. And Carmen will be running their shipping company in their absence."

This didn't sound good. At all. In fact, it made absolutely no sense.

"You trust her that much?" Mike asked, letting his incredulous tone tell what he thought of that.

"Yes," Igor replied. "Carmen is family."

Which explained a whole hell of a lot. "I see," Mike said. "Now I understand."

"Look, Mike. I like you a lot. But Lania is…"

"Special. I get it, believe me." Mike took a deep breath. "I would like to ask a favor, though. If Lania leaves me for you, I would like to continue working for you. No hard feelings." Ignoring the way it felt as if he'd sold his soul, Mike waited for Igor's response.

"That's an interesting proposition," Igor said. "I like

that you're able to choose your power and position over a woman. I always have a use for men like you."

"Glad to hear it," Mike replied, meaning it.

"You should also know that I have asked Carmen to find a spot for Lania," Igor admitted. "Once she agrees to become my partner, she will look out for my interests with Carmen's organization."

Which sounded as if Igor didn't entirely trust Carmen, family or not. Good. That gave Mike something to work with.

"Maybe so, but I'm also looking out for your interests," Mike pointed out. "And Carmen was talking as if she and Lania would be partners. Something about becoming more powerful." Though this last might be complete speculation, Mike figured something like that was going on right now behind the closed door. "A woman like Carmen will never play second fiddle to any man. And I think she wants Lania for herself."

The instant he said the words, Mike knew he was right. Carmen had looked at Lania with a mixture of cunning and calculated lust. And naive Lania probably had no idea.

For the umpteenth time, Mike regretted his impulsive decision to involve an innocent civilian. If things went south—and they very well could—he deserved to lose his job with the ATF. In fact, even if he managed to pull this bust off without a hitch, he'd be in a hell of a lot of trouble when they learned about Jennifer.

Since there wasn't anything he could do to change that, he had no choice but to focus on the job at hand. Right now, he felt like he was just barely hanging on by the skin of his teeth.

"I will consider what you've said," Igor finally allowed. "But Mike, if I find out you are attempting to play me for a fool, there will be consequences."

"I understand." He decided what the hell, might as well go for broke. "Igor, one last thing I want to toss out there. Lania and I are a great team. We do good work for you. Why mess with that? There are tons of other women out there." And then Mike held his breath, well aware he might have gone too far.

The strangled sound Igor made might have come from a place of anger, or a place of pain. Mike wasn't sure. Until now, he'd been careful to simply do the other man's bidding, proving himself a valuable asset over and over, until Igor increased his responsibilities. He and Lania had noticed Igor's growing infatuation with her, but until now it hadn't gotten in the way.

"You know what, Mike? I respect that you had the balls to tell me how you feel," Igor said. "I will take your words under consideration. You have proven your loyalty, so there's that. For now, remember that you still work for me. Not Carmen, not even Lania, but me. Understood?"

"Understood." Relieved, Mike thanked the other man and ended the call. He had no idea if what he'd done had helped, but at least Igor hadn't threatened to kill him. In the time he'd spent working for Igor, he'd seen the crime lord do that twice. Both times, the man Igor had threatened mysteriously vanished, never to be heard from again.

Realizing he'd started sweating, he took several deep breaths, hoping Lania would come out soon. This had always been a dangerous game they were playing, but now he felt as if they were walking on a rapidly fraying tightrope over a deep and yawning gorge.

The office door opened and Lania emerged, appearing dazed. She smiled when she saw him and strolled over, taking his arm. "Are you ready to go?" she asked, her brown eyes sparkling.

Struck dumb by her beauty, he managed to nod. Side by side, they left the warehouse and headed toward his car.

Neither spoke as he unlocked the Corvette and they climbed inside. Only once he'd started the engine and they'd pulled away did they both exhale loudly at the same time.

"That was surreal," Jennifer said. "Carmen is one scary lady."

He filled her in on his conversation with Igor.

"You told him Carmen likes me like that?" she asked, one brow raised.

"You couldn't tell?"

"Nooooo." She drew out the word. "As far as I could see, that woman gets off on power."

He let her think about it for a moment.

"You know, you may be right," she finally conceded. "She did give off an overly friendly vibe."

This description made him laugh. "*Overly friendly* isn't how I'd ever describe that woman."

"True." She tilted her head, eyeing him. "I can't believe you told Igor that you'd be okay with him stealing me away from you."

"I thought I was going to choke on those words," he admitted. "But I had to do something. He and Carmen are on the verge of edging me out. I've spent two years of my life on this case. Damned if I'm going without a fight, especially when we're so close."

"What about me? What am I supposed to do? I've got Igor after me on one side and Carmen on the other. Staying with you would be completely out of character for Lania."

"Stall them both as long as you can," he advised. "Maybe you can still pretend to be loyal to me."

"Really?" Feigning outrage, she lightly slapped at his shoulder. "After you basically told Igor you wouldn't fight for me?"

He considered telling her the truth—that he'd put his own life on the line before he'd let Igor touch her—but he decided not to. "I won't let you get hurt," he said instead. "I give you my word."

"Good." Sitting back in her seat, she sighed. "I just need to survive this so I can meet my sister."

"You will. And maybe you can help explain, because Laney is going to kill me when she finds out I involved you."

"She'll get over it." The confidence in her voice almost made a believer out of him. Almost. But then again, she didn't know Laney as well as he did.

"I wonder what happened to Samir and his friend," Jennifer mused. "They seem to have disappeared."

"Igor claims he sent them on another job. Since I was under the impression that it's their shipping company, I find that highly unlikely. Either way, Carmen is going to be taking over coordinating the shipping. The trucking company is on standby. Unless something crazy happens, this deal is going down without a hitch."

"And then we'll be free," she said.

"Then we'll be free." Echoing her words, he realized he wasn't entirely telling her the truth, which tormented him. Long after this case was wrapped up and delivered, he doubted he'd ever be free of Jennifer. To his surprise, he realized he truly didn't want to be. She was one hell of a special woman. Did he even stand the remotest chance of making a relationship with her work?

Arriving back at the condo, they walked to the elevator side by side, each lost in their own thoughts. Once inside, he pushed the button for the ninth floor. The elevator started to rise. And then everything went dark—all movement halted with a jerk and a jolt. They were stuck.

"What just happened?" Jennifer asked, fear mixed with shock in her voice.

"Looks like a power outage." For her sake, he tried to sound calm. This could be nothing, or it could be something very bad indeed. Getting out his phone, he used the flashlight app to locate the call button on the control box. He pressed it, and nothing happened. He tried again, with the same result.

Next, he tried his cell phone. Here inside the elevator, the cell reception appeared dismal. Not even half a bar. Despite that, he dialed 911 anyway. The call didn't go through.

Beside him, Jennifer started panting, sounding for all the world like a woman doing Lamaze. *Puff-puff-pant. Puff-puff-pant.*

"Are you okay?" he asked, concerned.

"I'm trying to be." *Puff-puff-pant.* "I am really claustrophobic. I can handle enclosed spaces for short periods, but I can't deal with this."

"You can," he assured her, reaching for her hand. "We're in this together."

Puff-puff-pant. And then once more as she clung tightly to his hand. "Come here," he said, pulling her close and wrapping his arms around her. "You got this. It's going to be all right."

"Is it, though?" Trembling, she spoke with her face pressed against his chest, her voice muffled. Her entire body seemed clenched stiffly. "This all seems awfully convenient. We meet with Carmen, you tell off Igor and now we're trapped in an elevator who knows how many floors up."

"I don't think this has anything to do with them," he said, despite the fact that he'd just been wondering the same thing. "I mean, come on, you're a hot commodity right now. Neither Igor nor Carmen wants anything bad to happen to you."

Instead of the puffing, she'd switched to deep, deliberate breaths. He took this as a favorable sign. "Maybe they've changed their mind," she ventured, her voice slightly less shaky.

"If they did, stranding us in an elevator wouldn't be their usual method of operations. They tend to use bullets or bombs or fire."

"True." To his relief, some of the tension leaked from her posture. "So you're saying this is likely a simple power outage."

"Yes. All we need to do is wait it out." He rubbed the small of her back, growing aroused despite the situation. He had no doubt she could feel his body's arousal pushing against her.

"Hmm." She squirmed, drawing a low groan from

him. "I have a better idea. Distract me." Still pressed up against him, she pulled him down for a deep, open-mouthed kiss, caressing his growing bulge. "I always wanted to do it in an elevator."

Just like that, she sent him over the edge. Frantic, he couldn't get enough of her. She matched him, equally urgent, channeling her earlier terror into reaching the height of explosive pleasure.

Pressing her back against the elevator wall, both their jeans halfway down, he entered her standing up. She came immediately and violently, her body clenching around him, almost making him lose his tenuous grip on control.

As he thrust himself into her, the lights came on. The elevator shuddered and began to move.

Too far gone to stop now, Micah continued to move, faster and faster until he reached his own release and emptied himself into her. It was only then that he real-ized he hadn't used a condom.

"Hurry," Jennifer urged. "We're almost to the ninth floor."

He pulled up his pants while she did the same. The elevator doors slid open as they were hastily adjusting their clothing.

As they stepped out onto their hallway, they realized two people stood near their unit waiting for them—Samir and Ernie, neither of them appearing too happy to be there.

Chapter Ten

"Uh, oh," Jennifer said, suddenly light-headed. She grabbed Micah's arm to steady herself. Micah tensed, stepping away from her, his hand automatically going to his holstered weapon.

She had a pistol in her purse, she remembered. Of course, with her luck, if she got rattled, she was more likely to shoot herself in the foot than actually do any good.

Lania would hit her target. But right now, even as she knew she had to be Lania, she didn't think she could actually shoot another human being. Even to save her life.

"Can I help you gentlemen?" Mike asked, legs spread slightly apart in a fighting stance. She admired the way he conveyed without saying the words that he wasn't going to be brought down easily. "Did you happen to have anything to do with the power being cut while we were in the elevator?"

"No. We were waiting in your hallway when everything went dark." Samir looked from him to Lania, his own posture nonthreatening. "We wish to talk," he said quietly. "Nothing more."

"Then talk." Mike didn't move.

"Here?" Samir glanced around. "Can we not go somewhere a little more private?"

"No way in hell am I letting you into our condo," Mike said, his voice flat. "It's right here or nowhere."

Ernie snickered. "I told you this was a waste of time."

"Be quiet." Samir ignored him. "We are in danger of losing everything."

Lania spoke up for the first time. "I take it Igor doesn't know you're here."

"No. And we'd like to keep it that way."

"You are aware we work for Igor?" Mike asked. "Because I honestly don't see what you'd possibly think we could do for you."

"That woman has taken over our shipping company," Samir complained, his tone bitter. "We have worked hard and long to make that company profitable. When Igor approached us about a very lucrative deal, I wish we hadn't listened. We should have known."

"Known what?" Mike asked. "Please don't pretend you're new to skirting regulations."

"Okay, okay." Samir shrugged. "We color outside the lines sometimes. But we have done everything Igor has asked, and now he's cutting us out."

That sounded eerily familiar, Lania thought. Igor appeared to be on the verge of doing the exact same thing to Mike.

"Why do you think we can do anything to help you?" Mike asked, his expression cold.

"Because we know Igor is about to do the same thing to you."

Lania laughed. "You know nothing," she said. "And even if that were true, any alliance the four of us were to form would be powerless against Igor and Carmen and their people."

Mike gave her the tiniest shake of his head, making her wonder if she'd gone too far. Just in case she needed to balance it out, she spoke again. "Plus, Mike and I are loyal to Igor. We would never do anything without his consent."

"Fool," Samir sneered. "You think you're gaining power and money. Instead, Igor will take everything from you, including your lives."

Gaze cold, Mike shrugged. "Then that's a chance we'll have to take." He unsnapped his holster, his hand lingering over his pistol. "You'd better leave, Samir. We don't want any trouble."

Instead of turning away, Samir took another step closer. "You do understand that we have nothing to lose, right?"

That did it. Lania reached into her purse, withdrawing her own small handgun. She flicked the safety off. "I don't take well to threats," she said.

"Hold up," another voice said. Igor himself emerged from around the corner. "Samir is just doing exactly as I requested."

"You're testing our loyalty?" Mike's tone warred between annoyance and admiration.

"But of course." Smiling broadly, Igor clapped first Samir on the shoulder, and then Mike. "I need to know who I can trust."

Then Igor turned to face Lania. She braced herself, certain she wouldn't like whatever he had to say.

"Put the gun away," he ordered, though gently.

Numb, she realized she still clutched the pistol.

Flicking the safety back on, she placed the weapon in her purse.

"Now," Igor said, his cool gaze boring into hers. "I will ask you for the last time. Have you made a decision?"

Dread coiling low in her stomach, she slowly nodded. Stepping over to Mike, she slid her arm around his waist. "Mike and I are a team." She braced herself for his reaction.

"I thought you might say that." And then Igor laughed. Not a forced sound, but one of true amusement. "And I think we would have gotten bored with each other. Mike here made some other good points." Still grinning, he gestured with a flourish. "I will keep you both as a team."

"What about Carmen?" Mike asked.

"I will deal with Carmen," Igor replied. "Right now it suits me to keep her as a partner. She brings a fresh influx of cash and an entire separate potential industry to the table. I believe her business will become quite profitable."

Human trafficking. Feeling queasy, Lania knew better than to comment. Mike squeezed her shoulders, giving her a warning, too.

"Well?" Rubbing his hands together, Igor glanced down the hall toward their condo. "Let's go inside and finalize the details. I hope to get all this done by the end of the week."

The end of the week? She didn't dare even glance up at Mike.

If he felt any reluctance to allow the crime boss inside their place, he didn't show it. Arm still around

Lania's shoulders, he led the small group down the hallway, unlocked the door and stepped inside. "Come in, come in."

Igor, Samir and the still-silent Ernie filed past. Lania took a deep breath and pasted what she hoped was a welcoming smile on her face. "Can I get anyone something to drink?"

"I have some very good single-malt scotch," Mike offered. Both Igor and Samir asked for that. Ernie said he'd prefer beer.

She went to get the beer while Mike took care of the scotch. For herself, she poured a glass of iced tea. No way was she taking any chance of clouding her mind with even the smallest amount of alcohol.

They were all seated in the living room when she returned. Igor looked up, his expression friendly rather than predatory. She wasn't naive enough to believe he'd totally stopped wanting her, but she was definitely glad he'd decided to quit the overt pursuit.

At least for now. She knew better than to let her guard down.

Taking a seat next to Mike, she listened carefully as Igor and Samir went over the shipping details. Apparently, Igor was allowing Carmen to believe she was running the show, but all the details would be hammered out before she even knew about them. Lania toyed with the idea of asking Igor if he really thought that was wise, but she decided it would definitely be safer to stay out of it. No doubt Igor had to be well aware what kind of ruthless woman Carmen appeared to be. He probably already had a plan in place to deal with her.

"What about Carmen?" Mike finally asked, surprising her. "I'm thinking you don't want to piss her off, especially since she's bringing another avenue of business to the table."

"Carmen is fine. She already knew she wasn't running the shipping operation. She really just wanted to size you two up and see if Lania might be interested in helping her run her operation."

"Too many games." Lania wasn't aware she'd spoken out loud until she saw the quick flash of shock on Mike's face before he wiped it clean. She swallowed hard. Now that she'd started, she might as well finish. "Why? Carmen is a capable, powerful woman. If she thinks for one second that she's being played, she won't stop until she's burned you down. Figuratively speaking, of course."

Igor studied her, his features shut down. She stared back, now certain she'd gone too far but aware she couldn't backtrack now. "Explain."

"Look, I don't know Carmen well," she said. "But from what I can tell, she's highly intelligent, personable and enjoys her power. She has a very high opinion of herself, and it's most likely justified. She will not take well to being played in any way, shape or form."

"I have no intention of playing her," Igor replied stiffly. "She has a very profitable business, and I am considering becoming a partner in that. That is where you come in, Lania. I want you to work with her on my behalf."

In human trafficking. Lania took great care not to reveal her disgust.

"I'd prefer that Lania and I continue to work together until this current shipment is finished," Mike said.

Narrowing his eyes, Igor glanced from one to the other. "I believe Lania is capable of deciding this for herself."

Lania lifted her chin, barely able to suppress a smile. Though she knew Mike didn't want her to get involved, to take this risk, if she could save even a few teenagers, the danger would be worth it. She had to at least try.

"I want to work with Carmen," she said, earning a sharp glare from Mike. "As long as she understands that my loyalty is not for sale."

This statement made Igor chuckle. "I'm quite sure you will find the nicest possible way to make her aware."

Slowly, she nodded.

"I'll be in touch," Igor said, eyeing Mike. "I want this shipment to go off without a hitch. I think we definitely have a better chance of that happening with Lania distracting Carmen."

"Sounds good." Mike and Igor shook hands. Samir stepped forward, his hand outstretched, too. Only Ernie continued to eye them all with a sullen expression. Judging by his expression, she could tell Mike briefly considered asking the younger man what his problem might be, but he evidently decided it wasn't worth the hassle.

Plus, she knew he really wanted these people out of the condo. It'd been impossible to watch each and every one of them a hundred percent of the time. Once they were gone, he'd have to call in a tech unit and have the place swept for bugs.

Igor gestured to Samir and Ernie, and they all three took their leave. Mike put his arm around Lania's waist and led her after them. On the pretext of walking their guests to the elevator, he got her out of the condo, too.

Once the elevator doors had closed behind the men, Micah steered Jennifer over to the floor-to-ceiling window. "We can't go back in the condo just yet," he murmured in her ear. "I'll be having a tech unit brought in immediately to make sure Igor and his men didn't leave behind any listening devices."

Eyes wide, she nodded. "What are we going to do in the meantime?"

He shrugged. "Go for a walk? Or we could go back in the condo, change into workout clothes and hit the gym."

"I don't want to go back in there until we know it's clean. The idea of someone listening to me is creeping me out."

"A walk it is, then. There's a nice little tapas place a couple blocks away."

Outside, the summer air felt even hotter after being inside in the air-conditioning. Arm in arm, they began to stroll down the street. There weren't many other people out at all, likely because of the heat.

"I don't like what Igor is trying to do," Micah said. "He's trying to divide us." He dragged his hand through his hair. "That's why he's so keen on you working with Carmen. I don't like it. Not one bit."

"I had to try," Jennifer explained, arm still linked with his. "I've watched documentaries on human trafficking. They're mostly teenagers and young girls, Micah. If I can help save even a few of them, it will be worth taking a risk."

"Have you ever thought you could end up one of

them?" His blunt tone shocked her. "They're drugged and sold all over the world. Most are never heard from again. You won't have me with you to watch out for you, and if you make one mistake, it's over."

Since Micah wasn't given to exaggeration, she knew she had to pay attention. Still, she thought he might be worrying a tad too much due to her inexperience.

"I'll be fine," she said with a confidence she didn't actually feel.

"No." Micah crossed his arms. "You won't. You've got to get out of this somehow. It's bad enough that I've involved you in illegal arms sales. But human trafficking is an entirely different ball game."

If she'd still been in her Lania character, she knew she would have laughed in his face and said something along the lines of he wasn't going to be telling her what to do. But as herself, as Jennifer, she suspected he just might be right. She hadn't been trained for this, and she didn't work in law enforcement. She worked in education.

"The thought of them trafficking human beings just sticks in my craw," she admitted. "Maybe it's the teacher in me."

"It's the human being in you," he replied, squeezing her shoulder. "I don't like it any more than you do. But we've got to focus on this case. It's the entire reason we're here."

"I know." She dipped her chin in agreement. "But I can't stop thinking about what those girls are likely going through. I have an opportunity to help. How can I turn my back on them?"

"Come here." He pulled her close and simply held

her. "Once this case is closed, we'll make sure the proper authorities are given the information to shut down the human trafficking ring. They're good at what they do, and I promise you, they'll get it taken care of the right way."

"What do you mean, the right way?"

Rubbing her back, he sighed. "To make this kind of arrest, the operation has to be carried out by the book. If rules are broken, the criminals can walk. I've seen it happen more than once. That's why it's important that you stay as far away from these people as you can."

Now she understood. "I see your point. But I've already told Igor I would do it. How on earth will I be able to get out of it now?"

"We're going to have to stall him." They'd nearly reached the tapas bar. He looked around to make sure no one could hear them. "Just long enough for this operation to go down and arrests to be made. After that, we can let trained professionals take over investigating the human trafficking ring." He opened the door for her. "Let's go eat and grab a drink. I've already texted to get the sweep done. They'll text me when it's over."

BY THE TIME they'd finished their drinks, Micah had already received the all-clear text. But seeing the way Jennifer had finally relaxed, he was in no hurry to head back to the condo. For the first time all day, her smile seemed natural rather than forced, and her brown eyes sparkled as they talked about everything and anything except for the case.

This was how it could be, he realized. Once they were no longer forced into playing roles, once danger no longer lurked around every corner, they would be able to be themselves and see where this thing between them might go.

Assuming Jennifer wanted to as badly as he did. He knew her primary focus would naturally be on finally meeting her twin sister and Laney's family. He also knew Laney would want to kick his ass for involving Jennifer, but hopefully once she got that out of her system, he figured, she'd eventually forgive him.

In the middle of telling him a convoluted story about her cat, the old lady next door and her best friend, Heather, Jennifer stiffened. "Don't look now," she muttered, cutting her gaze away from the front door. "But Carmen and another woman just walked in."

Micah swore under his breath. First Igor, Samir and Ernie, and now Carmen? No way this could be a coincidence, no way at all.

"Let me settle up the check and we'll get out of here," he said. "Hopefully without her seeing us."

"Too late." Flashing a weak smile, Jennifer—now Lania—pretended to do a double take. "Carmen? What a delightful surprise to see you here."

Carmen's cool and calculated gaze swept over them. Even in slacks and a sleeveless cotton blouse, she managed to look elegant. She wore her long, dark hair in an elaborate French braid and large gold hoop earrings. The equally well-dressed young woman with her appeared shy, careful not to make direct eye contact. "Are you following me?" she asked bluntly.

"Following you?" Lania laughed. "We've been here over an hour and have finished our meal. If anything, I'd have to ask if *you* were following us."

Carmen's heavily made-up eyes narrowed.

"We're just about to leave," Mike interjected. "Very good to see you."

With a regal nod, Carmen started to turn away. And then, because Lania clearly seemed to be ignoring the threat, she reached out and grabbed Carmen's arm. "Aren't you going to introduce us to your *friend*?" she asked, either blithely oblivious or pretending to be. "Or is this pretty young girl one of your relatives?"

Though Mike cringed inside, he kept it hidden. "Lania, honey. I think you've had too much to drink. Come on, let's go."

"Too much to…" And then, finally, Lania correctly interpreted the warning in his gaze. "Sorry," she mumbled.

Carmen sailed away without another word.

The waitress chose that moment to bring over the check. Mike handed her enough cash to cover the bill and the tip and told her to keep the change. Then he pushed to his feet and helped Lania up. "Let's go. Now. Don't even think about looking for Carmen."

Outside in the cooling afternoon air, Micah propelled Jennifer along firmly.

"Why'd you act like I was drunk?" she asked. "You know as well as I do that I only had two glasses of wine."

Micah sighed. "Carmen was about to go all crazy on you. First off, you grabbed her arm when she was about to walk away. In her mind, that was an almost unforgivable insult. Second, you asked about the girl."

Clearly not understanding, Jennifer frowned. "So?

I was just trying to be friendly. I thought maybe that might have been her niece or something."

He gave her a moment to let what she'd just said sink in. She might be naive, but she wasn't stupid. She'd figure it out.

"Oh." All the color drained from her face. "That girl is one of her…victims."

"I think so," he said gently. "Carmen probably brought her there to meet up with a potential client."

Jennifer looked up at him, her expression miserable. "I feel like I'm going to be sick. That poor girl. That's terrible."

"It is," he agreed.

"I really feel like I need to try to do something." She waved her hand. "If I don't at least try, I have a feeling I'm going to regret it for the rest of my life."

Torn, he wasn't sure how to respond. He knew that feeling well. In his occupation, it could be both a blessing and a curse. But Jennifer wasn't in law enforcement. She might intellectually understand the risks, but until someone actually found themselves in a life-or-death situation, they truly didn't know.

"You're a good person, Jennifer Glass," he said. "But I think this time you'd best leave it to the professionals."

She sighed. "I know you're probably right, but still…"

In response, he squeezed her hand. As they walked back toward the condo, he kept an eye out both behind them and all around them. Today had been just weird enough that he wanted to make sure no one else ambushed them.

Luckily, no one did. They made it back to the condo

uninterrupted. As they walked toward the elevator, Jennifer yanked him to a stop. "Sorry, but after what happened last time, I'm a little afraid to get in it now. Do you mind if we take the stairs? It's only nine flights up."

"*Only?*" He laughed. "Sure, I'm game if you are. Do you want to race?"

"You're on." She pointed to the door that led to the stairwell. "Let's go."

She took off running, Micah right behind her. She had no way of knowing that Micah often ran up and down the stairs for cardio. He actually enjoyed running. By the time they reached the sixth floor, she was seriously huffing and puffing.

Since he wasn't a fool, naturally he let her win.

She made it to their floor mere seconds before he did. Doubled over, trying to catch her breath, she glanced up and grinned at him. Her eyes sparkled, and the exertion had lent a pretty flush to her creamy skin. On top of that, the brief exercise definitely appeared to have lightened her mood.

He unlocked the door and ushered her inside. Brushing past him, she wrinkled her nose. "I swear I can still smell Igor's cologne."

"Can you now?" Pulling her close, he gave her a quick kiss. "He did have on more than usual. I guess he was trying to impress you."

This comment made her laugh. "I think at this point he's figured out that ship has already sailed." Her expression went serious. "We make a pretty good team, you and I."

His heart skipped a beat. "Does that surprise you?"

"I don't know," she replied. "Maybe a little. We sure

get along well, considering we were virtually strangers less than a few days ago."

He couldn't help but wonder where she might be going with this. Though he'd definitely begun to develop feelings for her, he knew better than to pursue them while in the middle of a dangerous undercover operation.

After would be a completely different story. Until then, he could only hope she'd begun to feel the same way as he. He'd never been much good at relationships, he knew. Until now, he'd never wanted to put in the time and effort. Plus, he'd witnessed firsthand the agony a law enforcement spouse went through when their husband or wife died in the line of duty. He couldn't do that to this woman.

"It's probably because you're so much like Laney," he said. Her face fell, making his gut clench. But he knew he'd said the right thing. Neither one of them could afford to have romantic thoughts right now.

"Am I?" she asked, her tone light. "You haven't told me much about her, other than that she's married and pregnant."

"That's because I don't want you to have any preconceived ideas about her." This part was the truth. She and Laney needed to get to know each other in real time. "Plus, she and I were simply partners."

She gave him the side-eye. "Surely you must have shared some personal information working undercover for two years."

"That's just it." He made his tone as gentle as he could. "We took great pains to keep things as professional as possible between us. It's a slippery slope when two federal agents bring personal emotions into the mix."

She looked down at that, and he knew he'd hurt her.

"What are you saying?" she asked. "That we made a mistake, you and I?"

"If we weren't in the middle of this operation, I'd say no way. But I'll be honest, Jennifer. You distract the hell out of me," he admitted with a small smile. "I think we need to cool it for now."

"For now," she repeated.

He braced himself for her to ask about the future, but instead she nodded. "One day at a time, Micah Spokane. One day at a time. For now, we catch the bad guys. Then we'll see."

Damned if he'd ever wanted to kiss her more. Since he couldn't, he settled on offering her a glass of wine. To his relief, she accepted.

"What's next, do you think?"

Considering her question, he shrugged. "Best-case scenario, this goes down without a hitch, Igor and his crew are arrested, and we're done."

"That sounds perfect." She took a sip of wine. "I hate to ask, but is there a worst-case scenario?"

"There always is." He grimaced, then shook his head. "But I don't want to jinx it. As long as you stay far away from Carmen, I think we'll be good."

"Easier said than done," she reminded him. He couldn't tell if she was joking or not. "That woman is a force of nature."

"So are you. We got this, you know. We're just about to cross the finish line."

She finished her wine and set the glass down. "No

more for me," she told him when he lifted the bottle with the intention of giving her a refill. "I'm going to go take a nice bubble bath and turn in early." A hint of sadness lingered in her eyes as she told him good-night.

It took every ounce of common sense he possessed not to follow her.

Chapter Eleven

Alone in her bubble bath, Jennifer wished she'd taken Micah up on a second glass of wine. She would have enjoyed sipping it while soaking. Still, he'd given her a lot to think about.

All her life, Jennifer had never been a particularly impetuous person. She considered herself a methodical planner, and routine was her friend. Part of the reason she took such care to stay on the straight and narrow was due to her knowledge of being adopted as an infant, and the fact that she knew nothing about her birth parents. She loved her adoptive parents and, not wanting to hurt them, she'd never made much more than a token effort to find out anything about her life prior to adoption. Even that small effort had been blocked by bureaucratic red tape, and she'd given up, perhaps too easily.

And now, because of a chance encounter in a sporting goods store, she found herself not only embroiled in a dangerous undercover operation but having steamy sex with a ruggedly handsome ATF agent. On top of that, she'd learned she had a twin sister and soon would be meeting her.

If, a few months ago, someone had told her this would happen, she never would have believed it.

Carmen and her weird fixation on Lania had the potential to seriously mess everything up.

While in her mind Jennifer knew Micah was right and she should stay far, far away from Carmen and her human trafficking operation, in her heart she couldn't stand the thought of so many young women and teens being held captive and treated as if they weren't even human.

But then again, what could she do? Even if she went with Carmen and saw the facilities with her own eyes, what then? In the end, she'd still have no choice but to step back and let law enforcement handle things. Why torture herself needlessly?

But what to tell Carmen? Both Igor and Carmen expected her to take part in learning the operation. Micah wanted her to stall as long as she could, and she would. But she also suspected Carmen would be persistent.

She wasn't wrong. Carmen called the next morning before Lania had even gotten her first cup of coffee. "Be ready in one hour," Carmen ordered. "I'm sending a car to pick you up."

"Wait," Jennifer began. But Carmen had already ended the call. "Dang nab it." Shaking her head, she went to find Micah.

"Did she say why?" Micah appeared genuinely worried.

"No, but you know why. What do you suppose would happen if I just didn't show up?"

"Nothing good." He thought for a moment. "Call her

back. Tell her you're sick. Make it sound bad. Vomiting, fever, the whole nine yards."

"She won't care, even if she does pick up." Still, she tried anyway. As she'd expected, Carmen let the call go to voice mail. Nerves had begun to set in, and to her absolute horror she realized her hands were shaking.

"I'm not sure I can do this," she admitted.

Micah pulled her in for a quick hug. "I don't want you to, but right now Carmen doesn't appear to be allowing you a choice."

Lania. She had to channel Lania. Only then would she stop being so darn afraid.

One deep breath, and then two. She stepped back, out of his arms, squared her shoulders and lifted her chin. "I've got this," she said. "I'll be fine. Now, please excuse me. I need to go get ready." She sailed off without waiting for him to reply.

After a quick shower, she blow-dried her hair and did her makeup before heading to her closet for something to wear. Since there were several expensive pantsuits, she chose one of those, along with a pair of kitten heels for easier walking. Costume jewelry instead of diamonds, and she made it to the kitchen with the intention of snagging some coffee with five minutes to spare.

Micah had already gotten a cup ready for her. All she needed to do was start the coffee maker. When he walked into the kitchen a few minutes later, she realized he'd dressed to go out. He wore a crisp cotton button-down shirt, khakis instead of jeans and a pair of what looked like Italian leather loafers.

"Where are you off to?" she asked, eyeing him while sipping coffee.

"I'm going with you," he stated, checking his watch. "No way am I letting you go into that viper's nest alone."

Though secretly relieved, she frowned. "Carmen's not going to like that."

"I don't give a damn if she likes it or not. We're a team, and I will tell her that if she questions my presence. Are you ready? That car should be pulling up in front of the building any moment now."

"Yes." She got to her feet. "I still don't think this is a good idea."

"Maybe not, but if you insist on going, I insist on accompanying you. I'm the one who got you into this to begin with. I'm not about to abandon you now."

Pushing away the warm, fuzzy glow she got at his words, she nodded. "Then let's do this." She squared her shoulders and marched over to the front door.

A sleek black SUV sat at the curb. When the driver spotted them, he jumped out and opened the back door. Lania got in first. When Mike moved to follow her, the driver caught hold of his arm. "I'm sorry, sir, but my instructions are only to pick up her."

Mike flashed a very intimidating glare. "Then your plans are going to have to change. I go with her, or she doesn't go at all." Without waiting for permission, he climbed into the back seat next to Lania. She grabbed his hand and held on tight, suddenly nervous.

The driver shot them a worried look before getting out his phone to make a call. A moment later he got into the driver's seat and passed the phone back to Lania. "She wants to speak with you," he said. There was no doubt whom *she* might be.

Lania accepted the phone and put it up to her ear.

"Hello, Carmen." Proud of how cool and collected she sounded, she continued. "As you can see, there's been a slight change in plans."

"This is not part of our agreement." The ice in Carmen's tone sliced through any hope Lania might have had of getting Carmen to accept Mike's presence without a fight.

"It's part of *my* conditions," Lania replied. "Mike and I work as a team or not at all."

"Then you're a fool," Carmen snarled. "You're also out. Hand the phone back to my driver and I'll instruct him to return you to your condo."

"Since we haven't left the condo, that won't be necessary," Lania said. "By the way, this is your loss." She handed the phone back to the driver. "We can get out now," she told Mike. "She's not fond of the idea of us being a package deal. I'm out."

Mike heaved a sigh that could only have been relief. He squeezed her hand, clearly unwilling to say anything until they were alone, and opened the door. Once they'd both gotten out and slammed the door closed, the SUV sped away.

"I gather she's pretty pissed?" Mike asked.

Grimacing, she nodded. "Furious. I'm not sure how this is going to play out."

He took her arm. "The only one we need to worry about keeping happy right now is Igor."

"I know, but…"

"Come on, let's get inside. I feel way too exposed standing out here in the open. Especially with the possibility that Carmen might go on a vendetta."

The idea made her blanch and hurry inside. "I'm sure

going to be glad when all this is over," she said while they waited for the elevator, which she'd decided she'd force herself to use.

For one heart-stopping second, she thought he might kiss her. But then the elevator doors opened and he looked away, gesturing for her to precede him.

Wondering at the huge sense of loss she felt, she did. At first, she intended to stand as far away from him as she could. But the instant the elevator lurched and moved, she grabbed hold of his arm and stood as close as possible.

"Are you okay?" he asked.

"I'm trying to be," she replied.

Luckily, it didn't take long to get to the ninth floor. The instant the elevator came to a halt and the doors opened, she rushed out, feeling slightly foolish.

Micah didn't comment; in fact, he acted as if he didn't even notice. Instead, he led the way down the hall to their unit and unlocked the door, stepping aside so that she could go past him.

She headed for the kitchen, intending to grab a water and hoping he'd follow her. Instead, his phone rang. He answered, retreating into his bedroom and closing the door.

Anticlimactic didn't even begin to describe the feeling right now. Clearly, she'd made a powerful enemy in Carmen. Though Micah felt Igor would protect them, Jennifer knew a woman like Carmen wouldn't easily forgive such a slight. She'd offered to make Lania— someone she viewed as subservient and weak—into a woman of power. To have Lania reject her offer and, as the ultimate insult, involve a *man*, would be a vicious twist of the knife.

No doubt Carmen would figure out a way to make her pay. And even once the ATF moved in on Igor and his group, unless Carmen got caught in the net, she'd still be out there, waiting.

Would Jennifer still have to worry about her once she went back to her normal life? She needed to get clarification from Micah on that one.

Pushing the troubling thought from her mind, Jennifer grabbed a water and carried it over to the bar to sit down and drink it. From here, she could look out the floor-to-ceiling windows at Denver and try to come to a place of peace with everything that was going on. The thought made her chuckle. Was such a thing even possible?

"Jennifer?" Micah called. He came striding into the room, phone in hand. "I just got off the phone with Igor. It's a go. Everything's in place." Excitement rang in his voice, nearly chasing away the shadows that haunted his blue-eyed gaze. "The trucking company will make the pickup tomorrow. I've—we've—got to go inspect all seven containers and seal them off. Once I've signed off on that, the trucks will hit the road. The containers will be brought to the shipping yard in Galveston, Texas, and should arrive in two to three days."

Startled, she frowned. "Texas?"

"Samir's shipping company uses that port as well as one out of New Orleans. He's got more contacts there in Galveston, so that's where they'll be going."

"I didn't think that far ahead," she admitted, more

troubled than she'd thought she'd be. "Are we traveling to Galveston, then?"

"Igor hasn't asked me to, but I'm going to try to get him to let us. I will definitely be placing tracking devices on each of the trucks, so we'll know their location at all times." He took a deep breath. "Even if I'm not there to personally watch everything be loaded on the ship, the ATF will have a team in place to sweep in and confiscate the containers full of weapons. There will also be agents here to pick up Igor, Samir, Ernie and Carmen."

She froze. "Carmen? To be honest, I've been worried about her."

"You're right to be. That's why I want to make sure she's caught up in the sweep when the arrests are made."

"While that will definitely be a good thing, I have to ask—if she's arrested, what will happen to all her captives?"

"I don't know. That's one of the things the top brass is working on. In a perfect world, they'd sweep in there and make the arrests simultaneously, but since that kind of thing is outside the ATF's jurisdiction, they can't."

"I hate red tape," she responded fervently. "These are people we're talking about here. Hopefully the bureaucrats will figure things out in time to save them."

He nodded. "Hopefully so, but I wouldn't count on it. Igor seemed unfazed when I told him what happened today with Carmen. Makes me wonder if he's regretting his decision to involve her." He took a deep breath. "Right now, we need to concentrate on the task at hand. We'll do what Igor asks and then work on seeing if he'll let us travel to Galveston to see the entire deal through."

Since physically being there for the bust seemed more dangerous, she secretly hoped Igor would turn Mike down.

Right now, though, all she could think about was how badly she wanted to make love with Micah again. Being around him so much, her desire for him had become an obsession.

What on earth had happened to her? She considered herself a sensible, often enthusiastic lover, though judging by her past relationships, she'd definitely missed out on *a lot,* to put it mildly. But never had any other man affected her the way Micah did. One look from those sexy blue eyes turned her insides to mush. She found herself staring at his arms, aching to caress the corded muscle there, and wondering if her desire was as transparent and obvious to him as it felt.

Intellectually, she understood the need to avoid distractions, to focus on the case. But that knowledge didn't help her late at night, when she lay in that huge king-size bed and longed for him. For the first time since this thing had started, she wondered what would happen once the operation had ended. Would Micah introduce her to her sister and then simply disappear from her life? She wondered how she'd survive the heartbreak if that happened.

Heartbreak? She froze, shocked despite already knowing somewhere deep inside. What the heck? When had she allowed her heart to become involved?

"Are you all right?" Micah asked, his expression concerned. "I'm not sure where you went just now, but judging from your expression, you were somewhere far away."

She blinked. What would he do if she told him her thoughts? Of course, she wouldn't. She might be naive and inexperienced, but she still had her pride.

"Sorry," she murmured. "I was just woolgathering."

"Woolgathering?" He laughed, giving her shoulder a light squeeze. "I love your choice of words sometimes."

Even that, the brief touch and the husky laugh, had desire zinging through her veins. She closed her eyes, took a deep breath and concentrated on not swaying toward him.

"Seriously, are you okay?" he asked. "Maybe you should go lie down for a little bit."

"That's a good idea," she replied, jumping to her feet so quickly she startled him. All she knew was how badly she needed to get away from him before she did something foolish. As she closed her door, she shook her head. She couldn't hide in her room forever. She simply needed to get a grip on herself and things would go back to normal. Or, she amended, what passed for normal these days.

STARING AFTER JENNIFER as she fled the room, Micah wondered what had gotten into her. Nerves, most likely, since they were so close to the end of this thing.

He needed to plan something for the rest of the day. Get her out of the condo, maybe make a shopping trip with a nice lunch. Or they could take in the Denver Zoo. Just getting out and doing ordinary things would do wonders to help calm her nerves.

And his, he admitted silently. This would be the largest weapons seizure of his career. But first, he needed to find out if he'd be going to Galveston to see the containers loaded on the ship.

Pulling out his phone, he called Igor. When he asked point-blank about heading to Galveston along with the trucking company, Igor laughed.

"Are you worried something will happen to one of those containers after you've signed off on it?"

"Yes." Mike kept his tone clipped. "It's my reputation on the line."

"Then you'd better double-and triple-check your inspection before you seal things up. I have my own crew shadowing the trucking company. Several of my men have been working there for months. And I already have people in place at the Port of Galveston. I've got this completely under control."

"Then I guess I'll be able to take a few days off," Mike said. "Recharge and all that."

"Don't forget to celebrate. Once that ship clears Texas waters, there will be a big bonus coming your way."

"I can hardly wait," Mike replied.

"Why don't you take Lania hiking?" Igor suggested. "Get out of the city and up into the mountains. Let her try out those new hiking boots."

Damn, the man forgot nothing. "That's a great idea," Mike allowed. "Thanks, man."

"Thank me later, when this thing goes off without a hitch." Igor paused. "And then maybe you and I and Lania will talk about taking over Carmen's operation. We'll have to get rid of her, of course, but I think it's doable."

As intriguing as that topic might seem, no way in hell Mike intended to touch on it. Not now, with so much else at stake. But he had to say something so Igor didn't seem suspicious.

"Good," he replied, infusing his tone with a bit of righteous, steely anger. "I for one will be glad to see that woman go down."

Again, Igor laughed. "You and me both, brother. You and me both." He hesitated a moment before speaking again. "Now, I want to ask you again about Lania. Would you be willing to share her for only one night?"

Rage instantly flashed through him, startling Mike with its intensity. "She's mine," he growled, feeling those words to the depth of his soul. "For as long as she wants to be. Lania does what she wants."

"And right now, she wants you." Frustration and amusement warred with each other in Igor's voice. "Fair warning, though. If that ever changes, I won't hesitate to go for my chance."

"Thanks for the warning," Mike said, ending the call. He understood Igor's fascination with her. He suffered from the same thing himself. Being around her had become a kind of sweet torture. He remained in a constant state of arousal. While she looked sexy as hell in the expensive dresses and sky-high heels, he found Jennifer the most appealing when she was lounging around the condo in running shorts and a T-shirt, barefoot with her hair in a messy bun.

Steeling himself, he went to her room and tapped on the door, intending to ask if she wanted to spend a few hours somewhere else.

"It's unlocked," she called out.

He opened the door, the words sticking in his throat as he took in the sight of her sitting in her bed with pillows propped up behind her, those long legs of hers seeming to go on forever.

"What's up?" She glanced up from her book, catching him staring.

"I really admire you," he said, meaning it. "Your courage, your compassion for the women that Carmen is using, and your mad acting skills. You came into this without the years of training your sister had, and you've done amazing."

Clearly pleased, she smiled. He felt the power of that smile like a punch in the gut. There was more he wanted to say, a lot more, like how he thought he might be falling for her, but now was not the right time.

"Well, since we're being honest, I admire you, too," she said softly. "I hope the ATF knows how lucky they are to have you."

That was all? Struggling to hide his disappointment, he nodded.

"I'm wondering, though," she continued. "You've been undercover before. Is it normal to have so much sexual attraction to your partner? Honestly, it's been a struggle to keep my hands off you."

He sucked in his breath and almost lost control of his ragged hold on his desire for her. Silently counting to ten, he waited until he could speak. "Ditto," he said, keeping his tone as light as he could despite the husky rasp. "And no, it's very unusual."

As if she had no idea of her effect on him, she

stretched, the languid sensuality of her movement strengthening his arousal. "Micah, come here."

He stared, half in disbelief, though his heart jolted. "What?"

"Come. Here." Patting the seat beside her, she eyed him patiently. "I think we both need to let off some steam."

Finding himself walking toward her without any conscious decision to move, he knew he still had time to save himself. The thing was, he didn't want to. Instead, he wanted to lose himself on her, with her, inside her. He damn near lost it even thinking about it.

"Stop thinking so much," she urged, reaching for him and pulling him down for a deep, drugging kiss.

This, he thought, rejoicing even as he allowed his desire to take control. *This. Her. Us.* Those were his last coherent thoughts for quite some time.

Later, when they were wrapped up in each other's arms, he remembered his plan to get out and do ordinary things. When he asked her, she chuckled. "I'm not a big shopper," she said. "But lunch and the zoo sound good."

"Not a big shopper?" he asked. "But when we met, that's what you were doing."

She gave him a slow smile that sent his pulse racing. "I wanted those hiking boots. I'd had my eye on them a long time, but they were way too pricey." Her expression turned pensive. "I still haven't had a chance to try them out. I hope I get to before winter."

This gave him a better idea. "Instead of shopping and lunch, how about we head up to Boulder and take a brief hike?"

This got her attention. Her face lit up. "I really like that idea. We could bring a picnic lunch, too." She sighed, her brown eyes sparkling. "I know! We can do Boulder Canyon, or Chautauqua Park, or even Realization Point. Have you ever hiked any of those?"

Though he hated to admit it, he had to tell her the truth. Hopefully doing so wouldn't dim her enthusiasm. "I'm not a hiker," he said. "I like to run, but mostly city streets. I don't even own any hiking boots."

To give her credit, she didn't laugh at him or even crack a smile. "There's always a first time." She cocked her head. "Or are you saying you don't really want to go hiking after all?"

"Oh, I want to go," he replied, meaning it. "But I'll need to get a pair of boots."

Her beaming smile was all the reward he needed. "Then I guess we will have to go shopping after all. And we'll make sure and keep the hike short and easy, at least until we both break in new boots."

They went to the same mega sporting goods store where they'd first met, which felt weirdly nostalgic, though Micah took care to keep that to himself.

Thankfully, this time, there was no sign of Igor.

Once he'd paid for his boots, they headed back to the condo to stock up on provisions for their picnic. They made the drive up to Boulder, which had always been one of his favorite places, even if he couldn't afford to live there. They decided to hike starting at the Bobolink Trailhead, west of Baseline and Cherryvale, which Jennifer promised would be not only scenic, but easy enough for them both to break in their new boots.

Though he nodded, he almost told her that she was all the scenery he needed. Clearly in her element, with her color high and her brown eyes sparkling, she glowed like some magical wood sprite.

"You're really into this, aren't you?" he asked, even as he considered bringing out his phone and snapping a few pictures.

"It's pretty obvious, isn't it?" She did a slow twirl, inhaling deeply and then exhaling. "I only just started hiking last year. While I love winter, I hate when the snow closes the trails. I've even thought about learning to use snowshoes."

Eyeing her in half disbelief, he laughed. "Don't tell me you aren't a skier? It seems like everyone heads up to Winter Park at the first sign of a decent snow."

"Nope." She shook her head, sending her long ponytail whipping around her face. "I took lessons and tried skiing a few times. But it's just not my thing. What about you?"

While he considered himself a pretty accomplished skier, he hadn't hit the slopes since he'd begun this undercover assignment. Thinking about that now, he realized he didn't even miss it. "I'm pretty good," he admitted. "Though I haven't skied for two years. Maybe I could teach you this winter."

This winter. She froze and then smiled while he tried to pretend he hadn't just hinted that he hoped to be around her after this case had ended.

Still, she didn't contradict him or press him, which he appreciated. "I'd like that," she finally said, turning away to gaze up the path and adjusting her backpack. "Are you ready?"

"I am. Let's do this."

He couldn't remember the last time he'd spent such an enjoyable afternoon. Outdoors, wearing jeans and hiking boots and a sleeveless tee, Jennifer's beauty far outshone when she pretended to be Lania in her designer dresses and heels. Laughing with her, watching her face as she pointed out her favorite rock formations, he realized his feelings for her had begun to deepen beyond mere sexual attraction. Any other time, with any other woman, such a thing would have panicked him.

Of course, there were no other women like Jennifer Glass.

"Here," she announced, pointing to a large, flat rock maybe four feet off the ground. "We'll have our picnic here." Climbing up, she pulled a blanket out of her backpack and spread it. "Come on. I've used this before. It's perfect for this sort of thing."

Though he couldn't help but wonder if she and her boyfriend had picnicked here, he decided not to ask. She hardly ever mentioned Caville. *What kind of a name is that, anyway?*

"Earth to Micah," she chided, still smiling. "You have our food in your backpack, and I'm starving. Are you going to come up here so we can eat?"

"Of course."

They ate and talked and laughed, and for that moment in time, the case, the danger, his job—everything—faded away. He felt lighter somehow. And when he leaned over to kiss her, she met him halfway.

And then his phone rang, ruining everything.

Briefly, he considered ignoring it, but in the end, the case had to take precedence over everything else. Reluctantly, he broke it off and dug his cell from his pocket.

"It's Igor," he said, still buzzed from the effect of her kiss. "I'd better answer."

Chapter Twelve

What a kiss. Touching her lips, Jennifer ached to wrap herself around Micah again. No matter what they said or promised, they couldn't seem to keep their hands off each other.

As usual, Igor somehow must have instinctively known when they'd finally relaxed and decided to ruin it by calling, Jennifer thought, watching Micah's expression change as he listened. While on a basic level, she knew this couldn't be true, she hated the way they were at the crime boss's beck and call. He acted as if he owned them. And in a way, she guessed he did. That didn't mean she had to like it.

This was, however, what she'd signed up for by agreeing to take her twin sister's place. She and Micah had a job to do. That job had to take precedence over anything else.

Micah continued to listen.

Scrolling social media on her phone, she saw one of Caville's friends had tagged him in a series of pictures when they were out and about over the weekend. They'd gone up to Estes Park, a popular tourist destination. In several of the photos, Caville had his arm around a busty redhead, who clearly enjoyed the attention, leaning in close in a proprietary manner. Clearly, they were a couple.

Instead of jealousy, Jennifer felt only relief. Caville had clearly moved on, and without even consciously thinking about it, Jennifer had done the same.

Glancing up at Micah, she realized his entire expression had gone tight. He clearly didn't like whatever Igor was saying to him. Finally, he ended the call, shaking his head.

"What's going on?" she asked, concerned.

"We have to go back to Denver," Micah told her, his voice as remote as his expression.

"Does Igor want us to do something?" she asked, already dreading the answer.

"Not yet," he replied. "He seemed a little crazed. Off the rails, actually. He talked fast, rapid-fire, making all kinds of accusations against everyone."

"Including us?"

Slowly, he nodded. "He sounds like he's panicking. He's lashing out, trying to figure out who would dare to try to interfere with his operation. Unfortunately, he's even more dangerous like this." He took a deep breath. "We have to go back. I can't take the chance of us being forty-five minutes away if he suddenly decides he needs us to do something right away."

"That makes sense." Reluctant to end the afternoon, she began packing up nevertheless. Micah helped her, lost in his own thoughts.

Once they arrived back at the condo, he excused himself, saying he needed to take a shower. Watching him go, she briefly considered joining him, wondering about his reaction if she did. But no, his mood had clearly soured. Instead, she decided she'd better cool her jets. For now, maybe for as long as she could, preferably until the end of this case.

She'd begun to have very real feelings for Micah. And she suspected he'd started to feel the same.

Something had shifted between them out there on the trails. While she and Micah hadn't ever traditionally dated, due to their being thrown together in a situation where they had to pretend to be in an already long-established relationship, today had felt like a date. They'd been relaxed and at ease with each other, their obvious pleasure in each other's company making the constant buzz of attraction even stronger.

She'd never experienced anything like this before. While she shied away from the *L* word, she could easily imagine it stemming from a relationship that started like this.

Clearly, neither Jennifer nor Micah could resist the other. Put them in close proximity and one of them inevitably reached for the other. Both of them, without actually saying so, appeared up for a physical relationship, and maybe something more.

Something more. She couldn't help but wonder if her desire for more might be one-sided, the stuff of dreams and fantasy. Even worse, due to the need to focus on the case, she couldn't ask him to discuss this.

For now, she figured she might as well enjoy it while she could, even though she knew once this case was over, if Micah disappeared from her life, it would hurt a million times worse.

In this instance, though, she thought, the pleasure really would be worth the pain.

After taking her own shower and changing into comfortable clothes, she wandered back into the kitchen. Micah was there, sitting on a bar stool and scrolling through his phone with a glum expression.

"What's wrong?" she asked, hoping Igor hadn't called again.

"Nothing yet," he answered. "I just wish I could figure out a way to take Carmen out of the equation. While I don't have proof, I can't shake the feeling that she's behind all this upheaval."

Grabbing a bottled water from the fridge, she took a seat next to him. "You're probably right. Is there anything I can do to help?"

Her question made him smile. "No, but I appreciate the offer." Eyeing her, he tilted his head, his gaze darkening. "On second thought, there is something. Come here."

Heart pounding, she walked over, standing in between his legs. Their time together was nearing its end, and they had to make the most of it.

"How about we continue where we left off earlier?" he asked, tugging her close.

Then he covered her mouth with his and kissed her.

As before, as always, passion instantly flared. She let it run through her, singeing her blood, electrifying her nerve endings. She couldn't get enough—not of the kiss or of him. Locked together, they stumbled to the bedroom, falling onto the bed, shedding their clothes as they went. They made love with a sort of intense need, letting desire take over, pushing away any and everything else.

She released her desperation, her worries and fears of uncertainty. She'd always been the type of person who had to have a plan, and this—all of it—felt a bit like jumping out of a plane without a parachute.

And she liked the heck out of it.

. She'd never realized how exhilarating taking a blind leap of faith could be. And then she closed her eyes, stopped thinking and gave herself over to making love with Micah.

After, she fell asleep in Micah's arms.

When she woke in the morning, his side of the bed was empty. Her body pleasantly aching, she sat up slowly, eyeing the bright sunlight streaming in from the floor-to-ceiling windows. Sated, content, she found herself actually wishing that this was real life instead of an undercover assignment. Though they might be pretending about everything else, this attraction between them was real.

The rest of it would go away soon. She couldn't help but hope Micah wouldn't.

"There's been a change in plans." Frowning, Micah strode into the room, phone in hand. Bare chested and barefoot, he wore only a pair of boxer shorts. Despite the way they'd gone after each other the night before, her entire body melted into goo at the sight of him.

"What do you mean?" she managed to ask, reminding herself to focus.

"I just got off a call with Igor. It's not good."

"It never is." She sighed. Real life, intruding again. "You sound worried."

"I am. I'm not sure what's going on, but Igor has heard rumors that the Feds are sniffing around. He's spooked. Everything has been shut down and put on hold until he locates the source of the leak."

She froze. Which would technically be them. Heart in her throat, she stared, realizing she really needed coffee. She got out of bed and padded to the kitchen to make a cup, using the time to get her scattered thoughts together. He followed her. "What are we going to do?" she asked, turning and eyeing him while her cup brewed.

"Nothing." Jaw a hard line, he shook his head. "Just lay low and do whatever Igor asks us to do. We've done absolutely nothing that could implicate us in any way."

Turning away to stir her coffee, she took a small sip, unable to entirely quiet her own nerves. "Are you sure we've done nothing? There's got to be a reason the rumor started in the first place." Another sip, and a deep breath before she allowed herself to meet his eyes. "I'm new at this, Micah. What if I accidentally did something?"

Instead of automatically offering reassurances that would mean nothing, he took a moment to consider. "Did you?" he asked, his calm quiet somehow more alarming than anger would have been. "Because if you did, please tell me now."

Thinking, she went over every interaction, whether with Igor or with Carmen, and shook her head. "I didn't. At least, not that I know of." One thing for sure, she'd never forgive herself if she'd somehow managed to mess this up. "It has to be something else."

Micah nodded, his tense posture appearing to relax

somewhat. "I have a feeling this all comes back to Carmen, and I said as much to Igor. I think she's setting out to get even any way she can."

"Maybe," Jennifer allowed. "But Carmen isn't stupid. She's powerful, but Igor is more so. I find it difficult to believe she'd jeopardize everything she's built in order to get revenge on a couple of minor players."

Her choice of words made him smile, his blue eyes crinkling at the corners. "Minor players, huh? Is that what you think we are?"

Confused, she shrugged. "Aren't we?"

"In their world, yes. But in reality, since we're going to be the ones to take this entire operation down, we're the biggest players of all."

Since his mood seemed to have lightened, she exhaled. Part of her wanted to invite him to climb back into the bed with her and strip off those boxer shorts. With difficulty, she managed to focus on the conversation at hand. "Still, if Igor is putting a freeze on everything, that means the end is no longer right around the corner." She wasn't sure whether to feel sad or relieved.

"Right. But we'll get there. Igor can't postpone the shipment forever. His buyers will grow impatient. If he's going to try and ferret out the leak, he'll have to act quickly." As if on cue, his phone rang. "It's Igor. Let me take this."

Listening to Micah's side of the conversation, she couldn't tell much. Micah only spoke to agree with whatever Igor said. At one point, he grabbed a piece of paper and wrote something. "Yes, sir, we'll be there," he said and ended the call.

"This is even worse." For the first time since she'd

met him, Micah sounded nervous. "He's sending us on a small shipment, hoping to set up Carmen and have the Feds tip their hand."

"What? As in, use us for bait and see if the Feds go for it?"

"Yes. However, they won't. There's no way they'd jump on something this small. Part of me thinks Igor has to know that. But he's thinking maybe he can draw them off enough that they'll let the big shipment slip through their hands. It concerns me that he's sending us with Carmen. That means Igor thinks we're expendable. He's willing to let us be the fall guys if the Feds do take the bait."

"Which means we'll be...sacrificial?" Horrified, she took a nervous gulp of her coffee, singeing her mouth. "If he's setting up a trap to draw out the Feds, that indicates he's willing to let us get arrested or killed."

Micah's gaze darkened. "That's right. In fact, he's expecting us to shoot it out if the Feds show up. Either way, dead or alive and arrested, we'd be the fall guys."

She groaned. "What are we going to do?"

"We'll do what Igor wants. But the Feds won't take the bait. I'll make sure of that. Maybe a no-show of federal agents will help reassure him. And us being willing to do this should assure him of our loyalty. It's a win-win."

A win-win. Willing her heart rate to settle, she dropped down onto a chair. "What about Carmen?" she asked. "Is Igor going to do anything to keep her from messing everything up?"

"I feel quite certain he will, though he hasn't confided in me exactly what." Micah appeared so worried that she couldn't help but get back up, intending to go to him and wrap her arms around him. She was careful to leave her coffee on the table, not wanting to spill it. Which turned out to be a good thing, since she managed to trip over her own two feet, which brought a reluctant smile to Micah's handsome face.

"Here." He reached out to steady her. "Be careful."

"Thanks." Taking a deep breath, she stopped just short of his arms and gazed up at him instead. "It's all going to work out," she told him. "I have a feeling it will be fine. Just wait and see."

In response, he kissed the top of her head. "Thanks," he replied.

While she was wondering if he might take it a step further, his phone rang, startling both of them. She honestly had begun to hate that darn phone.

Micah glanced at the screen and grimaced. "It's Igor again," he said, stepping back. "Proof of how bad his nerves are right now."

His and hers both, she thought.

Answering, Micah listened, his only response to what he heard a quiet "Yes, sir." When he ended the call, his bleak expression caught at her heart.

"He says he's got everything in motion. The shipment will leave Denver this afternoon. We're to get over to the trucking company and inspect the container and seal it."

"When?"

"As soon as possible. He wants us up there by noon."

She checked the time. Eight thirty. "That's doable."

"It is. But there's more." He swallowed hard. "Carmen is going with us. Igor's orders."

"Does she know that?" She made a face. "I'm pretty sure the last thing Carmen wants is to have anything to do with either of us."

"She won't have a choice, just like we don't. Igor wants us all to work together." The irony of this statement wasn't lost on her. "He's even given me the job of contacting her and asking for her help in uncovering the mole."

"Uncovering the mole? I thought he believes she *is* the mole."

"Who knows what he really thinks? It's entirely possible he believes we are. Either way, he's throwing us all into an impossible situation and waiting to see who sinks and who swims."

Feeling nauseated, Jennifer swallowed. "Are you going to call Carmen?"

"Since I don't appear to have a choice, yes."

"You don't sound really enthused about that," she said. "And I don't blame you. Would you like me to do it?"

He smiled at her, and her heart skipped a beat. Darned if he wasn't the most handsome man on this planet, running his hand through his already tousled hair. When his blue gaze touched on hers, she forgot all her fear and went hot inside.

"That's kind of you to offer, but you've already done more than enough. Plus, I think it's the aspect of me calling her and eating crow that might appeal to Carmen's power-hungry side. She's pretty pissed at you, so having your partner go crawling to her might work."

"That makes a sort of twisted sense," she allowed.

"But what if it doesn't? What if it isn't enough to appease her?"

"Then I'll have to call in reinforcements. You."

As it turned out, Mike's phone call was enough. He spoke in a halting, defeated voice that Lania knew would appeal to Carmen's thirst for vengeance.

"Yes, Lania is aware that I'm calling you," he said, the distaste in his expression not registering in his voice. "All right. Just one moment."

Holding out the phone, he shot her a look of caution. "Carmen wants to speak with you."

Swallowing hard, she squared her shoulders and took the phone. "Well, hello," Carmen purred. "Not so high and mighty now, are you?"

"What do you want me to say?" Lania asked, aware she had to be diligent not to say the wrong thing.

"Admit you were wrong and that you should have agreed to work with me in the beginning," Carmen goaded, barely even trying to restrain her glee.

Cool, calm and calculated, Lania reminded herself. "And if I don't?"

"Then I'll make sure Igor believes your boyfriend is a traitor."

The brazen statement hung there while Lania struggled to process it. Did Carmen know? Or was she only bluffing?

Lania decided to go with bluffing. "It's you, isn't it?" she said, bitterness tingeing her voice. "You're trying to destroy us and don't care if you take down Igor, too."

In front of her, Mike waved his hands and shook his head, silently cautioning her to be careful.

Instead of becoming enraged, Carmen only laughed.

"I like you, Lania. I really do. And I have to believe that you know better than to think I would do anything so foolish. Igor wants us all to work together to do a small shipment to try and draw out the traitor. This, we will do."

"Good." Gritting her teeth, Lania passed the phone back to Mike. "I'm done," she said, stalking away.

Micah found her a few minutes later, sitting on the edge of her bed, seething. She looked up, trying to get herself back to a calm place.

"Why are you so worked up?" he asked, sitting down beside her and bumping his shoulder to hers. "You have to think of this as a complex chess game."

All she could give him was the truth. "I really just want this to be over."

"You want your life back," he said. "I get it, believe me. But we have to believe the end will be in sight soon. Sure, there might be a hiccup here and there. But we'll get through this. Together."

Together. Lifting her head, she nodded. That would have to be enough. "Let's do this," she said. "But first, I need coffee and a shower."

"I'll make us something to eat," he told her. "We're picking Carmen up in two hours."

MAKING BREAKFAST WHILE Jennifer showered, Micah considered their partnership. While she and Laney looked almost identical, Jennifer had something her twin sister didn't. He couldn't really define what that was—some kind of spark, he guessed, that reached inside him and ignited a bonfire. He suspected Jennifer felt the same way. Grimacing, he shook his head. He sure as hell hoped she did. Because for the first time in his entire life, he was actually considering a different career. The kind where his woman wouldn't have to worry every day when he went to work. The thought both terrified and exhilarated him.

Later, they got into Lania's Mercedes, which they had to take since the Corvette only seated two, and headed over to pick up Carmen. Lania had gone awfully quiet, and he almost asked her if she was all right, but he didn't. Neither one of them was a big fan of Carmen, and he suspected Lania needed to gather her thoughts to prepare to deal with the other woman.

They pulled up in front of a modern-style house and waited.

Lania gave an audible sigh but kept her back straight and her chin up.

"Brace yourself," Mike murmured. "Here she comes."

They both watched as Carmen sauntered over to the Mercedes. Today she had on jeans and a sleeveless black top along with a pair of huge, dark sunglasses. Even dressed down, she managed to convey an air of elegance. Which probably meant her clothes had cost a lot.

Though he really didn't want to, Mike jumped out and opened the back door for her, managing a pleasant expression. In turn, Carmen flashed him a completely false smile, her bright red lipstick matching her long fingernails. She glanced at Lania as she slid into the car. "Let's do this," she said.

Since neither Mike nor Lania spoke, Carmen kept up a running dialogue all the way to the trucking company. Not only did this seem out of character, but her rushed speech and shortness of breath had Mike wondering if she'd taken drugs. In fact, her behavior specifically reminded him of his last phone call with Igor.

"When was the last time you saw Igor in person?" he asked, interrupting Carmen's monologue on various brands of trucks.

"Igor?" She blinked, momentarily appearing caught off guard. "Yesterday. Why?"

"What are you taking?" he demanded, infusing his voice with steel. "It's obvious you're on something. What is it?"

"None of your business," Carmen retorted, bouncing in her seat like an overstimulated child.

Instead of continuing to argue, he pulled the car over to the shoulder of the road and turned around to face her. "Get out. I'm not dealing with a coked-up druggie who could mess up the entire operation."

Carmen stared at him, her expression inscrutable. He'd bet if she removed the sunglasses, her pupils would be the size of pinheads.

"Get out," he repeated. "Don't make me drag you out of this car."

"You wouldn't dare." But she didn't sound too certain. "I'm calling Igor."

"Go ahead. And while you're at it, tell him how you showed up to carry out an important shipment all coked out."

"I…" Carmen glanced from one to the other.

Disgusted, he shook his head. "As if we can afford even the slightest mistake."

Lania watched the exchange with a small, tight smile. "I agree," she said, turning to glare at Carmen. "You call yourself a woman of power, yet you show up to work with us for the first time high? Get out."

Carmen looked from Mike to Lania, but she didn't move. "Let me call Igor. He will straighten this out."

Mike held up his phone and then pushed the call-now button. A moment later, Igor answered. He listened while Mike outlined his concerns. "Let me talk to Carmen," Igor said. Mike passed the phone over into the back seat.

"Hey, baby," Carmen drawled, shooting Mike a sly smile as she slipped her sunglasses on top of her head. "Yeah, you were right. It *is* good stuff."

Damn. Jaw tight, Mike glanced at Lania. Carmen had clearly gotten to Igor. Which made the fact that Igor had sent her on this particular mission an even bigger mystery. He tried not to gag while listening to her make cooing sounds.

"Here, Mike." Carmen passed the phone back. "Igor wants to talk to you."

"Listen carefully," Igor said, still sounding jacked up, but also serious as hell. "Do not give that woman any indication of what I'm saying, you hear me?"

"Yes, sir," Mike replied.

"She is using meth," Igor continued. "Not cocaine. And for all I know, she is addicted. She attempted to use this, and her body, to trick me, and as far as she knows, I fell for it."

Now this was the Igor Mike had come to know. Clearly, Igor hadn't allowed himself to fall for Carmen's schemes. While she thought she had the upper hand, he'd actually turned the tables and was playing her. Or was he? Mike couldn't ignore the very real possibility that Igor might be playing them off against each other. Plus, what about the drugs? Igor, too, had clearly seemed to be using something.

"I see," Mike commented, wondering if he dared to ask if Igor had also used Carmen's drugs. Telling himself he needed to pick his battles, he decided not to.

"I want you or Lania to keep an eye on her at all times," Igor continued. "And if you see her doing anything that might indicate she's selling me out, I expect you to deal with her."

Mike agreed and ended the call.

Now he understood why Igor had sent them all on this errand together. He had absolutely no doubt that Igor had told Carmen the exact same thing. Which meant if an unstable, drugged-up Carmen felt like it, she could gun down both Mike and Lania without facing any consequences.

He needed to warn Lania. But how, without Carmen overhearing? He decided to take the bull by the horns and be direct.

"Are you the mole?" he asked Carmen, crossing his arms as he faced her. She sat in the back seat, jiggling her leg.

She recoiled, clearly taken aback. "No. Are you?"

"Of course not. Though neither of us would actually admit it if we were, now would we?"

Eyes narrow, she glared at him. "What's your point?"

"Igor told me about the meth. He also gave me permission to take you out. I'm assuming he said the same thing to you about me."

She nodded. A slow smile curved her lips. "He did."

"Maybe he wants us all to go out in a blaze of gunfire," Mike continued. "Everyone but Lania, that is. He's made no secret of his desire for her."

Sunglasses still on top of her head, Carmen narrowed her eyes. "Everyone desires Lania." Bitterness colored her voice as she glared at Lania. "You need to learn to use that to your advantage."

"You need to help us make sure nothing happens to this shipment," Lania snapped back. "Come on, Mike. We have a job to do. I'll try and keep her out of trouble."

Her comment made him laugh out loud. He shifted into Drive and pulled back onto the road.

On the surface, everything appeared to be exactly as it was supposed to be. The weapons were all there, top-grade, high-capacity weapons. Mike inspected each crate before sealing it and watching it be loaded into the container. He made a notation after every crate, making sure the correct number was there, not wanting to take a chance that Igor's shipment would somehow come up short.

Then, once the container had been filled, Mike personally closed it, locking the sliding bolt into place. He tried not to remember the time he'd been shut inside one of these things.

Quiet for once, Carmen watched the entire process, her sunglasses once again covering her eyes. Lania stood next to her, arms crossed, her stance reminding him of a guard supervising a prisoner. Damn if he didn't like her. A lot. Far more than he should.

Now came the tricky part. If federal agents were actually going to swoop in, they'd either do it here or be in wait down at the shipping yard in Galveston. Mike had given explicit instructions asking them to stand down.

His office had gladly complied, because they wanted a big bust, not a minor one. Plus, no one liked the idea of Mike being set up.

The truck hauling the container pulled away without incident. Mike, Lania and Carmen all looked at each other. "Well," Mike said, rubbing his hands together briskly. "It looks like our work here is done."

Carmen sighed. Though still jittery, she appeared to be winding down. "This was a total waste of time."

"I'm just glad nothing happened," Lania said, her voice sharp. "It seems like Igor's worries were baseless."

"Good thing." Mike took her arm. "Come on, ladies. Let's get back to town. We can call Igor on the way."

Muttering under her breath, Carmen followed them back to the car.

As they pulled out of the trucking company parking lot and drove away, the light at the intersection turned green just as they reached it. "More good luck," Mike said, glad he didn't have to brake. Though the trucking company warehouse was located in a remote area northwest of Denver, he wondered at the surprising lack of traffic.

As he drove through the intersection, another car appeared, seemingly out of nowhere, driving too fast to stop, and broadsided them. The last thing Mike heard was the sound of the women screaming.

Chapter Thirteen

Jennifer came to slowly, the coppery taste of blood in her mouth. What had just happened? She hurt, felt bruised and battered and just…wrong. They'd been in an accident, she remembered, struggling to turn sideways to locate Micah.

Still strapped in, he appeared to be conscious, though dazed. "Micah," she called softly, forgetting to use his undercover name. "Are you all right?"

Slowly, he looked at her. It took a moment for his gaze to focus. "I think so. What about you? Your side of the car took the brunt of the impact."

He was right, though the other vehicle had hit behind her, on the back passenger door rather than the front. At that moment, she remembered there had been someone in the back seat.

"Carmen." Dang, it hurt to move. But she had to try. Unclipping her seat belt, she slowly turned around to view the crumpled metal that had pushed into the back seat. Carmen occupied a space maybe three feet wide.

Micah had managed to turn and do the same. "She seems to be in one piece," he said. "Though since she's covered in blood and glass, it's hard to tell."

"Should we even try to move her?" Jennifer—no, *Lania*, she reminded herself—asked.

"I think so. We've got to get her out of here," he replied. He got his door open and helped tug Lania toward him and out, too.

They both straightened slowly and stiffly, wavering a little while trying to stand. Remarkably, at first glance they both appeared unhurt, other than a few cuts and bruises, though Lania felt as if her entire body had been someone's punching bag. Looking at the crumpled back part of the car, she had a feeling that Carmen wouldn't be so lucky. If she was still alive, that was.

"I'm almost afraid to look," she admitted, getting out her phone. "I'm going to call 911." She glanced around. "Where's the other vehicle? The one that hit us. It's gone."

Blinking, Mike looked, too. Other than some pieces of metal and broken glass, there was no sign of the other vehicle. Which was weird. It had to have a lot of damage after plowing into them.

"I think it was a pickup," Mike said. "But I'm not sure."

"I never even saw it until it hit us," Lania agreed.

From the back seat, Carmen moaned.

"She's alive." Lania grabbed his arm. "We need to get her out of the car."

"Go ahead and call 911," Mike said. "Let me check on the extent of her injuries before I even attempt to move her." He managed to get the door open. "Good thing this Benz is built like a tank."

As Mike reached in, Lania peered around his shoulder, phone still in hand. She dialed 911, quickly gave their location and what had happened, and then, despite the operator's request to stay on the line, she ended the call. She needed to have both hands free in case Mike needed her help.

With the seat belt holding her in place, at first glance Carmen appeared to be in one piece. There was a lot of blood, on her face and head especially. She had a huge cut right above her forehead, still bleeding freely.

"I'm going to try and get you out of here," Mike said, releasing the seat belt. "Can you tell me where you hurt?"

"I…" Carmen struggled to open her eyes. She managed to get one open, though that gash on her forehead bled so much that Lania doubted Carmen could see through the veil of red.

"Everywhere," Carmen croaked. "What…what happened?"

Now they could hear sirens in the distance. "Help is on the way," Lania told her. "We were in a car accident. Another vehicle ran the light and T-boned us."

"Igor." Carmen managed to spit out the name. "He's behind this." And then, before anyone could reply, she passed out.

The ambulance pulled up, lights flashing, killing its siren. A police car followed. Mike leaned close. "Remember, use the identification I gave you."

She nodded. "That's all I carry with me these days."

Two paramedics approached.

"She's in the car," Mike said. "Still alive, but we're not sure how badly she's hurt."

Lania and Mike stepped back to allow the paramedics to take over. They lifted Carmen onto a stretcher and loaded her into the ambulance.

"What about you two?" a third EMT asked. "If you were in that vehicle, you probably need to get looked at, too."

Mike declined, asserting that he was fine. After a moment's hesitation, Lania did the same. She didn't feel bad, a bit bruised and battered and sore, so fine would be a stretch.

After the EMT returned to the ambulance, a uniformed officer approached, asking for their statements. "A tow truck has been called for your vehicle," he said. "It doesn't appear to be drivable."

For the first time, Lania wondered how they'd get home. When she asked out loud, the officer smiled. "I can drive you," he said. "Either to the hospital or home."

Micah cleared his throat, breaking the policeman's intense focus on Jennifer. "I think we'd like to go home, if you don't mind. We can take the other car to the hospital, if you could let us know where they've taken her."

"No problem," the officer replied, his tone a bit more businesslike. "I'll just need to take both of your statements and then we'll be on our way."

Once they both separately told him what had happened, they all piled into the squad car and headed back to Denver. Though the policeman asked Jennifer if she'd like to ride up front, she'd elected to sit in the back seat next to Micah. She didn't want to be too far away from him, especially after what had happened.

After being dropped off in front of the condo, she

and Micah walked inside, arm in arm. "He had the hots for you," he teased.

"No, he didn't," she protested. "He was just being friendly."

Micah snorted at her response. "He couldn't take his eyes off you. Not that I blame him."

Warmth spread through her at his compliment. "Thanks." She kept her tone light.

As soon as they were back inside the condo, Micah pulled out his phone. He eyed it for a second. "I need to call Igor."

"You do," she agreed. "Do you think there's any truth to what Carmen said?"

"That he was behind the accident?" He shrugged. "It's possible, but that's not really Igor's style. He's more likely to send goons with guns to take care of anyone he thinks is a problem. A quick bullet to the head is much more effective than a car crash."

She shuddered. "Well, call him anyway. It'll be interesting to hear what he has to say."

With a grimace, Micah pressed the button. A moment later, he left a message, asking Igor to call him back.

"Weird that he didn't answer," Micah said. "He's been acting so erratic lately. He told me he wanted an immediate call once the truck got on the road. I decided to wait until Carmen wasn't able to listen in, which is why I didn't do it before we left the trucking company."

"And then the accident happened."

"Right." Micah walked to the floor-to-ceiling window and looked out. "Let's go check on Carmen.

Though she's not my favorite person, I was driving, so I feel sort of responsible."

When they arrived at the hospital, they went straight to the ER. The charge nurse frowned and then asked if they were family. "I'm her fiancé," Micah lied. "And this is her stepsister."

"I see." The older woman frowned. "Let me see if the attending physician can speak with you first."

Jennifer and Micah exchanged glances. "That's not good," Jennifer said. "Is Carmen all right?"

But the nurse had already turned away without buzzing them through the locked double doors.

Just then Micah's phone rang. "It's Igor," he said. "Let me fill him in and see what he has to say." He walked away from the front desk and went outside to take the call.

Jennifer decided to sit while she waited. The triage nurse returned. "The doctor will be with you as soon as he can. Your stepsister is in the ICU. She's in serious condition."

Jennifer nodded. A kind of profound weariness swept over her. She'd begun to hate this entire setup—the pretending, the danger and the unspeakably cruel and evil things these people did to one another. The only good thing about all this was getting to know Micah.

Micah returned just as the ER doors opened and a male doctor wearing light blue scrubs stepped out. "Are you Carmen Montenegro's family?"

Both Jennifer and Micah nodded.

"Well, the good news is that she's stable. We were able to downgrade her from critical to serious. The bad news is that she's not out of the woods yet."

"What is the extent of her injuries?" Jennifer wanted to know.

"Miraculously, she has no broken bones. But she has swelling in her brain. That's what we're treating her for now." He sighed. "If the medication doesn't work, we may take steps to reduce her body temperature. We're hoping we won't have to operate."

"Are we able to see her?" Micah asked.

"Briefly. And only one visitor at a time." Motioning at the nurse to unlock the door, he waved a hand at Micah and Jennifer. "Follow me."

Walking quickly behind him, Jennifer wondered if Carmen would be awake or sedated. She also couldn't help but wonder, if in fact Igor had been behind this, if he'd send someone to the hospital to finish the job. Unfortunately, she couldn't voice this concern to Micah just yet.

The doctor led them down another hall, through a second set of double doors, and then stopped outside a room. "She's in here," he said. "She's been sedated, so she won't realize she has visitors. Please don't stay too long or disturb her in any way."

"We won't." Micah thanked him. He waited until the physician had walked away before turning to Jennifer. "Do you want to go first or should I?"

"I'll do it." Swallowing hard, Jennifer opened the door and stepped into the room. Though Micah was supposed to wait in the hallway, he followed her and then stopped just inside the doorway. She halted, too, taking it all in.

Looking impossibly small, Carmen lay unmoving in the hospital bed. Machines beeped and hummed, taking her vitals. She was breathing on her own, which was a relief. They'd done a good job cleaning her up, too, as well as bandaging her wounds. The fact that she had no broken bones seemed like a miracle. Clearly, she had to have hit her head hard.

"She looks totally different," Jennifer mused, keeping her voice down. "I'm not used to thinking of Carmen as vulnerable, but that's what she looks like now."

Again, she wondered if it had just been a horrible accident, or if, as Carmen had said earlier, Igor had arranged it. If so, he might have killed all three of them. But why? None of that made sense. For all she knew, this might have simply been a horrible accident. Hopefully, whoever had caused it would be caught.

She forced herself to take a step closer to the bed. While she and Carmen had never been close, nor would they be, she hated to see the other woman like this.

Should she speak to her? She remembered reading somewhere that people could hear you, even when they were in a coma. If so, what would she say?

Behind her, Micah squeezed her shoulder. "She appears to be in good hands. We really should get going."

Something in his tone… Jennifer nodded. "I wonder if we should try to locate any other family members?"

Steering her toward the door, Micah shook his head. "I don't think we need to get that involved."

While she understood what he meant, it still felt wrong.

They didn't talk again until they were inside the Corvette.

"What did Igor have to say?" she asked.

"He sounded shocked, of course." Micah shrugged.

"There are so many layers to everything that happens, it's like digging through a huge pile of...dirt."

The analogy made her smile, mostly because she knew what he'd almost said instead.

"This case really needs to be over," Micah continued. "It seemed so clear-cut, with the ending in sight, and now it's taken this huge detour. I have to believe Carmen has a lot to do with that. Everything changed once she entered the picture."

Slowly, Jennifer nodded. "But then why would Igor want to take her out?"

"That's what we need to find out." Micah sighed. "This is getting ridiculous. It's time to put an end to the nonsense. And that's what I intend to do."

THE NEXT MORNING, Micah woke with a renewed sense of purpose. He hadn't been joking when he'd said he'd had enough. He didn't like the way the ground seemed to be constantly shifting under his feet. Especially after two freaking years of sure and steady progress. Now it felt as if all that had been tossed into the wind.

He had to find out what the hell was actually going on. And the logical place to start was with Igor.

This wasn't the kind of thing that could be done over the phone. Nope, he'd need to meet with the man face-to-face.

"Where are you going?" Jennifer asked as he drained his coffee before heading out the door.

There didn't seem to be any point in hiding the truth. "I'm going to have it out with Igor."

Jennifer dragged her hand through her disheveled hair. She still wore the oversize T-shirt and shorts that she'd slept in, and her feet were bare. Any other time, he would have found her cuteness irresistible and urged her to take him back to bed. Now, though, he couldn't allow anything to distract him.

"Are you sure that's wise?" she asked. "We still don't know if Igor was the one who arranged the accident."

"No, we don't. But if Igor wants to take us out, he'll try. The only choice I have is confronting him. He admires confidence and people who take charge."

"Then I want to go with you," Jennifer declared. "I just need a few moments to change."

"I was afraid you'd say that. And I appreciate your offer to help. But this time, I'm going to do this alone. You've already been in too much danger. Take the day off. Do some binge-watching of your favorite show or read a good book. You deserve it."

She made a face. "Since my car is wrecked, I don't really have a choice, do I? It's not like I can go anywhere."

Careful to hide his relief that she didn't insist on going, he nodded. "It's safer here. Until I find out the truth about what's really going on, I don't want to risk you getting injured—or worse."

Her chin came up at that, though not before he saw the flash of hurt in her eyes. "I'm pretty tough," she replied quietly. "And since we've set it up all along so that we are equal partners, I don't think you going without me is going to help your case."

Damn it. Though he hated to admit it, she was right. Igor would no doubt find it odd if Mike showed up on his doorstep minus Lania.

He sighed. "Point taken. Go get changed and I'll wait. Since Igor isn't expecting me, it's not a problem."

"Be right back." She dashed from the room. Less than fifteen minutes later, she reappeared, dressed in a casual summer dress, with sandals. She'd even put on makeup and curled her hair.

He'd never met a woman who could do all that in such a short period of time. Not only that, but Jennifer looked as good as if she'd spent much longer on her appearance.

"What?" she asked, hands on hips, making him realize he'd been staring.

"You look amazing," he replied. "And I'm amazed how you can do it all so quickly."

This comment made her laugh. "I have a method. Are you ready to go?"

Suddenly reluctant, he stalled. The urge to protect her, for however long he could, overruled everything else, even his common sense. "Don't you want to have a cup of coffee first? Maybe something to eat?"

She cocked her head. "What's wrong with you? I thought we needed to get going."

"We do," he admitted. "But before we go, promise me you'll be careful."

"I will." She smiled. "Though I can't actually speak for Lania."

It shouldn't have bothered him that he knew exactly what she meant, but it did. That was the problem with these kinds of deep undercover operations. Sometimes the role you were playing took over.

"Just try and rein her in," he said, grabbing his car keys. "Let's go get this over with."

They made the drive over to Cherry Creek in silence. Mike wondered if Lania felt nervous. If so, he couldn't blame her. He wasn't entirely certain this was the right thing to do. But he needed to get things moving again, and hopefully this would help. Plus, even though he didn't even want to think about the possibility, if his cover had been blown, he needed to get the hell out and away before he or Jennifer got hurt.

The instant they pulled up in front of the lavish estate, several armed men surrounded their car. They wore their weapons discreetly, under their windbreakers, making sure to move just enough to alert Mike to their presence.

He gave his name and explained that he didn't have an appointment but felt sure Igor would see him. In this, it seemed he was correct, as after conferring with their boss, they said they'd escort him to the house.

"I've been expecting you," Igor said when his men showed Mike and Lania into his office. He sat behind his huge, elaborately carved mahogany desk, hands behind his head.

Mike gave a slow nod. "We just checked on Carmen in the hospital. She's in serious condition."

"Is she?" Igor's sharp gaze missed nothing. He looked from Mike to Lania and back again. "Sit," he ordered. "Would either of you like something to drink?"

Both Mike and Lania sat, though they declined the offer of a beverage. Igor took a sip of his drink. "I'm glad both of you escaped the accident without serious injuries."

"Thanks. We are, too." Mike wasn't going to go there. Not yet. He wanted to deal with the other business first. "I wanted to talk to you about the smaller shipment I signed off on. It went well, without a hitch."

"It did," Igor agreed, his expression giving nothing away. "Clearly, the information I received about an informant was wrong."

"Clearly," Mike drawled, crossing his arms. "And because I'd really like to get paid, how about we get that other shipment taken care of while Carmen is out of commission? It seems to me all the problems started when she got involved."

Igor stared, his eyes narrowing. Finally, he sat up straight and slammed his hands on top of his desk. "I like the way you think," he said. "And you're right. Carmen is nothing but trouble. Let's get the ball rolling. The sooner we get those guns to the coast, the sooner we all get paid."

It took every ounce of self-control Mike possessed not to jump up and fist-bump the air. Instead, he flashed Lania his most savage, ruthless grin. "We're going to do this," he said.

"Damn right we are," Igor seconded. He actually seemed pleased, something Mike hadn't seen often. "Let me make some calls and get things moving. I'll let you know when I want you back out at the trucking company to do your inspection of the cargo."

"Perfect." Mike pushed to his feet, holding out his hand to help Lania up. "I think we've got some getting ready to do."

"You do that." Standing also, Igor gestured toward the door. "And this time, try not to wreck your car." Grinning, he cracked up at his own joke.

Mike shepherded Lania out of there as quickly as he could without appearing to be rushing.

"What's wrong?" she asked while they were getting into his car.

He shook his head. "The way Igor was acting back there? That's what I'm talking about. In the entire two years I've worked with him, I've never seen him make a joke. Not once. I always figured he just didn't have a sense of humor."

"Okay," she replied, clicking her seat belt in place. "But maybe that's a good thing. Perhaps he's loosening up a bit more because he trusts you."

"Maybe, but somehow I doubt it."

She made a face. "You sure sound grumpy," she teased. "I'd think you'd be more excited. The end is once again in sight."

He leaned over and kissed her then, a quick press of his mouth on hers, promising more later. "I hope you're right," he said. "The sooner the better."

Two days went by without word from Igor. Micah didn't want to worry, but he couldn't help but wonder about the delay. After they'd left their meeting with Igor, he'd assumed he'd be hearing from the other man in hours, not days.

The delay—for whatever reason—was driving him straight up a wall. Worse, he couldn't do anything about it. It would be bad form to press Igor, especially since Igor had made it plain he'd let Mike know as soon as he'd set everything up.

Now, though, it felt more like Mike had been cut out. He couldn't imagine why Igor hadn't yet contacted him.

Each and every scenario that played out in his mind seemed worse than the other.

While forty-eight hours of nothing to do turned Micah into a pacing, grumbly fool, the peace and quiet appeared to have the opposite effect on Jennifer. She'd happily settled into one of the chaise lounges on his patio with a book and had barely budged. "I finally feel like I'm on a bit of a vacation," she told him, which made him feel guilty, since he knew she was actually on her summer break.

He made an attempt to join her, grabbing the latest bestselling thriller from his nightstand, but his restlessness made it impossible to concentrate on the pages.

The morning of the third day, he remembered Carmen. "Maybe we should check on her," he said to Jennifer over coffee. He'd come to enjoy this little ritual they'd developed—coffee together, sometimes in the bed they'd shared, more often in the kitchen, talking over their plans for the day.

Jennifer made a face. "This is going to sound awful, but do you think we can just call? I really don't want to go visit her again."

He couldn't help but chuckle. "I hear that. Let me call the hospital. I bet they wonder why her so-called fiancé hasn't been to see her at all since day one."

This comment had Jennifer shaking her head. He called the hospital, identified himself and winced as they put him through to Carmen's room.

However, the nurse answered. He asked a few questions, made up some story about his job making him travel out of town and got the update on her status.

"Well?" Jennifer asked, getting up to make herself a second mug of coffee. "How's she doing?"

"Carmen's on the mend, according to her nurse. The meds were successful in stopping her brain swelling, and they've brought her out of the medically induced coma. They've got her moving around a little and are hoping she can be discharged in a day or two."

"Coma? I thought she was just sedated."

He shrugged. "I don't know. But more importantly, the longer Igor keeps stalling, the less likely it will be that we can get that shipment done before Carmen gets out of the hospital."

About to head to the shower, he stopped when his phone rang. "Igor," he said, his heart skipping a beat. "Finally."

"I bet you wondered what the hell was going on," Igor said, sounding tired. "It's been a lot of work trying to get everything coordinated again." He went on to complain about sellers refusing to hold his previous orders, having to work new deals and now having to reschedule everything from the trucking company to the dock time down in Galveston. From the way he talked, anyone listening in would assume this to be a completely legitimate business operation.

"You should have called me," Mike replied. "I would have helped wherever you needed me."

"I know, I know. I got it handled. And finally, we're almost good to go," Igor said. "I'm hoping to be able to send you out to the trucking company bright and early Thursday morning. You'll be doing exactly what you did with the smaller shipment."

"Let me know for sure and I'll be there," Mike said.

"Will there still be seven containers?" Which would mean he'd need one more tracking device. He'd only had seven and had sent one with the smaller shipment just as a test case. From all reports he'd received, the device was working perfectly.

"Yes." Igor coughed. "I'm waiting on confirmation from one more manufacturer before I can say we're good to go. Meanwhile, I've got to try and keep Carmen from finding out. I don't want her there."

"Carmen?" Alarm bells went off. "Is she out of the hospital?"

"She's not but claims she's getting out soon. Since she regained consciousness, she's made several phone calls threatening me." He sighed. "She clearly feels that I was behind the accident."

Mike so badly wanted to ask the other man if he had been, but he knew better. Right now, he couldn't afford to say anything that might jeopardize his role in the shipment. He just wanted all this over.

"You'd think she'd know better," Igor continued. "If I want someone dead, they're dead, usually from a bullet in the brain." He took a deep breath. "Let me talk to Lania."

Startled, Mike's first instinct was to refuse. Then, thinking better of that, he held out the phone. "Lania, it's Igor. He wants to talk to you."

Her eyes widened, but she accepted the cell. "Hello, Igor," she said. "Of course it's wonderful to hear from you. What's up?"

She listened again. "You know Mike and I are a team. We can talk about this other opportunity, but together. I see. Yes, I'll think about it. Thank you."

Ending the call, she passed the phone back to Mike. "He's back at it again," she said. "I'm guessing since Carmen is out of the picture. He wanted to talk to me about forming a partnership with him. You heard my response."

Mike swore. "Whatever you do, stall him until after Thursday. We can't piss him off. Not now—not when it's so close."

"I told him I would think about it. He didn't specify a time frame—in fact, he told me to take all the time I needed."

Though Mike nodded, he couldn't help but think this wasn't good. For Igor to stir things up this close to a major shipment seemed worrisome, to say the least.

"We just need to hang in there," he said out loud. "Thursday, the shipment leaves Denver. From that point, it's out of our hands. All we can do is sit back and wait."

"I hope Igor doesn't somehow screw this up," Lania said.

"Me, too," Mike agreed. "Me, too."

Chapter Fourteen

The phone conversation with Igor had been unsettling, to say the least. Jennifer didn't understand why the crime boss couldn't seem to follow a normal, straight trajectory. Why not finish with one thing before starting another?

Still, now that everything had been okayed and was almost good to go, she felt optimistic that the end might finally be in sight. As long as Igor didn't do anything stupid, she had hopes that she could get back to her real life soon.

The thought brought a pang. Would Micah remain in her life once this had ended? While she hoped he would, she didn't want to talk to him about what would happen afterward, as she didn't want to jinx it.

Two more days went by without them hearing from Igor. This appeared to drive Micah crazy, judging by his pacing and all-around grumpiness. Though worried, Jennifer caught up on her reading, got a little sun and even accompanied Micah to the building gym. To counteract this, she'd also baked a delicious apple crumble, and she and Micah had enjoyed every decadent bite.

Mike checked with the hospital and learned that Carmen had been discharged, they suspected mostly by sheer dint of will. Though Lania hadn't heard from her—a blessing for which she was glad—she occasionally wondered how the other woman was doing. Since she couldn't bring herself to worry about a human trafficker, she considered Carmen's absence a godsend.

As for herself, after the accident Lania had felt a bit bruised and battered, but nothing major. Mike claimed he felt the same. They knew they were lucky not to have been more seriously injured. Mike claimed he still didn't know if Igor had been behind the wreck or not. While Lania had her suspicions, in the end it didn't matter.

As it inched closer to Thursday, they both got a bit jumpier. Waiting on Igor to give them the order to head up to the trucking company to inspect the outgoing shipment was a form of torture, especially since Igor made no other contact.

Every time Mike's phone rang, he started, but so far Igor hadn't called. Once that happened, everything would be underway. Igor's operation would go down.

And if there was any way they could tie Carmen into it, Lania hoped she'd go down, too. Or at the very least, her trafficking operation would come under scrutiny, making it impossible for her to operate.

Micah's phone rang. This time he stared at it in disbelief. "Finally," he said. "It's Igor."

Answering, he listened. Apparently, Igor had a lot to say, because Micah never got another word in. Finally, he managed to speak, saying only "yes" before ending the call.

"Well?" she demanded.

"Igor wants to see us," Micah said, not bothering to hide the excitement in his voice. "I think things are finally going to get underway."

Jumping up, she high-fived him. "Awesome." She couldn't help but grin. "It's about time. When are we meeting with him?"

"He wants us to head over there now. He's got some final instructions he wants to go over." He grinned back. "And then come Thursday, we'll be good to go."

"Fingers crossed." She looked down at her denim shorts. "I should change first."

"Igor said to come as we are." Micah shrugged. He wore a pair of khaki shorts. "This time we're meeting him in one of his warehouses. I'm ready if you are."

"These shorts are too short," she said, thinking of the way Igor undressed her with his eyes. "Let me get a sundress and sandals."

Back in the huge closet, she picked the plainest sundress she could find. It was navy blue, and while it might be high fashion, the way it hung in a straight line reminded her of a tent. With this, she pared white sneakers. Glancing at herself in a mirror, she felt satisfied she looked as far from sexy or even attractive as she could get.

Even though Micah's eyes widened when he saw her outfit, he didn't comment. They climbed into the Corvette, Jennifer glad to have the longer length of the dress.

The warehouse was located near where they'd first gone to see Samir and Ernie.

"Are you ready?" Mike asked as they pulled onto the street that went between the various buildings.

Lania nodded. "I am."

"I'm not sure what he stores in there," Mike said.

"Maybe some of his guns?" she asked.

"Possibly, but that's doubtful. It wouldn't be wise to keep a lot of weapons in one place, though it could be a stopping place as he funnels them through for shipping."

She guessed they were about to find out.

Once at the warehouse, they parked. Stepping out of the car, they walked to the back door and knocked. Slowly, the metal door opened, and they stepped inside. Two men holding some kind of large and dangerous-looking guns stood inside.

"Igor has asked that you follow me," one said, speaking to Mike.

"And you are coming with me," the second told Lania.

Right away, she balked. "We'd prefer to stay together," she said. "Igor knows we work as a team."

The guy didn't budge.

"We go together," Mike reiterated. He took her hand and squeezed it, which she interpreted as a warning.

The two armed men looked at each other. "He wants to meet with each of you separately," the first one said. "We were not told why."

Mike appeared torn. She could tell what was going through his mind. He didn't want to blow this, but why on earth would Igor decide to do something like this now?

"It's okay," she said, pulling her hand free. "Hopefully, this won't take long and we can get on with business."

Slowly, Mike nodded. She watched as he walked

away, waiting until he'd disappeared from sight around a corner before turning to follow her own escort.

He took her to what appeared to be some sort of storage room, with a concrete floor and walls, filled with boxes and metal shelves, and left her.

She didn't like meeting Igor alone. Not just because she had a lingering fear that she might mess up, make a mistake and reveal herself, but because she flat out didn't trust him. Not before and especially not now, when he'd been acting erratically, likely due to him using drugs.

"There you are." Igor's booming voice startled her, making her jump. She collected herself quickly, putting on her cool, composed face.

"Igor." Hoping she sounded pleased to see him, she stayed put to keep her distance, but he crossed the room and took both her hands in his.

Air-kiss it would be, then. One for each cheek, European-style. As she moved in to do exactly that, Igor yanked her up against him, hard.

"Come here," he growled, planting his mouth on hers.

Instinctively she knew if she struggled, it would only arouse him. Men like Igor were all about power, and her best chance would be a nonreaction. If that failed, she could use some of the moves she'd learned in that self-defense class she'd taken.

Lania kept her lips locked closed, her body stiff as stone. Igor pressed her back against the wall, grinding against her, his arousal obvious. Nauseated, she thought she might puke. Instead, she swallowed hard and turned her face to the side. "Let me go, Igor," she demanded. "You know I don't want this."

When his gaze locked on hers, a chill snaked down her spine. His pupils were the size of pinpricks, which mean he'd taken some sort of drug.

"I don't care what you want," he told her, smirking. "You have spent months playing the tease, so now it's time for payback."

"I don't want to hurt you," she warned. "Let me go."

"Hurt me?" He chuckled. "As if you could. Go ahead, try. That will only make things more interesting."

Dang, she'd been right. She brought her knee up, intending a sharp jab in his groin. Instead, he kicked her leg away and slammed her back into the wall, pinning her between his body and the wall, and then put both hands around her throat. "Try that again and I will choke you," he said. "That is a promise, not a threat."

Trying not to panic, she thought back to the self-defense class. They'd practiced a similar scenario, except the choke hold had come from behind. There had to be a way to adapt it to this situation. But for the life of her, she couldn't figure out how.

She had a choice—pretend to go along with Igor, let him think he had a chance with her and then get away at the first opportunity she got. Or continue to struggle and likely he'd inflict bodily harm on her.

Pressing his mouth on hers, he forced his tongue between her lips. She bit him. Hard.

He backhanded her across the face so hard she thought her cheekbone was broken. While she was still reeling from the blow, he brought his hands back tight around her throat.

"Bitch." He spat the word. "You will pay for that." As he tightened his grip around her neck, she began to struggle in earnest. Twisting. Turning, desperately trying to get away. She couldn't breathe. He was going to freaking kill her!

Just as her vision started to go gray, Igor suddenly stiffened, releasing her as he slumped to the floor. Doubled over, she tried to pull air into her aching throat, rasping and wheezing.

"You're welcome," a voice said cheerfully. Carmen? Dazed and dizzy, Lania looked up to see the other woman standing over Igor's prone body, holding a baseball bat. "He's going to have a hell of a headache when he comes to."

Carmen appeared well, though pale. She moved a bit slower than usual and wore a baseball cap that didn't quite hide the bandage on her head.

Both horrified and grateful, Lania wasn't sure how to respond. "Thanks for saving me," she managed, the rasp in her voice a testament to the soreness in her throat. "But there's going to be heck to pay after this."

"Heck?" Carmen's elegant brows rose. "Heck to pay? Who says that? What's wrong with you?"

Crud. Shaking her head, Lania managed a shaky laugh. "Someone who just lost all oxygen to their brain. You know what I meant. There's going to be *hell* to pay." It took every ounce of self-control she possessed to keep from blanching at the swear word.

"No, there isn't. Because Igor is no longer in power. I'm seizing the reins of his little group right here and right now."

Rapid speech. Jerky, movements. Lania glanced at

the other woman. Yep. Carmen's pupils were dilated. Clearly, she was using again. Great. Just great.

Quickly, Lania made herself focus on what Carmen had just said. "You are? What about all his men? How are you going to get them to work for you?"

"I'll have their boss. None of them will want Igor the great and powerful to be hurt. Of course, he will be, in the end. But I think you know that." Carmen smiled, though the movement of her mouth seemed more like a snarl. "He tried to kill us. The wreck was no accident. Now he has to pay."

Lania nodded. "Naturally." She thought for a moment, absently rubbing the spots on her neck where Igor had choked her. "Does that mean you're going to kill him eventually?"

"Maybe." Carmen prodded Igor's motionless body with the pointy toe of one shoe. "Though I think I would find it far more entertaining to lock him up and make him watch me take over his organization. Slow torture might be fun, too. Then, when I don't need him anymore, I'll kill him."

Lania must have blanched, because once again Carmen eyed her suspiciously. "You look weird," Carmen said. "Maybe you'd better sit down."

Something in the other woman's demeanor warned Lania she'd better be more careful. Still, she allowed herself to drop down into a chair, still massaging her neck. "It hurts," she allowed. "Igor deserves to pay. In fact, I'd like to take part in torturing him."

This statement had Carmen laughing. "I knew I liked you." She moved closer. "If you're good to me, maybe I'll let you do it."

Slowly, Lania managed to nod. She reminded herself that she was playing an amoral opportunist, with loyalty only to one person—Mike. Speaking of Mike, she really hoped he'd show up soon and get her out of this situation that was growing more and more impossible by the moment.

"There you are." Mike burst into the room, sounding way too chipper. He skidded to a halt, taking in the situation in a glance—from Igor unconscious on the floor, to Carmen holding the baseball bat and finally Lania with darkening bruises on her throat.

"What happened here?" he asked quietly, his expression deadly serious.

"Igor tried to rape your girlfriend," Carmen said, her tone casual. "When she resisted, he started choking her. He would have killed her if I hadn't knocked him on the back side of his head."

His gaze found Lania, not bothering to hide the quick flash of rage. "Is this true?"

Slowly, she nodded. "Yes. And Carmen and I are taking over Igor's operation. And you, too, of course. Are you in or out?"

"Taking over…" Mike looked from Lania to Carmen. "I assume this is your idea?"

She stared him down. "Do you have a better one? If we let Igor go, he's going to kill me for knocking him out. Plus, I don't think Lania will be any safer."

"She has a point," Lania concurred. "And I feel Igor needs to pay for what he did to me." She shuddered, not even having to pretend. "If Carmen hadn't saved me…"

Jaw tight, he nodded. "I get it," he said. "But I really don't want to jeopardize any shipments we have in the works."

"You mean the big one?" Carmen asked. "The one that was supposed to leave tomorrow?"

Lania looked down so she didn't make eye contact with Mike. Carmen knew about the shipment. Which meant either Igor had lied and set them up again, or Carmen had someone on the inside.

"Yes, I knew." Carmen correctly took their silence for what it was. "Igor thought I wouldn't find out. He was going to cut me out. But I have my own way of finding out things."

From the floor, Igor groaned. When he stirred, Carmen kicked him hard in the side with her boot. He didn't move again.

"Darter," Carmen called. A large, hulking brute of a man stepped into the room. "Darter, I need you to restrain Igor here. Once that's done, take him to the cellar, to that place he uses for prisoners sometimes. Lock him up in there and report back to me."

"Yes, ma'am," Darter replied. He removed a pair of steel handcuffs from his belt. Shoving Igor's hands behind his back, he slapped them on. Then he picked up the smaller man, slung him over his shoulder and stalked from the room.

Mike watched him go. "What are you going to do if some of Igor's men see and try to help him?" he asked.

"Let them try." Carmen didn't appear concerned. "Igor's men don't like him any more than you or I do. They know the old ways. If I take him down, I'm now the boss."

Lania kept her head down, not quite sure what to

make of all this. Would the sudden shift in power totally mess up the shipment, which in turn would endanger the ATF bust? Or might it not mean that Carmen would also get caught up in the web of arrests? Now that would definitely be something Lania could get behind. She raised her head to find Carmen, hands on her hips, eyeing Mike.

"Your turn, Mike," Carmen said. "Are you in or are you out?" She still held the baseball bat loosely, though Lania doubted Mike would let her get a chance to use it.

"I'll need to think about it," Mike said, crossing his arms. "I don't swear my loyalty lightly."

"Loyalty?" Suddenly furious, Lania jumped to her feet. "Look at what that man did to me." She bared her throat, letting him see what had to be awful bruise marks. "How dare you even think about backing that monster after he tried to rape and choke me?"

Mike swallowed and looked down. When he raised his head again, she saw the resolve in his steely gaze. "You're right, Lania," he said. "My apologies." He turned to Carmen and inclined his head. "You can count me in."

"Good." Smiling now, Carmen gestured toward the door. "Let's go to the room Igor was using for an office. It'll be mine now. First order of business is to make sure this shipment goes smoothly. And I believe the best way to do that is to let them believe Igor is still in charge."

THE NEXT MORNING, after making a full report the night before to the special agent in charge, Micah got ready to head out to the trucking company. Carmen had insisted that everything should go as planned. Mike tended to agree with her, but since he trusted her even less than he trusted Igor, he couldn't help but worry.

In fact, until the cargo had been seized, the arrests had been made, reports filed and this operation could be called safely in the books, he wouldn't be able to let down his guard.

Worse, every time he saw the bruises on Jennifer's throat and thought of what Igor had nearly done to her, he wanted to find the man and take him apart with his bare hands.

"I'm fine," Jennifer had protested when he'd asked her if she wanted to go to the ER. "Just a few bruises, but I don't think he did any lasting damage."

He'd taken her in his arms then, holding her close and smoothing the back of her hair until she stopped shaking. He hated that this had happened to her, and he feared she might experience a little PTSD for a while.

From now on, he vowed, he'd shield her and protect her. She'd never feel unsafe again, as long as he had anything to say about it.

They'd clung to each other all night, making love and cuddling until they both fell asleep. When he woke in the morning and saw her lying there, those purpling bruises marring her creamy skin, rage warred with tenderness. He'd failed to do the one thing he'd sworn to do after getting her involved—protect her.

Right then and there, he'd made a vow. He'd make damn sure she didn't get hurt again. By anyone.

At least the assignment was nearly over. They'd inspect and sign off on the shipment, and the wheels of justice would be set in motion. If all went according to plan, all the bad actors would be rounded up. He planned to take Jennifer out to a fancy restaurant to celebrate, as well as discuss if she wanted to make plans for a future with him in it.

He knew with unshakable certainty that he couldn't live without her.

"Are you ready?" Jennifer asked, striding into the kitchen in her full Lania outfit. This time, she'd chosen what she'd jokingly referred to as a power pantsuit, complete with low heels and a crisp white blouse. She looked competent and cool and sexy as hell.

He nearly told her so, but at the last moment he held his tongue. Neither of them needed even the slightest distraction right now.

"Just about," he replied. "Do you want me to make you a coffee to go?"

She held up a stainless-steel mug with a lid. "I already did."

This made him smile. "Such a normal-sounding conversation, considering what's about to go down."

"True." She shrugged. "I'm just thankful Carmen didn't insist on going with us."

"Me, too. On the bright side, we won't have to deal with her too much longer."

On the drive to the trucking company in the four door, back-up Ford that he'd been forced to use since the Mercedes was out of commission, Lania went silent, clearly lost in her own thoughts. He got it, since inside he was a bundle of nerves. Unusual for him, but there'd been absolutely nothing normal about this assignment. Now, they were so damn close. They couldn't afford to have anything go wrong.

If he was a wreck, he could only imagine how Lania felt.

She sighed. Reaching over, he squeezed her bare shoulder, marveling at how silky her skin felt. "We're in the homestretch," he told her, hoping he sounded reassuring.

"I know." She gave him a wobbly smile. "I can hardly believe it."

"We've got to do something about Igor," he said. "If he's locked up and Carmen is in charge, there's a chance he could weasel out of facing charges."

"What?" Lania sat up straight. "That would defeat the purpose, wouldn't it?"

"Yes."

"I see. Then what are you going to do about it?"

He took a deep breath. "We've got just about enough time. Let's swing by the warehouse and see if we can figure out a way to free him. As long as Carmen isn't there, we might actually have a shot. Since she expects us to be at the trucking company, doing this now might be our safest bet."

"I'm not sure I should be involved in that," she said, her entire posture tight. "I don't think I can. That man tried to rape me and nearly killed me. Personally, I'd prefer he stays locked up and rots."

"I agree." Setting his jaw, he swallowed back the wave of rage that went through him every time he thought of what Igor had done. "And you're right. I think I already have enough evidence to prove his involvement. I won't free him. I just want to check on him. Basically, make sure he's alive. You can wait in the car if you want."

Though she appeared troubled, Lania didn't try to dissuade him. "We'll see," she replied.

When they reached the warehouse and parked, he looked around. Everything seemed normal—the parking lot half-full and workers coming and going.

"I'm coming in," she told him.

Nodding, he squeezed her shoulder. "I promise you, I won't let him hurt you again."

"I'll hold you to that."

"We're going to bluff our way inside," he said. "Just follow my lead."

Slowly, she nodded.

They got out of the car at the same time. Mike took her hand, and together they walked inside the building. To his surprise, no one stopped them. In fact, though several people glanced their way, their arrival generated no attention at all.

Working by memory, he led Lania to the room that used to be Igor's office. He wanted to go there first, just in case Carmen might be inside.

But the office was empty.

"Can I help you?" A tall factory worker with long gray hair pulled back in a ponytail stood in the doorway. "Are you looking for Igor?" he asked.

"We are," Mike replied. "Or Carmen. Is she around?"

"She was, but she left an hour ago," the guy said, scratching his head. "And none of us have seen Igor for days. Not sure what's going on with him."

Mike barely restrained himself from glancing at Lania. So this guy didn't know that Carmen had taken Igor prisoner. "Does this building have a basement?" he asked.

The man frowned. "I think so. Why?"

"Do you mind if we look there?"

"Suit yourself." The guy pointed. "There's a stair-well over there."

No one stopped them as they made their way toward the metal door. Mike half expected it to be locked, but it wasn't. Inside, he located a light switch, illuminating the passage down.

Once they reached the bottom, another switch provided light. Looking around, he saw most of it was the typical industrial basement—gray concrete floor and walls. Only a portion of it had been finished out. "There." He pointed. "Looks like they built a couple of rooms. That's the only place down here where she could be keeping Igor."

As they walked toward the area, Lania held back.

"Are you all right?" he asked, stopping. One look at her expression told him she was not.

"I feel physically ill," she rasped, grimacing. "I'm sorry, but I can't deal with seeing Igor again right now."

"Don't be sorry. I get it." He glanced around. The only way in or out appeared to be the staircase they'd used. Still, he didn't want her standing out in the open. "Wait over here," he said, leading her around a large stack of boxes.

Once he felt satisfied she'd be partially hidden, he walked toward the two makeshift rooms. As expected, when he tried the doorknob of the first one, he found it locked. "Igor?" he called out, keeping his voice low. "Igor, are you in there?"

No response. Not even the slightest sound. Which

meant either Igor wasn't down here or he wasn't able to respond.

Mike moved down toward the second and last office. This doorknob turned easily. Inside, he found a room with a cot, a stool and nothing else. Definitely no prisoner.

He checked his watch and cursed. They were running out of time, since they were expected at the trucking company.

Trying the first door again, he debated attempting to pick the lock. Instead, he rattled the door, calling for Igor again.

Nothing.

"What's going on?" Lania appeared. "We've got to go or we're going to be late."

She was right. Nothing else mattered as much as making sure that arms shipment went off without a hitch. Not even finding Igor. That would have to wait until later.

"Come on." He took her hand, and they hurried toward the stairs, emerging into the bustling warehouse.

No one bothered them as they made their way toward the exit. Once in the car, Mike drove faster than normal to make up for lost time.

"Do you think Igor was in that locked room?" Lania asked.

"Who knows? If he was, he's either unconscious or she's got him gagged." He shook his head. "Hopefully, he's in there. We'll find out when the bust goes down and we start rounding them up."

They arrived at the trucking company. Unlike last time, the parking lot was empty and the place appeared deserted. Yet in the area behind the fence, there were seven semitrucks, all of them loaded with shipping containers.

Relief flooded him. Finally, even with Igor out of commission for the moment, it looked like this deal was actually going to happen.

Except he couldn't shake the ominous feeling that something was off. Over the years, he'd learned to trust his gut instinct.

"Wait." He grabbed Lania's arm. "I could be wrong, but if something seems sketchy, I want you to run. Don't worry about me or what might be happening, just get out and get away as quickly as you can."

Eyes huge, she locked gazes with him. "What do you mean? What could go wrong now? It's almost over."

About to open his mouth and explain, he froze. "Damn it."

Lania followed the direction of his gaze. Carmen had opened the door and walked out of the building, heading straight toward them.

"It took you long enough to get here," she declared, her razor-sharp stare missing nothing. "I was just about to start without you."

"I thought you'd decided to let us handle this alone," Mike said, careful to keep both his voice and his expression neutral.

Carmen shrugged. "I decided it might be better if I supervised. I'm not entirely certain I can trust you."

The blunt insult had to be a test. His best reaction would be not to react.

"You should be," he said, his tone terse. "I always do what I say I will."

"As do I," Lania interjected.

"Well then, neither of you will mind a little supervision, will you?"

What could they say? Absolutely nothing, he realized, without garnering suspicion.

"Just stay the hell out of our way and let us do our jobs," Mike finally growled.

This made Carmen laugh. "Come on, then. Let's get this show on the road." She spun on her stilettos and strode ahead of them, her long, dark hair swinging with her movements.

Inside, the empty building set off even more internal warning bells. When Mike had been here to oversee the smaller, test shipment, there had at least been a few employees.

"Where is everyone?" he asked, keeping it casual.

"Out," Carmen replied. "I decided the less witnesses, the better. The only ones here are the drivers. The containers were loaded at the manufacturers and brought here. All we need to do is inspect and then seal them." She held up a clipboard with several sheets of paper attached. "I've got the shipping manifests here."

Mike wondered if she knew that the shipping manifests were inaccurate. Lying about the contents was how Igor got away with so many illegal shipments. Most of the weapons that were going out today would not be shown on any kind of paperwork. Too dangerous.

But it wasn't his place to educate Carmen. If she planned to run Igor's operation, then she'd better know exactly what the hell she was doing.

As long as she didn't completely mess things up, he'd stay out of her way. The most important thing was getting these containers on the road.

Chapter Fifteen

Lania watched Carmen closely. Earlier, Mike had said he had a bad feeling about this. Which meant she would need to be extra careful, staying quiet and out of everyone's way. Even if doing so wouldn't hold true to Lania's brash personality.

Mike began the painstaking process of inspecting the contents of each shipping container. Lania wasn't sure how many cartons each one held, but it looked like a lot. The huge metal containers sat individually on what looked to be specially designed trailers. Two workers assisted him. Ignoring Carmen's clipboard, he consulted the information he had stored in his phone, opening every single crate and checking out the contents before having the men hammer the crates closed.

Once he'd finished with a container, that too was shut and sealed, and the truck carrying it was given the okay to drive off. Clearly, this would take a while. At least she'd worn comfortable shoes.

"You're awfully quiet," Carmen said, strolling over to stand next to Lania.

"Am I?" Lania shrugged. "I prefer to let Mike do his thing without interruptions."

Carmen eyed her. "You're acting weird. Did what happened with Igor mess you up?"

Despite her skipped heartbeat, Lania maintained her composure. "Maybe." She considered, weighing her next words. "Yes. It freaking did." Exhaling sharply, she rolled her shoulders. "Actually, I'm really glad I don't have to see him again right now."

"I understand that." Staring at Mike while he worked, Carmen appeared lost in thought. "Once this shipment is gone and you and Mike get paid, what are your plans?"

If she only knew. Lania gave a casual shrug. "I'm not sure. What are you offering?"

Carmen's sly smile seemed feline. "You know I have other business interests. You and I have discussed this. I would seriously like you to consider running one of them for me."

The human trafficking. It had to be.

"I'll need to be well paid," Lania declared, careful not to reveal her revulsion. "Depending on what you need me to do, the amount of money will definitely help me make a decision. Let me know when you're ready to talk specifics."

Carmen chuckled. "Of course, of course."

They fell silent again, continuing to watch Mike.

He appeared to be halfway through the second container. Proof that this was going to take a while. And, since the other woman didn't walk away, Lania resigned herself to the fact that she'd have to continue to make small talk with Carmen.

Careful, careful.

"I wish my father could see this," Carmen mused.

"He always told me I could be whatever I wanted. He worked for one of the cartels in Mexico for years before he was killed. He'd be so proud of what I've accomplished in such a short time."

Proud. Instead of snorting, Lania nodded.

"What about you?" Carmen asked. "Are your parents still alive? Are they aware of what you do for a living?"

Since Mike had told her it was best to always stick as close to the truth as possible, Lania did. "Yes, both my parents are alive. And no, they have no idea about any of this." She waved her hand toward Mike.

"Really? What do they think you do?"

Crud. Now she'd backed herself into a corner. She could make something up or change the subject. She decided to go with the latter.

"I'd prefer not to talk about my parents," she said in as lofty a voice as she could manage. "Instead, I want to discuss your plans for Igor."

If Carmen found the abrupt change in subject odd, she didn't say so.

"Who cares about Igor?" she asked instead. "He can rot in hell for all I care."

"True." Lania glanced sideways at the other woman. "But I want to personally make him suffer."

Carmen chuckled. "I'll make sure you have your chance, as long as you agree to continue to work for me."

Though Lania nodded, she made sure not to verbally commit to anything. She really didn't get why everyone seemed so hot to have her around.

Mike closed up the second container, signed off and that truck pulled away.

"This is going to take all day," Carmen commented. "Would you like to go somewhere with me and have a bite to eat?"

"No, thanks." Lania gestured at Mike. "How about we all three go once he's finished?"

"I don't get you." The sharp edge to Carmen's voice felt like a warning. "What is your obsession with him? You can do so much better."

"Can I?" *Keep things light*, she told herself. "I disagree. But taste in men is such a personal thing."

"True." Carmen's eyes narrowed. "But I have heard stories about you. Igor says you've taken other lovers in the past."

"What's your point?" Lania snapped.

Her response appeared to amuse the other woman rather than anger her. "Why not Igor?" Carmen asked. "You had the perfect opportunity to increase your power. Why did you not take it?"

Lania didn't have to fake her shudder of revulsion. "No. Just no."

Carmen laughed again and finally moved away to confer with a couple of her men.

Watching Mike work, Lania almost wished she'd thought to bring a book. Except she suspected doing so would have been completely out of character for Lania. Nothing left to do but wait for Mike to finish and hope Carmen didn't try to start up another conversation.

Finally, the very last truck pulled up. From a distance, even Mike seemed exhausted. Yet he continued his painstaking examination of every single crate, made his notations, sealed it and moved on to the next.

When he stepped outside and gestured for the men to close up the container, Lania felt like cheering.

"Ah, he's finished." Carmen walked up alongside her. "Very good. Now I'd like to see both of you inside before you leave."

Lania nodded, though she wanted to groan. She'd had visions of her and Mike going somewhere to eat and celebrate. Instead, they were being summoned to the wannabe queen's office so Carmen could flex her newfound power.

Carmen strolled off without another word, disappearing inside the building.

When she told Mike, he rolled his eyes. "Let's just hope this doesn't take long," he said. "I'm starving."

"Me, too." Slipping her hand into his, she shoulder-bumped him. "Good job doing that inspection. You were really thorough."

"That's because you can't make a single mistake on a shipment this important. Igor gets that. I'm not sure Carmen does."

Hand in hand, they entered the building. The place still seemed suspiciously empty, as if most of the workers had found a sudden need for an extended break. Framed pictures of various semitrucks decorated the walls and the reception desk sat empty, despite the ringing phones.

"You don't suppose she did something to these people, do you?" Lania asked, suddenly uneasy.

"Other than cruelty for cruelty's sake, there wouldn't be a point," Mike offered. He too appeared on edge, making her remember his premonition earlier.

"Maybe we should just go," she offered. But right

at that moment, Carmen appeared, gesturing them to go ahead of her.

They walked down a narrow hallway decorated with more framed truck photos and into a large office at the end of the hall. Clearly, it belonged to the trucking company owner, and a large nameplate on the door that read J. A. Beasley proved it.

"Where is everyone?" Mike asked casually, stopping just inside the doorway. "It sure looks like everyone vacated the place in a hurry."

Since he didn't take a seat, Lania remained standing also.

Carmen walked around the massive desk and dropped into the chair on the other side. "I requested they give us the day," she said, her voice cool. "We didn't need to have any witnesses."

"Can't argue with that." Mike crossed his arms. "What's up, Carmen? It's been a long day, and I'd like to get going."

"Sit." Carmen gestured toward two chairs across from the desk. "This talk is long overdue."

Careful not to look at Mike, Lania dropped into one of the chairs. A moment later, Mike took the other.

"I have made your lady friend an offer," Carmen said, looking at Mike. "Now I'd like to make you one."

Lania relaxed slightly. She hadn't been too sure where this was going, but it sounded as if Carmen had decided to trust them both.

"Mike, I've decided that you will join Igor." The curve of Carmen's brightly painted lips turned into a smirk. "Men, take him away."

Three hulking brutes entered the room, weapons

raised. Mike jumped to his feet, bringing out his pistol. A second later, heart pounding, Lania pulled hers out, too, hoping her hands didn't shake too badly. Both she and Mike trained theirs on Carmen.

"Standoff," Mike drawled. "Shall we all start shooting and see who's left standing?"

Taking in the situation, Carmen began clapping, a slow, methodical sound that grated on Lania's already frayed nerves. "Bravo," Carmen said. "Now I know whose side you're really on, Lania. So much for loyalty."

"I've made no secret about where my loyalty lies." Somehow, Lania managed to keep her voice cool and her arm steady. "Mike and I are a package deal. We're a team."

"You are willing to die for him?" Carmen asked. "And give up your opportunity for revenge against Igor for what he did to you?"

Instead of replying, Lania simply stared the other woman down. "What are you going to do, Carmen? Are you willing to risk your life?"

"For this?" Carmen waved her men down. "I will let you two go. For now. But you'd better watch your back. I will not forget this."

Mike didn't move. He kept his gun trained on the other woman. "I need my payment now," he said. "In cash."

Carmen frowned. "I don't have any money. Your agreement was between you and Igor."

"Since you are taking over his business, I expect you to honor it. In fact, how about you come with me?" He moved swiftly, going around the desk before Carmen could move. Her men brought their weapons back up, but too late. Mike held Carmen up against him, pistol pressed against her temple.

In retaliation, the guards attempted to grab Lania. She spun, glad of her self-defense class and *situational awareness*, and brought her own gun up in front of her. She hoped like hell she'd managed to depress the trigger enough to release the trigger guard like Mike had shown her. If she didn't, she was probably going to end up shot or worse.

"Let me go," Carmen ordered, her voice a vicious rasp. "Who the hell do you think you are?"

"You're coming with us," Mike said. "We're going to free Igor. I am going to get paid. If he's the only person who can do that, then we go to him."

MIKE COULDN'T BELIEVE how well Lania had handled the situation. Working as a team, acting as if she was a well-trained agent, they hustled Carmen out of the trucking company building and into the Ford. He found a length of rope in the shipping department and grabbed that, using it to secure her hands behind her back.

Spitting mad, Carmen cursed at him in both English and Spanish. "You will pay for this," she declared. "My people are loyal to me. They won't let you keep me prisoner. You'll see."

Mike and Lania exchanged glances. "What makes you think we're taking you around your people?" he asked.

"Because that's where Igor is and you know it," Carmen shot back.

"We don't need you to get in to see Igor." Mike made a quick decision. "Though we might be able to use you as leverage. How many of your people would be willing to stand by and watch your head get blown off?"

"I think we should let her wait in the car," Lania put in. "I can watch over her." She smiled. "Don't worry. I won't hesitate to put a bullet in her head if she tries anything."

Mentally, Mike had mad respect for his partner's phenomenal acting skills. On the surface, though, all he did was nod. "Sounds like a plan," he said, putting the car in Reverse. "Let's head back to the warehouse and free Igor. I imagine he'll be so pleased, he might even pay us extra."

Carmen inhaled sharply. "You are a fool." She directed her ire to Lania. "I think you are the mole," she announced. "I don't have proof, only suspicion. But I'm usually right."

"What makes you think that?" Lania asked, her tone calm. "I have been nothing if not loyal to Igor, as well as Mike."

"You won't swear. I would never trust someone who says *heck* instead of *hell*."

After a moment, both Mike and Lania laughed.

"That has got to be the weirdest thing I've ever heard," Lania finally said. "Personal preference, Carmen. Nothing more."

"It's stupid," Carmen insisted, lapsing into silence for the rest of the drive.

Once they reached the warehouse, Mike parked away from the building, under a large evergreen tree that provided ample shade. "Wait here," he said. "I'm leaving the keys in the ignition in case everything goes south. Otherwise, don't take your weapon off her, understand?"

"Got it." Lania nodded. When he got out, she slid into the driver's seat, though she turned around to face Carmen, keeping her pistol balanced alongside the headrest. "Make a move," she invited. "I dare you."

Carmen's gaze narrowed at Lania's savage tone, but she kept herself still. Even with her hands tied, she could still launch herself at the front seat, and Mike leaned in and whispered that to Lania. "Got it," Lania responded. "Now go find Igor."

He kissed her cheek and took off. Back inside the warehouse, he didn't bother with any of the employees and took off for the staircase leading down to the basement. Once there, he went directly to the locked door from before and slammed into it with his shoulder. The door shuddered but didn't break. In the past, he'd had better luck busting down a door with a well-placed kick, so he tried that.

Three kicks later, the door frame finally separated, and he pushed the door open. He located a light switch and turned on the light. Igor lay on a cot, curled into a ball and completely unresponsive.

"Igor," Mike said, gently shaking the other man's shoulder. "Wake up."

Nothing. Checking out the back of Igor's head, he realized after seeing all the blood that Carmen hadn't treated the place where she'd clubbed him.

He needed professional medical help, like yesterday.

Swearing, Mike rushed out of the room, leaving the door unlocked. The second he got to the top of the stairs, he started looking around for a landline phone. Best if he called 911 anonymously. That way, Igor could get the help he needed to survive without jeopardizing the case.

He found one on the first desk he saw. Punching nine to get an outside line, he dialed 911. Keeping his voice low, he told the operator exactly where to find Igor and his condition. Then, leaving the line open, he placed the phone on the desk next to the cradle and strode toward the front door.

Back outside, he headed toward where he'd left the car. But the nondescript, four door Ford, along with Lania and Carmen, was gone. His heart stopped. Surely not. It couldn't be. Slowly, he turned, surveying the lot. He must be looking in the wrong place.

But no, the parking spot under the towering evergreen tree was empty. And he saw no sign of the vehicle anywhere else in the entire area.

Lania and Carmen were gone.

"Damn it." Mike wanted to punch something, anything. He never should have left a woman who barely knew how to handle a pistol with one of the most dangerous women in the cartel.

His cell phone rang. "What?" he snarled, not bothering to hide his fury.

"I have your little girlfriend," Carmen said. "She's in one piece, for now. I suggest a trade."

"A trade?"

"I need Igor. You go get him and bring him out. Call me when you have him, and I'll be back to do the exchange."

In the distance he could hear the sirens, signifying the ambulance's approach.

"That's impossible," he replied, his voice flat. "He's

in bad shape. I've already called 911." Lifting the phone away from his ear, he held it up so Carmen could hear. "The ambulance is almost here."

"Then your lady friend is dead."

A shot rang out, nearly deafening him and stopping his heart. "Carmen?" he asked, frantic. "What did you do?"

Instead, Lania's voice came on the line. "It's me," she said. "I shot her. There's so much blood. It's everywhere. Oh, jeez. I'm not sure she's even alive."

Lights flashing, the ambulance pulled into the lot and parked right by the front door.

"Listen to me," Mike said. "Can you get back here?"

"Yes, I think so." Her voice trembled. "I'll have to push her over."

"Do that. And get here. An ambulance is here right now for Igor. There's a chance we can get them to look at her."

"On my way." She sounded a bit better. Still shaky, but as if she'd managed to wrestle herself into some semblance of control.

A minute later, the Ford coasted into the parking lot and pulled up alongside him. Yanking open the driver's side door, he took one look at Lania covered in blood and just about lost it. "Are you all right?" he asked, his heart pounding, taking in the situation.

"I think so. This is her blood." She pointed. Carmen lay unmoving in the back seat. "I don't know how, but she somehow got her hands untied. She jumped me. I couldn't make myself pull the trigger." Her beautiful brown eyes filled. "I'm sorry. I just couldn't."

Reaching into the back seat, he checked for a pulse. When he found one, he told Lania, "She's alive."

"Thank goodness," Lania breathed. "What are we going to do?"

He reached a quick decision. The trucks with their illegal cargo were in motion. Both of the ringleaders were injured. They couldn't let Carmen die. While he'd prefer not to, exposing their true identities right now shouldn't endanger anything.

"Slide over," he ordered. Lania immediately complied. Getting in, he drove over to the ambulance. They'd already loaded Igor inside and were working on him before heading toward the hospital.

Pulling up in front of them, he jumped out of the car. He ran over to the back and pounded on the door. "ATF." Flashing his badge, he pointed over to the Ford. "We have a gunshot victim. She's in pretty bad shape."

The paramedic glanced from him to Igor, whom his partner was trying to stabilize. "Same incident?"

"Yes," Micah lied. Since he knew ambulances often took two patients if they'd both been injured in the same incident, he felt the little white lie was justified in this instance.

The EMT jumped down and went to check Carmen out. Lania had shot her in the shoulder, and the bullet had passed clean through, into the back seat. But Carmen had lost a lot of blood. They'd need to transport her to the hospital along with Igor.

"We'll need to have Denver PD meet us there," the young man explained. "Any time we have a gunshot wound, we need to file a report."

"That's fine," Mike agreed. "However, this is still

an undercover operation, so I'll need you to keep my identity quiet. We'll follow along behind you and get all that handled."

As soon as Carmen had been loaded up, Mike called the special agent in charge to fill him in. He didn't mention Lania, just stuck to the facts without going into detail about how Carmen had been shot. His boss wasn't too happy and decided he'd make a call to Denver PD himself so the operation wouldn't have to take a chance of getting exposed until the trucks arrived in Galveston and the bust went down. "I'll send one of the other agents to meet the police," he said.

"Thank you," Micah replied. All he wanted to do at this moment was take a still visibly shaken Jennifer home. A hot shower to wash off the blood, a shot of whiskey and a good meal would do wonders to help her feel better.

The ambulance pulled away, lights flashing, siren running. Micah followed, except when the ambulance turned left, he went straight.

"Wait." Jennifer pointed. "I thought we were—"

"My boss will sort things out with the police. He doesn't want to take the chance of screwing things up until everything's over."

She nodded, the movement robotic. "Does he know about me?"

"Not yet," he answered. "He will, soon enough." Sooner than Micah would have liked. Because he would have to make a report, and then the SAC would learn what Micah had done.

"I can't believe I shot her." She took a deep, shaky breath. "I hope she doesn't die. I'm not a murderer."

His heart ached for her. If he hadn't been driving, he would have taken her into his arms and held her close. "She's going to be fine," he reassured her. Now was not the time to tell her that if she had killed Carmen, it would have been in self-defense. "You got her in the shoulder, a clean shot. She's lost a lot of blood, but they'll be able to fix her up as good as new. Just in time for her to be arrested."

Back at the condo, Jennifer appeared to have regained some semblance of self-control. Dry-eyed, she allowed Micah to help her out of the car and to the elevator. She didn't speak again, not until they were inside the condo with the door closed and bolted securely behind them.

"Micah…" A ton of heartbreak was in her voice.

"Come here." Finally, he pulled her into his arms, his voice as fierce as his heart. "It's all right. It's going to be fine."

"Maybe so." With her face pressed against his chest, her words were muffled. "But I'm not sure I am. I've changed. And I'm not sure it's for the better."

He hadn't thought he could feel worse, but hearing her say that shattered him. "I'm sorry," he told her. "I never should have involved you."

Raising her head, she looked him straight in the eye. "Don't ever say that. I wouldn't have missed this for anything."

"Seriously?" Damned if he'd ever understand women.

"Yes." She cocked her head, the glint in her gaze sending his heart rate into overtime. For the first time, he wondered if he might really have a chance to forge some sort of relationship with her. Or—a contrasting thought sobered him—was this her way of saying good-bye?

On tiptoe, she pressed her mouth against his. "I met you, and I wouldn't give that up for anything. This undercover thing has been way outside my comfort zone, and I've learned a lot." Her expression sobered. "I've just got to come to grips with the idea of shooting another human being."

"Carmen would have killed you, you know," he pointed out. "You didn't have a choice."

She nodded. "I know, but there's always a choice. I made the best one I could at the time. I've just got to convince myself it was the right one."

Unsure of what to say, he covered her mouth with his. Now might not be the time to talk about the future, but at least he could show her how he felt.

"ARE YOU READY?" Micah poked his head into Jennifer's room, where she'd finished packing. The light in his blue eyes made her mouth go dry. She wanted to throw herself into his arms. Instead, she looked down and forced herself to focus on the task at hand.

"Just about," she replied. The ATF had told her she could keep any of the expensive designer outfits that she wanted, but she had little use for that kind of clothing in her ordinary life.

A lot had happened since she'd shot Carmen, who had fully recovered and now sat behind bars. The containers full of illegal weapons had arrived at the port in Galveston, and the ATF had moved in as they were being loaded on the ship. Igor and several of his top men had been arrested, as well as Samir and Ernie.

And most importantly of all, the undercover assignment was officially over.

The ATF had been furious with Micah when they'd learned of Jennifer's involvement. Privately, Micah had told her he hoped they'd ask him to resign, but that didn't happen. Instead, he'd been placed on administrative leave while an investigation was underway. Apologies had been made, and not only had the ATF offered Jennifer monetary compensation, but anything she'd worn while playing the role of Lania.

She'd defended Micah, explaining that she'd been fully aware of the dangers when she agreed to take on the undercover assignment. It had been exciting, she'd claimed, startled to realize this was only the tiniest white lie. *Life-changing* and *exhilarating* were a couple of the other descriptions she'd given, and she'd apparently improved her acting skills, because the powers that be appeared to believe her. That might be, she admitted privately to herself, because most of what she'd said was true.

And finally, Micah had put her on the phone to Face-Time with her twin sister, Laney, still bedridden and pregnant but glowing.

Staring at her twin felt like looking into a mirror. A wonderful, magical mirror. Overcome by emotion, Jennifer couldn't speak at first. Her eyes filled with tears. "I never knew," she managed. "I always felt as if a part of myself was missing, but I had no idea you even existed."

"I'm sorry." Laney wiped away her own tears. "Ever

since I found out, I've agonized over whether or not to contact you. From what I could see, you appeared to have a happy, well-adjusted life. I was afraid to upend it."

Jennifer shook her head and then waved away the regrets. "It doesn't matter now. What does is that we've finally found each other." She cleared her throat, trying to get past the lump.

Slowly, Laney nodded. "You're right. Still, my decision cost us time together. I'll do my best to make that up to you when I can." Looking down, she gestured at her huge baby bump, smiling. "As you can see, I'm a little preoccupied right now."

This made Jennifer laugh. Now that the ice had finally been broken, they could move past the initial awkwardness and truly get to know one another.

"I heard you had quite the adventure," Laney teased. She too had been furious with Micah, but she'd gotten over it fairly quickly once Jennifer spoke up for him.

Over the course of several phone conversations, Jennifer and Laney had hit it off, discovering they had quite a bit in common. They'd even made plans to get together in person once Jennifer had settled back into her regular life. Jennifer couldn't wait. She hoped Micah would come with her. Not only did he know Laney well, but Jennifer, too.

"It's a well-known phenomenon that twins, even if raised completely separately, turn out to have similar habits and beliefs," Jennifer told Micah.

He'd nodded, his expression unconvinced. "As far as I'm concerned, you and Laney couldn't be more different," he said. "You're both amazing, in completely different ways."

The offhanded compliment made her smile.

They still had not had a conversation about the future. She supposed that was because neither wanted to ruin how easy and natural things were between them.

"Let's do this." Closing her suitcase, she took one last look around the bedroom she and Micah had often shared. The condo had been lovely, but nothing about the life they'd pretended to have there was real. Well, nothing except her growing feelings for Micah.

He grabbed her bag, then leaned in for a lingering kiss. "You were the best part of this entire assignment," he told her. She waited for him to say more, but instead he hefted her bag and turned away, grabbing his own on the way out the door.

He'd be driving her to her town house in Longmont next. For some reason, she felt nervous about him seeing it.

"Why?" he asked, turning to glance at her over his shoulder, making her realize she'd spoken her thought out loud.

"Because where I live is completely different from this." She waved her hand at all the plush luxury. "I'm just a regular person, a schoolteacher. I could never in a million years afford anything like this place."

He laughed. "That's good, since it turns out I'm a regular person, too. I can't wait to see your place. I have a feeling I'll be seeing quite a bit more of it in the weeks and months to come."

Hearing this, her spirit soared. "What about you, Micah? Where do you live?"

"At the moment, nowhere. With the exception of the Corvette, which I own, I put my stuff in storage when I took this assignment. I had a hunch it would be a long one. Turns out, I was right."

Side by side, they walked to the elevator for the last time. "What will happen to all that furniture?" she asked, gesturing back toward the unit.

"Oh, it will stay there. The entire condo was rented, furnishings and all. I imagine the owner will either return home or rent it out again."

Stepping into the elevator, she clung to him, partly out of habit and partly because she couldn't get close enough to him, ever. "If you don't have a place to live," she offered, "you're welcome to stay at my place for however long you need."

He swallowed, his expression shuttered. "That's kind of you, but I would hate to impose."

Was she wrong? Were her feelings all one-sided? She'd never been a bold person until lately, but she refused to believe that.

The elevator doors slid open. Jennifer stabbed the button to close them. Turning to Micah, she cupped his face in her hands and pulled him down for a kiss. As usual, by the time they broke apart, they were both breathless. And back at the ninth floor.

"Sorry," she said, anything but. Pressing the button for the lobby, she smiled up at him, her confidence growing. "Micah, I've never felt like this about anyone before. I wouldn't mind seeing where this goes."

This time he smiled back. "I didn't want you to think we were moving too fast."

She shrugged. "We've moved quickly ever since the moment we met. Why would that change now?"

They barely made it to the parking garage before he took her in his arms. "In that, I'm one hundred percent in agreement."

* * * * *

COMING SOON!

We really hope you enjoyed reading this book.
If you're looking for more romance, be sure to
head to the shops when new books are
available on

Thursday 7th
July

To see which titles are coming soon, please visit

millsandboon.co.uk/nextmonth

MILLS & BOON

LET'S TALK
Romance

For exclusive extracts, competitions
and special offers, find us online:

MILLS & BOON
A ROMANCE FOR EVERY READER

- **FREE** delivery direct to your door

- **EXCLUSIVE** offers every month

- **SAVE** up to 25% on pre-paid subscriptions

SUBSCRIBE AND SAVE

millsandboon.co.uk/Subscribe

MILLS & BOON
Desire

Indulge in secrets and scandal, intense drama and plenty of sizzling hot action with powerful and passionate heroes who have it all: wealth, status, good looks…everything but the right woman.

MILLS & BOON
MEDICAL
Pulse-Racing Passion

Set your pulse racing with dedicated, delectable doctors in the high-pressure world of medicine, where emotions run high and passion, comfort and love are the best medicine.